"Ya know, Harper, out here tonight because, well, because of times together—remember those?"

Remember them? I still fantasized about those "other times." The first time, I came out of a bar bathroom and acted on pure lust. I grabbed Brody's collar and pulled his lips down onto mine. One minute I walked out of the restroom, and the next ten minutes we feasted on each other like it was our last meal. It was the best damn make-out session I ever had, until our next one.

The other time happened at Marti and Declan's wedding. We danced to a slow, bluesy song. Our bodies moved together in one grinding motion. Brody led and coaxed my more-than-willing self into a coat room for another round of passion.

Both sessions ended as abruptly as they began. Both times, we didn't reunite during the night, nor any other nights that followed. I was probably another chink in his seasoned armor, or he, in my amateur sheath. There were so many reasons why we wouldn't work out, so many reasons I didn't want us to work out.

"Yes, I remember *those times*," I admitted. "I didn't need a reminder tonight."

"Reminders are good." He chuckled. "I thought tonight might be a chance to reminisce with our mouths, you know, as some people do."

# Praise for Betsy Dudak

Colorado Romance Writers
Award of Excellence Finalist

~*~

"Ms. Dudak has without a doubt the greatest sense of humor! She grabs you with her quirky way of looking at life and love from the very first page and maintains the momentum until the end."

*~Angela D Me*

"I look forward to future titles by this author."

*~Marie Drake, Marie Reads and Reviews*
*(5 out of 5 hearts!)*

"Elizabeth does an amazing job of describing everything."

*~Super\*BETA\*Reader*

~*~

## Reviews for *WHAT THE HECK, DEC?!*:

"...so funny and quirky, with a great cast of extremely crazy, kooky, hot and sexy characters."

*~kstar0330*

"This Book is Brain Candy."

*~rickter*

"Great characters, smoldering scenes, and tons of witty observations that will have you giggling out loud."

*~Hopelessly Devoted Bibliophile*

"A very humorous, strong female lead character with loads of personality..."

*~Susan Reviews*

# Wanna Bet?

## by

## Betsy Dudak

**Wanna Bet?**

Cover Art by *Diana Carlile*

The Wild Rose Press, Inc.
PO Box 708
Adams Basin, NY 14410-0708
Visit us at www.thewildrosepress.com

Publishing History
First Champagne Rose Edition, 2019
Print ISBN 978-1-5092-2745-7
Digital ISBN 978-1-5092-2746-4

Published in the United States of America

## Dedication

This book is dedicated to the man who called me a creative writer with "all the voices" in my head, my husband, Peter. Even in your death you will forever remain my romantic muse.

Chapter One
The Bet

Kissing is an art form, and I was kissing a da Vinci. He knew when to tease, when to command, and when to retreat in gentle agony. I sighed and whimpered and moaned, all from his mouth on mine. It was the third time in ten months our lips found each other, and *every* time our passion created masterpieces.

When we came up for air, I pulled in my lips to taste his lingering spice.

"We shouldn't be doing this." I clasped my hands behind my neck and looked up into the early evening sky. "No. No. No. We shouldn't be doing this at all."

"And what exactly shouldn't we be doing? Having fun?" He spoke low and soft. His gray, wolf-like eyes, stared at me through a fringe of blond lashes.

"Yes." I sighed.

"We're at a party. We're supposed to have fun." Brody shrugged.

"Not this kind of fun," I said.

"Look at it this way, Harper. It's like we're playing pin the tail on the donkey, but in this case, we are pinning our lips together and without blindfolds—although blindfolds are a great idea."

"Seriously?"

"Sure. I like blindfolds. Oh, wait. Too soon? Okay, we can save blindfolds for another time." He chuckled.

I remained somber. "Come on. That was funny."

"None of this is funny, Brody. We're in the backyard of a housewarming party, playing tonsil tag like two overly hormonal teenagers, and being a tiny bit rude to Marti and Declan. You remember them? The host and hostess? Your brother and sister-in-law? And what about our dates, the ones we left in the house to get our horny on? Will they get a chuckle out of this?"

"What do they say about ignorance being bliss?" Brody laughed.

"I don't find any of this is funny."

"Come on. Not even a little bit?" He held up his index finger and thumb an inch apart. When I glared at him, Brody shook his head. "Tough crowd."

"Guilty crowd." I plopped down on a wrought iron chair which offered cool relief from the August night's heat. "What is wrong with *us*?"

"Calm down."

"Calm down? Really?" I asked in exasperation. "Why do we keep doing this, Brody? Why is it every time we see each other, every single time, we greet one another by smashing our open mouths together?"

"Our tradition?"

This time I snorted out a laugh. Brody smiled as he scraped an identical chair against the patio's cement and parked it next to mine. He sat and folded his arms across his slim, muscular frame. Underneath the cuffed sleeves of his blue and white pinstripe shirt, the edges of tattoos showed. My stomach fizzed at the sight of them. I am a sucker for muscular forearms, especially muscular, inked forearms. A slight breeze wafted Brody's crisp, woodsy scent toward me. I fought to keep my nose off his neck to take deeper breaths of him.

"Ya know, Harper," Brody started, "I followed you out here tonight because, well, because of our other times together—remember those?"

Remember them? I still fantasized about those "other times." The first time, I came out of a bar bathroom and acted on pure lust. I grabbed Brody's collar and pulled his lips down onto mine. One minute I walked out of the restroom, and the next ten minutes we feasted on each other like it was our last meal. It was the best damn make-out session I ever had, until our next one.

The other time happened at Marti and Declan's wedding. We danced to a slow, bluesy song. Our bodies moved together in one grinding motion. Brody led and coaxed my more-than-willing self into a coat room for another round of passion.

Both sessions ended as abruptly as they began. Both times, we didn't reunite during the night, nor any other nights that followed. I was probably another chink in his seasoned armor, or he, in my amateur sheath. There were so many reasons why we wouldn't work out, so many reasons I didn't want us to work out.

"Yes, I remember *those times*," I admitted. "I didn't need a reminder tonight."

"Reminders are good." He chuckled. "I thought tonight might be a chance to reminisce with our mouths, you know, as some people do."

"Some people do not." I snickered in shock.

"Okay, like we do. I'm glad I followed you. I mean, if I didn't, we wouldn't have—"

"I know what *we wouldn't have*, and that's my point—one of them anyway."

"And why isn't your boyfriend—"

"Date," I corrected.

"Randy, is it?"

"Randall."

"Why isn't your date, Randy, out here with you?" Brody replied with a smirk. "He could have done what we just did, with you. Not me. He's not my type."

"Good to know." I pushed air out through my nose. "You know, I only came out to cool down. I should have never started dancing. Dancing makes me hot and—"

"Oh, you're hot, all right." When he saw my eye-roll, he winced. "Bad line?"

"Terrible."

"I won't use it again." He shrugged. "I'm glad you danced. I liked watching you. You dance well."

"I'm okay."

But I was more than okay. I did dance well. I practiced every morning. For forty minutes, I danced to stay in shape, or to stay in *my* shape, on the curvy side, as in the last time single-digit-sized clothing fit my body, my age was in the single digits. I wore a nice, comfortable size twelve or fourteen, depending on the fashion. Not bad for a mother of two.

"Doesn't matter, Brody." I rubbed my temples with my fingertips. "You can go in now. I think our make-out session is over."

"We can begin it again, you know."

When he leaned into me, I nearly took what he offered. He studied my face and stared at my lips. I sent a silent plea for him to take them into his mouth, devour them as before. I leaned closer, to encourage him when the slam of the screen door jerked me back.

"There you are, Brody. I couldn't find you in the house." The voice held thick a Scottish accent.

"Guess what? Ya found me, Ma." Brody held humor in his response.

"What are you doing out here?" she asked.

"Trying to make out with Harper," he whispered, but yelled back, "I needed some air."

"And Harper's out there with ya, now?"

"Yup." Brody traced his fingers on my bare thigh. I grabbed them and bent his fingers back. He flinched from the pain.

"Hi, Mrs. Reed," I called out with a laugh.

"Hi there, Harper," she responded. "It is hot inside, now isn't it?"

"It is. Wanna join us?" I asked and snickered when Brody hung his head in exaggerated disappointment.

"Oh no. I just threw some garbage out for Declan," Mrs. Reed volleyed back. "Don't be too long, Brody. Da wants to hear you and your brothers sing 'Danny Boy' before he leaves. You know how he is. It must be sung by his boys at every event, doesn't it? He'll always be my sweetheart from Ireland, I suppose."

"'Kay, Ma. I'll be in shortly."

"Oh, and your young man is looking for you, Harper."

"Shit," I mumbled. "If you see Randall, please tell him I'll be right in, Mrs. Reed?"

"I will, dear."

When the screen door closed, I whipped around to Brody and pointed to the house. "See. Anyone could have come out and caught us, including our—"

I let the words drop as we both knew the end to the sentence. I should have gone back inside and return to

5

Randall. Instead, I shifted in the chair and wrapped my arms around my knees. I glanced over at Brody. He grinned and showed off those marvelous mutations in the Reed family gene pool—his dimples.

"What?" I asked.

"You're so beautiful, so uniquely beautiful."

"Uniquely beautiful, huh?" I pushed out a scoff. "Isn't that what a mother says to her ugly duckling daughter before telling her she will, one day, grow into a beautiful swan?"

"No, it's what I say when I want to describe a woman who stands out in a crowd, a woman, who among other beautiful women, demands my attention—a woman like you."

Now that *was* a great line. I mean, I don't consider myself unattractive, and my eyes, a shade close to violet, are unique. But if the tabloids were correct, Brody Reed, the well-known former lead singer to one of the hottest indie bands of the past decade, dated many attractive women with unique and beautiful traits. When I looked into his eyes, I almost believed him. Almost.

"You know why I am so damn attracted to you?" he asked. "It's the confident way you move, your maturity, and—"

"Oh shit. You did not just use the word *maturity*?" I hissed. "You mean old, right?"

"No, I mean maturity, a true woman."

"Brody, these are all lines you keep feeding me here."

"They're feelings, not lines, Harper."

"Yeah, right." I jeered. "It doesn't matter anyway. I am not what you want."

"And what do you think I want, Ms. McReynolds?"

"You want a woman who is young and thin, maybe blonde, but definitely young and thin, the thinner, the better."

"I do?"

"Of course, you do. Most men do."

"Uh oh. You're anti-men." Brody gave me a side glance.

"I am not," I protested.

But Brody wasn't wrong. After the crap I went through at the hands of my ex, anti-men was the kindest word to describe me.

"Let me ask you something, Harper. Why did you come out here tonight?"

"I told you. I needed to cool down after dancing."

"Needed to cool down." He repeated my words as he scratched the golden stubble on his square jaw. "Or, maybe you thought we might end up like always? Maybe you wanted to get away from Randy for us to greet each other in our traditional way, you know, mouths open."

"Puh-leeze," I said. "Don't flatter yourself. I wouldn't purposely do that to Randall. He's a nice guy."

Randall Prescott was a nice guy, a sweet, dependable, nice guy. He was decent looking, in a semi-dorky way. He worked hard, drew a steady income, and was reliable. He listened attentively as if I mattered. I was comfortable, unafraid, and relaxed around him. After the chaos of my past, I needed Randall Prescott.

"A nice boyfriend does it for ya?"

"Well, duh." I sounded like my teenaged daughter. "And Randall is not my boyfriend. He and I are still in the dating stage. We have not ventured into boyfriend territory."

"Okay. I get it." Brody put up his hands.

"There's nothing to get other than I am a horrible date, and so are you." I scooted to the edge of the chair and looked at him. "Why aren't you with your date—what's her name?"

"Her name is Z."

"Z." I sniffed. "What kind of name is Z?"

"It's short for Jasmine."

"Well, don't be judging Randall because Z's no prize."

But Z was a prize, and all the men who were at the party, and my friend, Esther, kept their eyes on the prize. Z was tall and thin with blonde hair, bee-stung lips, and big boobs. Sure, her attributes were enhanced, but I don't think any of the men, or Esther, cared.

"I'm not judging him, and Z's okay. But I'm not with Z because I'm out here with you right now."

"Making you as shitty a date as me."

"Probably."

I stood and walked away from him. I needed distance to sort out my feelings without Brody's gray eyes watching me. He came up alongside me, tilted his long body back on the fence, and crossed his feet in front of him. I kept my gaze on the ground.

"Dig the kicks, cowboy." I pointed to his pair of gray, scuffed-up boots.

"You don't like them?"

"No, actually, they are great."

"With a great story."

I waited for more, and he disappointed me when only silence followed.

"Come on, Reed. Don't leave me hanging here."

"Okay, but only because you asked." He looked at me and winked, a wink which made my body liquefy. Damn it. "One night, after a concert in Mexico City, I wandered off to explore with a friend of mine, Reggie."

"Ohhhh. A special girrrrl." My words came out like the sing-song of a kindergartner teasing a classmate about a crush.

"No, the drummer for our band, but interesting where you went. Anyway, we ended up in a town called Something-Tula. Not sure of the exact name or how we got there. A fifth of tequila probably clouded my mind. I remember the last part of the name was Tula because I corrected Reggie every time he said tulip."

"Sounds like Gracie." I snorted.

"Gracie?"

"My five-year-old daughter. She's always making up words." I could have gone on, but I didn't want to give him glimpses into my kids. "Anyway, you went to Tulip, I mean Tula, and?"

"And there was an old man on a street corner, selling boots at one in the morning. Weird to be out selling only boots so late, I know. I looked at all the boots, and I kept coming back to these." He nodded down to his pair.

"You must have liked them."

"I did, but there was something else. The old man saw my interest and said something. Now my Spanish is not the greatest—ya know, a few years in high school—and I didn't catch all of it, but I think the old man said they'd give me good luck. And, for some

9

reason, I believed him."

"The tequila?" I asked.

"I thought so too, at the time." His almost awkwardly broad shoulders lifted in a half shrug. "But I tell you what, when I tried them on, goddamn if they weren't comfortable like I had broken them in for years. I bought them on the spot."

"The next morning as we traveled to the airport, I made our driver take a detour to the old man's corner. I wanted to ask him more about these boots because I doubted my inebriated mind. Hell, maybe even buy another pair, but we couldn't find the place. Reggie and I laughed it off convinced we were so drunk we forgot. I don't know. A part of me wants to believe maybe he never existed, and somehow I was meant to have these boots."

"Huh" was all I could say as I fell deeper into Brody's hypnotic story.

"What? You don't believe me?"

"I will give you this," I murmured. "It is a great story."

"One I never told anyone."

"Why?"

"Because I think people will have the same look you have right now, the one of disbelief."

"You always have Reggie to back you."

"Reggie died of a heroin overdose, six months after our Mexico City gig." Brody didn't look at me but rather spoke his words into the night's darkness.

I gazed in the same direction. "That sucks."

"It does."

We didn't talk for a few minutes. Perhaps because we wanted to give the memory of Reggie some respect;

perhaps we didn't know what else to say; perhaps both.

"Let me ask you something, Harper." Brody looked at me. "Why do you think we have never gone further? And I don't mean just sex. I mean, why aren't we each other's Randall and Z?"

"I don't know, but I can guess."

"And?"

"And…" I chose my next words carefully. "We're different. I'm a single, suburban mother of two. You're this crazy-famous rock star. The two worlds shall never meet."

"I'm not crazy-famous. Crazy, maybe. And I'm so not a rock star." He sneered. "I was in a band with a few years of success."

"Brody, you sold out arenas and won a few Grammys. You're famous enough."

"Maybe." He turned to me and traced a finger down my neck to my collarbone, where he massaged it. And God help me, I let him.

My eyelids drooped, and my breaths grew shallow. I enjoyed the feel of his touch, until I let out a plea so unconvincing, I doubted it myself. "Stop."

And he did stop. I moved away, ducking around his body. He was dangerous.

"You know what I think?" he asked. "I think we're both afraid to act on this attraction."

"My reasons aren't complicated."

"You mean, besides me being this famous rock star?"

"Yes." The ground held my stare. "But I'm not sure if you want to hear them."

"Try me."

"Well, for starters, I am thirty-four, which makes

me what? Six? Seven years older than you?"

"Six."

"That's a lot of years, Brody," I said. "And I am a single mother of two girls."

"*So?*"

"So, I have to think of them and what they need. They need what you can't give." I pointed to the house. "They need what's in there. They need Randall."

He did not argue or question me. When I looked at him, I expected to see a reaction on his face. Instead, I saw an expression as blank as the undecorated wall in Declan and Marti's new house. And so, I continued.

"My reality is I have a thirteen-year-old daughter with a bad attitude who fights me at every turn. She is entering her last year of middle school. Middle school. The true definition of hell on earth. I have another daughter starting kindergarten. She's adorable and beautiful and represents everything right in this world. And she has some disabilities, reminding me the world is not always right. I spend a lot of time trying to hold it together."

"But Randall fits into all of this?"

"Yes, of course." I let out a deep breath. "Randall is nice and kind and comfortable and stable—all the things I want. All the things I need. My relationship with Randall is predictable. It helps me hold together what I have. He is what I can handle. Honestly, I can't handle you, not with everything else I have in my life."

"Wow."

"Come on. Your reputation precedes you. I read the tabloids. I watch celebrity shows. You like women, you like to party, and—"

"I don't party anymore, sugar. I am sober now and

have been for a long time. Don't pin that on me." His eyes narrowed, and his words were sharp. "What you read in the tabloids or see on those shit TV shows? They're not me. They're an exaggeration of me meant to entertain."

"I'm sorry." And I was. My words hit his Achilles' heel, smack dab in the middle. His face softened. "Why do you think we never got together, Brody?"

"I think because I always felt all the reasons you just gave me. And, I think, I see the walls you built because of some fucked-up things in your past. And maybe you're right. Maybe I'm not the one to try to climb them. But, in the meantime, I'd like to be friends."

"Friends?" I sneered. "Like you could be friends with me."

"Wow, someone has a high opinion of herself."

"We make out every time we see each other." I laughed, and he smiled. "Come on. Do you even know how to be friends with women?"

"Sure, I like women."

"I bet."

"Okay, I will take that bet." He held out his hand.

"What bet?"

"I bet I can be friends with you, Ms. Harper McReynolds."

"Not what I said." I turned toward the house. "Nice talking with you tonight, Brody."

"Hold on there, thirty-four-year-old, weight-of-the-world-on-your-shoulders woman." He grabbed my elbow to stop me. "I will take your challenge, unless, secretly you're scared to be my friend. Maybe you think *there's no way I can only be friends with this gorgeous man with the cool kicks."*

"Really?"

"I'm just saying, maybe you're thinking about sex with me right now and well—"

"Okay. These will be our rules." If he wanted a bet, I'd give him a bet. "We'll give it three months, until Thanksgiving. In those three months, we can only be friends. We can hang out, but no dates. There is a difference. You need to treat me like a friend, a bud, a pal. We can't have our traditional greetings."

"Hard to break tradition, but okay." Brody nodded with a grin. "And if I do cross that line? Then what?"

"You will lose your dignity."

"Well, there's that." He looked down at his feet in thought and then up at me. "No. If I lose, you can have these boots. You like them. I like them. And I'm *that* confident I can be, and always remain, your friend."

"Brody, I can't take your boots."

"Who said you will?" He lifted his eyebrows.

"And what about you?"

"Me?" I asked.

"Yes, you. What do you have important to you?"

"You mean if I fall madly in love with you, thus begging for sex and losing the bet?"

"Nooooo, I thought more along the lines of if I win and can stay friends. What do you lose, Harper?"

"Well, I already lost my virginity. And you can't have my kids."

"Not sure if I would know what to do with them." Brody grabbed me by the shoulders and looked down at me. "I'll tell you what. If you lose, you'll have to come to my parents' Thanksgiving dinner, with my entire family there, and admit to me, and everyone else, you were wrong. You will have to say how horrible you feel about thinking less of me, and I can be friends with a woman."

"I will?"

"Yes. Oh, and wear something nice."

"Why?"

"Dunno. I'd like to see you look all knock-out-ish."

"Not a word."

"Shhh. Deal?"

"I have to crash your Thanksgiving dinner, with all your family?"

"Yes. And confess how wrong you were. Don't forget the part about looking all knock-outy-ish."

"I don't know." I hesitated. "Seems, steep."

"What's the matter? 'Fraid you're gonna lose?" Brody grinned. "Harper McReynolds, are you already thinking there is more between us? Hell, I only want to be friends."

"I bet."

"So, the bet's on?" Brody held out his hand.

"Yes." I smiled up at him and shook his hand. "The bet is on."

"Good." He kept my hand in his. "When do we start?"

"As soon as we enter the house. You have to treat me as your friend and no talk of our bet in front of Randall or Z, or anyone."

"Okay. Can I seal this bet with our traditional kiss?" He moved toward me. "For old time's sake?"

And because I knew I wouldn't taste him for some time, if ever, and I wanted one last chance to commit it all to memory, I whispered, "Yes."

As soon as I responded, his mouth took mine with

sweet tenderness. He drew my lips inside his mouth to suckle and nibble, while mocking my need for him. I groaned with impatience. As I tasted more of this delicious man, a screen door creaked open.

"Brody?" His mom's voice echoed in the yard. "Your da and I are leaving."

We laughed against each other's mouths and then withdrew.

"I'll be there in a minute, Ma." His eyes held mine as he tucked strands of hair behind my ears. "Bet's on, sugar."

I could only bring myself to nod as Brody left me standing in the yard, wondering who would lose the bet.

Chapter Two
Teenagers

"Momma. Momma." My shoulders rocked back and forth. I sank deeper into my bed and hoped the morning had not come yet. "Wake up, Momma. You're having a knifemare."

I propped one eye open and a pair of blue, semi-crossed eyes peered at me behind light pink glasses. Those baby blues needed extensive surgery in a few years in a desperate attempt to prevent blindness. My heart squeezed, like it always did, at the thought.

"You awake?" she asked, as her massive head of blonde curls flopped one way and then the other with every move of her head

"I am now," I yawned.

"Did I awake you?"

"Yes." I grabbed Gracie into a hug and tickled her neck with kisses. She exploded into giggles.

"Good." She pulled the covers away from me and snuggled up to me. "I wath athcared becauthe you kept thaying thomeone'th name in a thpooky voice."

With every s, her tongue slipped through one missing front tooth. "Did I?" I took in her scent of morning and little girl, the aroma of newness.

"Yeah, thome mothster named Brody."

I let out a snort. "Brody is not a monster, honey." He was a lot of things, but not a monster.

17

"Oh good. Who ith he then?"

"Brody's a friend." There. A word I had to get accustomed to saying.

In the nightmare Gracie thought I dreamed, Brody and I kissed, a fabulous, lingering kiss by a fence. The kiss led to Brody bending me over said fence as he took me from behind. It was a great, wet dream until the shake of a five-year-old woke me out of it and brought me back to my senses.

"I never heard of him, Momma." Gracie played with my fingers.

"He's a new friend. He's Mr. Declan's brother."

Gracie adored Declan and Marti. I became close with both during my fourth year at Noteah Middle School in the suburbs of Chicago. I was its administrative assistant when they landed jobs there— Marti as a sixth-grade teacher, and Declan as the school's social worker. Along with Esther Nittlebaugh, the school's art teacher, Marti and Declan quickly became part of my small circle of friends. The circle apparently grew with the addition of Declan's brother, Brody.

"Oh. You athcared to be Brody'th friend?" Gracie asked.

"No." Hell, yeah.

"Then why did you keep thaying his name like you wath?"

"Dreams are weird sometimes."

"Yeth. Like bemember the dream I had about..."

As Gracie recapped her ice cream mountain dream, I drifted off, thinking about the night before. When I got back to the house, Randall asked where I had been. I told him I went outside to get some air, which *was* the reason I went out to the backyard in the first place. Randall placed his hand my forehead and said he thought I had a fever because I looked flushed—thank you very much Brody Reed and your damn good kisses. Randall suggested leaving, and I almost agreed, before Esther grabbed me for another dance in the front room. For the rest of the night, I concentrated on having a good time.

The party thinned, and people moved outside to gather in a circle in the backyard. Some sat in chairs, and others plopped themselves on blankets or mats on the ground. Brody brought out his guitar and sang a few songs. His voice, his melodic raspy voice, sliced through me like a winter chill. When I let a shiver escape, Randall wrapped an arm around to warm me up.

From time to time, I caught Brody's gray eyes peering into me as if trying to dig out my secrets. By the third song, I did something I don't usually do, I lied. I leaned in and told Randall I felt ill. When we walked to the car during my fake escape, Brody's voice drifted over the fence and onto the street in a tease to call me back.

"Bemember, Momma?"

"Hmm?" I fell back to reality. "Oh. Yes, I do, Gracie. I remember."

"Crathy dream, right?"

"Very crazy." Her belly grumbled, and I poked at it. "Someone's hungry."

"Me." Gracie moved the blanket aside and stood up on my bed. "I'm thooooo hungry."

"Good." I sat up. "Then I will make us some breakfast. How do chocolate chip pancakes, bacon, and strawberries sound?"

"Fantathtic."

Gracie used my bed as a trampoline, the top of her baby doll pajamas parachuting up with each jump. As I watched in amusement, my heart squeezed. She and her sister were my life, and Randall Prescott fit into it very nicely.

"Morning, family," Josie, my thirteen-year-old, barely awake child, mumbled as she shuffled into the kitchen. I placed pancakes onto empty plates around the table.

"Morning, sunshine," I teased with forced enthusiasm.

"Humph," Josie responded, her half-opened eyes looking up at me. I waited for the day when she flipped me off, and sometimes, I'm not sure I blamed her.

I poured myself my version of coffee—half diet cola and half regular cola over ice. Early on, when my ex-husband told me to drink diet cola because of my "growing waistline," I snuck in some of his regular cola, my secret defiance, and the taste grew on me. Five years later, I still drank my concoction of regular and diet cola.

"Hi, Jothie." Gracie bit into her bacon. "We had fun yethterday with Aunt Hannah, didn't we?"

My little sister, Hanny, was brilliant and assiduous in her career. At twenty-eight, she had worked her way up at a successful Chicago accounting firm. She made beaucoup bucks and spent too much of it on my daughters. She had stuffed animal tea parties with Gracie and put on fashion shows with Josie. Twice a month, they spent the night in her tiny, cramped, over-priced Chicago condo by Lake Michigan. Beautiful was too weak of a word to describe Hannah. She was stunning, at least in her big sister's eyes.

"Always do." Josie slithered down into her seat and drank the glass of orange juice in one long gulp. "I wish we could have spent the night."

"She's working this morning." I placed two pancakes on Josie's plate. "She told you before you went there."

"Thanks, Mother. I forgot." Josie held the same sardonic trait as me, yet in her teenage angst, she did not know how to stop before crossing over into disrespect.

"Watch it." I pointed the spatula at her.

"I said I *wished*. I already knew. Whatevs." Josie played with the ends of her brown hair as she spoke, a sign of discomfort but not of retreat. "I am just saying—"

"Hello." A familiar, gentle voice called up my back steps.

"Come on in," I called.

I went to grab another plate and a mug of coffee. I don't drink coffee, but I have always kept a small pot on for Nonnie.

Nonnie was my friend, my pseudo grandmother, and my landlord. I have known Nonnie most of my life. She and her husband, Henry, lived next door to me growing up. She was my refuge from an unstable mother. Hanny, my brother Hayden, and I spent many of our nights and days there when we didn't know the whereabouts of our mother.

When Henry died, Nonnie moved to Noteah with her sister, Mona. Mona, divorced from her third husband, convinced Nonnie to buy a two-story home together. Mona lived upstairs, and Nonnie settled on the first floor. When Mona married her fourth husband and moved to Florida, Nonnie stayed, leaving the upstairs vacant. Five years ago, when my girls and I fled my ex, we took sanctuary in the apartment, and we have lived here ever since. Nonnie was an esteemed family member, and as such, Josie knew to respect her.

"Good morning, dear." Nonnie kissed the top of Josie's head.

"Morning." Josie's eyes darted to mine in a challenge.

"Nonnie." Gracie jumped out of her chair and hugged Nonnie's midsection. "Oh, good morning, my Nonnie."

"Good morning, my Gracie Girl." Nonnie smiled and ran her fingers down Gracie's hair as she clung onto her.

"I love my Nonnie. I love her tho much." Gracie spoke to herself, a habit she had from the moment she could talk.

"Here." I pulled out a chair as Gracie went back to her seat. I set her hot mug of coffee and an empty plate on the table. "Sit. How long have you been up?"

"Oh, a few hours. I had to change the bird feeders and say my morning prayers." Nonnie smiled, lighting up her wrinkled face. "You got your stove fixed."

"Not fully. Just the burners. I'm still waiting on a part for the oven."

"Let me call a repairman." She grabbed my hand. "Or maybe Hayden could fix it."

"I know how to repair things. Remember how I fixed your plumbing?"

"Yes, but Hayden is a mechanic. He can probably

fix it faster."

"I love my brother dearly, Nonnie, but he is not the most reliable."

"He's busy. He runs a great business with those motorcycles he repairs."

"He does, but he also has too busy a social life."

"He's young. He should." Nonnie adored Hayden, and she never wanted to hear anything negative about him, which included anything about Hayden's semi-manic night life.

"I suppose," I said.

"And you need to get out more, Harper." Before I had a chance to defend myself, Nonnie asked, "How was the party last night?"

How was I supposed to answer? Good? Odd? Passionate? I am a horrible person to Randall? I settled with "Good. Their house is nice and in a great neighborhood."

"Is Marti getting big? How far along is she again?"

"She's almost five months, and yes, she is getting big." I put some pancakes on to her plate. "She's finally starting to feel better, too. Her morning sickness stopped."

"Good." Nonnie nodded.

"Grathy called me last night." Josie's interruption caused silence to fall over the room like a curtain falling on a mundane act.

*Grathy* was what my girls called my mom. Since she demanded her own children to call her Kathy, no way my mother allowed my children to call her grandma. But I didn't want the girls to call her Kathy. After a "discussion" with her, she came up with Grathy—Grandma and Kathy combined. She thought it was clever. I thought it was stupid, but as Nonnie pointed out, it was a compromise.

My mother never called her kids or grandkids to catch up or check in. She always had a reason, and never a good one. She either wanted to borrow money or for me to bail her out of jail. She once called Josie crying and said she needed rent money, as if a then ten-year-old could help her out.

"Really?" I glanced over at Nonnie. "What did she want?"

"She talked to my dad," Josie said.

"She did?" My entire body tensed, my stomach tumbled, and my blood boiled.

"Uh-huh," Josie continued. "Grathy said Dad might be coming to Chicago and thought maybe I could get together with him. What'cha think?"

"I think." I hesitated and gave some thought to my next words. "I think, I'll have to think about it."

"I knew it!" Josie's yell bounced off every wall in the kitchen. "I told her you wouldn't let me see him."

"Josie, I told you I would think about it."

"Which means he can't. I don't know why you just can't say, 'Sure, Josie. He's your father. Of course, you can see him.' "

"You know why."

Josie *did* know why. Her memory of running to a neighbor's house in the middle of January, barefoot, without a coat, holding her broken ribs and asking for help while her father continued to beat on me would never be erased.

"I don't want to thee him." Gracie shrugged. "I don't care if I can't, Momma."

"I know, baby." I smiled.

"Grathy didn't say he wanted to see you, Gracie." Josie's words stung with the hurt and anger. "Just me. He wants to see me. In fact, you are the reason—"

"Josephine Lee Young," I interrupted. I knew what was coming next. She would blame Grace for our divorce and possibly his violence toward us. The last words flying out of Alan's sick mouth before Josie fled the house were "this wouldn't be happening if it weren't for the goddamn baby you're carrying. The one I never wanted."

"What?" She shrugged. "I'm being truthful."

"Are you? Or are you spitting back what you heard your father say?" I knew the minute those words vomited out of me, they were wrong. I looked over at Nonnie. Her expression told me she agreed with me. "Sorry. I shouldn't have said that."

"It'th okay, Momma." Always the peacemaker, Gracie smiled.

"No, it is not okay, for either of us."

"Fine." Josie got up from the table, pushing her chair to the floor as she did. "I will lie. He does want to see Gracie. He doesn't think it's her fault we're not a family anymore. And he doesn't think you're the b-word."

"Josephine." Nonnie's voice was barely audible. The shocked look on her face hurt me more than Josie's words.

"What? Grathy told me. She did. She said my dad thinks Mom is the b-word, Nonnie. I believe her because Grathy treats me like an adult. She doesn't keep things from me." And yet another problem with my mother. "I defended Mom and Grace to her, but now, I don't know why."

"Josie." I pinched the bridge between my nose. "Pick up the chair and go somewhere before we both regret any more words."

"Fine. I'll go to my damn room." Josie picked up the chair and glared at me. "And I'm going to Maggie's house this afternoon."

"Are you asking me or telling me?"

"You already said I could."

"Sure, before you threw this hissy fit. No way can you go to Maggie's house now."

"You're not being fair."

"No Maggie's house," I said and added as an afterthought, "I am keeping your phone for the rest of the weekend."

"Good luck finding it."

"Oh, I found it on the toilet tank this morning. I didn't want it to fall in, and now I'm keeping it."

"Shit." Josie stomped out of the kitchen and slammed her bedroom door.

I sat in the aftermath of Hurricane Josie, trying to grasp my daughter's swirling words. I didn't blame Josie, not entirely. My mother provokes the worst out of anyone, especially a teenage girl trying to hang onto positives about her father.

"Josie needth to put money in the thswear jar." Gracie's eyes widened behind her glasses, and her tongue touched the gap of her missing front teeth.

"Yes, I suppose she does."

"What did Jothie mean, Momma? About me?"

I looked over at Nonnie and saw the same hurt I swallowed. One day, I would have to tell Gracie about her dad, but leave out a few things. I pushed "one day" as far out as possible.

"Josie is upset," I said cautiously.

"Becauth of her dad?"

The *her* before dad was not lost on me. Gracie didn't think she had a dad. She didn't understand yet how conception worked. In her make-believe world of magic kingdoms and talking animals, Gracie only knew people existed. She saw pregnant women, even Marti, but she never questioned it. She understood fathers, but she also knew not everyone had one.

"Because of a lot of things, Grace." I sighed.

"I heard Uncle Hayden telled Nonnie he'th not a nithe man, and I'm a believer of him becauthe Uncle Hayden doethn't lie."

Hayden hated Alan. Hayden spent a few weeks in jail for beating the shit out of him.

"And another thing—" Josie reappeared in the kitchen.

"Josie, please." I pointed past her. "Go to your room."

"I want to live with Dad!" Josie screamed and exited in a performance worthy of an Oscar.

Silence filled the room. I took long, deep gulps of air. Nonnie sipped her coffee, and Gracie scraped her fork against her plate. Anxiety tightened my chest. I worried Josie was her father, temper and all, and I blamed myself for her future.

"Momma, my cartoon'th on." Gracie broke the silence and grabbed my hand with her sticky one. "Can I go watch it?"

"Sure, girly girl." I kissed her forehead, relieved for the diversion. "Go ahead."

"Yeth." Gracie pumped a fist into the air and scurried out.

"I'll help you with the dishes." Nonnie tried to stand.

"I've got them." I patted her shoulder. "Sorry you had to see that. Josie's a—"

"A teenage girl who is confused, and your mother doesn't help."

"Ya think?" I sighed.

"Problems in paradise? I heard Josie downstairs when I came in."

My sister, Hannah, looking flawless, glided into the room like a ballet dancer. Her hair, the shade of honey when the sun shone on it, was pulled back in a lazy ponytail. She hid her gemstone green eyes behind a pair of oversized, black-framed glasses. A loose, below-the-knee sundress covered her willowy frame.

"Josie is upset," Nonnie answered as Hannah planted a kiss on top of her head.

"Figured." Hannah nabbed a piece of bacon and bit into it. "Did Josie tell you Kathy called?"

"Yes, which is how it all began." I narrowed my eyes at my sister. "Wait. Why are you here? Weren't you supposed to work this weekend?

"Computers are updating. The boss lady forgot." Hannah rolled her eyes. "Waste of a fun sleepover. Anyway, I had nothing else planned, so ta-da, I'm here. What's going on?"

"A nightmare." I got up and filled a mug of coffee for Hannah. I placed it in front of her and sighed. "Kathy told Josie her father wants to see her, and Josie is insisting on it."

"You're not going to let her see Alan, are you?"

"Of course not, Hanny." I shook my head. "He's playing a mind game, trying to intimidate me, not caring about the impact on Josie. He doesn't want her. Alan only cares about Alan and bullying people. And, of course, Kathy feeds into it. She never backed me on anything, let alone Alan. She needs to stay out of my life."

"Was she ever in it?"

"No, but for some reason, she is smack dab in it where Alan is concerned."

"None of this matters now, does it?" Nonnie played with the crumbs on the table. "You know what you need to do."

"Can't you do it?" I half joked.

"Only you can talk to Josie. She needs to remember who Alan was, and you have to let Gracie know. Maybe it is time to see Sabrina."

Sabrina Foster was Josie's and my therapist. At first, we had appointments with her twice a week. Later, once-a-month sessions, and then down to four times a year. It had been three months since Josie saw her last. I knew I needed to call for an appointment soon.

"Maybe." I shrugged. "I will set it up soon. I don't even know where or how to start."

"Which is why Sabrina would help." Nonnie's smile warmed me.

"I know." I rubbed my face with my hands. "Can we change the subject?"

"Absolutely." Hannah grabbed another piece of bacon and pointed it at me. "Did Randall have a good time yesterday? Did everyone like him?"

"I think it went well." I rolled up a pancake and dipped it in syrup. "They all seemed to like him. Ester and Marti told me they liked how his eyes lit up when he told stories about me, or the girls, like he knew

Gracie and Josie were important to me."

"Wonderful." Nonnie patted my hand.

"It is." I wondered if Brody's eyes would even flicker. "He and Declan hit it off well, so well, in fact, Declan asked him to be on his basketball team as a sub. I guess one of the guys got hurt."

"Oh, I'm glad. Randall is a great catch as they said in my day," Nonnie said. "Last night, when you were finishing getting ready, I told Josie to roll up the hose and Gracie to pick up her toys outside. Randall went out with them to help the girls. I watched them from the window. They were running around and laughing, even Josie. They looked like they were having fun. That's an important quality in a man, laughing with children."

"I know." I sighed.

"Then how come I feel like I'm selling him to you?" Nonnie asked.

"You're not." I shook my head. "He's great, and I'm not."

"Oh, that's not true." Nonnie rubbed my shoulder.

"If you only knew," I mumbled.

"Educate us." Hannah took another piece of bacon.

"Never mind," I said and sipped my soda. Two sets of eyes stared at me while I swallowed. "Ah, hell. I kissed someone else last night."

Nonnie raised an eyebrow. "Who?"

"Brody Reed, Declan's brother." I played with the sweat beads on my glass.

"Oh." Nonnie didn't have to express her disappointment in me. I saw it in her eyes

"You moshed it up with Brody Reed?" Hannah's laugh boomed. "Holy shit."

"Hannah, language," Nonnie chastised.

"Sorry, but Nonnie, this man's a beautiful-looking, sexy as fu"—she looked at Nonnie—"as heck, a rock god, and my sister moshed with him."

"Stupidly." I shook my head. "God, I'm an idiot."

"Does Randall know?" Nonnie asked.

"Is he a good kisser?" Hannah inquired.

"No, Randall does not know." I sat back in my chair and looked at my fingers on my lap. I chose to ignore Hannah's question.

"Are you going to tell him?" Nonnie grabbed my wrist. "You're not going to break up with Randall, are you?"

"What? No. I like Randall. I do."

"But not enough, huh?" Hannah lifted an eyebrow.

"Shut up. No. I like him. Enough. More than enough," I explained before I exhaled. "It's a long story."

My cell phone buzzed.

"You're not a teenager, Harper. You shouldn't be doing stupid." Nonnie gave me the warning look she gave me as a child when she reprimanded me.

"I know."

The phone hummed again.

I snapped it up. I didn't want to hear Hannah gush, or for me to have to explain anymore to Nonnie because I didn't know if I could.

"Hello?" I shouted into my cell.

"Wow. What a greeting." Brody's voice came through my phone, sending an unexplained explosion of goosebumps over me. It pissed me off. "Everything okay?"

"No actually, it's not." I glared at Hannah who continued to laugh and glanced over at Nonnie who still

waited for an explanation. "Your timing is off."
"Or maybe, sugar, my timing is perfect."

Chapter Three
And Then Brody Called

"Let's start over. Hello, pal," Brody said with false enthusiasm.

"Why are you calling?"

"You're not getting it. Your response should be, 'Hello, friend.' "

"Brody—"

"I'm checking in as any good friend does, and it sounds like you can use one. Wanna talk about it?"

"No." I took a sip of my cola concoction. "So, I guess this is goodbye."

"You know I'll keep calling you back. I'm that type of friend, Harper McReynolds."

Despite my mood, I snorted.

"Listen." I glanced over at Nonnie. "How about I call you back? I have company."

"We're not company, and we're leaving." Nonnie pushed on the table to lift herself up. She rubbed my back as she went past me. Hannah didn't budge. "Come on, Hannah. Give your sister privacy.

"I'm not going anywhere. I want to know more."

"Hannah Marie." Nonnie gave her *the look*.

"Okay." Hannah sighed and got up from her chair.

"And Harper…" Nonnie kissed the top of my head. "Figure out what you want."

"But, Nonnie," Hannah said, and looped her arm in

33

Nonnie's. "It's Brody Reed."

I watched them leave and didn't talk for a few beats.

"Sugar, you still there?"

"Yeah." I sighed out. "I am."

"Something happen?"

"Just disappointed one of the most important people in my life and shocked my sister." I paused. "Wait. How did you get my phone number?"

"It wasn't easy. I knew Marti would ask way too many questions, and Declan would probably say he'd have to ask you and it would have spoiled the surprise. You are surprised, right?"

"Sure."

"Good," Brody said proudly. "Strong friendships are based on surprises."

"You pulled that out of your ass."

"No, no. I read it somewhere once."

"Yeah, right." I giggled. Giggled. Damn, I annoyed myself.

"Anyway, I did some detective work; namely, I looked at Declan's phone. His password's too easy, pathetically easy. Who uses their birthdate?"

"You're not being a detective; you're being nosy."

"Whatever you want to call it. Tell me you're not happy to hear from your new pal."

"Brody, my sister and Nonnie know."

"What's a Nonnie?"

"She's my everything, and she and Hannah know we kissed, and now Nonnie thinks I'm not a good person. She didn't have to say it, but I know she is probably thinking it."

"Part of your shitty morning? Knowing about us

and our fabulous, seeing-beyond-the-stars kiss?"

"Seeing beyond the stars, huh? Are you sure you're not laying it on too thick?"

"Never. Is it?"

"Yes."

"Other things, too?"

"Yes."

"Wanna tell me about it?"

"No."

"Can you say more than one word?" Brody asked.

"No." He chortled, and I smiled, feeling better. "Suffice it to say, besides them knowing, I'm dealing with an ex who is the biggest dick—not *has* the biggest, mind you, but *is*—and a thirteen-year-old girl who sometimes is the greatest kid in the world and then other times—"

"Not so much?"

"Not so much."

"Sounds thirteen to me." He took a long drink of something.

"Maybe." I brought my leg up on the chair, wrapping an arm around my knee. "But her asshole for a father doesn't help."

"Why's that?"

"Alan's a piece of shit ex, father, and man." I let the subject drop. I didn't want him in my past, especially the part with Alan in it. "Why are you up this early?"

"I guess we're changing subjects. I am an early riser."

"In more ways than one, I bet."

"Ms. McReynolds, I feel violated."

"Yeah, right." He slurped in my ear. "You are also

a loud drinker."

"I do enjoy my cups of coffee in the morning."

"Cups? As in how many?"

"Normally, one before my workout and then about four, five, ten more."

"Brody Reed," I admonished.

"Not proud of it. And don't tell me you don't do caffeine."

"No, I do." I looked down at my second glass of cola/diet cola concoction. "But not as much as you, and I hate coffee."

"First of all, that's a blasphemous thing to say. Second, I keep the coffee people in America in business."

"So, you are, if anything, an American and a religious one at that." I moved around the kitchen, cleared off plates, and put the butter away. "What kind of workout do you do?"

"Let's see, kickbox about six days a week, and I swim on Sundays. Sometimes, I'll run with my brothers. The workouts serve my ADD well."

"I don't think you're kidding."

"I'm not." He took a sip of coffee. "I would get into all sorts of trouble if I didn't exercise."

"You must have been a handful as a kid."

"As a kid, a teenager, an adult, I am just a handful."

"I'm starting to think so." I snorted.

"Your turn. Tell me, how do you get your rocking body? And I mean it in a friend-telling-another-friend-her-body-is-great sort of way."

"Mmm. I'm not sure friends say that to each other."

"What? My brother Declan notices. He's your friend."

"There you go. Making up stories. Declan does not—"

"According to his wife, he does. Of course, Marti is a tiny bit insecure."

"Ya think?" I asked.

"I think. I mean, I love Marti. We are friends, but her insecurity would turn me off if we were more than friends."

"She's young."

"She's not much younger than me."

"I know. Again, Marti's young."

"You are an ageist." Brody clucked. "It doesn't matter. All that does is what Declan thinks of Marti, and he loves her hard. Maybe now she's pregnant with a girl, she'll realize how—"

"Wait," I bellowed. "Marti's pregnant with a girl?"

"You didn't know?"

"No." I grinned when I thought how Marti told me she wanted boys because, after listening to my Josie stories, said they seemed be less trouble.

"Ah, shit. I have a big mouth," Brody mumbled.

"No worries. I won't say anything."

"You mean we're sharing our first secret? We really are friends. Can we have a sleepover next? Maybe have a pillow fight in our underwear?"

"Don't push it, Reed."

"Damn."

"You know," I said, "Declan once told me you were shy. You don't seem shy."

"I'm quiet with people, especially when I don't know them well. And in a crowd, I shrink back."

"Really? But it goes against your rock-star status."

"Rock star, huh?" Brody chuckled. "Why do you keep using that word?"

"Okay, performer."

"Better, and performing is behind me. My quiet got in my way, I suppose, which is why producing and writing songs suits me better."

"I understand. I have a sister who is quiet. I think you and Hanny would hit off. But first, you would have to promise me you'd treat her well."

"Nah, it'd never work," Brody said.

"Because you can't promise to be nice to her?" I teased. "I'm rethinking this friendship."

"I treat women well, very well." His "very well" came out all sexy, and my belly tumbled. "Do you believe me?"

"Yes," I said, almost moaned, and then coughed. "Then, why? You'd like Hanny. She's smart, funny, and beautiful."

"Well, if she resembles you, I am sure she is, but sugar, our friendship would suffer."

"How?"

"Whenever we'd get into a fight, you'd have to choose a side, and it'd always be Hanny's, thus ruining our friendship. You didn't think this fixing up thing through, Ms. McReynolds." Before I said anything more about Hanny, he jumped in. "Here's why I called. How would you and your girls like to go to a Cubs game?"

Josie loves sports—loves to play them, loves to watch them. Some would call her a tomboy, but not a word I like to use. It suggests girls are different if they are athletic and enjoy competition. The feminist in me would not agree. I think Josie is Josie.

"A game, huh?" I chewed it over.

"Oh, and I have a ticket for Randy too."

"Randall." I exhaled. "His name is Randall, and you know it."

"Sorry." He chuckled. "I have a ticket for him."

"Sounds like fun." I battled to keep my excitement level low. Sure, I loved seeing my girls happy, and they would be ecstatic. Josie watched Cubs games all the time with Nonnie. Gracie would love anywhere hot dogs were sold. And I had never been to Wrigley Field, one of the must-see places in Chicago. "Okay. When?"

"Tomorrow."

"Tomorrow?"

"Tomorrow. Are we going to start singing Broadway songs?" I laughed so hard the soda I sipped shot out through my nose. He joined in with his own, light laugh. "How about it?"

I thought for a moment about the grounding I gave Josie. I thought about her cruel words to both her sister and me. I thought about the lesson I would not be teaching her. I thought about how this might cool some of her anger toward me. And, sure, maybe I wanted her to like me again. I know. Bad mom.

"Sure. Randall won't be able to make it. He has a company golf outing tomorrow."

"What does he do for a living?"

"He's chief financial officer for his family business."

"What kind of business?" Brody slurped again.

"They make glass windows for high rises." I rushed through the explanation. It made Randall appear pompous and, I don't know, compared to Brody's lifestyle, boring. "So what time?"

"Wait. One more question. Why aren't you going to Randall's work thing?"

"Because his work thing came up before we started dating. Besides, we're not quite there yet."

"There? Without sounding Dr. Suessy, there where?"

I snorted. "You know, *there,* where I get to know his friends, his family, his coworkers. Randall met my friends for the first-time last night, and we were outside making out. God, I feel so shitty thinking about how I treated him."

"Yeah, yeah. You're horrible." Brody dismissed my words. "Has he met your kids?"

"Yes."

"So, you're *there* with him, but not *there*?"

"You got it." I snickered.

"Um, sure?" Brody questioned. "Declan and Marti liked him. They said he was easy to talk to and a good match for you. Even my da liked him. Everyone liked him."

"Because Randall is a likable guy. Maybe you should have talked to him last night."

"And how would I start a conversation? Your girlfriend is a great kisser?" Brody sniffed, and I snorted a laugh. "Okay, I will pick you and your girls up around ten thirty."

"You don't have to drive here. We can meet you there."

"But I want to drive."

"Seriously, we can—"

"Stop. Just say, *Okay, Brody. We'll be ready.*"

"Okay, Brody. We'll be ready," I said robotically.

40

"Huh. Easier than I thought." Brody chortled. "Oh, Bryn will be there."

"Bryn?"

"You know my sister Bryn, right?"

"I've seen her a few times. I'm not sure we've ever talked."

"Well, now's your chance. She's dating the guy who plays third base for Milwaukee."

"Cooper Milo?" I was stunned.

"You know him?"

"Well, I've heard of him, but who hasn't?" I've watched enough baseball with Nonnie and Josie to know some of the players.

"I didn't," Brody said. "I don't watch baseball."

"But Cooper Milo? He's been the league's MVP three years running, Golden Glove for two. He's been to the World Series three times.

"The what?"

"This friendship may not work." I smiled. I found myself smiling, a lot, with Brody. "How did they meet?"

"I don't know. Not something I ever asked, but you can when you see her. Although I will tell you, she's not the most outgoing person in the world, nor the friendliest, but she's my twin and—"

"Bryn's your twin sister? How come I didn't know?"

"I guess you didn't investigate my family tree thoroughly."

"If at all." I pulled myself up on the counter and got comfortable. "No, what I mean is why didn't Marti or Declan ever tell me?"

"Well, you're lucky Marti says anything about

Bryn."

"Why?"

"Marti and Bryn have this love-hate thing going on. Bryn is very protective of Declan."

"Why?"

"You know, you sound like a little kid with your whys."

"Why?" I smiled yet another smile. "Seriously, why does Bryn feel a need to protect her older brother?"

"That, sugar, is one long-ass story." Brody shut down the conversation. I took the hint and continued with casual.

"You and Bryn close?" I prodded the conversation along.

"We are. I think most twins have a special bond. When we were younger, we had our own language. I don't remember it, nor does Bryn, but my brothers told us it was very annoying."

"They are just jealous of your close bond."

"I have done some shitty things to break any type bond with my siblings, but we're getting back on track." He sounded sad, almost embarrassed. He paused then asked, "You're not going to ask what the shitty things were, Harper?"

"I don't ask what, only why." Brody chuckled on the other end. "Besides, I figure if you wanted to tell me, you would."

"Thank you." Brody breathed a sigh of relief. "Tell me more about your siblings. I know you have a sister who is funny, smart, and beautiful."

"Hannah. You forgot, she's your age. You're missing out, Brody."

"Not settling for second best, Harper."

"Brody, we—"

"Any other sibling you want to fix me up with?"

"Well, I do have a brother, Hayden, who is also smart and handsome, but something tells me you wouldn't be his type."

"Is he curvy? I do like curvy."

"He has a normal build but is completely heterosexual."

"Ah, well, thanks for looking out for me."

"What are friends for?" I teased.

"Hey, I need to tell you something. You know the date I brought to the party yesterday?"

"XYZ?"

"Z," Brody corrected me.

"What about her?"

"She's one of Bryn's best friends. And the last time the three of us were together, you and I were, you know, *together*, and—"

"Oh shit." I laughed. "You think I'm gonna tell Bryn we made out? What am I going to say? '*By the way, Bryn, I had my tongue in your brother's mouth Friday night, and I know XYZ is your good friend and all, but we're good, right?*' "

"It might be an icebreaker."

"In such a good way, too," I scoffed. "Does it bother you Nonnie and Hannah know?"

"No, but it does you."

"I'm trying not to let it." I sighed. "It's hard. Not so much Hannah, but Nonnie. I know she was so disappointed, and I hate to disappoint her. She's like my fairy godmother, my guardian angel, and a grandmother to my kids, all rolled into this one

43

beautiful woman, and I don't want her to ever think bad of me."

"She's your role model. I get it. Did your mom die?"

"No, my mom is very much alive," I said. "She wants to be called by her first name, Kathy, so Grandmother is not a title she would want nor a role she would ever embrace, at least not the way a grandmother should."

"Meaning?"

"Meaning Kathy hates getting old and doesn't accept her illness. And now, let's move on." No way did I want to open that decaying can of worms.

"How's your dad?"

"I don't know my dad. He was any one of eight men, none of whom I've ever met."

"Come again."

"Here's the short of it. Kathy followed a Grateful Dead tour the summer she graduated high school. She rode a bus belonging to one of her friends. Kathy decided it would be fun to see which man dirty danced the best. Not sure who won, but I know I wasn't the prize."

"No shit."

"No shit. Kathy told me all of this when it was probably inappropriate to tell me." I told him too much and needed to change subjects. "What about you, Reed? I bet you had a great childhood."

"It had its moments." Brody hesitated for a minute before he continued. "I inherited the alcoholism gene from my mom. You do know I'm a recovering alcoholic, right?"

"Uh-huh."

"Yeah, I guess most of America knows. The tabloids made sure of it." Brody words were sharp. "Anyway, my mom's drinking didn't make for a great childhood. If it wasn't for Cal—he's my oldest brother—it would have been shittier."

"I'm sorry, Brody." And I was, very sorry.

"Yeah, well, it happened. I understand it more as an adult, and it's not really my stone to throw at her." He jumped subjects. "So, tell me, what are you wearing? As a friend, I am interested in your wardrobe."

I laughed, not because it was funny, but more because it gave us relief in a subject matter hard for both of us.

"Black lace bra, matching crotchless panties, garter belt, and six-inch spike heels. You know, what the typical suburban mom wears on a Saturday morning of cleaning." I giggled, but Brody didn't join me. "Brody? You okay?"

"Yup. The damn visual you gave me sent me somewhere else for a minute."

"Again, only friends here, Reed, and speaking of friends, please don't tell Declan and Marti about us, about what we did in the backyard last night."

"I won't, but my mom knows."

"What? How?" I nearly knocked over my soda as I jumped off the counter.

"She told me as much."

"Nooooo." I gasped.

"Yessss." He mimicked my gasp. "Don't be so surprised. It wasn't very dark outside."

"Damn it. How do you know? What did she say?"

"I didn't give her a chance to say much. I told her it

was none of her business. Not exactly those words, but she got the point. Hey, it happened. Don't sweat it."

"But I do." I had to think this through. "Can't you explain to your mom that, for a minute, we let horny take over?"

"I'm not talking about being horny to my mom." Brody had a point. "Harper, you can spin it any way you want. If you're worried about Z or Randy finding out, I say, so they find out."

"Didn't you just tell me not to tell Bryn?"

"I didn't want Bryn to—" He paused. "Shit, I don't know."

"See. Not easy."

"Look, all I know is I'm good with what happened last night," Brody said. "I wish I felt bad, but I don't."

"Well, I'm feeling a whole lot of guilty here, Brody."

"So, you keep saying. Hey, we acted on an attraction, and now it's done."

"Because the attraction went away?"

"Well, no, but I do have a bet to win which means we have to be done."

"Right." Even as I agreed, disappointment trickled in. I mean, the man could kiss. "And you're a nice man, Brody Reed."

"Don't let it get out, okay?"

"Another secret we'll share."

"Another one, huh? We're getting even closer to a sleepover." I snorted, and he chuckled. "Oh, and Harper, when you see my sister tomorrow, remember, she can be very protective of me, and um, she can be very annoying, too."

"Noted." I jumped off the counter. "The game will

be fun."

"Momma." Gracie came in her bathing suit on backward. "Can I go thwiming?"

"I have to go." I ran a hand down Gracie's hair and pulled her into me. "I have a little girl dying to swim."

"You have a pool?" Brody asked.

"No. Just a hose."

"I'm a bit confused."

"Exactly my Gracie." I smiled down at her.

"I think I like her already." Brody chuckled. "See you tomorrow then."

"See you tomorrow, my lead pipe in hand in case Bryn gets out of control."

"Tough broad, Ms. McReynolds."

"You don't know the half of it, Mr. Reed."

"Bye, Harper." His voice was low, dangerous, and sexy as hell.

"Bye, Brody," I choked out.

## Chapter Four
## Waiting Is the Hardest Part

"Are you looking forward to the game tomorrow?" Randall asked.

I had my back pressed against Randall's chest in a comfortable lounge on my couch. His arm draped around me, and our fingers intertwined. The comfort of our bodies against one another reflected the ease of the night spent eating pizza and watching a movie about a dog and his owner. With Gracie tucked into her bed in a deep sleep, and with Josie spending the night with Nonnie—something we all agreed would allow Josie and me some time to bandage both our open wounds— Randall and I were alone in my living room.

"Cubs games are always fun. I wish you were coming too, but I understand." I kissed the top of his hand. "Are you okay with me going?"

"Why wouldn't I be?"

"I don't know." But I did know. My guilt ate away at me all evening like a stomach ulcer. I held an internal debate all night long on whether to tell Randall about my kiss with Brody.

"Do you want me to be jealous?"

"What? No?" I moved to give him my full attention. "Are you?"

"A little." Randall shrugged. "I wouldn't have brought it up if I wasn't."

"But why?"

"You spent some time alone with him yesterday, and now you're going to a Cubs game?" Randall gave a half smile. "It just seems odd to me. I didn't even know you two were friends."

I stared at Randall, not knowing my next words. My chance to tell him we kissed and then made the stupid bet presented itself. And yet, I wanted to lie and tell him Brody and I were old friends, and yesterday we reconnected. I didn't know what to say, and luckily, I didn't have to say anything.

"I suppose it's none of my business who you make friends with and what you do with them," Randall continued, "but it's Brody Reed. I mean the man is attractive."

"You *are* jealous." I grinned, hoping to lighten the mood. Randall didn't return my smile. I reached up and brushed his brown bangs to the side. "Randall, if Brody wanted to be with me in any other way than friends, would he have extended the invite to you or ask me to bring my kids? And if I wanted to, would I have told you about it?"

"No." Now he did smile. "I suppose not."

"No." I kissed his lips. I knew I had to be careful with my next words. I didn't want to lie or tell the entire truth. I stayed somewhere in the middle. "Look, I met Brody through Marti and Declan, a few times. Last night, I danced a lot in a hot house. I went outside to cool off. Brody was there. We talked."

So far, I hadn't lied. We *did* meet through Marti and Declan. We *did* talk, among other things. Of course, I didn't tell him about the "other things."

"And the more we talked," I finished, "the more we

connected, *as friends*."

"I don't mean to sound suspicious, Harper."

"No, no. It's okay, Randall. I understand. But I'm dating you, and Brody is dating a stunning woman."

"Did you know she is a lingerie model?"

"Figures," I mumbled. When Randall tilted his head in question, I let out a strangled laugh. "It figures an ex-rocker would be dating a lingerie model."

"Yeah, kind of a cliché." He laughed with me.

"You have nothing to worry about, Randall. Brody and I are just friends, okay?"

"Okay." He let go a puff of breath which held a hint of garlic from the night's pizza.

"Okay." I lifted my lips to kiss him, a soft light kiss, until he pulled me in to kiss me harder, with passion, maybe with a jealous passion.

Randall wasn't the best kisser. His kisses were wet and not creative. He did not tease or nibble. His kisses were repetitious and awkward. The description of great kissing, "he made my toes curl," didn't apply with Randall. When we kissed, my toes did not have a coil in them. To be fair, he wasn't awful either. He got better with time. I believed Randall's lack of skill corresponded with his lack of experience. He tried, though. God love him, he tried.

Randall's hands roamed up my shirt to my breast, and I grew excited. I straddled him and rubbed myself against his growing erection. I was hot and thought Randall had the potential to be as good as—damn you, Brody Reed. You ruined it.

I stopped my grinding and ended the kiss.

"Did you hear that?" I asked, my eyes widened as if a burglar just entered my apartment.

"Hear what?" His hands still played with my breasts.

"I think I heard Gracie." I took Randall's hands out of my shirt and got off his lap.

"I don't hear anything."

"No, wait." I put my finger on his lips to quiet him. My lie went on far enough. "No, you're right. I must have heard something else."

"Come back to me, my honeybun."

His words were corny but endearing. And when I looked at him, with his short hair ruffled, his glasses skewed on his face, his lips red from kissing and his arms stretched out to me, I smiled. He was so darn cute. It wasn't fair of me to put too much emphasis on a kiss.

"Randall." I cozied up to him. "I don't think I'm ready for us to have sex yet."

"Okay." He rubbed my back. "Let me just hold you."

Cupping his face, I kissed him long and hard. He wrapped his arms around me. "Thank you," I said.

"For what?"

"For being kind and understanding."

"You're welcome." Randall stroked my hair. "What did I ever do to deserve someone as beautiful as you? I am very lucky you chose me."

Guilt grew heavy on my chest, settling into me like a blanket wet with regret. "Randall, I—"

"Let's not talk." He pulled me in closer. "Let me just hold you."

And he did, for the next half hour. When he let me go, he kissed me on my forehead and told me to sleep well, without anger and with a genuine concern, and then he left.

\*\*\*\*

"You're wearing *that*?" Hannah spit out the words like vinegar splashed on her tongue.

"What's wrong with what I'm wearing?" I looked down at the Cubs T-shirt I'd borrowed from Josie, my comfortable cutoff jean shorts, and my red canvas shoes.

"You look, I don't know, un-Harper-like. Normally, you dress in something vintage and have more makeup on. You're scaring me here."

"Boo." I lunged at her and laughed when she flinched. "We're going to a baseball game, not a red-carpet event."

"At least wear your hair down."

"No." I purposely swung my ponytail when I walked out of the bedroom, Hannah at my heels. "Why are you here anyway, Hanny?"

"You're kidding, right? Brody Reed is coming to your house—for you. He moshed with you. I still can't get over it."

"Imagine. Brody Reed moshed with me, despite the hump on my back, and my wart and then there's my cackle."

Hannah hit my shoulder. "You know what I mean."

"Drop it, okay? We will not be moshing again. Just drop it."

"Is Randall okay with this?"

"I didn't have to ask him for permission, you know. But yes, I did tell him, and he told me to have a good time."

"Good." Hannah plopped down on an overstuffed loveseat in my front room. "When's Brody's coming over?"

52

"In a few." I scurried around the room, picking up the dolls Gracie placed on the floor and the furniture. Grabbing them, I threw them in a basket on the enclosed porch. "Seriously? You are going to sit there and wait for him."

"What part of *its Brody Reed* do you not understand?" She threw one of Gracie's dolls at me.

"Momma, I wanted my dollth to thtay there. They're having a thleepover while I'm gone." Gracie came into the room, a yellow and blue striped shirt over a pair of red checked pants barely fitting over her belly. She loved the shirt and the shorts, but she busted out of both.

"They'll have a sleepover in the basket." I kissed the tip of her nose as I walked by her, my hands full of another group of dolls. "In the meantime, sweetie, you're gonna have to pick out something else to wear."

"Why? I love thith outfit." She hugged her body tightly.

"I know, but it's getting too small for you, which is a good thing. It means you're growing."

"My little sister is growing up." Josie walked into the room and started to pick up the doll outfits scattered on the couch. She wore a pair of rolled-down basketball shorts, a Cubs tank top, and flip-flops. A baseball cap held back her thick, brown hair showing off all her beauty. She looked so much like her father—big cocoa eyes, high cheekbones, and a scattering of freckles. Even her thin build was her dad's. However, she inherited her round, full lips and sarcasm from me.

"I don't want to change." Gracie didn't whine often, but when she did, it was like a dog whistle, almost too high of a pitch to hear. Her whines usually happened after Josie and I fought.

"I'm sure you don't," I acknowledged, "but you're gonna have to."

"But I look pretty in thith one."

"You look pretty in any outfit."

"Momma, I don't wanna wear—"

"Grace, please." I held back a snap. I knew my nerves should not be taken out on anyone, least of all my five-year-old.

"Come on." Josie dropped the doll clothes into the basket. "I'll help you pick out a new outfit."

"Who is she and what did she do with Josie?" Hannah asked when the girls left the room.

"I know, right?" I shrugged. "We talked this morning about respect and boundaries."

"And that's all it took?"

"Well, that and I told her if she did anything to disrespect me, she would not be going to the Cubs game."

I put the last of the dolls in the basket and looked around the room. My front room was a mix of old and new. When I fled my ex, I couldn't very well carry my furniture with me. In our divorce settlement, I got the deep rose-colored couch I fell in love with at a resale shop right after Josie was born. An afghan Nonnie crocheted exploded in colors of reds, pinks, and white and hid a grape juice stain on its arm. The two overstuffed chairs in dark purple—Nonnie brought them down from her attic for us—were the most comfortable pieces of furniture in the room. My television rested on a chipped, wooden chest I purchased at a garage sale. On one side of the TV, a grandfather clock, from the early 1900s, chimed the time of ten thirty. I'd rescued the clock from the curb my mother put it on when she "grew bored with it." On the other side, a tall, ladder-back chair Hanny gave me one Christmas. With framed pictures of the kids' artwork and photographs scattered on the walls, my living room was comfy, but most importantly, it was our home and our haven.

"Harper has lived upstairs here for about five years. Or is it six? Let me think." Nonnie's voice came from the kitchen. "No, it's five years."

"Sorry to have bothered you, ma'am. I should have asked which doorbell to ring."

I held onto the back of the sofa to steady my racing heart when I heard Brody's voice. Crap. And then it dawned on me. "Shit."

"What?" Hannah whispered.

"I forgot to brush my teeth," I whispered back.

"Not a problem at all," Nonnie's said. "It's hard to tell which doorbell belongs to which floor anyway. I keep telling Harper we need to label them. But then again, I wouldn't have been able to meet you, now would I?"

"No, ma'am."

"And here she is."

"Hi." I ran past them, my hand over my mouth. "I'll be right back."

After I made certain my teeth were squeaky clean, my breath minty fresh, and my lips painted a light shade of plum, I took some deep breaths. I nodded to myself in the mirror and walked back into the front room.

Brody sat on the couch surrounded by the dolls I put into the basket a few minutes earlier. Gracie sat on one side of him and told a story about each of them. Josie sat on his other side, bombarding him with question after question about his old band, Sun Also Sets. Nonnie sat in a chair and scrutinized him with stares. And Hannah had not moved from her spot on the overstuffed loveseat, her long leg swung over its arm. She inspected Brody as if he were a painting.

"And thith ith Princtheth Penelope. She'th my favorite." Gracie held the doll close in front of Brody's face. He reeled back to get a look.

"Did Tosh write most of the music?" Josie shifted her position to face Brody. "He said in an interview once he did and then in another one, Lonnie said you did and—"

"Hi," I blared, knowing I needed to save him.

"Hi." He stood up and smiled. Okay, I understood why Hanny inspected him like art. He *was* a masterpiece.

He wore an away game Cubs jersey over a pair of navy-blue cargo shorts. Tattoos sleeved his right arm in colors of greens, reds, yellows, blues, and black. A shamrock with lettering on each petal covered most of his forearm. His blond hair hung loosely to his collar, where a pair of mirrored sunglasses dangled from the opening of his jersey.

"Hi," I repeated.

"Hi," he responded.

"You met everyone?" I grabbed my purse off the entertainment center.

"I did."

"I 'troducthd him to my dollth, didn't I?" Gracie asked.

"Every last one of them." He winked at me. A

flush crept from my throat and exploded onto my cheeks. Shit.

"You're Mithter Declan'th brother, right?" Gracie's head flopped to one side.

"I am." Brody looked down at her.

"Mr. Declan is nithe."

"Yes, he is." Brody smiled. "But I'll tell you a secret. I'm nicer."

"Momma said I can't keep thecretth from strangerth."

"I'm not a stranger."

"Yeth, you are. I don't know you."

"True, but—" Brody ran his hand through his hair. I let out a snort. He looked at me. "A little help here."

"Gracie, Mr. Brody tried to be funny. He didn't really mean it was a secret."

"Oh, a joke." Gracie forced out a giggle.

"I know, not a very good one." I bent down to be eye to eye with Gracie. I looked up at Brody while I spoke. "You see, Mr. Brody thinks he's funnier than he is. Let's go with it. We don't hurt his feelings."

"Smart ass," Brody mumbled between smirking lips.

"Oh, Mithter Brody, you can't thwear." Gracie shook her head. "You need to put money in our thwear jar."

"Swear jar?"

"Oh yeth." Gracie nodded.

"You don't have to." Josie rolled her eyes. "We have a swear jar. We put money in it every time we swear."

"Nonnie and me never thwearth." Gracie shook her pigtails. "Nuh-uh. Momma and Jothie do, and

57

thometimeth Aunt Hannah. Uncle Hayden doeth a lot, but not me and Nonnie."

"It's a stupid rule," Josie spat.

"No, actually," Brody corrected, "it's a good one."

"I suppose," Josie agreed as fast as she called it stupid. "Mom puts in as much as my Uncle Hayden. She's bad. Nonnie says she swears like a truck driver and then lectures about how swearing is a sign of ignorance."

"Nonnie has a point." He dug into his pocket and pulled out his wallet. He peered into it and asked, "Will a dollar be enough?"

"Uh-huh." Gracie's eyes grew behind the thick frames of her glasses.

"Put your money away." I pushed his hand. "You're taking us to a game."

"Rules are rules," he said.

"But you didn't know about it." I shook my head. "Not taking it."

"I try not to swear," Josie jumped in, "but it's hard when you have a mother who swears, like, all the time."

Nonnie laughed. "Okay, Josie, your mother does not swear all the time."

"Yes, she does, Nonnie," Josie snapped. When I narrowed my eyes at her, she looked down and mumbled, "Well, you do."

"Ith thith good, Momma?" Gracie climbed off the couch and showed off a pair of red biking shorts with a baby doll tank top in colors of blue, red, and white, the same outfit she wore for the Fourth of July.

"Better than good. Perfect." I smiled.

An awkward silence came into the room like a fog waiting for light. Brody rocked back on his heels and stared at the ground. Nonnie watched him with the interest of a father with a shotgun. Josie played with Gracie's hair, and Gracie's eyes drooped in pleasure. Hanny caught my eye and mouthed *Do something*.

"We should probably go," I said, slicing through the silence.

"Well, have a nice time," Nonnie said.

Brody looked at Nonnie and then Hannah. "Do you two want to come with us? I'm sure I can dig up extra tickets."

It was a suck-up move, and maybe over the top, but Nonnie appeared pleased, and I thought, *Well played, Mr. Reed, well played.*

"Oh, how nice." Nonnie blushed. "But no, thank you. I'll watch it at home."

"Hannah?" Brody asked. "I'm sure—"

"Thanks, but no." Hannah smiled. "You kids go and have a good time."

"And we kids should go, or we will miss warm-ups," Josie interjected.

"Have a nice time." Nonnie shook a crooked finger at Josie and Grace. "And you two behave."

"We will. And watch for us." Josie gave Nonnie a huge hug and took off toward the door. "Come on, Gracie. I'll race you to the car."

"Josie alwayth winth," Grace said to only herself.

"Josie," I called after them, "please get Gracie's car seat out of our car."

"Got it."

"Be nice to her, Harper," Nonnie said.

"I will try to be patient." I turned to her, aware of Brody behind me, and hugged her.

"Good." Nonnie looked over at Brody. "And you,

too. Be nice to my girls, especially Harper."

"I promise." Brody put his head down and shuffled his feet. I snorted out a laugh.

"And don't be so obvious about staring at Harper's ass in front of my nieces," Hannah threw out.

"Okay." Red surged into Brody's cheeks.

"Yeah." I gave his shoulder a small poke. "My friends don't stare at my ass."

"Oh, I'm pretty sure Esther does." Brody opened his stance and waved a hand to have me walk in front of him.

"No, she doesn't," I said.

"No, she does," Hannah confirmed. "You've got a great ass. It's not the typical mom flat ass."

"Nonnie." I sent her a pleading look. "Help me out here."

"Have a good time," Nonnie called out with a laugh.

"Wait." When I stopped suddenly, Brody's hand fell to the small of my back. The heat of it seeped through my shirt. I tackled the shiver wanting to escape. Shit.

I turned into him and his gaze. Warmth from his body melted my insides. I took in deep breaths of his mint gum. For a few beats, we both looked at each other, no movement, no words.

"Uh—" Frazzled for a moment, I didn't remember why I stopped. "Oh, I have to grab a bag of Gracie's change of clothes, just in case."

"Of?" Brody finally dropped his hand.

"She sometimes has accidents." I walked past him toward the front porch. Both Nonnie and Hannah had grins on their faces. I pointed to Hannah and between clenched teeth said, "Stop it."

"What?" She put her hands up in self-defense. "I said nothing."

I yanked the bag off the couch and walked by her with a glare.

"Have a good time with your, um, friend," Hannah yelled after me.

Chapter Five
The Friendly Confines

The ride to the ballpark was a smooth one until we hit a bump. It was a small bump, yet it cracked a door into my past.

A Bob Marley song came on the radio, a favorite of mine and my girls. Josie and Brody began to sing with it, and at the chorus, Gracie's off-key voice joined in. My head bobbed up and down to the melody.

"Do you know this song?" Brody glanced my way.

"She does." Josie's hands floated in the air to the musical part.

"Then come on." Brody grabbed my hand and started moving it back and forth. "Join us."

"I can't sing." I snorted.

"Sure, you can. Everyone can sing."

"I can sing, but not very well."

"Says who?" Brody smirked.

"My dad," Josie chimed in.

"Did he now?" His jaw sawed back and forth, and his smile dropped.

"He did." I looked out the window.

Josie let out a nervous chuckle. "Once he warned her if she ever sang in front of him, it wouldn't be pretty."

"Well"—Brody spoke over the chorus—"I think singing is fun, no matter how it comes out, and you shouldn't give a damn what anyone says."

"Thwear jar," Gracie piped in.

"Right." Brody winked at her in the rearview mirror.

"Give it a rest, Gracie." Josie shook her head.

Because I didn't want pity from Brody, for Josie to think an abusive man stopped me from singing forever, and to stop the fight brewing between the girls, I whipped my head toward Brody, and I joined in. For the rest of ride, Brody and Josie tried to keep up with the out-of-tune, flat singing of Gracie and me. And for the first time in a long time, I loved singing.

When we entered the ballpark and found our seats, five rows back on the third-base side where the Cubs' pitcher warmed up, an excitement snuck into me causing giddiness. Those were emotions I had not experienced in a long time. I took a deep breath to calm myself.

Josie and Gracie made a beeline to the back of the dugout to seek out autographs for themselves and Nonnie. I sat down next to Brody. He didn't say much and looked lost in thought since we entered the ballpark.

"If I said, 'a penny for your thoughts,' I think I would have more money than the swear jar."

"I think you'd be right." Brody grinned.

"You okay?"

"Yup." He looked out at the ballpark to gather his thoughts. I let him collect. "You know, Harper, I had a great time in the car. Your girls are—"

"Not very shy, are they?"

"Nope."

To prove my point, Josie and Gracie danced in the

aisle to an overplayed Taylor Swift song—Gracie with the seriousness of a nun and Josie with the craziness of a clown. Brody and I laughed.

"They could entertain me all day. In fact, I—" His words dropped as he looked past me. I followed his glance. There stood a thin, legs-up-to-her-chin, puffy-lipped lingerie model. Z looked at him like a lioness ready to pounce on her prey. I sucked in my stomach and sat taller.

"Hi, Brody," she purred.

"Z." Brody got up from his seat. "I didn't know you would be here."

"I'm Bryn's plus one. Disappointed?" She leaned over me, planted a kiss on his lips, then wiped her lipstick off Brody's lips with her thumb. No doubt about it, Z marked her territory.

"Surprised." Brody pulled back.

"Why didn't we sit in the box seats like Bryn wanted to?" Z asked.

"Where is Bryn?" Brody asked.

"She'll be here." She glanced down at me.

Brody nodded toward me. "Do you remember Harper from Declan's party?"

"No, I don't." Without so much as a "how are you?" or an "excuse me," Z stretched her long legs over me and took a seat on the other side of Brody.

"Hey, bro." Bryn came down the row.

Bryn Reed stood a few inches taller than me, yet she was so self-assured, she seemed much taller. Her eyes were the same deep blue as her brother Declan's with a midnight-black jungle of lashes. She wore her dark hair short, pixie short, with wisps of curls throughout. It accentuated her alabaster skin and her full, rose-colored lips, the same shade and shape as Brody's. She jutted her jaw out to me. "Harper, right?"

"Yes." I gave one nod. "Bryn, right?"

"Uh-huh." She stood, looking down at me.

"Are you gonna sit or stare at my friend all day?" Brody scratched his stubble.

"How 'bout if I sit and stare?" Bryn lowered herself. Her glare never moved off me.

"Brody, you'll never guess who I saw." Z began her story, taking Brody's attention away from me. I looked over at Bryn. I wanted to smile, but I didn't think she would smile back. I ended up looking away.

"I hate when my brother gets all 'I don't deserve privileges,' " Bryn said.

"I don't know. I like these seats." They were the best seats I ever had.

"Not me. Brody never uses his fame to get anything. Z uses hers to get them into places, but Brody? He doesn't like the thought of being treated differently. Most times, I think he's right, but on a day like today, air conditioning with a cold beer would be heavenly."

"Hmm," was my response.

Silence fell over us like an uncomfortable, scratchy blanket, until Bryn spoke again.

"You have kids, right?"

"Two." I pointed at the rows ahead of me. "They're trying to get autographs now."

"I didn't think you had one so old." Bryn's eyes focused where I pointed.

"Yup. She's getting ready to go to graduate college soon." I nodded, my sarcasm in full glory.

Bryn didn't smile. "I'll sit here until they come

back."

"From college? It'll be a while, but okay." I saw a small smile creep and then retreat on Bryn. Brody chuckled. I wondered if he laughed in response to my remark or something Z said. "I don't care where you sit."

Z giggled a cute, very girlie giggle which caught my attention. I watched as Z picked up Brody's hand, held it to her lips, and began to suck on his finger. I almost vomited. I mean, come on. PDA is one thing; it's another to announce to everyone this is what I'm going to do to my boyfriend's penis. Brody squirmed in his seat, either from her brazen show of affection or a growing hard-on. Whatever the reason, he pulled his hand away.

"Not now, Z," he admonished.

"Poo." Z folded her arms across her chest. "You're no fun."

"Z's demonstrative with Brody." Bryn broke my glance, my look, okay, my stare. I darted my eyes back to my girls. "It takes some getting used to."

Cooper Milo, with the sun reflecting off his cocoa brown skin, signed autographs near Josie and Gracie. Josie put out her program, and he grabbed it. He said a few words and smiled down at Gracie as they both talked up a storm to him.

"Is he a good guy?" I tried another attempt at conversation.

"Milo? Sure." Bryn shrugged. "And he's a good lay."

"Bryn." Brody shook his head. Apparently, he had one ear in on our conversation, which brought me back to his first chuckle. I needed to stop obsessing over its reason.

"What? He is." Bryn put her feet up on the seat in front of her. "You know, men can say a bunch of shit about their conquests, and no one says anything. Women do it, and we're sluts. Double standards there, bro."

"True, but I don't need to hear about my sister's sex life."

"Then don't listen."

"Brody." Z grabbed his face and moved it toward her. "You know I'm only going to be in town a few more days. Can't you break your meeting tomorrow?"

"No, I…"

I lost the rest of the conversation when Bryn stunned me with her next words. They were quiet ones, and ones only meant for me.

"I know about you and Brody."

"What about us?" I asked as I fought to remain calm.

"Really?" Bryn's eyes danced up and down my face and then into my eyes as if she were looking for something in them. "Okay, I'll play. I know about you and Brody making out in the backyard on Friday. And I know about the make-out session at Cal's bar. And my cousin saw the you two in the coat room at the wedding."

"Brody and I are friends." I willed myself not to flinch.

"If you say so. From my experience, friends don't normally grope one another." Bryn shrugged.

"Bryn, sometimes things are not what you think."

"No? And what do I think?"

"I'm just saying appearances can be deceiving."

"You know, part of me wants to kick your ass because if I told Z, she would want to but certainly couldn't do it herself. She'd be too afraid to break a nail. Besides, I think you'd be the one getting the best of her."

"Kick my ass? What are you, twelve?" I scoffed. I regretted my next question. "And what does the other part want to do?"

"The other part wants to ask why Brody would leave a renowned, beautiful model, a woman every man wants and one he's been dating off and on for two years, alone at a party, full of men, mind you, to make out with a, well, a nearly plus-size mother and housewife."

"You know how to talk so purdy, don't you?" I asked in a saccharine-sweet voice.

"Well, you are a mom, aren't you?"

"What's your point?"

"I wonder why all of a sudden you and Brody have this, this friendship, as you are both calling it, and just how long you've had it?" I didn't respond. "And where is Randall, your boyfriend?"

"At his work golf outing," I snapped. "What business is this of yours anyway?"

She ignored my question. "Let me give you a warning, Harper. My brother has a history of playing with things that don't belong to him."

I got up. Now it was my turn to look down at her. "You need to talk this over with Brody, not me."

"I don't know if Brody would tell me anything. And I'm talking it over with you."

"Because you think I would?" I forced out a laugh laced with bitterness.

"I thought I'd try."

I gave a fake smile. "None of this is any of your business, including what you think you saw at Declan's party or at Cal's or whatever your cousin told you."

"Oh, honey, Brody is my twin brother and Z is my friend. Of course, it is."

"Oh, honey, you are one condescending bi—" I stopped myself and moved past her. "Excuse me. I have to get my girls."

"Where ya going?" Brody called after me.

"To get hot dogs for the girls." I didn't even look back when I spoke.

"Here, let me give you money for them."

"No." I whirled toward him. "I've got it."

As I reached the end of our row, Brody snapped at Bryn. "What the hell did you say to her?"

****

For the rest of the game I attempted to keep Gracie entertained. She grew restless before the seventh inning stretch. Josie enjoyed every pitch, grounder, catch, and out. During the sixth inning, a foul ball came toward us. Brody, Josie, Gracie, Bryn, and I jumped up in surprise. Z was too busy talking on the phone to move. As the ball neared us, I tried to step in front of Gracie and Josie, but instead tripped over the legs of my seat and fell back into Brody. His hands grabbed my hips and steadied me. His thumb pressed on my exposed skin above the waistband of my shorts. The heat of his hands and the roughness of his thumbs callouses on me caused a stutter in my heart.

"Watch it!" I screamed.

Josie, with the instincts of a cat, took off her hat, poked it out in front of Gracie and caught the ball.

Everyone around us went wild. People applauded and whooped it up as Josie took bows.

"Well done." Brody laughed. His hand found a resting place on the small of my back.

"Oh my God!" I yelled and grabbed both girls into a hug. As I bent, Brody's hand fell to my ass and withdrew quickly.

A small crowd began to gather and then grew bigger. At first, I thought the crowd was there to compliment Josie on her catch. It only took a few beats to remember the true reason. The ever-growing crowd's attention centered around the celebrities we sat with, Brody and Z. People pushed up against them like horses released out of a gate.

For the next twenty minutes, Brody and Z signed autograph after autograph. Brody said something small to every fan handing him a pen and paper. Z, on the other hand, signed and gave the signature back as if she were paying taxes. When it didn't let up, Bryn asked security to clear the area. They did, and Brody shrugged apologies.

On the ride home, both girls were quiet. Josie had her headphones plugged into the MP3 port in the back of Brody's Jeep, and Gracie, with her thumb hooked to the side of her mouth, fell fast asleep.

I didn't want to talk. I hadn't wanted to speak since my conversation with Bryn. The whole afternoon was odd. I was uncomfortable as Z staked her claim on Brody by a hand hold or a snuggle into him. When Brody tried to talk to me, Z grabbed his attention with a whine of his name or a planted kiss. Maybe our friendship was like Bryn inferred—a play thing. I didn't want to be played.

"You want to stop somewhere to eat?" Brody threw against our wall of quiet.

"No," I said with irritation, and quickly cleared my throat. "No, it's been a long day."

"I can pull into a drive-thru, grab something quick."

"No thanks." I tried to be light. "One more thing in any of our mouths, and I think we'd bust."

"Nothing like ballpark hot dogs, huh?"

"Nothing."

"Gracie thought so, Josie thought so twice, and how many did you have?"

"One."

"One," he repeated. It became quiet for a few more minutes. Brody tried again. "With all the ice cream and cotton candy, I hope Gracie doesn't get sick."

"Me too."

Brody nodded and looked toward the road. We spent another five minutes in silence.

"Are you angry at me for some reason?" Brody's slanted sideways at me.

"No." The more accurate adjectives were aggravated, bewildered, and confused at what the hell I was doing with Brody.

"Sugar, I am sorry Z took up my time. I only wanted to spend it with you and your girls. I didn't know Bryn was bringing her."

"Doesn't matter." I sighed.

"You sure?"

"She's your girlfriend. I get it. We're friends, right? Why would I be mad?"

"I dunno, but you are."

"But I'm not."

"Why are you so quiet then? Since the ballpark, you—"

"Bryn knows." Not the real reason, but I needed to give him something.

"Knows what?" he asked and then raised his eyebrows. "Oh shit."

"Yeah, shit." I fell deeper into my seat. "She told me she knows, even about Cal's and our coat room grope. I don't know how she knows about Cal's—"

"We weren't too discreet."

"Well, now she wants to kick my ass."

"Bryn won't kick your ass. She can be—"

"A good friend and loyal sister. I get it." I nodded. "Bryn also warned me you're playing with me. I'm too old for games, Brody, even with friends. I need loyalty in my life, not mind games."

"I'm not playing." Brody's jaw sawed back and forth.

"I hope not."

Another blanket of silence floated between us and stayed for a few minutes. Tinny music blared from Josie's earphones. Gracie stirred in her back seat. And Brody lightly drummed on the steering wheel to a beat unheard by me. He stopped and glanced over at me.

"You know, we can't do anything about it now, Harper, and I can't keep convincing you our time together at Dec and Mart's didn't cross any line. If what we did upsets you so much, tell Randall. What's keeping you?"

"Because if I do, he may not want to be with me anymore, and I want to still be with him."

"Okay, then don't tell him." Brody shrugged. "Let it go. We're friends now, only friends. And hey, our tradition was broken this afternoon."

"You're right. We broke it." I snorted and then took a deep breath in. "I don't know. Are we supposed to pretend those kisses didn't happen?"

"Oh, I know they happened, but I'm not making a big deal of it." Before I said anything, he held up a hand. "Let me get this straight. You accuse me of not being able to be friends with a woman because I'm this shallow guy while you're the one who perhaps can't handle friendship. I guess I won then."

"What?"

"You heard me. I won the bet. Now you'll have to go to my family's Thanksgiving. It's a ways off, but—"

"Don't be looking all victorious." I punched his arm. "I didn't say you won."

"Sounded like you were conceding, which means I won."

"I'm not conceding."

"Sure, you are." He grinned at me, showing off those damn dimples.

"Oh, the bet's still on, Reed. Those boots are going to look great in my bathroom."

"Bathroom?"

"Sure, they can hold extra toilet paper rolls."

"My boots, the ones with the great story, may end up in your bathroom as toilet paper holders?"

"Absolutely."

"Now I'm working double time."

Our laughter quieted down. My head fell on the window, and I stared at the asphalt road going by.

"You know, "I said, "maybe we should tell everyone about our bet."

"So, they can convince you how having my boots

in your bathroom is not a good idea?"

"Wait and see, Mr. Reed." I reached over to touch the shamrock on his right arm and, for some reason, began to trace it with my fingernail. "Nice tats by the way."

"Thanks." He lifted a half grin.

"What do they all mean?"

"Well, the ones on my left arm were done at different times in my life. Some tell the tale of a concert or an album. One has the date of my sobriety, and there are a few tattoos about things in nature I dig," Brody explained. "And the one you're tracing with your fingernail, in a very unfriendly—" I jerked my hand away as he chuckled. "I got on my parents' thirtieth anniversary. Declan, Cal, Bryn, and I got them done together. Cal has one on the inside of his arm, Declan on his bicep, me on my forearm and Bryn on her calf. It's our initials on the leaves—Bryn and I share a leaf—and then on the stem is the date they got married. It is meant to remind us we're all part of each other."

"Wow. Beautiful."

"I suppose it is." He glanced over. "How about yours? I've caught a glimpse of one or two."

"Well, I have a tiger. It starts here." I pulled up my sleeve high enough to expose my shoulder. "And goes around to my back. It reminds me of strength and courage—things I need to be reminded of in life."

"Why?"

"Let's say it was my divorce gift to myself." I shifted in my seat and picked up my top to show off the two hearts intertwined on my rib cage with initials and dates. "This one represents the loves of my life."

"Two old boyfriends?"

"No." I slapped Brody's arm. "Gracie and Josie."

"I know." Brody laughed. "Any other ones?"

"I have a butterfly one you may never see, Mr. Reed. It was during my 'I'm sixteen, and I can do whatever I want' stage. The tattoo doesn't have any meaning other than being cliché."

"Sixteen? Underage, weren't you?"

"Didn't say I got it done legally." I raised my eyebrows. "When I think about it now, I realize I was only three years older than Josie, and I would kill her if she got one, especially where I did."

"You have me intrigued, Ms. McReynolds and mystery among friends is always good. I read it in a teen magazine."

"You do tend to read a lot, don't ya?" I asked with humor. "How about you? What was your first tattoo?"

"My first one was of a guitar, not very original either, but at least I was eighteen and legal."

"Always following the law there, Mr. Reed?"

"Um…" He hesitated. "Can I plead the fifth?"

There was another quiet pause. It was natural and warm this time.

"Bryn isn't a bad person." Brody gnawed on his thick bottom lip.

"As I said, she seems like a loyal friend and sister. I get it. You don't need to keep defending her to me."

"I *always* feel a need to defend her. Not a lot of people like her. She has this tough edge to her, but she has some kindness in her. She doesn't show it too often. She sees a lot in her job and—"

"What does she do? Marti makes it sound very mysterious."

"It's not." Brody cringed. "I know this is going to

sound contradictory, but I can't say. It's up to her."

"All right. I won't ask." I turned in my seat full of fascination. "With those muscles on her, I think she's a personal bodyguard for someone famous."

"I can't—"

"I know, say. I don't mean to keep digging, but does everyone in your family know?"

"Don't mean to dig but will." Brody looked at me and winked. The flush from his earlier wink crept up in me again. "Yes. We all know, as does her friends, so it's not a huge secret. It's actually not one at all. Still, it's up to her to tell people."

"I bet she's an agent of some kind, isn't she?" I put up my hand. "Promise. I won't ask anymore."

"Thanks. And thanks for understanding about Bryn. I guess it comes from being a sister yourself."

"Exactly."

"Are you protective, too?"

"I can be a mother hen, yes. My siblings have always needed protection."

"How so?"

The words fell from my mouth like stale food. "My mom is bipolar. She's never been the best about taking her meds. When she does, she is funny, gentle, caring, and understanding. She still has her vain moments, like not wanting to be reminded of her age. But growing up, when she stayed the course of meds and therapy, she was a good and loving mom. Then there were the times, way too many times, when she went off track."

"Not the best mom?"

"Not the best mom," I answered. "In the throes of her mania, Kathy becomes unpredictable, even dangerous. Growing up, I protected Hanny and Hayden through manic episodes scarier than any Wes Craven movie. Thank God for Nonnie during those times. She was our refuge. Nonnie and her husband, Henry, lived next door to us, and sometimes when things got way out of hand, we'd run over to their house."

"A tough illness."

"It is. One Hayden inherited, and I worry about him sometimes. Sure, he's better than Kathy about taking his meds, still I'm concerned he—" He gazed at me, and I didn't want to say more. "And I'm done talking about all this."

"You open up and then shut down a lot, Harper."

"To use your word, yup." I shifted uncomfortably in my seat. "And Z? What's your story with her?"

"Let's see. I've known Z for six years, but we've been dating for two, on and off. When I met her, we were into our get drunk or high stages. She's still in it. She does enjoy partying."

"Sucks for you."

"What does?"

"Having a partier as a girlfriend."

"Not really." Brody shrugged. "But it is the reason Marti doesn't like her. She thinks Z should be a bit less of a one around me. Well, and when Z drinks—how do I say this—she's not very nice, especially to Marti and Cal."

"Cal? But he is one of *the* nicest people."

"He is. Though sometimes he takes the big brother thing a bit too far."

"I understand. It's part of being the oldest sibling," I said. "How long have you been sober?"

"I've been sober four years, ten months, three weeks, and two days."

"But who's counting?" I laughed, but quickly stopped when he didn't join in.

"Oh, sugar, when you're an addict, you always count the days."

"I guess you do." I touched him again, and this time my fingernails raked up and down his forearm. An explosion of goosebumps appeared on his arm. I yanked my hand back as if I touched a hot pan. Damn it. "Does it bother you I asked?"

"No, not at all. What else do you want to know? I'm an open book. Take advantage of it."

"Okay." I peeked in the back of the Jeep to make sure the girls were not paying attention. "Why don't you enjoy performing anymore? What happened to your band? And why no more albums?"

"Wow. When you ask, you ask."

"Too much?"

"I set myself up. Let's see. I do perform live every now and then at Cal's bar. No, I don't play in big arenas anymore because I'm done with the travel, the waking up in different cities every couple of days, the not being home with my dogs. I'm plain tired of the road. I don't think I ever had the personality for it. I like the low key of being Brody Reed, the producer slash writer." Brody held up two fingers. "Second, my band broke up when Reggie died of an overdose, and the lead guitarist, Bobby Blues—a stupid made-up name—ran off to Sweden to avoid tax-evasion charges."

"Which would explain the no more albums."

"Which would explain no more albums," Brody echoed.

"Why didn't you ever go solo?"

"Because of all the reasons mentioned. Make

sense?"

"Sure." I stared at him.

"What?" He glanced at me and then back to the road.

"You seem to know yourself pretty well."

"Oh, sugs, I'm not so sure if I do."

"No, I mean it. Most people would live off their name or their fame or whatever. You've chosen a life, I don't know, more comfortable for you. Maybe I do have you pegged wrong. Maybe you aren't this fame mongrel, trying out the next best model or girl."

"Is that what you think?"

"I did. You can't really blame me." I looked out the window. "You were linked to this model or that actress. You were shown living it up at this bar or that party. It looked like you led a pretty wild life. Then I stopped hearing anything about you, probably when you were working on getting your life back on track. As I'm getting to know you, it surprises me how regular you are."

"Well, fiber helps." I snorted out a few laughs, making Brody grin. He glanced back when the Jeep came to a traffic-jam standstill, and I followed his gaze. Josie smiled at him and moved her head back and forth to the music. Gracie slept.

Brody looked at me for a beat and then focused on the road. "You know, I have done a lot of shitty things in my past, Harper. During my high, my buzz, my whatever, I hurt people. And I was a shit to women. There were women I used. They used me, too, I suppose, and always consensual use on each of our parts. It's probably why Bryn told you I play with women. I mean, I was scummy sometimes. I had many, too many, one-night stands. Promised to call women and never did. Hell, I even stole other men's women and didn't give a shit about it. Not such a great thing to do, huh?"

"No, not a great thing to do."

"Thanks for being honest. Most people from my past pitied me or told me what they thought I wanted to hear."

"Well, those were scummy things to do—to the other person, to you, and to the women."

"Yup. I've tried to reconcile it, you know, accepted it as part of my past, a past I spent drunk or high. I apologized for being a dick to many people. Some forgave me, others have not. And I don't blame the ones who haven't."

"Uh-huh."

I knew people changed, and I knew people changed once addiction let loose its grip, but I wondered if deep down Brody was the same, drunk he used to be. I wondered if sober Brody still toyed with people for shits and giggles. And I wondered why I had this draw to be friends with him, despite reservations screaming at me.

"And now you are thinking what a dick I am."

I softened my voice. "No, just thinking in general."

"And in general, what are you thinking about?"

"I don't want to tell you because I'd only lie."

"Fair enough," Brody said.

"What about Z? She still stuck by you during your rehab, right?"

Brody thought for a moment. "Z and me? We're complicated. We're not always good together, but then sometimes, we're great."

"I bet," I teased.

"Nah. Not the sex part, but the companionship part, or friendship or, hell, I don't know what you call it. Maybe it's codependency on one another," Brody said. "I mean, I know I like her; it's not like I don't."

I fell silent with more thoughts.

"Come on, tell me what you think, Harper," Brody said. "No need to hold back. I'm a big boy."

"Okay." I hesitated for a minute. "I think you had a rough past, one I don't know everything about, and I'm not sure I want to. And I think your past would be another reason why you and I wouldn't work out, other than as friends. I don't need or want drama or knowing the man I am with had a life I may not like."

"Ouch."

"Ouch," I agreed. "Listen, I am all for knowing you as a friend. But if it's a struggle for you to keep your sobriety or make amends for what you did in the past, or even talk about it, and then there's your complication with Z, well, a relationship with you—"

"Whoa. I never said anything about being in a relationship with you. I never said I want to be committed to you. I mean, we both know our physical attraction is off the charts. But a relationship? I never said anything about a relationship. Don't jump there. Fun? Sure. I'm all in for fun."

"But at my age, with my two girls, I'm not in anything for fun anymore."

"Friendships can't be fun?"

"You're right. They can."

"So Randall is the serious you want?"

"Maybe." I shrugged. "I want dating to be easy, not hard, not a struggle, not full of baggage."

"Damn. And I thought I had the pity thing going with women." I didn't miss the bitter sarcasm.

"Brody, I didn't mean—"

"You know, my past isn't the prettiest, sugs. And Z represents a lot of my past. She's a smudge on an otherwise dirty glass, and I'm not going to excuse any of what I did. Pasts sometimes suck."

"I get sucky pasts, Brody. You didn't corner the market on them."

I knew he wanted to ask me more, but the girls stirred as we drew nearer to the house. We pulled into the driveway where a black, four-door sedan awaited our arrival. Randall Prescot leaned against it.

## Chapter Six
## You Remember Brody

As I approached Randall, I didn't know what to do. A kiss on the cheek would have been cheesy and a handshake, silly. He erased my doubt when he kissed me, opened mouth on my closed lips.

"You remember Brody." I nodded in Brody's direction.

"I do." Randall offered his hand to him. "I think we met at the party."

"We did," Brody agreed and shook his hand.

"Oh, Mithter Randall, we had tho much fun." Gracie almost doubled over in delight.

"You did?" Randall squatted in front of her. "Did you eat a lot of ice cream?"

"No." Gracie's eyes grew big as she shook her head. "But I ate hot dogth and popcorn and cotton candy."

"Wow. Do you have a tummy ache?" Randall asked.

"A little bit." She squished her face.

"Aw. Well, at least it's only a little bit." Randall brushed her nose with his finger and stood up. "And I saw a replay of your catch, Josie."

"You did?" Josie's eyes lit up as if she were about to blow out birthday candles.

"Yes. The TV station showed it on the after-game

replays."

"Seriously? They showed it on replays? Awesome." Josie took off in a jog. "I'm gonna go see if Nonnie saw us, too."

"Wait for me, Jothie."

"Girls," I called after them. "Isn't there something you want to say to Mr. Brody?"

Josie jogged backward. "Thanks. I had an awesome time."

"I'm glad," Brody replied.

Gracie stopped, looked toward the house, looked toward us and then back at the house. She ran back and threw herself onto Brody's legs in a hug. "Thank you, Mithter Brody. It wath tho much fun."

"You're welcome, Gracie." His long fingers stroked her hair, and I swallowed hard.

"Wait for me, Jothie." Gracie let go and ran toward the house.

My attention went back to Randall. An uncomfortable silence fell, and Randall looked from me to Brody and back to me again. Brody rocked back on his heels. I stared at the bricks on my house.

"They showed it on replay, huh?" I asked when the quiet grew too deafening.

"Yes, a lot." Randall groped for words. "They showed Brody and Z a lot, too. You were the talk of the broadcasters."

"I'm sure we were." Brody wasn't cocky, rather truthful, and a little embarrassed.

"Josie's great catch brought out all the autograph hounds," I added.

"Yeah, sorry about that," Brody said. "I didn't think about the attention a Cubs game might draw to you and your kids. I was hoping for a good time is all. And I thought I was doing pretty well not being recognized until your kid had to make a spectacular catch."

I snorted. "Sure, let's go with blaming Josie."

"The broadcasters were confused if Brody was there with Z or Harper," Randall continued. "They even joked how Brody dated two women. They talked about Z and wondered about Harper. They thought perhaps you are his other girlfriend."

I cocked my head and looked over at Brody. "When did I become your other girlfriend?"

"I guess right before our other engagement."

"Ah, well, I suppose they were going to find out about us before the other wedding, and then there's Laramie and Cutie Pie."

"I assume they are our other kids," Brody replied playfully.

"Yes. Our other twins."

"Twins, huh? I always forget. Who picked out those names?"

I smiled. "I did."

"And I let you?"

"Absolutely."

"Probably because I thought Gracie and Josie were great names. Foolish of me."

"Well, they got them now. Next time you will have to be a more active other father." I shrugged. Brody shrugged. And Randall stood there emotionless. I grabbed his hand. "Come on, Randall, this is funny. They were probably kidding. I mean, Z is Brody's type, not me."

"Not true. Z and I don't have other twins," Brody

mumbled.

I choked on a laugh. "Randall, nothing happened."

"Everything was on the up and up, Rand…all." Brody caught himself. "The press likes to blow up things. I am well-known, single, and sitting with two attractive women. They're gonna say what they're gonna say. Once a reporter announced my engagement to Bryn. I think he was fired once it was revealed she was my sister. It's all ridiculous. I am disappointed it took away from Josie's catch. Man, what a great catch."

"Aw." I looked at Brody. "Thanks."

"Why are you thanking me? You didn't catch it."

"No, but I birthed the catcher."

"True, but you—"

"You know, I thought so, too," Randall interrupted. "I thought *it's nothing*. It's the announcers making something out of nothing, and then I saw your hands on my girlfriend's hips."

I held down a shiver from the memory of the heat of Brody's hands and his thumb on my bare skin.

"I had them *there*?" Brody shrugged. "And I missed it? Huh, I think I would have enjoyed it, too."

"Stop. You're not helping." I stepped in front of Randall and smiled up at him. "Look, if Brody's hands were on my hips—"

"They were," Randall responded.

"Okay." I put my hand to his chest, and it was then I noticed his yellow short-sleeve shirt tucked inside a pair of pleated khaki shorts. The outfit looked like something a fifty-year-old man on the golf course might wear, not the casual look of a thirty-five-year-old. But it was Randall's look, and I was attracted to his dorkiness. "It was by accident. When the ball came toward Gracie,

I jumped up. Brody jumped up. When we jumped up, it probably looked like—"

"His hands were digging into your hips?"

"Wait." Brody put up a hand. "Did I touch her hips or dig into them? Please help me remember."

"Don't listen to him." I gave Randall another reassuring pat. "It may have *looked* like something, but it wasn't anything. My girls were there and Brody's girlfriend, who, I might add, was all over him."

"You noticed?" Brody asked.

"How could I not?" I turned to Brody. "She either hung on your arm or hung on you for dear life. I mean anyone ten rows in front or ten rows in back knew Z branded you as her man. I think a shirt saying, 'I'm with Brody Reed' would have served better, but I'm not sure they come in crop tops."

"Oh, wow, Harper. Meow." Brody purred.

"No, I'm not being catty. I'm being—"

"It looked like Brody was with *you* and the broadcasters seemed to agree," Randall said, and brought my attention back to him. He shook his head.

"Come on, Randall. You know it wasn't like that." When I placed the palm of my hand on his cheek, his expression mellowed.

"I know." Randall smiled sheepishly. "I'm being silly."

"Very silly," I agreed. "There is nothing to be worried about."

"You're right. It sure looked real to me, and you both smiled like—"

"I thought of the catch, nothing else." I interrupted and let my fingertips fall from Randall's face.

"Rand...all, you jealous little boyfriend, you."

Brody smirked. "Women like a little jealousy in men. It shows they care. Good going, guy."

"Well, I don't know." Randall's nose whistled in a laugh. A pink hue colored his cheeks. "I am surprised by my reaction. I suppose I am jealous. "

Brody nodded. "Sounds that way to me."

"You can't blame me though," Randall added quickly.

Brody slapped Randall's back. "No, I get it. Another man's hand on your beautiful girlfriend? Most men would be a little jealous. I would. Randall, you may get lucky tonight."

"Brody." I shook my head, and I moved in closer to Randall. "Although, he's right. I like this little jealousy of yours."

"Really?" Randall brought his mouth down on mine, and again, he gave me a full wet kiss. His mouth opened, mine remained shut. It was strange. Not because he never kissed me before, but because he did it in front of Brody. I looked over at Brody, a bit embarrassed. His wolf eyes stared into me. I didn't look away, until Randall spoke. "Well, you all looked like you had fun."

"We did."

"Good." Randall forced out a laugh. "I've been ridiculous."

"Don't worry about it." I grinned. "Think about it though, Randall. Brody's dating a lingerie model. To think he would go after a secretary, with two kids no less, is pretty ridiculous."

"I don't know. You're as beautiful as her." Randall beamed, and my heart warmed.

"Listened to him, Harp," Brody said. "Jesus, you

are way too hard on yourself."

"I'm not. I'm truthful. I mean if Z and I walked into a room of twenty men, where would the men's eyes go and stay? Onto Z. Randall is nice, but deep down, I know he would glance Z's way."

Randall said nothing as if the truth would hurt me.

"Wow." Brody pulled his hand through his hair and repeated. "Wow."

"Anyway, Randall, did you come over to talk about the great Josie catch?" My attention left Brody.

"And to return the DVD you lent me."

"Did you like it?"

"I fell asleep watching it." Randall's laugh escaped through his nose.

"Oh." I couldn't hide my disappointment.

"Sorry, sweetheart." Randall grabbed my hand as if sensing the change in my mood. "Really. I'm not into documentaries. You know how I like action movies. I tried though."

"Thanks for trying." I forced a smile.

"What DVD did you lend Randy?" Brody folded his arms across his chest, this time not correcting himself.

"I prefer Randall."

"What movie is it?" Brody showed an impolite side I never saw in him.

"The new Harris John documentary," I said in a huff.

"The one about single motherhood in America?" Brody nodded. "I heard about it. Good?"

"Excellent, actually," I answered, and forgot about Brody's rudeness as I talked about the movie. "One woman described exactly how I feel. She came from a single mother, didn't want it for herself, but ended up in it because of the choices she made and stayed in a marriage a lot longer than she should have. Great film."

"I'd like to watch it," Brody said.

"I like the war, shoot-em-up type of films," Randall interrupted.

"Randy," Brody growled, "Harper was talking about this movie."

"Don't." I sent a "shut up" glare to Brody. "I can defend myself if it bothered me. I don't need you."

"Maybe you did." Brody shot me an amused smirk. "Can I borrow the DVD sometime?"

"No," I snarled.

"Too bad." Brody shrugged his large shoulders. "I like John's style, especially in the documentary on the unfair stereotypes of the poor in America. Did you see that one yet?"

"No."

"One-word answers again? You need to up your vocabulary there, Harper."

"Okay, how about three words? You're being rude." I lifted an eyebrow.

"It's a start. Tell you what. I will lend you my movie if I can borrow yours.

"I didn't say I wanted to borrow it."

"Do you?"

"I suppose." But I more than suppose. I knew.

"Okay, then. Deal?" Brody held out his hand. When I looked down at his long-fingered paw, I took a calming breath to steady my racing heart. He had great hands.

"What? Not gonna shake it? Should I spit in my hand before I shake yours?"

"I think a shake, minus your spit, will be enough." And despite my anger, he did what he always did. He made me laugh.

"Deal." Brody grinned and grabbed my hand with his. He held it longer than necessary, or I held onto his longer than necessary. We held on to each other longer than necessary. I enjoyed the jolt racing through me from his touch. I watched Brody's eyes grow darker as they watched mine. Randall's voice broke our connection.

"Well, I'll go get the DVD then. It's in the front seat of my car." On his way, Randall turned to me and walked backward. "Oh, and I made a reservation at Horton's for five o'clock on Wednesday, okay?"

I plastered on a phony grin. "Sure."

"You like their salmon, right?"

"I do."

"Great." Randall turned and held up a finger. "Oh, and another thing. I got our tickets for the opera in the mail today. We're still on, right?"

"Uh-huh." I nodded.

"I am glad you're giving it another try," Randall said. "Where do you want to go after?"

"I don't know," I said.

"Right. Well, I'll pick out a place, just in case."

I watched Randall continue to his car. His shorts rode a little too high on his thighs, and his butt widened in them. But he was Randall, and he was my comfort.

"I had a great time today." Brody interrupted my stare.

"I did, too. Thank you." I looked over at Brody. "The girls will be talking about this for days, weeks maybe."

"Not years?"

"No, they have short attention spans."

Brody chuckled. "Sorry if Z made you uncomfortable."

"But not sorry you were rude to Randall?"

"I was?"

"Come on. You know you were." I put my hands on my hips. "If we're going to be friends, Randall will be part of our friendship. You have to stop being rude to him."

"You mean I have to call him by his full name?" When I sneered at him, Brody held up his hands. "Okay, I'll try."

"Seriously, Brody, you have to—"

"Well, I should probably get going. Randy wants to spend time with you." Brody put his fingertips to his mouth. "Oops. How rude of me to interrupt."

"Idiot."

"You know…" Brody leaned into me, his arms still folded across his chest. "Randall certainly wanted me to know all of your plans. I get it. He's marking his territory."

"I'm not his territory." I gave Brody a small shove.

"Sure, you are, just like you said I was Z's."

Randall came back to us and handed me the unwatched DVD. I, in turn, gave it to Brody. Brody took the DVD and held it out to his side as if to pass it off to someone else.

"Oh," Brody said and grabbed it back to his chest. "I thought we were playing a game of pass the DVD, like hot potato."

I snorted out a laugh so loud, I put my hand over my mouth in embarrassment. Brody grinned and

Randall scratched his head.

"I'm going to get Gracie's car seat out of Brody's car." I hiccupped out the last of my laughter. "I'll meet you upstairs. I think I have some leftover ham casserole if you want some. The girls and I are stuffed so I won't be making anything else."

"I'd love some. Your ham casserole is the best," Randall replied.

"Good." I rubbed his arm.

Randall nodded a goodbye to Brody and headed into the house.

"Maybe I should stay and have some of the ham casserole too," Brody said. "Randy did say it's the best."

"Go to hell." I shook my head and walked over to his Jeep.

"What? I'm repeating what Randall said."

"You're a jerk." I tried not to smile, but one crept out.

When we reached the car, Brody tossed my DVD into his front seat and bent in the back to take out Gracie's car seat. I watched as the material of his cargo shorts clung to his muscular ass cheeks, and thought, *I envy those shorts.*

"Thanks again, Brody." I coughed to get myself together. I couldn't let lust take over, not with Randall a few feet away in the house. Not ever.

"You already thanked me enough." Brody set the car seat down by my feet. His silver eyes gazed into mine. "And for the record, if you walked in the room with Z, my eyes would go to you and stay on you. But then again, you are my buddy."

"Smooth. A liar, but smooth."

Brody didn't even crack a smile. Instead, his stare explored my face and rested at my lips. I knew what would come next. I didn't want it to happen, but I couldn't stop it.

Brody leaned his head down and took my lips between his with the softness of a butterfly kiss. When he tried to move away from me, I pulled him down by his Cubs jersey and took his lower lip in between mine. I nibbled on it like a piece of forbidden chocolate. My tongue poked out to lick what I nibbled. Brody caught my tongue with his mouth and brought it in.

I stroked the velvety softness of his tongue, pulled back, then came in again to caress more slowly teasing him in a dance of stroke and retreat, stroke and retreat. I captured his tongue to suck on it with the gentleness and slow speed of a bee pulling out nectar. A low, guttural moan of pleasure escaped him.

When I deepened our kiss and became the aggressor, entangling my fingers through his thick, blond tresses, Brody drew me into him even more. He splayed his fingers on my ass and hauled my abdomen into his growing erection. I scraped the back of his neck with my fingernails, and his groan echoed into my mouth in appreciation.

The quiet giggles of Josie and Nonnie drifted out the front door, poking me with a reminder we were not alone. I pulled away from Brody with the quickness of a kid ripping her hand out of a cookie jar.

"Fuck. Shit. Damn it." I backed away from Brody and leaned against his Jeep to slow my breath.

"Damn is right, woman." Brody gently touched his lips as if he didn't want to erase me from them.

"What the hell did I just do, again?" I pulled in my

94

lips to lick off his deliciousness.

"Hey." Brody stuffed his hands in his pockets and tried to pull down the tightened material around his crotch. "We were keeping up our tradition."

"This isn't funny," I protested. "You should have stopped me."

"So, it's my fault?"

"Yes."

"Oh, no. You're not getting my boots, for what did you say? Toilet paper?"

"Maybe." I laughed.

"Nah, uh. I didn't break any rule. You attacked me. I had to defend myself."

"I know. I'm such a horrible person."

"Sugs." Brody stood in front of me and tilted my chin up. "Don't worry about it. It's okay."

"No. It's not okay." I inhaled deeply and looked up at him. "And, by the way, this, what we just did, doesn't mean I'm going to give up Randall for you, especially not for you. Randall is steady, and like I told you, it wouldn't work and—"

"Thanks for a nice day, Harper." Brody pulled away from me and yanked open the driver's side door. "Until you just ruined it."

"No, what I meant was—"

"I know what you meant." Before closing his door, Brody shot me one last look. The hurt in his eyes slapped me hard in the chest.

"Brody—"

"I'll talk to you soon, sugar."

Brody's Jeep burned out of my driveway, and I stared at its taillights until they were out of sight. The bang of the screen door disrupted my gaze. Randall's shadow came over me, and he draped his arm around me. I stiffened in guilt.

"He's a nice guy."

"He was rude to you."

"I think he was trying to be funny." Randall kissed the top of my head. "How about we go inside? You can heat up your famous ham casserole."

## Chapter Seven
### Randall's Passion

During the days following the Cubs game, there were rumblings on the Internet about me and my connection to Brody, but not a lot. Brody's celebrity status had dimmed in the years since Sun Also Sets broke up. Maybe because he didn't play anymore concerts, sing anymore number-one songs, or grace anymore covers of gossip magazines, and the trolls had short attention spans.

It helped that hours after the Cubs game, one of the sisters from the reality family, with first names starting with N, kissed a famous and incredibly talented yet married actor, thirty years her senior at a televised awards show. It took the spotlight right off Brody and Z. Brody was relieved, and Z was angry. Go figure.

The night after the Cubs game and my most recent attack on Brody, I focused on making the night great with Randall. I concentrated on pushing the kiss I shared with Brody aside and putting Randall front and center. It took some doing, but one long talk with myself in a bathroom done in whispers over running water, and I convinced myself I was swept away in gratitude for Brody and the Cubs game, nothing more

Randall and I eased into it with a board game and ham casserole with the girls. He made silly mistakes, sending Gracie into fits of giggles and Josie teasing him. He took it all in stride, laughing and joining in on the fun.

After the game, I put Gracie to bed. She fell asleep two pages into *The Dinosaur Who Went to School.* Josie went downstairs to spend time with Nonnie, recapping the highlights of the game. She, too, eventually fell asleep on Nonnie's couch where Nonnie insisted on keeping her.

Randall and I settled into a snuggle, then into kissing. Every time a spark of comparison with Brody ignited, I blew it out with thoughts only of Randall. Our kissing led to a slide into second base. While Randall fumbled with my bra hook, I let out a yawn. I tried to cough over it, but Randall wasn't an idiot. He chuckled and said he understood I needed sleep. Randall left at eight o'clock and suggested I turn in early, which reminded me, once more, Randall Prescott was a kind man. And I was a Brody-horny-induced horrible person.

Randall and I went out for dinner the next Wednesday night to Horton's Steakhouse. It was a nice steakhouse on the outskirts of Noteah with secluded booths and a view of a manmade pond. It was my third time at Horton's, each time with Randall. He ate there so often the staff knew him by his first name. Randall's chest filled out with every greeting.

"You know," I said after taking a sip out of my lemon martini. I am not a drinker, but I do like Horton's lemon martinis. "You've never really talked about your first marriage."

Randall played with my hands from across the table. "What do you want to know?"

"Her name, why you ended the marriage, and how

many years you were married to her." I shrugged. "I don't know, everything."

"You haven't told me much about your marriage either."

"I told you I was married eight years and his name was Alan. I left him because it didn't work out between us. He was controlling."

"Okay." Randall picked up his scotch and took a long sip. "Her name was Jean. We were married for twelve years, and she died from brain cancer three years ago. She was the love of my life."

The world around me faded. Dishes clanked against each other, forks dropped, the buzz of people's conversation, all of it, faded. I assumed Randall was divorced, like me. I assumed his divorce and marriage were messy and the reasons why he avoided any discussion about either. To find out his wife died, and he was married for twelve years, took me aback. Sadness came over me.

"Oh, Randall." I put my other hand over his. "I'm so sorry."

"Thanks." He avoided my eyes. "I never said anything because it's too hard for me to talk about her."

"Twelve years is a long time. Were you high school sweet—"

My question was cut short when the waiter came to our table and placed our dinners in front of us. Randall withdrew his hands from me, and from any more conversation about his ex-wife. The rest of the evening we talked about his job, the food, the lemon martini, and my girls. We never ventured back to discussions of exes.

At the end of the night, we went back to my house,

like we always did. Randall never offered his house, which was odd to me, but okay. I liked being in my own home if or when Josie and Gracie needed me.

This night, the girls spent the night with Hannah. In a few weeks, they would be back to school. They were grabbing as much time with their aunt as possible. My house was empty—except for Nonnie downstairs—and a perfect time to be alone with Randall.

As we sat on the couch, I moved close to Randall and snuggled up against his broad chest. Our hands intertwined, and my leg fell over his lap.

"Harpie?" It was a name he called me from time to time. I think he found it endearing, and I grew accustomed to it.

"Yes?" I stared at his fingers and compared them to mine. Randall's hands were larger and plumper than mine. His fingers were not too much longer, but masculine, nonetheless.

"Are you on birth control?"

"Yes," I answered. I started back on birth control my second week of dating Randall. "I also have condoms in my purse."

"It's been a long time, and I have tested clean, but if you still want me to wear a condom, I will."

"I would."

"Does this mean we're going to have sex tonight?"

"I guess it does." I smiled.

"Well, if you are ready, it would be nice."

I never saw a brighter smile from Randall.

"Yes, it would." I climbed on top of him and straddled him. Looking down at him, I unbuttoned the top of my sundress in seductive slowness.

"No, wait." He grabbed my hands. "Can we go into

your bedroom?"

I didn't give him an answer. Instead, I got up from his lap, pulled him up, and led him down the hall to my bedroom. When we entered, he turned me around and kissed me. It was a tender kiss, not full of neediness or desperation or even passion. He unbuttoned the rest of my sundress and it pooled at my feet. I slipped his jacket off his shoulders and hurried with the buttons on his shirt, pushing it off his chest. He did not look away from me when he removed his pants.

I watched the heat rise in Randall's eyes, and it ignited my own passion. I ached for him to touch me, any part of me. Instead, his hands stayed at his side, balling up the edge of his boxers in his fists.

I moved in and ran kisses along his jaw. "Touch me," I pleaded.

My hands roamed his torso, scraping my fingernails along the tufts of his hair on his chest and lower. He grew harder underneath my touch. I pushed him backward, onto the bed. I kept my eyes locked on his as I took off his shorts.

"Put your hand on me." He commanded softly. A little tingle climbed up my spine from his demand.

"I will." I stroked his thighs, traveling upward, closer to his fully erect manhood. "But I think, someone needs to get a condom on before we do too much more."

"I know." His voice grew heavy with pleasure. "I know. Just a little bit longer. Please."

I went back to pleasing him, stroking him, feeling powerful.

When I touched his erection, he shouted, "Yes. Yes!"

"Randall, let me put a condom on you, and you can—"

But it was too late. Randall shot up from the bed with his eyes squeezed closed. A loud, primal scream escaped him along with the spill of his seed. He fell back on the bed. His chest rose with each gulp of calming breaths. He let out a small laughter of pleasure.

"Oh, Harpie." His words were jagged. "That was fantastic."

Stunned, I got up from the bed, and stood naked except for a pair of yellow underwear. I looked around the room as I listened to Randall laugh some more and steady his breath. I didn't know how to feel, what to say, how to act. Should I have been angry because he didn't reciprocate? But maybe he didn't know how to stop. He did say it had been a long time.

He got up and wrapped his arms around me and drew my head to his chest. The cologne he wore earlier in the night mixed with his sweat and sex.

"Thank you." He kissed the top of my head and walked around me. "Next time, it's your turn. I promise."

*Next time? There's going to be no this time? Can't we take turns? Can it be mutual pleasure?*

I said, "Oh, okay."

"I'm going to get going. It's late. But I am glad I came tonight." He chuckled at his own corny pun. Maybe another time, it would have been cute, but now, not so much. I grew angry, and the feminist in me yelled, *Say something...now.*

"Randall." I turned and grabbed my bra off the floor. "You know, next time, we should please each other during sex."

"But we didn't really have sex, did we?" Randall pulled on his pants.

"Actually, I thought I'd give you foreplay, and then you'd give me some, and then—"

"We need to be spontaneous, Harpie." He kissed me on the forehead. "I'll call you tomorrow."

"No." The feminist demanded her appearance and flew out of my mouth. "Listen to me!"

"Okay," he said tenderly.

"Next time." I took a calming breath. "Next time, can we please, I don't know, please each other? And maybe you can wait on…on…you know, until we are both ready?"

"Of course. I'm an idiot." He rubbed his hands up and down my arms. "I'm sorry. To be honest, I haven't had sex since…well, it's been too many years. I suppose I just got carried away. I should have been more sensitive to your needs. I am sorry."

"When was the last time? With Jean?" I grabbed my robe off the hook on the door and put it on.

"Yes." Red flushed his cheeks in embarrassment. A and a lump formed in my throat. "Pathetic, huh?"

"No, not at all." I wrapped my arms around his midsection.

"I just loved her, you know? And for a long time, I didn't want sex with just anyone. I wanted a woman who I could trust. A funny and smart woman, not to mention great looking. A woman like you."

"Oh, Randall. That's so sweet." I sighed.

"It's true," he said. "I'm sorry. I need more practice I guess."

"Well, thank you for the compliment. And I'm sorry too. I didn't mean to get upset." I hugged him tighter. "I'm honored you shared all of this with me."

"Of course." He placed his chin on the top of my head.

We stayed in each other arms for a few more minutes. Both of us were quiet. My heart swelled with sympathy and compassion for this man, a man who loved his wife so much he waited to share himself until the right woman came along.

"Harper," he whispered. "I think I may be developing really strong feelings for you."

I could have left it alone and kept holding him, feeling all the good about him, about us, but I needed to say something. I chose my next words carefully.

"Randall." I looked up at him. "A lot went on tonight. We are starting down a more serious path. Your emotions are high, and you are probably feeling a whole lot of other things you can't put into words. Can we see where it goes?"

"Sure." He smiled, but it didn't catch his eyes. "I do need to get going."

"You do." I nipped his mouth. "Because you're right. It's late, and we both have to work tomorrow."

Chapter Eight
How It's Done

Ten days before school was scheduled to open, I spent the morning answering phone calls, preparing students and teachers schedules, sorting through mail and scheduling building meetings for the upcoming school year. While I did all these things, I played one of Brody's old CDs as a member of SAS Hannah lent it to me.

I'd never listened to the group before. Life was different for me when SAS was famous. My pregnancy and divorce kept me busy. I didn't have time for music, other than the same old ones I listened to when I danced. I missed out. As the first song played, I understood their popularity. Brody's rustic, melodic, even sexy voice mesmerized me. The falsettos he threw in and the talent of the SAS musicians only added to Brody's talent. He belonged in music.

As the morning wore on, teachers trickled in to set up their classrooms before the first day of school. Many of them stopped to say hello to me. Since Declan's office was across the hallway from my desk, I helped him get his files together for the new slew of sixth graders.

"Thank you," Declan said before he put the last of his files away.

"Welcome," I answered.

He looked up at the clock. "You have a taste for pizza?"

"I always have a taste for pizza."

"Good. I'm gonna order in a few minutes. Meet me in Marti's classroom in about half an hour."

" 'Kay." I got up from my chair. "How much do I owe you?"

"Owe me? After all the work you did for me, Harp, I owe you. The pizza's on me."

"I'm so in."

Right before noon, I walked into Marti's classroom, shouting, "I'm here. Break up anything you may be doing."

I had to yell it. I caught Declan and Marti too many times moshing—as Hannah called it, and I needed to make my presence known. Sure enough, they withdrew from each other like teenagers being caught at a drive-in.

"You do know this is a school." I shook my head in exaggerated disdain.

"I do." Declan grinned a smile the devil of lust would envy.

"I know." Marti ruffled Declan's hair. "I can't get enough of this guy."

"Give it twenty years." Esther walked in behind me, her floppy patchwork skirt and oversized jean shirt flowed behind her.

"I don't think I'll ever tire of her." Declan sat on the edge of the desk and grabbed Marti into him. "Besides, my parents still grope each other after thirty-five years of marriage."

"If you look like your da in thirty-five years, I'll be groping." The room became quiet, and we looked at

106

Marti. "Wait, that didn't come out right. I meant Dec's da is great-looking, and I'd grope him. Wait, no I mean—"

Declan kissed the top of Marti's head. "Babe, I think you should probably quit while you're ahead."

"Probably." She let go of one of her husky laughs, and it filled the room. I saw a small flare in Declan's nostrils. He told me once the thing that pulled him to Marti more than anything else was her laugh. He called it pure and sexy as hell. I agreed it was genuine and had to take his word about it being sexy.

"Ladies." Marti played with Declan's hand. "Are you up for a Girls' Night In on Saturday?"

"Girls' Night In?" I asked.

"You know," Marti explained, "instead of going out, we stay in."

"I'm up for one." Esther sat down on one of the students' desks.

"Maybe," I said. "Randall said something about going out on Saturday."

"You two are getting pretty serious." Esther chomped on her nails as she spoke.

"Randall and me? Noooo. Phfft." I waved my hand like I was batting away flies and smiled nervously. "We're still in the finding out about each other stage. Not serious at all. Not at all. No commitment. Nothing like that. Noooo."

If I said it aloud and reminded myself Randall and I weren't serious, I could clean out some of the guilt. I could kiss other men, including Brody. Okay, so maybe not men fifty feet from Randall. But I needed to rein it in.

"I like Randall," Declan said. "He's a nice guy, and

we'll see soon how he plays basketball."

"He'll understand if you tell him you can't come out Saturday because you have plans with a girls' night in, right?" Marti pleaded with me with her big brown eyes.

"Sure," I responded. "There's nothing to understand. We're not serious or anything."

"You've said." Esther popped her finger out of her mouth. "A few times."

I slid Esther a side glance. "But I'll still have to see if I can get someone to watch Josie and Grace."

"Great." Marti clasped her hands together in excitement. "Declan has a bachelor party to go to, and I thought, while he's out with the boys, I can stay in with the girls. What do you think?"

"Who's getting married?" I asked.

"My cousin, Ewan." Declan rubbed Marti's stomach in an unconscious, protective habit. It warmed me to see it.

"And he's Scottish, so all the Reed boys will be wearing kilts." Marti wiggled her eyebrows up and down.

"Woohoo." I let out a whistle. "I'm coming over just to see those Reeds' legs."

"Speaking of legs, where's the pizza?" Esther looked at her nails.

"What does one have to do with the other, oh weird one?" I tugged on one of her dreadlocks.

"It takes legs to walk and carry in the pizza," Esther replied.

"Brody's bringing it." Declan glanced at the clock. "He should be here soon."

"Brody's coming?" I played with one of my

earrings.

"Yes," Marti answered with a smirk. "And look at you trying to be all casual. We know, Harper."

"Know what?" This time I looked at them with the best poker face I could muster.

"We know about you two making out at our party." Marti kissed Declan's lips before settling back in a chair near him. "And stop trying to lie. You'll never be good at it."

"I didn't lie about anything," I said. "And what did you hear?"

"What Marti said," Declan answered as he grabbed a chair and straddled it. "Bryn told me."

Marti shrugged. "She pretty much tells Dec everything, and Dec pretty much tells me everything."

"And then Marti told me." Esther gnawed at her nails.

"Ah, hell." I let out a deep breath. "It meant nothing. We're just friends."

"You sure?" Declan looked at me.

"Oh, don't be pulling your social worker moves on me. We are."

"Brody told me about the bet, too." Marti rubbed her belly. Between her and Declan, their baby was going to be very loved.

"He wasn't supposed to." I held back my anger.

"He had to tell me. I asked him why suddenly he asked you to a Cubs game, and well, he spilled."

"He'd never be a good spy." Declan shook his head.

"How did you know about the Cubs game?" I held up my hand. "Don't tell me. Bryn."

"Sure, but I saw on the Internet the mysterious

woman next to Brody. I Google Brody occasionally." Marti smiled.

"And you're okay with this?" I looked at Declan.

"What? My wife's stalking my brother?" Declan asked.

"Stop," Marti protested. "I read everything on Brody."

"Oh, well, as long as you read everything on him, that's better," Declan teased.

"You know I do. He's my friend and brother-in-law. Why wouldn't I?" Marti kissed Declan full on the mouth. "Besides, I'm in love with Brody's brother."

"Does Cal know how you feel?" When Marti slapped him playfully, Declan laughed and kissed the top of her head.

"Anyway, I think it's fun, the two of you have this bet, but—"

"Martina, don't get involved." Declan warned.

"Yeah, like I ever listen." Marti's chuckle was as deep as her laugh. Declan grinned.

"Go on," Esther said. "But?"

"Don't egg her on." I pointed a finger at Esther.

"But"—Marti ignored me—"I think Brody might lose and might lose big. And not only his boots. He may get hurt."

"Why?" Esther asked.

"Do you know what 'don't egg her on' means?" I questioned.

"Well, Est, I think he's always had this thing for Harper. I mean it's obvious." Marti and Esther nodded. "Harper thinks we don't know, but we do. We know they also got hot and heavy at our wedding and at Cal's bar."

"Come on. How discreet can she be?" Esther asked. "Making out in the hallway of a busy bar."

"And," Marti added, "did she actually think Declan's teenage cousin would keep a secret like a coatroom make-out session?"

"I know!" Esther exclaimed. "What was she thinking?"

"I guess I'm not even here." I looked at Declan.

"I'm sorry, who are you?" Declan narrowed his eyes at me.

"And"—Marti looked at Declan and then me—"I think you, Harper McReynolds, are too guarded to let Brody in. You settle for comfort, and Brody is uncomfortable, but in a good way, in an artist type of way. So, Brody will be left losing the bet and maybe his heart."

"True," Esther jumped in. "Or Harper will be hurt because she didn't let him in."

"Good point," Marti agreed but then shook her head. "No, I think it'll be Brody with the biggest heartache."

"Again..." I looked at Declan. "I'm not here."

"I thought you left." He grinned.

"No, I'm serious." Marti's face exploded with expression. "The Reed men come from a very humble, hard-working environment. They are devoted to each other and their friends. They live simply and don't want too much. Brody's career forced him into a glamorous ritzy and rich world, which Z was part of and more. But Brody needs strong and normal. Besides you are beautiful—"

"With a great body." We turned to Esther, and she smiled. "Come on, she does. You do."

"True." Marti pointed to Esther. "And you are what Brody wants. Brody needs—"

"I heard my name like six times as I walked down the hall." Brody came into the room carrying two pizzas. He wore a white pocket T-shirt and ripped-up jeans with a pair of dark-brown work boots. Even dressed casually, he looked sexy as hell, a sexy-as-hell friend. Brody looked over at me and grinned his crooked grin that called out his deep dimples.

I had not seen Brody since the Cubs game. We texted a few times and even had a short conversation once. I don't know if I avoided him, or he avoided me. Whatever the reason, we avoided each other.

"We're saying what an asshole you are, and nobody disagreed. Huh." Declan got up to grab the pizzas from his brother. Brody flipped him off. "Now that just hurts."

"Hey, Marts." Brody bent down and kissed Marti on the forehead.

"Hi, handsome," Marti replied.

"Esther." Brody kissed her cheek.

"Hey, Brody." Esther talked between clenched teeth while chewing on a fingernail before getting up to help Declan and Marti ready the pizzas. "We were just talking about you, your bet, and your make-out sessions, as in plural, with Harper."

"Plural, huh?" Brody raised an eyebrow at me, and I did a slight shake of my head in warning. I didn't want him to mention the one after the Cubs game. "Details, please."

"And," Marti added, "how I think you will lose the bet because, deep down, you like Harper. You like her."

"We were having quite the conversation, huh?"

Brody's dimples dug into his cheeks as he came over to me and bent down. He planted a kiss on my cheek, inches away from my mouth. My eyes drooped. I wished his lips were closer to mine. "Oh, and here. Not sure if you had anything to drink." He set down a Super Sip in front of me. "Half and half, right?"

Stunned, I nodded. I dated Randall for months and he never once got it right.

"Did you get anchovies?" Marti looked over the pizzas. "You remembered. Thank you."

"Anything for my niece." Brody winced. "Shit. Sorry."

"You're having a girl?" Esther squealed and grabbed Marti into a hug.

"You really suck at keeping secrets." Declan punched his brother's arm.

"I deserved that." Brody shook off the pain.

"Yes, we are," Declan confirmed. "Esther, you can't say anything to anyone."

Conversations exploded in the room about the pregnancy and different names for girls while I nibbled on a slice of pizza. I wasn't hungry. I wasn't sure why. I tried to blame it on the fatigue from another new school year, or my night with Randall. But I knew my guilt returned when I saw Brody and ruined my appetite.

"You look good, Harper." Brody sat down beside me. His voice was low as the conversation continued.

"Thank you."

"Why are you quiet?" Brody took a big bite of his pizza, tomato sauce dripping from the side of his mouth. I wondered if I licked it what would it start. I shook the thought out of my head. "The gossip about us wearing you out?"

"I guess."

"And you're still feeling guilty? Like a horrible person?"

"Yes. A little." I lied, a little. "And I'm tired. Long week. Long night."

"Randy stayed the night after, where was it, Horton's?"

"You remembered?"

"Sugar, he made it a point to tell me. The salmon was good then?"

"It was okay." I picked off a mushroom and put it in my mouth. I wanted to change subjects. "And the night before, I got up with Gracie. She had a nightmare about the Cubs mascot chasing her with ice cream, a recurring one since the game."

"Oh." Brody let out a laugh. "Sorry, probably not funny."

"No, it is." I snorted, too. "Poor thing."

"I had a great time, sugs."

"I know. You told me, a few times—on the phone, in texts."

"Worth repeating in person. Don't you have an opera coming up?"

"I do," I admitted, as if I were going to a dentist appointment. "I don't even know the name of it."

"You're not excited, huh?"

"I don't like operas. I try though."

"For Randy?"

"Yes." I didn't even bother correcting him. "He keeps thinking I have to give it more time. He told me it was like learning to like beer. It takes a couple of times before you develop a taste. Maybe he's right."

"Or maybe he's wrong." Before I responded a defense, Brody moved on. "Harper, I have to tell you something. I may cheat on this bet a bit."

"How? We gonna sleep together?" I smirked.

"No, but I like how you think. No, I am gonna cheat because, well, I'm going away for a week."

"You are?" I tried to mask my disappointment.

"Yup. I have to fly out to LA and then to Jamaica."

"You do have a rough life." If I didn't know myself better, I would have sworn I was pissed or jealous. I did know myself quite well. I was both.

"It is when you don't want to go." Brody took his napkin and wiped his mouth.

"Why? Because they're such crappy places to visit?" I needed to rein it in.

"No and yes. I mean, Jamaica's beautiful, but LA has always been trouble for me. But I promised Z I would attend a premiere with her in LA of some new movie. She has friends in it. It'll probably be a crap movie, but I promised."

"And promises can't be broken." I bit out. I coughed and plastered on a relaxed face, hoping the tone would come through. "And Jamaica?"

"And in Jamaica—" Brody stopped. "Well, how do I say this without bragging?"

I touched his leg. "Brody, as long as we've had this friendship, I've never known you to brag."

"Well, you do know me the best." He squeezed my hand before I pulled it back. "Well, I am going to Jamaica to meet with Henry Knight."

"The R&B guy?"

"Yes." Brody took another bite of pizza.

"For?" I prodded.

"For, well, I'm writing a song for him. I got the tracks down, and I wrote some of the lyrics, but we're gonna see how it all sounds in his Jamaican studio."

"Wow." It was a loud *wow*.

"What wow?" Marti took a sip of Declan's cola. He looked at her. "What? It was a sip. A sip won't hurt, baby. I have my lemon-lime."

"What wow?" Esther repeated.

"Brody's going to Jamaica to meet with Henry Knight," I answered, still stunned.

"The R&B guy?" Esther's eyes grew.

"Uh-huh."

"Wow."

"Oh, he's written for a bunch of people." Marti's delight showed on her face, like a mother talking about her child. "He wrote for Mallory Tufts."

"*The* Mallory Tufts?" I continued my shock. "*The* hottest country singer?"

"The same." Marti smiled. "Her song 'Till Next Time'—Brody wrote it. Wrote the lyrics and the music."

"Wow." I looked over at him.

"I know," Marti continued. "And the Releases' song 'One Moment from Then'? Sure, Brody—"

"Marts." Brody tried to interrupt.

"And you know what else? Right now, three, yes three, of the top twenty songs on the pop chart—one on the top twenty R&B charts, and one on the country chart—were all written by one Brody Reed, music and lyrics. Well, he co-wrote the country one. He even produced a few of them, whatever producing means in music." Pride beamed from Marti's eyes. "Of course, he won't tell you, but they are. Cal told me. Cal's the only one Brody shares this with."

"Really?" I looked over at Brody.

"Sure, Cal and I are tight."

"I mean about the songs?" I snorted out a laugh.

"I guess." Brody got up and threw away his plate. I didn't know if he was angry, embarrassed, or both.

"In fact, I bet he wins a Grammy this year. I bet he—"

"Martina," Declan interrupted her. His gaze glued on Brody. "Don't, okay? If Brody wants to tell her, he will."

"But..."

"Babe, you are embarrassing him." Declan rubbed Marti's back.

"Oh." Marti's voice softened. "I didn't mean to. I'm sorry, Brody."

"No worries." Brody forced a smile and sat back down.

"No, it's not okay." Marti's eyes glistened with tears. I remember those hormones. "I know I have a big mouth sometimes and—"

"Marti, I'm good." Brody sent her a wink.

"Well, I'm stuffed." Esther got up and stretched. "And I need to get back to my classroom. I have to watch an hour-long video on washing paint brushes before the school year starts. A district requirement because, you know, we art teachers need to be taught the importance of washing them and the correct way to do it."

"I should be going, too." I begin to clean up. "I have a lot of work to do."

"And I'm heading out. Got some packing to do." Brody got up and glanced over at Marti. His face softened as he went over to her and crouched down. I couldn't help but look at his thigh muscles as they expanded in his jeans. "Marts, I'm good. I just don't like to talk about myself too much. I appreciate how proud you are of me, really, thank you."

"I *am* proud of you. But I probably shouldn't have said anything. It's your story to tell."

"Nah. It's all good. You tell it well." Brody smiled, and Marti laughed.

"Thank you." Marti hugged her brother-in-law. "I love you, you know?"

"I do." Brody kissed her forehead before he stood up. "Love you, too."

"Safe trip." Declan grabbed his brother into a hug.

"Thanks." Brody handed him a set of keys. "Take good care of my bitches."

"Your what?" I dumped the plates and napkins into the trash can.

Declan laughed. "We're taking care of Brody's two dogs while he's gone."

"And here I thought you had a brothel or something." I smirked.

"Now *that* I would brag about." Brody grinned.

Brody and I walked down the hallway, the heels of my shoes clicked on the tiles with every step. Marti and Declan stayed in her room, insisting they would finish the clean-up and probably to mosh. Esther walked with us, passing a few classrooms before she ducked into hers.

"So, you're gonna be wearing a kilt soon, huh?" I asked.

"Yup. It's not my first time, you know."

"No?"

"Nope." Brody put on a fake Scottish accent. "On my mother's side, we have worn them for other events."

"I would love to see you in one."

"Maybe one day I'll show you." Silence passed between us as we walked. Brody looked like he wanted to compose his thoughts, and I waited for them to come together. "You know, sugs, in order for me to maintain this bet, I'm gonna have to call you and call you often."

"Like you'll be pursuing me in a creepy way?"

"Is that wrong?"

"On so many levels." I hesitated before adding, "I'd like that."

"Good."

"Brody…" I hesitated. "Please don't feel like you can't tell me these things, you know, your accomplishments. If we're going to be friends, you can open up to me about your accomplishments. It won't be bragging, and you do have a right to feel proud of yourself. It's *huge* to have your success."

"Thanks." Brody looked at the ground and then shot me a look through his lashes. I noticed this shy move of his more, and it endeared me to him, more. "It's just, well, it doesn't normally come up in conversation."

"No? Can't work 'hey, I have all these songs in the different top-twenty music charts' into conversations?"

"I try, but it never seems to flow." Brody smirked. "Thank you."

"For?"

"For being a good friend."

"You bet." I snorted. "And Brody?"

"I know."

"No, you don't."

"You're going to say you didn't mean to attack me *again* after the Cubs game, and horny got a hold of you *again*, and Randall is who you want, and we really need to break our tradition, and you didn't mean to hurt my feelings, and you really want us to stay friends."

"Okay, so maybe you do." I smirked.

Brody draped his arm on top of the doorway to the front office. He looked around the empty hallways and then back at me. Leaning into me, he took my bottom lip and, with the softness of a feather, kissed it. A moan escaped me. I wanted to call it back, but it fled and ran free into the area surrounding us. Brody smiled against my lips before kissing my upper lip. I caught my moan this time and backed away, my hips bumping into the door's wooden frame. Taking both lips into my mouth for the taste of him, I let out a long breath.

"And that, pal, is how it's done, without the guilt or feeling like a horrible person." He grinned, calling out his dimples one last time before he went on his way.

I stood there, breathing as hard as if I'd run a marathon, from a mere chaste kiss.

Chapter Nine
A Night at the Opera

Labor Day weekend flew by with the speed of a fighter jet. Gracie was over the moon and on another planet for the start of kindergarten. The night before her first day, she got out of bed three times. Once, she touched her outfit and beamed with approval. Another time, she double checked the contents of her backpack. On Gracie's last trip out of bed, she made sure there was enough cereal for the next morning.

Josie's feelings on beginning a new school year were neutral. She had concerns about her advanced classes but brushed it off as soon as she mentioned it. Like most eighth graders, excitement for school died a little more each year.

Randall and I didn't see each other very much the week leading up to the start of school. He had contracts due before Labor Day, and I believed he still held some embarrassment about our "sex night" and used work as avoidance. My own exhaustion from beginning a new school year, both at work and at home, gave me little time to care.

We did talk every day, never about that night. Once, I broached the subject of sex, ready to talk about my unfulfilled needs. Randall immediately changed the subject to our upcoming opera date. Our conversations stayed on more banal topics like his job flow, the start of basketball with Declan, my girls, and Nonnie. Sometimes, our chats bored me, but I told myself boredom was part of a developing relationship, however much that idea bothered me.

True to his word, Brody stayed in touch, mostly through texts. *Our messages went back and forth like a tennis ball during Wimbledon. He sent me silly texts about our bet, light texts on the weather and detailed texts on his time in LA. I sent back messages containing updates on Gracie and Josie, outlines of my chaotic work schedule with the new school year and new music I listened to during my morning dance workouts.*

We even had a series of funny texts about our "tradition." I laughed so loud at my desk, my boss had to remind me of the inappropriateness of having my cell phone out during school hours. And as much as I hated to admit it, she was right. So, I made many bathroom trips to steal glances at my phone. I felt like my sixteen-year-old self who sneaked into the bathroom for cigarettes.

****

"And I told them, I don't think the budget would hold if we keep the union." Randall's words slurred as he took another long drink of his vodka on the rocks.

It was Friday night after Labor Day. We sat in a fancy downtown bar. One more performance had convinced me I hated opera. Sure, the singing, the scenery, the music, and the costumes were stunning. I even enjoyed dressing up in my best clothes. I enjoyed all of it, until the novelty of the beautiful voices, the magnificent scenery, the melodic music, the breath-stealing costumes, and my uncomfortable dress wore off. It was my fourth opera, and like every other time, fifteen minutes into the show, I was done.

An evening in sweats, on my couch, sucking down a big bowl of ice cream, especially on a Friday after a long work week, was more favorable than my attempt to follow a story sung in a strange language. My internal dialogue's argument to enjoy the uniqueness of an opera did not squelch my longing for my comfy clothes and cold, creamy, calorie-rich indulgence.

"You know?" Randall had the rock glass by his mouth.

"Uh-huh," I answered after twenty minutes of Randall's talk about sales. Throughout Randall's discussions of business, I listened without comments or interest. He didn't notice or didn't care. "Randall, can we please go home? It's been a long week, and I'm exhausted."

"One more." He drained the last of his drink and stood up at the bar. His eyes tried to catch the bartender. The bartender gave a quick nod. Randall looked at me with puppy dog eyes. "Please?"

"But Josie has an early game tomorrow."

"It'll be fine." The bartender set another drink in front of him.

My cell phone rang, and I looked down.

"I have to get this." I picked up my phone. "It's Josie."

"Absolutely." Randall smiled, and I returned one of my own.

"Hey, Josie. What's up?"

"Hey, Mom. When are you coming home?"

"In about an hour. Why?"

"Can I spend the night at Maggie's? I know it's late, but her mom will pick me up. And, yes, I know, I have basketball tomorrow. I'll be fine." I was never one of those sports moms who insisted on sacrificing fun for the sake of the game. The game itself was supposed to be fun.

"Yes."

"Yes?"

"Yes." I took a sip of my wine. "And only if Gracie can spend the night with Nonnie."

"Of course, I will make sure Gracie can spend the night with Nonnie." Gracie's giggles erupted in the background as Josie repeated the words for her benefit, not mine.

"She's still up, then?"

"Yup. We finished playing with her dolls, and now she is already for bed."

"Good babysitter."

"Thanks. And I asked Nonnie a few minutes ago."

"Let me guess, and she said yes."

"I wouldn't have called if she hadn't." Josie would be a brilliant salesperson one day, like her father. "And, I know, since I didn't babysit her until you got home, I won't get the full amount."

"You babysat her enough. You'll get it."

"Did I tell you I've always liked you the best out of all my other moms?" Josie asked.

"Wow. I have stiff competition, too."

"I know." We both laughed.

"Jos, have a great time and—"

"Smart choices, yes, I know," Josie said. "One time, Mother, be creative and tell me not to make the stupidest choice ever, like joining the Marines."

"I'm pretty sure you would have to be a little bit older than thirteen."

"I can look mature."

"True." I snorted. "Okay, have a great time and don't join the Marines."

"You'll miss me when I'm in the—" Josie gasped. "Oh wow."

"What?" I faked a gasp.

"It's Brody!"

"Where?" This time I did not fake it.

"On ME, like now."

ME, or the Music Entertainment channel, was one of Josie's favorite channels. It reported on gossip in the current music world, as well as played music videos. ME was part of our cable subscription. Cable was a luxury, one we couldn't afford if it were not for Hayden. Every year, my Christmas gift from him was cable subscription. I think it was more the girls' gift than mine, especially Josie and her love for ME.

"Brody's on ME right now, at some premiere. They're talking to that model Z, and he's right next to her. Pretty cool, huh?"

"Pretty cool," I admitted.

"How would you know? You're not watching it."

"True."

"Well, I've got to go. I'll see you tomorrow, Mom. Love you."

"Love you, too, baby girl."

With a click, she was gone. Disappointment washed over me. I wanted to keep talking to Josie because I knew as she crept more and more into her teenage years, our phone calls would be less and less, as it should be, but not like I wanted it to be.

My eyes darted over the bar area for a TV. I found one perched at the far end and signaled for the bartender. He nodded and began pouring me another glass of white wine.

"No," I screamed over the noise and pointed to the TV. "The Music Entertainment channel, please."

"Sure." He picked up the remote and switched the channel.

"What's going on?" Randall asked. I pointed to the TV.

I couldn't hear anything. I watched as lightning of flashbulbs erupted around Brody with Z draped over him like an accessory. Brody treated the press to strangled smiles but gave a I-don't-want-to-do-this vibe when he stuffed his hands into his pockets and held a steady stare to the ground.

His ensemble of a shiny silver suit with a thin, black tie and a pale-yellow shirt showed off every packed muscle. It clung to him as if it knew its purpose was to reveal every inch of his sexiness. I snorted aloud when I saw his gray cowboy boots hiding under the hem of his pants. When Randall looked at me in question, I waved a dismissive hand.

Brody Reed looked hot and steamy. The gobs of gel used to slick back his hair disappointed me, just a little. I liked when his hair flowed unrestricted and the waves of his mane framed his armor gray eyes. With it held back, he lacked the rawness of his looks even though his eyes still shone like a wolf on a hunt. No matter how his hair was done, Brody Reed still simmered with sensual beauty.

"Oh, my." The words freed themselves before I had a chance to shut my mouth on them.

"Right?" A woman, close to her fifties, sat next to me. She peered at the screen over her martini glass. "I could cougar him all day."

"We know him." Randall leaned over me to the woman.

Heat from embarrassment, or maybe the wine, or both, rose on my cheeks. Randall heard me. I wanted to add more casual words, to cover up what fell out my mouth, but the woman spoke before I could.

"You do?" She raised her eyebrow lazily.

"Yes." Randall pointed to me. "He's friends with my girlfriend."

"Friends? Lucky you," said Martini Woman, her voice husky with humor. With her eyes still on the TV, she continued, "I heard he's a bit cocky though."

"He can be," Randall agreed. "He thinks he's funny, too."

"He is hilarious, and he's not cocky at all," I snapped. "He's very generous too."

"She's just saying that because he took her and her girls to a Cubs game." Randall tried to be funny, but I didn't laugh.

"Wait a minute." Martini Woman hung open. "You're the woman from the Cubs game with him. The one—"

"Yes, I am." I didn't want to talk anymore to a stranger about Brody. I got off my stool and said to Randall, "I'm going to the restroom. When I get back, I think we should leave. And I'm driving. I think you had too many."

Randall and Martini Woman talked more about Brody as I walked away. I began to understand what Brody told me, the night of Marti and Declan's party, about how people held opinions of him without knowing him. Even people like Randall, who talked to

127

him a total of ten minutes, passed judgement on Brody.

When I completed my escape to the restroom, I closed a stall door and sat down on the toilet, fully clothed. I took out my phone and began to text.

—S*aw u on TV. U r wearing my toilet-roll holders.*—

After I hit send, I rubbed away the headache threatening to vise-grip my forehead with my fingers. The night annoyed me. I would never like opera no matter how much I tried. Randall's comments to Martini Woman, especially his implication I used Brody for Cubs tickets which he disguised as a joke, angered me. His order of a third drink irritated me. And the desire I held the entire night for a pair of sweats, T-shirt, and ice cream had not waned.

I knew Randall wanted to attempt sex again. He whispered throughout the opera how he bought condoms and how much better he'll be this time around. Randall might have thought his suggestions were amorous or playful, yet the thought of more hours spent awake after an exhausting day frustrated me.

I took a deep breath in. I needed to think about all the reasons why I liked Randall before I lost it completely.

In the first place, far and above anything else, I dated Randall Prescott because he was an established man, secure about himself, and kind to me. He had a slow temper—a massive asset after the hell I had lived. He had his own charm, a little clumsy but endearing. He liked my kids, and he was kind to them as well. He had an attractiveness which drew me to him in the first place. And most importantly, I saw myself in a long relationship with him. Randall had his flaws, sure, and I had mine. Imperfections made up a whole person, and I had to, wanted to, embrace all of Randall, including his flaws.

Satisfied with my pep talk, I nodded and left the stall to wash my hands—a habit after I left any bathroom stall even if I did business in it or not. As I dried them, my phone buzzed. I took it out and looked at the screen. I smiled when I opened the message.

—*U saw me?*— Brody texted.

—*Yup. Josie watches ME & texted me.*—

—*Where you at?*—

—*I'm at a bar. Made bartender turn it on.*—

—*Made him? How?*—

—*I'll never tell.*— I laughed as I pushed the keys with my thumbs. —*Seriously, how's it going?*—

—*Sucks. Don't like it.*—

—*Thought so by yr look. I mean, u look good but uncomfortable.*—

—*Thanks, and very. Well, gotta go. And thanx for the laugh, sugs.*—

—*A power of mine. Try to have fun. U r in Hollywood, Baby.*—

I walked out of the restroom lighter and happier. I put my hand on Randall's back. "Ready to go?"

"Sure." He downed the rest of his drink and handed Martini Woman his card. "Let your son know to call me. I'll see what I can do for him."

"Thanks for being so nice, Randall." She beamed a smile. "I was telling your boyfriend my son is looking for a job. He agreed to talk to him. You're dating a great guy there."

I looked over at Randall. "I think so."

While we walked to the car, I thanked the gods of

martinis and bathroom stalls for the reminder I was, in fact, dating a great guy. I grabbed Randall's hand and snuggled into him.

On the drive home, I thought about sex with Randall. With Josie at a girlfriend's house overnight, and Gracie asleep downstairs at Nonnie's, the night was perfect for another go at it.

I put my hand on Randall's thigh and smiled. My nails lightly scratched a path up to his crotch. I made circles on his pants and teased him with each stroke. Randall sucked in a breath, but his penis remained limp. It seemed like a case of liquor dick, and after a while, I gave up.

When we got upstairs to my house, Randall took off his jacket, loosened his tie, and took off his shoes. He sat down on my couch and lounged back.

"Fun night, huh?" he asked. "You looked nice tonight."

It was the only compliment Randall gave me all night. In fact, Randall didn't dole out too many compliments, especially about my appearance, in all the time we dated.

"Why, thank you." I straddled his lap and outlined his ear with my fingernail. "You know, the girls are gone tonight. It's just you and me."

"Yeah?" A smile spread across his face.

"Yes, and we"—I kissed his cheek—"can"—I kissed his other one—"have some fun."

"Sounds good." He went in for a kiss and then retreated. "I can't, Harper. The room is spinning. I mean, really spinning."

"Aw, I'm sorry, Randall." I patted his chest and got off his lap. "Let me get you a glass of water."

"That'd be nice." He leaned to the side of the couch, until his head hit the cushion. He nestled into a fetal position.

"And a pillow and blanket," I said to myself.

I came back into the room, covered him with a blanket, put a pillow behind his head, and took off his glasses. He looked childishly content while he slept. I smiled and kissed him on the cheek. "Goodnight, Randall."

I dressed for bed and padded into the kitchen. Grabbing a spoon. I took the ice cream out of the freezer. Finally, my ice cream craving was met. I sat down on the overstuffed chair and flipped on the television. For the next hour and a half, while Randall snored, I watched a bad 1980s horror movie. While I shoveled rocky road into my mouth, I snorted out laughs. When the movie ended, I kissed Randall on the cheek again, turned off the television, and headed to bed. I buried the empty ice cream container in the garbage to hide any evidence of my indulgence.

Before I got into bed, my phone rang. My heart leapt into my throat whenever the phone rang late, and with Josie at a sleepover, my heart almost fell out of my mouth.

I answered it with an anxious. "Joze?"

"Noze."

"Brody." I sighed.

"Sorry am I calling too late? Did I scare you?"

"I thought you were Josie."

"Shit. I didn't think," Brody said. "I was taking a chance you might still be up, and if you weren't, I was going to leave a message. I didn't even think about your kids. Shit. Is Josie okay?"

"Yeah. She's at a friend's house, and I thought…it doesn't matter."

"I am sorry. I should let you go." There was a desperation in his voice, and I knew, no matter how tired, he needed to talk.

"No, it's fine. I'm up. Something wrong?"

"I shouldn't—"

"Brody, what's wrong?" I repeated.

"Nothing."

"I'm not gonna ask you again."

"No? I thought we can keep doing this." He tried to be lighthearted, but it missed.

"Brodes, tell me."

He hesitated, then took a deep breath in, releasing it slowly. "I wanted to drink tonight, Harper."

"Oh."

"And now I scared you. First, I called you late at night and made you think I was Josie, and now told you this. Fuck."

"No, it's fine," I assured him. "You didn't, right? Drink?"

"No. Damn if I didn't want to, but no." He swallowed a crack in his voice. "Right now, I am in my hotel room with a bottle of water. Before I got here, I asked the wet bar to be cleaned out, except for water. I think I'm on my third bottle."

"Start from the beginning. What happened?"

"LA happened. I'm telling you, sugs, this town and me? We don't get along so well." He paused, and I waited for him to continue. "Before the premiere, we went to a hotel room of one of Z's friends. There were about eight people, and all of them drank a shitload of champagne. Z told them we had nothing in our room

132

and suggested a glass wouldn't hurt me. She doesn't fucking get it. One glass would destroy me."

"And you didn't drink anything. That's great."

"But the draw was strong, Harper." His voice quavered. "And then in the limo on the way to the premiere, they snorted coke. Z offered me some. Pretty fucked up, huh?"

"Pretty fucked up," I agreed.

"When we got to the theater, Z stumbled, more than a few times. Everyone wanted a photo of her, so I held her up." That explained why Z draped herself over him. "And then, when we got into the theater, she and her friends do more coke in the bathroom."

"Wow. She was pretty messed up. How was she during the movie?"

"You don't want to know."

"Bad?"

"She tried to blow me." He sucked in a breath in regret. "And I shouldn't have said that."

"It's okay, Brodes. I'm a big girl." I tried to make light of it.

"I'd say more of a curvy woman, but okay." Finally, there was a smile in his voice.

"Tomayto, tomahto." I snickered. "What happened after the movie?"

"Well, after, she was pissed at me for, you know."

"Pushing her away?"

"Yeah, and then she insisted we go to a party. I told her I wanted to get back to the hotel room. She went off on me in front of all her friends, called me an asshole. She told me I changed. I was no fun. Blah, blah, blah."

"How did you two leave it?"

"I walked a mile, back to the hotel. I don't know,

Harper, I think I'm done with Z. I mean, why do I date someone who compromises my sobriety?"

"Other things compromise your sobriety, too, Brody. Not just Z." I startled myself.

"Meaning?"

"Nothing. I shouldn't have said anything."

"Come on, what do you mean?"

"Brody, why, I mean, why would—" I struggled with the words. "Why do you perform at Cal's bar?"

"Why do you ask?" There was anger in his words, anger I never heard from Brody before. It didn't scare me as much as it surprised me.

"Never mind." I probably crossed a line. "So how was the movie? What exactly goes on with premieres, anyway?"

"Don't change the subject. Finish what you started."

"Don't order me around," I snapped.

"I'm not," Brody bit back, then took a calming breath. "Please, Harper, continue."

"Well," I hesitated. "I admit I don't know anything about the rules of NA or AA or sobriety, but it seems to me, you are around temptation all the time. Why? To test yourself? To set yourself up to fail?"

When there was only silence, I bit my lip. "A bit too harsh?"

"Yes," Brody answered.

"Look," I began. "I know you think you're helping your brother out by playing at his bar, but it's a bar, Brody. A bar serves liquor, and everyone drinks the liquor. I wonder why a recovering alcoholic—"

"And addict."

"Okay, and addict, would be around a bar."

134

"I like to sing every now and then. And, you're right, it helps out Cal."

"I'm sure. You probably bring in a lot of business."

"I do." I didn't take it as cocky but as a matter of fact.

"All right, but I've been at Cal's bar when you didn't sing, and he was busy." When he didn't say anything, I continued, "And I get it. You like singing. But what about singing at a small venue or coffeehouse? Why a bar? Again, I think Cal would understand."

"Shit. I've got to go, Harper."

"Don't hang up on me now," I bit into the phone. "What? The conversation gets hard, so you hang up?"

"Maybe, as someone once told me, your timing sucks."

"Or, as someone else responded, maybe it's perfect timing," I answered back.

"You know, Harper, you don't know everything." Brody struggled to hold onto his patience. "I perform at my brother's bar. Not some random one. Do you think my brother would let me drink? Especially Cal who saw my ugly side when I did?"

"Not my point. I asked why you test temptation?" I crossed another line—hell, I jumped over it—but I needed to finish. "Look, you hang out at a bar and date a woman who likes to party. Something is wrong with these choices, Brody."

There was silence on the other end. I knew he was still there, and I gave him time.

"Fuck. I'm so pissed off."

"Kind of figured you'd be at me," I answered.

"Not at you." His breath whistled through his nose.

"Listen, I am going to go, Harper. It has everything to do with what you said, but not what you think."

"I'm confused."

"I want to find a meeting."

"A what?" And then it dawned on me. "Oh. An AA meeting?"

"Or NA. I went to one this morning, but I need one now."

"Brody, I'm sorry if I added—"

"You added nothing. This is all my shit. And thanks, Harper. I needed to talk to you tonight."

"And you're sure you're not mad?

"Truthfully? I am mad I have to look at things—myself, Z, and so many fucked-up situations. But you personally? No."

"Damn, I was trying to push your buttons."

Brody's chuckle sent some light into the deepness of our night's conversation. "I will talk to you soon, okay?"

"Okay." Randall's retches into my toilet boomed into the room. Great.

"Is someone sick there? I hear some nasty things in the background."

Lies ran in my head—no, it's the television, yes, it's Gracie, what noise. I tried to think of response to avoid the Randall issue. I went with the truth. "It's Randall. He drank too much and now—"

"Now he's blowing chunks? Kissing the porcelain god? Upchucking? He's—"

"Yes, all those things. We went out after the opera, and he had one too many. I drove his car home, and now he's spending the night. He's not a drinker."

"Noooo," Brody said in fake shock.

"Well, it's one of the reasons I like him." I cringed at the asshole thing I said to someone who called me about his struggles with alcohol. "I didn't mean—"

"No worries. I should go."

"Okay. Bye, Brodes."

"Bye, sug."

Chapter Ten
A Ride in the Squad Car

At three thirty in the morning, I heard it. At first, I thought it was a noise outside. I had been asleep for two hours, and I was disorientated. After Brody called, I started in on another gallon of ice cream. I knew tomorrow I'd have to break my no "exercise rule" on the weekends.

The noise grew louder with a bang that rattled of my back door. My heart pounded with every boom, boom. I leaped out of bed and hustled past Randall. Red lights flashed across the walls of the front room as the knocks continued.

"What's happening?" Randall sat up. He rubbed his eyes with the palms of his hands.

"I don't know." I picked up my pace. "I hope not Nonnie."

I ran down the stairs and threw open the door of the back porch. A police officer, in his mid to late twenties, stood behind Josie. Her eyes were focused on the ground. Another police officer, a woman, probably ten years older than me, stood at her side.

"What the hell? Are you all right?" I grabbed my chest and looked at both officers. "Is she all right?"

"Ma'am, your daughter was at Triton Park, alone," said the male cop who looked bored out of his mind. "We picked her up about fifteen minutes ago. She broke curfew."

"She what?" This was all too surreal for me. "What was she doing there?"

"She won't tell me." The male cop moved his neck back and forth to crack it.

"Josie?" I pinched her face in my hand and turned it to me. "Wanna tell me?"

"Joining the Marines?" Josie lifted her eyebrows.

"I am not in the mood for jokes."

"She did tell us she lives here, and she left a sleepover with her friend Maggie," the neck cracker reported. "Then she talked with Officer Tanner here for a while. She's better with kids than me."

"And?" I looked at Officer Tanner.

"Do you want me to tell her, or do you?" Tanner's eyes shifted from me to Josie.

"Can I flip you for it?"

"Josie, this is not funny," I said, and Officer Neck Cracker tried hard not to smile.

"Can we come in?" Officer Tanner asked.

"Of course. Please come in." I opened my stance to let them in. As we walked up the stairs, Nonnie clung to her door with a look of horror on her face.

"Harper, what happened?" Nonnie asked. "Is Josie okay?"

"Josie is physically fine, but that might change," I spat between clenched teeth. "She snuck out of her sleepover, and these officers picked her up."

"Josephine," Nonnie admonished.

"What?" Josie shrugged. "I'm fine. Nothing happened."

"What's going on?" Randall came to the door, his shirt out of his pants and his tie still loosely around his neck.

"Are you Josie's stepfather?"

"No." Randall reeled back as if he'd been asked if he had smallpox. "Oh, no."

"No, just some man spending the night with my mother." Josie swept past me and gazed up at Randall.

"Officer Tanner, why don't we all sit down?" I tried to gain control of an out-of-control situation. "Nonnie, everything's good. We'll talk in the morning. Go back to bed."

"Are you sure?" Nonnie looked at me.

"I'm sure." I looked at the bored, neck-cracking cop. "Can you please turn off your flashing lights outside?"

"Ma'am, I—"

"Just do it, Billy," Officer Tanner jumped in. "In fact, wait for me in the car, okay?"

"Sure." He turned and headed down the stairs past Nonnie and nodded. "Night."

"Thank you," I threw after him.

"Just doing my job." He waved back without a glance.

"Nonnie, it's fine."

"Okay." Nonnie looked confused and worried. My heart melted. "Okay. We'll talk in the morning?"

"I promise." I looked at Randall. "Are you, what I mean is, would you—"

"I should go." He yawned and sent a stream of lousy breath our way. Officer Tanner grimaced.

"Yeah. It's probably a good idea. You okay to drive?"

"I'll call for an Uber." He picked up his jacket. "I'll wait downstairs for it and give you some privacy.

Call you later?"

"Sure." I rubbed his arm. "Thanks."

"Bye, Harper." He went in for a kiss but pulled back and thought better of it. "Bye, Josie."

"What? Not gonna wait around for my jail sentence?" Josie asked.

Randall's eyebrows rose, brushing his hairline.

"Let's see what a comedienne you are in a few minutes," I said.

"Um, I'll be going now." Randall strained to get out. "Um, yeah."

When he left, Josie tried to stare me down, but I was a champion on the stare downs. Her eyes darted away from me and onto the floor.

"Please sit down." I pulled out a kitchen chair. "Can I get you anything? Water? Soda?"

Officer Tanner smiled. "No, I'm good."

"Do I need to be here?" Josie asked. "I'm tired."

"You do, but your attitude doesn't. Lose it." I pointed to a chair. "Sit down."

"Whatever." Josie slid down on the chair.

"First of all," Officer Tanner said, her hazel eyes full of kindness, "I think Josie needs to know how lucky she is she didn't get hurt. It's dangerous for her to be in the park this late."

"Right. In Noteah." Josie rolled her eyes.

"In Noteah," Tanner repeated. "It's not a crime-free town, Josie. Triton Park has had its share of robberies and drug busts."

Before Josie responded, I shot her a look. "Right now, Josie, your role is to keep your mouth shut, keep your eyes still, and listen to Officer Tanner. You are not to say anything unless asked and with a normal tone.

Do not make this any worse than it already is, got it?"

She nodded her head.

"I will ask you again, do you have it?"

"I've *got* it," she said in a whisper and looked down at her hands. "Maybe now's not the time for a grammar lesson. Yes, I understand."

Officer Tanner looked over at her. "You know, Josie, you weren't this funny when we picked you up, were you?"

"I know." Josie's eyes stayed glued on the napkin she played with in her hands.

"No, in fact, Ms. Young—"

"Please call me Harper." I didn't want to correct her and explain I didn't hold the same last name as Josie.

"Okay, Harper. Josie here wasn't tough or funny at all. She was in tears."

Good, I thought. I normally would have jumped in, grabbed my child into a hug and soothed her. This time, Josie needed to be scared.

"She should have been. I hope a ride in a squad car scared the shit out of her." I leaned back. "Josie, what were you thinking? What were you doing out there?"

"Nothing." She shot Officer Tanner a sideways look.

"You can either answer your mother's question truthfully or I will. It's up to you."

"I have rights," Josie snapped.

"Not as a minor you don't." Officer Tanner drew closer to crowd Josie. "I thought your mother said your attitude wasn't welcome here. Again, do you want to tell her or should I?"

"I was waiting for Dad to pick me up." I barely

understood her mumble at first, and then it hit me like a steel beam to my gut.

"You were what?"

"I didn't know he was going to be late," Josie answered. She tried to sound trite, but her attitude started to soften.

"Why don't you start from the beginning?" Officer Tanner suggested.

"I was born—"

"Josephine." I slammed my opened hand on the table. Josie jumped, and Officer Tanner watched me. "I will not tell you again. This is not funny, this is not a joke, and you will answer all questions honestly. Got it?"

She nodded as her eyes widened. I don't get angry very often at my kids. I left a hostile relationship, and I would not let my kids grow up with anger. But I reached my ends—my wit's end and the end of my rope.

"Good. Now start from the beginning."

"Dad texted me yesterday." She tried to steady her voice, but some cracks came through. "And he said he wanted to see me on Friday."

"Why the hell would your father text you? We went over this."

"Why don't you let Josie finish her story?" Officer Tanner suggested.

"You're right," I agreed while reining in my emotions. calm. "Go on, Josie."

"Anyway, I told him I had to watch Gracie because you were going out. He said he was only gonna be in town on Friday. I told him maybe I could say I was going to a sleepover at Maggie's and, you know, get

Nonnie to watch Grace."

"You used Maggie?"

"I dunno." Josie shrugged. "I asked her if I could spend some time there and then you know, sneak out. She said yeah, but we had to keep it from her mom."

"And what about when Maggie's mom didn't see you in the morning?" I dug deep into Josie's eyes.

"She'd tell her mom I got sick and you picked me up." Josie grabbed my hand. "Mom, you can't tell her. Maggie will get into trouble."

"Go on." I pulled back and folded my arms across my chest.

"He told me he'd pick me up at Triton Park, and he said he would be there around eleven o'clock."

"You waited in the park for three hours?" I puffed out a breath. "Josie."

"What? You said I wasn't allowed to see him."

"You know why." My temper rose with my voice. "We have a restraining order against him. He can't see you or me or Gracie."

"He made a mistake, Mom. It's been five years. He's almost done with therapy, and you said you would see if this year he could see us." Josie's voice rose.

"I said with someone, Jos. Supervised. I would not allow him to see you and Gracie by himself, ever. And I doubt he's changed."

"Aren't you always the one telling me not to judge? You're judging. He's changed."

"Obviously not too much. He had you wait for three hours for him and never came," I shot back.

"Probably lost track of time." Josie began to cry. "He's my dad, and you can't keep me from him."

"I am not keeping you. I'm trying to protect you

from him, Josie." My voice softened, and I grabbed her hand.

"He's not who you say he is, Mom." It was now Josie's turn to pull away. She got up from her chair and bent down toward me, her face inches away from mine. "He's nice to me. He said you always made him lose his temper, but I don't. He said he hit you because you made him angry. And when he hit me, he said it was an accident. He didn't mean to hit me."

"Oh, baby girl, he didn't only hit me, he beat me. And nothing he did that night was an accident which is why I left. You know this. You saw this."

"But it's been five years. Why can't you let me see him *now*?"

"Because I don't believe he's changed, and I need to protect all of us," I said. "Tell me, how did he get your cell phone number?"

"It doesn't matter."

"Josie," Officer Tanner jumped in, reminding me of her presence. "I think you need to tell your mom how he got it."

"No, because she'll take away my phone and then my dad can't contact me at all."

"Oh, Josie." I rubbed her cheek. "I'm taking it away anyway. It's better if you tell me."

Josie shook her head no. And then it hit me.

"It was Kathy, wasn't it?" I fell on the chair. "Shit, Kathy gave him your number."

"And Kathy is?" Officer Tanner looked from me to Josie.

"Of course." I spoke more to myself than anyone in the room. "She had him text you because like you told me, Kathy still keeps in contact with Alan."

"And who is Kathy?" Officer Tanner asked again.

"My grandmother," Josie answered.

I wanted to add, *and the wicked witch of any direction*, but I didn't.

Josie continued, "She called me. My dad wanted my cell phone number and asked if it was okay. I said yes, and she gave it to him."

"Damn it," I said between clenched teeth. "Kathy should have asked me, not you."

"Come on, Mom. We were going to find each other sooner or later. There is something called the Internet. But when Grathy told me he wanted to see me, I wanted to see him."

"Oh, Josie."

"Ms. Young, um, Harper." Officer Tanner stood up. "Why don't you let Josie go to bed? I think she's had a long night. You can talk more in the morning."

I blew air out of inflated cheeks. "Probably a good idea."

Without a word, Josie walked out of the room. I sat back down. "Fucking bastard."

"I think I'll get us some water." Officer Tanner walked over to the cabinets and helped herself to two glasses. She filled them with tap water. "You know, my sister has teenagers, and they are a handful."

"What are their ages?"

"Let's see." She placed a glass in front of me and held onto the other. "A boy, fifteen, and a girl, thirteen. Hard ages."

I took a sip and looked at her. "And does your sister have an abusive ex and a mother who knows no boundaries?"

She laughed. "No, neither one of those."

"Didn't think so." I let out a strangled laugh. "Now what happens? Court date? Should I get a lawyer?"

"Probably would be a good idea. Your ex broke his visitation rights."

"Oh, he has none," I scoffed. "What about Josie?"

"Nothing." Officer Tanner shrugged. "We're not going to file any charges."

"Will Officer Look-So-Bored agree?"

"Billy?" She smiled. "He will. Less paperwork."

"Thank you." I relaxed. "I mean it. Thank you. It's been hard lately for Josie. I'm not sure why."

"Well, it's an age where they start to notice boys. She's probably wondering about the male figures in her life. Good or bad, your ex is a figure. Kids sometimes block out the bad. I suppose we all do. It's called survival."

"Well, I'll never forget."

"Good." She downed the rest of her water. "Can I give you some advice?"

"Sure." I wasn't in the mood for advice, but I didn't want to piss her off because she had been kind to me. "Before you start, I have a therapist appointment scheduled for Monday. Josie has a regular therapist, and I know she needs help. She saw her therapist once every six weeks for the past half year, but now I'll make her appointments more regularly."

"Okay, good." She put the glass in the sink. "Go easy on her. She's confused and scared and in need of you right now, even though she's pushing you away."

"I have to punish her."

"Yes, but the way she cried tonight, I think she's already punishing herself." She came up to me and leaned down. "Ms. Harper, I hear lots of cries in my

147

profession. Some are fake, some are out of fear, and some out of hurt. Your daughter's cry tonight was not made up. It was full of fear, and she is hurting, make no mistake, she's hurting."

"Okay." It barely came out. I fought the tears threatening to fall. "Thank you. Really. Thank you."

"You're welcome." She headed toward the door and stopped. "Oh, and Harper?"

"Yes?"

"Was that your boyfriend who hightailed it out of here?"

"Randall?" I shrugged. "I know what it looked like. But he never spends the night. I am well aware of my kids and how it would look. But tonight, he had a few too many, and I didn't want him to drive home. He slept on the couch."

"Not why I asked." She faltered. "For what it's worth, I question any man who doesn't stick around when cops show up at the door."

"He asked to stay. I said no."

"Maybe you shouldn't have, or maybe it wasn't the time for him to listen."

"He's a nice guy."

"Okay, not my business." Officer Tanner pulled out a card and set it on my counter. "Let me know if you need anything, anything at all."

"Thanks, again."

"Oh, and you can drop Officer Tanner. Lana is fine."

When she left, I put my head down on the table and began to cry, something I hadn't done in a very long time, but needed to, for a very long time.

Chapter Eleven
Stress and Cigarettes

I stood there eyeing the spot where I kept a pack of cigarettes. Just for emergencies. The stunt Josie pulled called for a glass of wine and at least one smoke, possibly two. Nobody knew—not Hannah, not Hayden, not Nonnie—and especially, not my kids. Four to six times a year, I smoked and every New Year's Eve I replaced the old pack with a new one.

When Officer Lana Tanner left, my cigarettes called me. But before I answered, my phone rang. It was Maggie's mom.

"It must be so hard to be a single mom." Not even a hello first. Maggie's mom went right to false compassion. Her voice was sickly sweet, and if I were a diabetic, I would have gone into a coma.

"Thanks, but Josie shouldn't have—"

"No, she shouldn't have, but I understand. I am sure you struggle to raise your children without a husband to help. I don't know and probably will never know since my husband is great—to our kids and me. But I have read articles on the struggles on single parenting."

I burst into laughter. This was a ridiculous conversation. Not only did Maggie's dad think himself as the lady's man of Noteah and slept with any woman who agreed, Maggie's mom never even talked with me enough to care.

"Sorry." I coughed. "It's been a long night."

"Oh, I can only imagine. You know, Josie's not a bad girl."

"Thanks."

"Oh sure, she has a smart mouth. Not to me, mind you. She's always polite to me," she went on. "But I have heard how she talks to the other girls. If you don't mind me saying, I kind of knew one day she would get in trouble for it."

"Is there a reason why you called?" I pinched the bridge of my nose.

"Yes, and please know this was hard for my husband and me to decide. It won't be easy on Josie, I know, but we have to do what is right."

"And that means what exactly?" My patience thinned.

"Maggie cannot hang around with Josie anymore. Josie's just not a good influence on Maggie. She lies, gets arrested, and she used Maggie. Even you have to admit it's not right."

Even me. Me, the single mom who had it so tough, had to admit my daughter was liar, a criminal, and a user.

"I do agree about one thing. This will be hard on Josie. Maggie and Josie are good friends, and it's hard to lose a friend in middle school." I didn't let her jump in. "Listen, I have to go. It's been a long night."

"I hope—"

I hung up on Maggie's mom. I had enough. After I hung up, the urge for the wrong type of craving was still there. I fought against it, and I lost. Scowling, I got up and dragged a kitchen chair toward the cabinet above the refrigerator. I stood on the chair to grab a pack of cigarettes hidden inside an old chipped mug from my childhood. I sat down on the kitchen counter by the open window and lit up. I inhaled, coughed, inhaled, and coughed. Why I thought this would relax me, I didn't know, until it did.

When I finished my cigarette, I thought about lighting up another one until a coughing jag came on and killed the thought. Instead, after I sprayed the room with deodorizer, and I put my headphones into my phone jack, cranked up my music and danced. Best stress relief of all. I danced until my legs hurt, my ass ached, sweat drenched my T-shirt, and I nearly collapsed from exhaustion.

My fatigue only lasted through two glasses of water, and then I cleaned. I cleaned the front room until all dust bunnies were dead. I scoured the kitchen and the bathroom as if I needed to scrub away my past. I washed the floors until every shoe mark were memories. Finally, I collapsed onto a kitchen chair with a glass filled with cola/diet cola mixture.

"Hello," Hannah greeted me with a kiss on the top of my head. The hour hand clicked onto the seven.

"You're up early."

"Nonnie called. I couldn't go back to sleep." She shrugged. "And how are you holding up? How's Josie?"

"What did Nonnie tell you?"

"The cops brought Josie home, but it seemed to be okay. What gives?"

I filled her in on every detail. Hayden would eventually get every detail from Hannah. The three of us, from childhood, never kept anything from each other, especially about each other.

"I probably should fill Nonnie in soon, huh?"

"Probably should." Hannah rubbed her thumb over my knuckles. "Nonnie is family."

I nodded. "Did you call Hayden?"

"Yup. He said he would be here after work to hear the details."

"He doesn't have to come." I got up, more for something to do than anything else, and grabbed a bowl of strawberries out of the fridge.

"But he will," Hannah said. "And then he's gonna wanna look for Alan."

"That's what I'm afraid of."

"You're right, you know. Alan doesn't want to see Josie. He is more interested in using her to get to you. Be careful."

"I know." I pointed a berry at my sister. "I also know Hayden will never find him. The snake in the grass probably has already slithered back to the hellhole he came from."

"Do you have Josie's cell?"

"I took it away from her last night, or this morning, actually."

"Use it. Pretend you're Josie." Hannah popped a strawberry into her mouth. "We'll find out where he is."

"No. I'll do it the legal way. I'll show my lawyer all the texts and then—"

"And then pay the lawyer a mint for a judge to slap his wrist with a year probation and say, 'Bad Alan,' like the last time? Sucks."

"What's better? For our brother to beat the shit out of him, again, and get jail time, again?" I shook my head. "No, if I truly believe in karma, it'll all work out.

"But what if—" My cell phone buzzed and moved on the table. I ignored it. "Ya gonna answer it?"

"No. Although it might be Randall. Hmmm." I thought for a minute.

"He's not here? I thought I saw his car parked up front."

"It is." I pulled myself up on the counter. "He got drunk last night. Threw up and slept most of it off. Anyway, he left once the cops came."

"Seriously? He didn't stay? Aren't you pissed?"

"No." The phone went off again. Again, I ignored it. "I told Randall to go. Teenagers are scarier than zombies."

"He should have stayed."

"He did ask." This time my phone pinged four times and indicated four different text messages.

"At least look at the texts." Hannah tried to grab the phone, but I beat her to it.

"This bugs you, doesn't it?"

"Don't you even want to know who it is?"

"Apparently you do. Me? Not so much."

"What if it's Marti or Esther?" Hannah's big green eyes shot up at me. "Oh, wait. What if it's your new friend Brody?"

"I can't talk to him about this."

"Why?"

"Why would I? I haven't even talked to my old friends, Marti and Esther, about this, but I will my new one? Besides, he called me last night and—" I stopped. I was close to my sister, but I didn't want to break a confidence. "Well, let's just say he's having issues of his own and doesn't need mine, and I don't want to hear any more of his."

"It's called sharing with a friend."

"Nope, not gonna happen." I opened my mouth, and Hannah tossed a strawberry into it.

"Is Josie still sleeping?"

"I think she may be faking it. Can't imagine her sleeping through the tornado of cleaning I did." I chomped down on the strawberry. "I am gonna get her ass up in a few."

"Don't be too hard on her. She's probably hurting, too."

"Hanny, she broke curfew, lied to me, and waited in a park for three hours. I will damn well be hard on her." When Hannah looked at me, I lifted a hand in surrender. "But I will do it calmly. Maggie can't hang around with her anymore, which means—"

"Nor will Katie because she'll side with Maggie. Josie will lose both friends." Hannah shook her head. "Shit."

The phone pinged and then rang.

"Damn it, Harper. Answer the phone." Hannah grabbed it, pressed the button, and pushed it into my face.

"What?" Not my best greeting.

"And good morning to you, too, sugs." His voice slid over me like the hands of a trained lover. I wanted to hate it.

"Yeah, whatever."

"Hey, you okay?"

"No, Brody, I'm not, but after all your calls and texts I thought I'd better answer."

"I haven't done either. Is someone else stalking you?" He started to chuckle, and when I didn't join in, he stopped. "I probably woke you. Go back to sleep."

"I wasn't sleeping. If I were, I'm up now."

"Are you always this crabby in the morning or is something going on?"

"No, nothing's going on." Hannah's eyes drooped at me in judgment.

"So, you're crabby in the morning," Brody said. "Coffee can cure that, sugs."

"Why are you calling?"

"Right to the point, huh. Okay, I wanted you to know I took your advice. I told Z I needed time and space to think about us. I didn't break up with her. I distanced myself. I am leaving this morning from LA, early, and chilling in Jamaica."

"Okay" was all my stressed-out self could push out.

"I'll be there for a few days and probably come back on Friday. I told her I'd talk to her then."

"Great," I said with as much enthusiasm I could mustard, which wasn't much at all.

"Sugs, what's wrong?"

"Nothing."

"I thought we already established you are not a good liar."

"Nothing is wrong, Brody."

Hannah mouthed *Really?*

I flipped her off.

"I didn't sleep well is all. I had a shitty night."

"Randall?"

"No," I barked. "I can have a shitty night without Randall. I have kids you know, and sometimes kids fuck up, which makes for a shitty night. It's not always about a man. What's with you? Life's not a middle

155

school drama. There's much more to it, you know."

Hannah's eyes grew big. There was silence on the other end. I rubbed my face with my free hand.

"Harper, I know," he spat back at me. "Damn. I didn't think you'd throw last night back at me. Lesson learned."

"Oh shit, Brody, I'm sorry." My voice cracked as I fought against the urge to release all the emotions of the night and swallowed hard. "I'm sorry. I'm a bitch, a real bitch. I had a shitty night and didn't sleep. I'm tired, so tired of so many things." I acted like a middle school drama queen.

"Tell me what's wrong." He skipped a beat. "Are you crying?"

"No." I inhaled deeply and clutched my tears like feathers in the wind. I had to get myself together. I was not weak. "But look, I gotta go."

"Something's going on."

"I'll tell you later." Maybe, I thought. "Right now, my sister's here, and I need to talk to Josie and—"

"Is Josie okay?"

Not after I kick her ass, I thought, but responded, "Yes."

"Are you—?"

"Yes." The word shot out like a bullet. I took a deep breath and repeated it with more calm. "Yes, I'm fine. I'm glad you're taking time to think about Z."

Hannah looked at me like "really?" I shrugged. I didn't want to talk about myself, so I deflected his questions by commenting on Z. It was a great avoidance move.

"I'm still not sure—" He stopped. "You do know you can tell me what's going on, right?"

"You are persistent, aren't you?"

"Basics from Stalking 101."

This time I did laugh.

"It is a long story. Right now, you have to catch a plane, and I have to get the ass of a teenage girl out of bed and, well, maybe kick it."

"You can't kick her ass. Mine? Randall's? Maybe. But your girls' asses? Never."

"You are probably right."

"All right, I'll let you go. But I will call you later, okay?"

"If you want."

"One of these days you're going to say, 'Yes, Brody, I need you. I need—' "

"I can already see your boots in my bathroom."

"I need a friend," Brody finished. "I think you will be losing this bet with your mind always going there and the way you attack me every time we—"

"Bye, Brodes."

"Bye, Harper."

Hannah tilted her head toward me and smirked.

"What?" I spilled the rest of my drink into the sink.

"What? Phbbbt. You were in a piss-poor mood when I got here, and now after the phone call with Brody, you're all smiles."

"Shut up." I threw a dish rag at her.

Chapter Twelve
Kathy and Corn Muffins

"We should call Kathy." Hannah muted the TV and looked at me.

Hannah and I sat in the living room. We stared at a Saturday morning television show on elephants without interest. My efforts to push Hannah out the door failed. I was glad she stayed. I needed company. I needed her company.

"Let's not and say we did."

"Come on, Harper. You have to eventually, and now is as good a time as any, especially while you are pissed."

"Hanny, I don't—" But Hannah already dialed and plopped down next to me.

"She should be up by now. If she ever went to bed. I have a feeling she's off her meds."

As Hannah put her cell on speaker phone and Kathy's phone rang, I took the short time to decide what I wanted to say. I *wanted* to scream, but I knew it would be wrong. Her connection to Alan alarmed me. She could not be made my enemy. My instincts told me to remain calm.

"Hello?" Kathy's voice sang through the line.

"What the hell, Kathy?" I didn't listen to my instincts. My temper flared.

"Good morning to you, too, Harper."

"Hi, Mom," Hannah threw in.

"Mom? I don't know a mom. I know a Kathy."

"My mistake. Hello, Kathy." Hannah rolled her eyes.

"Hi, my Hanny. Tell your sister to settle down, will you?"

"Don't tell me to settle down, Kathy," I snapped. "Why did you give Josie's number to Alan?"

"Getting to the point, aren't you?"

"Not in the mood to chitchat. You should have asked me."

"Harper, Alan has a right to at least talk with his daughter. He—"

"He gave up all rights the minute he bashed her against the wall."

"He did not *bash* her." Kathy scorned. "Always the dramatics, Harper. Just like your father."

"You have no idea who my father is," I bellowed.

"True. But I know I met him at a Grateful Dead concert, and all Deadheads are dramatic."

"Unbelievable." Hannah groaned with shake of her head.

"All I'm saying is Alan did not *bash* Josie. He—"

"She ended up with three broken ribs from him." I held back the volume of my shout. "I can't believe I have to defend myself to you."

"Well, if he did, and I'm not saying he did—"

"He went to jail for six months, Kathy," Hannah screamed.

"Yes, but it was *only* six months. If it were as bad as you say, Alan would have gotten more time," Kathy said in victory. "He really wants to see his daughter, and I think now is the time you should let him. He was respectful of the order you wrote up—"

"Which is why he only got six months, Kathy," Hannah bellowed again.

"Stop yelling, Hannah. It's not very becoming of a woman," Kathy scolded. "As I told Josie, Alan has changed. He followed your order and never tried to sneak to see her. Hell, he hasn't even contacted you or the kids until now, has he?"

"No, but—"

"No. Exactly," Kathy repeated. "Harper, he's had time to reflect. Did you know he's doing yoga now?"

"Kathy, Alan can be doing transcendental meditation for all I care, but he will never see Josie again. Don't get involved. You hear? This is none of your business."

"Of course, it is. I'm Josie's grandmother. I have rights."

"Wait?" Hannah jumped in. "Did you just admit that you are a, gulp, grandmother?"

"You're not being nice, Hannah." There was a hitch in her voice. Yes, my mother would not get emotional about her granddaughter's three broken ribs, but she would at the reminder of her age. "And now, I am going to hang up."

"Kathy, don't." Hannah pleaded with her while I silently begged for Kathy to hang up.

"You know, when I leave for Bermuda—"

"Bermuda?" I exclaimed.

"Oh, right. I didn't tell you girls. I'm going to Bermuda with Larry in a few hours."

"Few hours?" Hannah asked. "When were you going to tell us?"

"I don't know. I didn't think about it. What does it

matter? I'm telling you now."

"Who's Larry?" I asked.

"I didn't tell you about Larry? My mind is so scattered sometimes." Hannah and I lifted our eyebrows in disbelief. Our mother was scattered all the time. "He's a ski instructor, and he set up a business in Bermuda. He asked me if I wanted to go with. I thought, why not?"

"Wait." I stared at the phone. "When did you meet this guy? What kind of business? He does know there is no snow in Bermuda, right?"

"I met Larry three days ago. We're in love." Kathy gushed like a teenager talking about her crush.

"Three days ago? Kathy, seriously?"

"What? Life's too short to count days. Oh, did I tell you? Larry sells logging equipment."

"Hold on. You just told us he's a ski instructor." I wanted to end the conversation, but something about manic Kathy always drew me in.

"I know because he is that too." Kathy was confused by my question. "Anyway, we leave this afternoon. I probably won't see you until maybe after the new year. You don't have to call me until then because I have Larry now."

"Kathy, when's the last time you took your meds?" I asked. I knew the answer as sure as I knew I would call her before the new year. That's how we rolled.

"None of your business. I'm fine. Great in fact. I do yoga now because Alan told me all about it. And you know, it helps my...my..." Kathy always had a hard time using the word "bipolar," so I helped her.

"Kathy, you are bipolar. Hayden is bipolar. You told me your mom was bipolar," I reminded her of all these facts. "It's a disease, a disease that runs in our family. There's nothing to be ashamed of, and one of the ways you can help yourself is through meds. How many times do we have to go through this?"

"Oh, you and your labels. I feel great. In fact, better than great."

"So, you did stop your meds." Hannah pursed her lips in frustration.

"You know, you girls insult me too much. I'm really hanging up this time. Goodbye."

"Wait, Mom, Kathy," I called into the phone, but she was gone.

For a while, Hannah and I stared at her cell phone. I started with a small chuckle, which led to more chuckles. The chuckles rolled into waves of laughter. Hannah joined in.

"She is off totally off her meds." I laughed out.

"Totally," Hannah agreed, barely able to get the word out. Eventually, the laughter died. "What the hell is wrong with our mother, Harper? How did the conversation start about you and finish about her?"

"It's always all about her. I am surprised we aren't more fucked up than we are."

"Because of you. You brought me up, not her." The clock's ticks were the only noise in the living room. There was always a reflective hush during our discussions about Kathy. "Do you think she'll be okay?"

"I don't know." I shrugged. "If not, well, I've never been to Bermuda before."

"I wonder how the hospitals are down there." Hannah smiled sadly and stared out the window. "Remember when Nonnie took us to see her in

Detroit?"

"When she was picked up naked, outside the baseball stadium, claimed the general manager asked her to be a distraction for the opposite team? How can I forget?"

"Or the time you drove Hayden and me to Atlanta for the weekend?"

"To pick up Kathy at a church where she professed to be the second Virgin Mary?" I shook my head.

"You were only, what? Seventeen?"

"Just turned. And I didn't tell anyone we went, not even Nonnie. Boy, was Nonnie ever mad at me for taking you two."

"You always took good care of us." Hannah picked up my hand and squeezed. "And you take good care of your kids, Harp. You are not Kathy. You are a good mother."

"Sometimes, Hanny, I'm not so sure."

****

Josie eventually woke up, or, rather, I woke her up. She was sheepish and when we talked, I told her about the conversation with Maggie's mom. It sent Josie into a tirade as to why I was a horrible mother. She bellowed she needed to call her dad because he would understand. I explained a) I had her phone, and b) I blocked and deleted Alan from her phone. I morphed into the worst mother *ever*, which was quite an accomplishment. It meant I was worse than Kathy.

By four o'clock in the afternoon, I was exhausted. I had only slept a couple of hours and pushed my body to extreme fatigue. Not only did I dance and clean, in the early afternoon I cooked. I loved to bake and cook. It cheered me up. One reason I looked forward to the weekends. Saturday and Sunday were my days to cook meals for the rest of the week.

Josie moped around the house and made sure every slammed door, every "this sucks," every "I have no friends," and every "you're not fair" served as reminders of my worst-mother-ever title.

I called Josie's therapist, Sabrina, later in the morning. On short notice, she agreed to carve out two hours Tuesday morning, not only for Josie but also for Gracie and me. Sabrina thought situations were becoming a little bit more "front and center" with Alan, and we, as a family, needed to talk about it. I agreed. Even though it was the start of the school year and the appointment would delay the start of our day for all of us, this was more important than missed school or work hours.

In the evening, two big pots of chili simmered on the stove. Once chilled, I put both into the freezer to be thawed and served for Friday Chili Night with Hayden and Hannah. Josie sat at the kitchen table and did not help. Instead, she shot daggers at me with arms folded.

Gracie knelt on another chair and helped me make the four dozen corn muffins. I snuck shredded carrots and broccoli bits into two dozen of the muffins and filled the other two dozen with jalapeno and cheddar cheese. Gracie brought down the chocolate chips.

"Let'th put them in too. Pleathe?"

"I'm not sure, Gracie Girl." I kissed the top of her blond mop of curls.

"You alwayth thay to apperiment."

"I do, don't I?" I shrugged. "Okay then, go and experiment."

My cell phone erupted into a chorus of "I'm Every

Woman," my ring tone. Gracie and I danced as I picked up my phone. I looked down and saw Randall's number. He had not called me since he left the night before.

"Hello, Randall." I dipped my finger in flour and put it on Gracie's nose. It sent her into fits of giggles. Josie smiled.

"Hi." Randall pathetic voice came over the line. "I have a nasty hangover."

"I can imagine." I laughed.

"I missed lunch with my mom and my golf game, maybe one of the last times before it turns cold."

"That sucks. But I'm glad you made it home okay," I said. "Uber was a good choice."

"I didn't want to risk it. Although, by the time I made it home, I was sober. So sober in fact, I started my hangover." He chuckled.

"I should have given you some water or something when you left, but I did have company."

"Right. Shit." His tone was rueful. "Sorry. I should have asked. How did it go with the police? What happened?"

"Well." I looked over at Josie. She joined Gracie and measured cornmeal. "I can't really talk now."

"Because I'm sitting right here, Randall," Josie shouted without glancing up.

"What she said." I grabbed a towel off the stove's handle and hurled it at Josie. She laughed. Her mood had lightened.

"Later, then?" Randall asked.

"Yes."

"Promise?"

"Yes."

"Let me just ask you this, is she okay?"

"Define okay," I said mirthlessly. "No, she's okay…for the moment."

"Sorry." Randall's sincerity seemed genuine.

"Me too." Fatigue rammed my body, and I nearly buckled from its blow. "Randall, I should go. We're cooking and baking, and it's not a good time."

"Sure. I understand. I'm headed back to bed, maybe grab something to eat. Are you sure you're okay? I can come over."

"No. Don't. We'll talk later. Go and get some sleep. Eat something too."

"All right." His voice hitched. "Harper?"

"Yes?"

"It'll be all right. Teenagers do stupid things. Their minds are underdeveloped. They just don't think. Now, I don't know what Josie did, but I'm sure it wasn't the end of the world. You probably are just over-reacting."

"Randall." I blew out in agitation. He lectured me on something he knew nothing about. I mean, he wasn't a father or a teacher or even a coach. His platitudes angered me. Yet, I knew it came from a good place, from a kind place, from a Randall place. I needed this conversation to end before I blew up.

"I'm just saying, Harper. I know moms worry over silly things and—"

"Oh shit. My muffins are burning." And there it was, a lie. To hold off a yell or an argument, I lied. Not my proudest moment. "I have to go."

I hung up without a response and leaned my forehead against the refrigerator.

"Why did you lie to him?" Josie's question hit me from behind.

"Why did you listen to my conversation?" I lifted my head.

"Didn't you teach me never to answer a question with a question?" Josie spit out with disdain. She probably hated me, but when I looked into her girl-woman eyes, my heart swelled, and my love for her became all too much.

"You're right, I lied. I lied because I didn't want to get into a fight." There. At least I told someone the truth.

"About me?" I saw the hurt. I knew she liked Randall.

"Josie, no." I smoothed out her hair. "No. It was about—doesn't matter. I shouldn't have lied."

"No, you shouldn't have." Josie shrugged. "Too many people lie, you know?"

I knew she didn't mean only me. I knew she thought about Alan and how he left her at the park.

"Sucks, doesn't it?" I whispered. "Not really fair."

"Momma, look," Gracie shouted into the room before Josie answered.

"What?" When I saw the two empty bags of chocolate chips, I knew she dumped them into two dozen raw corn muffins. I sighed out a "Gracie."

Josie tried to hold back her laugh, but it spilled out of her.

"Don't laugh at your sis—" I began to choke on my laughter.

"What?" Gracie brows furrowed in confusion. "I apperimented with all of them."

Josie and I roared harder in harmony. If all else failed, even with messed-up lives and unresolved issues, there would always be laughter.

Chapter Thirteen
In Need of Some Therapy

"Do you understand, Gracie?"

Sabrina's blue eyes softened as she spoke with Gracie. Sabrina Anderson, in her mid-40s had a kind demeanor with a no-nonsense approach to therapy, probably to life. Sabrina's specialty is domestic abuse. She treats not only the victims but also the children of the victims. Josie and I saw Sabrina a month after I left Alan. The emergency room doctor who treated Josie for her broken ribs, gave me her card. It was the first time Gracie came with us.

I sat next to Gracie on the loveseat. She played with my fingers as Sabrina spoke. Josie draped herself over the arm of an overstuffed chair next to us. Sabrina sat closest to the door. An oriental rug was positioned between all of us.

"Yeth." Gracie didn't look at Sabrina.

"What do you understand?"

"That my dad is not nithe. And—"

"He is nice." Josie charged in with an interruption.

"Josie, this is Gracie's time to talk," Sabrina reminded her. When Josie folded her arms over her chest, Sabrina's attention went back to Gracie. "And?"

"And Jothie thneaked out to thee him."

"How do you know your dad is not nice?" Sabrina asked.

"Becauthe onthe I heared Aunt Hannah talked to Uncle Hayden. She said he hitted Momma. Uncle Hayden thaw me and told me nithe men don't hit women." Her eyes grew big. She looked at Sabrina. "Oneth I hitted Jack at thchool because he wanted to play with me and Marina, and I only wanted to play with Marina. Momma told me it wasn't nithe of me. Hitting is wrong. I told Jack thorry, and now he'th my friend. Maybe my dad and Momma can be friendth too?"

I swallowed hard and looked at Sabrina like a drowning victim waiting to be saved.

"I don't know, Grace, but I do know your mom and Uncle Hayden are right. Hitting is wrong." Sabrina smiled. "Do you hear a lot of stories about your dad?"

"Yeth." Gracie looked back down at our entangled fingers.

"How do you hear them?"

"I dunno."

"And what kind of stories do you hear?"

"Well, like—" Gracie glanced at me sideways.

"Honey, I told you. You can tell Miss Sabrina anything. Don't worry about Josie's feelings or mine. Be totally honest with her, okay?" I winked at her.

"Okay." She blinked both eyes and turned to Sabrina. "Momma told me the reathon my dad doethn't live with uth, and why I can't thee him, is because he getth angry and he hitted her. Jothie said he hit her onthe, too, and broke her but now he's thorry. Uncle Hayden calls him an athhole."

I nearly spit out my gum. "Honey, Uncle Hayden—"

"Go on." Sabrina gave me a look meant to quiet

169

me. "What else?"

"Momma told me one time she and my dad loved each other, and Jothie and me were part of their love. But my dad didn't be nithe to her and Jothie so we can't live together. I never met my dad, but I don't think I want to." She shook her head. "Nuh-uh. Not if he's an athhole, which I know is a thwear, and Uncle Hayden put money in the thwear jar. Oh, and latht week Jothie told me my dad hated me."

I looked over at Josie, who shot a look outside the window as a tear streamed down her face.

Sabrina frowned. "I bet that made you sad."

"I don't know." Gracie shrugged. "Nonnie told me onthe when I thaid I hated Marina'th mom because she wouldn't let her come over, you can't dethide if you don't like thomeone if you don't know them. Reverthe my judgment, Nonnie thayth."

"Reverse?" Sabrina looked at me.

"Reserve." I smiled.

"Ah." Sabrina held back a smile.

"Yeah, and my dad doethn't know me. And I do like Marina'th mom, now, after I met her."

"Ah. Well, Nonnie has a point. Your father doesn't know you. If he did, I'm sure he would like you, don't you think?" Sabrina asked.

"I think tho." Gracie nodded her head. "Jothie told me my dad didn't want me, but Momma said my dad thayth mean thingth when he'th mad."

"We all do sometimes." Sabrina's voice was like a mother's, lulling her newborn to sleep. I imagined everyone opened up to her.

"I know, because one time I gotth tho mad at Jothie and called her ugly, and she'thnot." Gracie lifted her hand at Josie. "Look at her. She'th the prettietht gull I know 'thept Momma."

"Thank you, Gracie Girl." Josie squeezed her sister's hand. "I know you didn't mean it, and Daddy probably didn't either. I shouldn't have said anything."

"Ah, it'th okay."

"Gracie, you are a sweet girl." Sabrina smiled.

"I know." Grace smiled back.

"Thank you for being here today." Sabrina smiled. "Is there anything else you want to tell me?"

"Yeth." Grace nodded, in excitement. "The new Princeth Penelope movie ith coming out on DVD. I'm tho 'thited."

"That is exciting," Sabrina agreed. "Do you think Prince Preston is finally going to get his dragon?"

"I don't know. He wanth it tho, tho, tho bad." Gracie giggled. "You're pretty."

"Thank you, Grace." Sabrina's eyes showed what many people's eyes show when they are around Grace, affection. "Is there anything else you want to tell me about your mom, or Josie, or Nonnie, or your Dad?"

"Well—" Gracie looked around the room. Her bottom lip quivered. "I don't like when they fight. It makes me athcared."

"What scares you?" Sabrina asked.

"The yelling. I'm athecared Jothie might hit Momma thometimeth, like my dad."

My stomach jumped into my throat, and I fought back the tears. This little girl heard and saw much more than I ever thought. My heart burned with regret and sadness for her. I placed my lips on the top of her head and kissed it over and over.

"Has she?" Sabrina asked. "Has Josie ever hit your

mom?"

"No." Gracie shook her locks of golden curls.

"Has Josie hit you?" When Sabrina asked, my head jerked toward Josie.

"Oh no. And Jothie told me she won't ever, never ever, and if anyone ever did hit me, she would kick their ath. I made her put money in the thwear jar."

"Sounds like Josie loves you."

"I know." Gracie smiled. "I love her, too."

"I know," Josie murmured.

"Thee." Gracie pointed at Josie. "She'th a great big thithter."

"She is," Sabrina agreed. "Why would you think she would hit your mom?"

"I don't know." Gracie looked up at me.

"Gracie, go ahead. I told you. You can tell Sabrina anything."

"Becauth…" Gracie hesitated. "Becauth I hearded Momma telling Aunt Hannah onthe Jothie is like her dad, temper and all."

My chin dropped to my collarbone. I fought back the urge to vomit. I needed to remember how small my house was and the cruelty of my tongue.

"Harper?" Sabrina looked at me.

"Gracie, I probably did and—"

"And it's the reason you hate me." Josie pinned me with a glare. "Because I remind you of Dad, and all the shitty things he's done to you. Thanks, Mom. I love you, too."

Sabrina put her hand on Josie's knee. "Josie, we'll talk about this later, but it's still Gracie's time."

"Whatevs."

"Grace, Josie does remind me of your father." I

wouldn't let anyone jump in to stop me. I spoke louder and faster. "She is funny, like your dad. She has his build—thin and athletic. She has his beautiful brown eyes. And, yes, she does have his temper, but—"

"See." Josie threw her hands up.

"But," I repeated, "she uses it differently. Josie uses it to stand up to people, to protect her little sister, to be her own person, to stop anyone from walking all over her and her family. She uses it to make sure she is heard, and you know what? I admire her for those qualities so, so much."

I kissed Gracie's head and left the couch to squat in front of Josie. I willed her to look at me, but she didn't. "I once loved your father, Josie, and all those good qualities you have of his, I also loved in him."

"Yet you left him," Josie scoffed.

"Yes, I left him because he hit me, and hit me hard. He hit you. I didn't want you to grow up and think it was normal, for you or me. I didn't want you to think it was okay because maybe he would change."

"I know he's changed, and you can help him change some more."

"Oh, Josie, I tried. I tried."

"Josie." Sabrina's gentle voice cascaded down my back like a soothing waterfall. "A person has to change on their own. It's not anyone else's responsibility."

"I guess." Josie shrugged.

"And Pumpkin Toes…" I had not used Josie's nickname in a long time. It made her finally look at me. "I couldn't take the abuse anymore. I couldn't hope he'd change. In the end, I didn't think he'd change, and for the good of you and Grace and myself, I had to leave him. And I have to continue to protect the two of you and myself. Bottom line, Josie, we're not getting back together, and I'm sorry if this hurts you, but you can't see him, not alone anyway."

"I will when I'm eighteen. You can't stop me then."

"No," I agreed. "I can't. But until then, I can, and I am going to."

"Mom, why don't you talk to Grace, too?" Sabrina reminded me.

Sometimes, the squeaky wheel does get the most attention, and Josie's wheel cried out for lots of it. In the meantime, the one who ran smooth and steady still needed a little bit of oil.

"And Gracie—" I went to sit down next to her. "I think Josie and I can promise you, we will not hit each other. At times, we get loud. We need to work on our inside voices. But I promise you, I will never hit Josie. I am sorry for what you heard, baby. I am. Will you come to me when you overhear something or get afraid? Please?"

"Yeth." Gracie grinned and showed off her gums of her missing two front teeth.

"Gracie Girl?" Josie whispered. It made all of us look her way. "I won't hit Momma. I scream at her and act all mad and stuff, but I wouldn't hit her. She's our mom. I respect her, and I love her. You don't hit someone you love. You know, even when I'm mad or in a bad mood, you can come to talk to me. I'm your big sister. Okay?"

"Yeth. Would you play dollth with me? You haven't played in a long time."

"Maybe." Josie smiled which warmed up her entire face.

"Anything else, Gracie?" Sabrina asked.

"Yeth." Gracie looked at her with profoundness. "Do you think Printhe Prethton'th uncle will ever be friendth with King Paul again?"

"I don't know." Sabrina seriously considered the question. "I guess we will have to wait for the movie to come out."

"But Christhmath ith tho far away."

"Okay, I think it's probably a good time to talk with Josie alone." Sabrina rose from her chair. "Harper, if you want to take Gracie to the waiting area, there are new toys out there she might like."

"There are?" Gracie sprang out of her chair when I stood up. "Anything with Princeth Penelope?"

Sabrina smiled. "I think we do."

"Yeth." Gracie skipped toward the door.

"I love you, Pumpkin Toes." I got up and ruffled Josie's hair. It brought a half smile out of Josie as she looked out the window. I kissed the top of her head.

As I left the office, Sabrina grabbed my hand. "This was good, Harper."

"Sure." I glanced back at Josie. "But she's really hurting."

"I know." Sabrina offered a weak smile.

****

I read the fifth Princess Penelope story to Gracie, who sat on my lap and sucked her thumb. I thought of pulling it out but stopped. If I sneaked a cigarette during a stressful time, she was allowed a thumb in her mouth.

Josie came out of the office. "Ma, Sabrina wants to see you."

"Okay." I scooted Grace off my lap. "You okay?"

"Ish." Josie shrugged.

"We were reading the last of the Penelope books." I leaned in to Josie. "You're welcome."

Josie laughed and grasped my hand. "I'm sorry I snuck out."

"I know you are." I kissed her cheek.

"Still a little upset at Josie?" Sabrina sat in her oversized chair, writing down notes as I walked in.

"No." I plopped down on a chair. When she glanced up at me in disbelief, I let out a long breath. "Okay, I am. How do I get over this? I can't believe she snuck out to see Alan. You know how dangerous it would have been if he saw her? He might have…" I scrubbed my face.

"But she didn't, and he didn't." Sabrina stopped writing and looked up at me. "Josie is confused right now. She's a middle school girl who wants to be like everyone else, and everyone else, in her world anyway, has two parents. Josie's memories of Alan are fading. She's held onto the good, the same good you saw in him. She's held onto what your mother told her and is hoping he has changed."

"I don't understand how she forgets. I mean, the last night with him—"

"She was eight years old, a long time ago for her. And we do tend to block out the hurtful, soften it, or hope it's over with. It's a coping skill."

"Where do I go from here?" I shook my head. "I can't allow Alan to see her. If he gets angry at me and takes it out on her, I will never forgive myself."

"It's illegal for him to see her alone, sure." Sabrina leaned in. "But have you thought about more supervised visitations?"

"He never wanted them before." I shot up from the chair and looked out the window. "He's just playing mind games. Why now? I don't know."

"Doesn't matter the why. Josie wants to see him, Harper. You have to let her, or else she will keep sneaking out. Do you think she hasn't thought of other ways?"

"Why? What did she tell you?" My head swiveled so fast toward Sabrina I thought I ripped a tendon.

"You know Josie has not given up. You know as well as I, she is tenacious."

"Shit. I do." I played with the arm of the chair and concentrated on the pattern. "How do you think we can make this work?"

For the next ten minutes, Sabrina told me about how to arrange visitations, the lawyers I needed to look up and assured me, in all the cases she knew of, these types of visitations work the best for both child and parent.

"What about Gracie?" I asked. "He doesn't want to see her."

"Gracie appears to be okay with it." Sabrina moved forward on the chair. "I would like to see Gracie more regularly, maybe once a month, just to check in on her."

"Really?" This suggestion surprised me.

"If Josie sees Alan, then things may start to get confusing for Gracie. Okay?"

"I suppose it makes sense."

"Good. I think you should bring Josie back on Friday. I have an early-morning opening."

"Okay." It would mean Josie would miss the first half hour of school, and I would be an hour and a half late for work, but I knew the necessity of it.

"Good. Now Josie told me Randall left when she came home with the police Friday night?"

"Yes. I told him to leave. I suppose you want me to tell you why I did."

"Only if you want to."

"Because this is my shit. I don't really need his support."

"How serious are you with him?"

"I don't know." I shrugged. "We're getting there. This stuff is all too early."

"He doesn't know anything about you and Alan?"

"Some."

"Hmmm." Sabrina shifted in her seat. "I have to wonder, Harper, are you afraid if you tell him all of this, he'll leave?"

"No. He's a nice guy and he doesn't need my past messing up what we have, you know?" I looked down at my hands.

"Josie told me you lied to him to get off the phone."

"I did, but only because I didn't want to start a fight."

"What did he say when you told him about what happened with Josie? Was he supportive?"

"I told him we'd talk about it later," I muttered.

"But he did ask, right?"

"Yes."

"I see."

"Oh, come on, Sabrina. Don't get all therapisty on me. What does 'I see' mean?"

"It means, Harper, you need to be more open with him. You can't pretend you're something you're not by hiding your past or any part of you," Sabrina answered.

"Josie also told me about Brody Reed."

"Doesn't surprise me. She does like him," I said. "Brody's a new friend."

"Tell me about him."

And I did. For the next twenty minutes, I did. I explained how I knew him, the bet—which we both laughed about—the Cubs game, our conversations and texts, Z and, yes, even all our make-out sessions. If I told my kids to be honest with Sabrina, I had to follow my own advice.

"*The* Brody Reed." Sabrina's mouth rounded in an O. "Cool."

"He's a nice and funny guy. I'm sure he'll be a great friend."

"But not a boyfriend?"

"Definitely not a boyfriend," I said.

"Why?"

"For so many reasons. I don't know if Brody will ever be truly interested in all of me. Sure, he's fun and we have a phenomenal physical attraction, but he's six years younger than me with some major baggage of his own. I mean, he's a musician. Not a lot of stability there, which is not great for my kids."

"But Randall is?"

"Sure. Randall is stable and nice and, I don't know, professional. He has a steady job and is right for my situation."

"Your situation as daddy to your kids." Sabrina nodded. "How do you feel when you are with him?"

"Like everything is okay. It's strange. I laugh a lot around him. I laugh around him more than I do with anybody else. I forgot how great it is to laugh, to really laugh. He brings lightness to any situation. He doesn't take things too seriously, yet he knows when to be serious. Or at least I am starting to see that he does. He listens to me and is interested in me. He asks me questions, you know?" I smiled. "And when we kissed, even the chaste on-the-lips kisses, my whole body explodes with passion. And I hate it."

"Why? He's the perfect man."

"Because we can only be friends because, you know, I'm dating Randall, and he has Z."

"Wait." Sabrina held up a hand. "I thought you *were* talking about Randall."

"No. Brody." Bewildered, I tilted my head. "Isn't that what you asked? How I feel when I'm with Brody?"

"No, I asked a follow-up question about Randall."

"Oh." Heat scorched my cheeks.

"Does Randall have any of what Brody does?"

"Randall's a nice—"

"—man. You've said, a few times now." Sabrina put down her pad and looked at the clock. "Harper, we have to wrap it up here, but I want to tell you a few things."

"Go for it."

"Well, you may have to open up more around Randall, if, in fact, he is the partner for you. And don't be afraid. From what you said, Randall's not Alan. You don't think he will hit you, do you?"

"What?" My eyebrows touched in confusion. "No."

"Good. Then there's nothing to be afraid of. What's holding you back from showing him everything about yourself? A question for you to think about." Sabrina stood. I joined her. "We'll see you and Josie on

Friday. It'll be Josie's appointment, but maybe I can see you the week after?"

"Sure." I walked toward the door, to the giggles of Josie and Gracie.

"Oh, and Harper."

"Hmm?" I turned back.

"I think you like Brody much more than you let on and perhaps it scares you."

"Oh, Sabrina, all Brody would end up doing is breaking my heart."

"And that scares you?"

"I do have kids, you know. Can't afford to go around with a broken heart."

"You know, my grandma—a woman probably as wise as Nonnie—once told me the only way something can be broken is if it's touched." Sabrina lifted an eyebrow. "Just a thought."

## Chapter Fourteen
## Flowers to Boot

"A lot of crap happening, huh?"

I sat on my overstuffed chair and played with the fringe of a blanket that draped over the armrest. It was Wednesday night, the girls were in bed and the clock neared midnight. I finally spilled Josie's story to Brody, who was still in Jamaica.

My session with Sabrina stayed with me. I thought about Randall, Brody, opening myself up more, and my fears. After I spent a few more days in avoidance through text and conversations, Brody asked me one last time what happened with Josie, and I broke my silence. It was wonderful to purge out the poison.

"All of it sucks." Brody let out a deep breath. "How are things going now?"

"Let's see. Josie had crappy first days at school because only one friend still talks with her, and for a thirteen-year-old that means your life is nearly over. Gracie is asking more questions about her father, a father she otherwise cared nothing about. Kathy called Hanny from Bermuda. She pleaded a case of only trying to reunite the family, which my sister and I found funny since Kathy never had an inkling about the meaning of family. And Randall and I haven't talked about the night since it happened."

"Why?"

"It's more me than him. He's asked; I don't tell. Bad, huh?"

"Up to you if you want to tell Randy." I smirked at his ongoing joke with Randall's name. "So, your life's been one big clusterfuck lately."

"You pretty much described it better than anyone has so far."

There was silence on the other end. I wasn't sure if Brody didn't know what to say or he regretted our conversation.

"You still there, Brodes?"

"I'm still here." He exhaled hard and long. "Can I ask you some questions, Harper?"

"I suppose I opened myself up for some. Go ahead. Shoot."

"I think your marriage was, um, your ex-husband was, um, not so nice, huh?" I knew what he wanted to ask. I didn't know if I wanted to talk about it. Yet, I knew I couldn't turn back.

"No, he wasn't. And I think you want to know more."

"Yeah." Brody skipped few beats. "I mean, it may be obvious, and I'm not sure if I should even ask—"

"Alan hit me. He beat me. He abused me. He was an asshole to me in every way possible."

"Shit," he mumbled. "And the kids?"

"Did he hit them? He hit Josie, a hit there, a slap there. Nothing too much. It's how I justified anyway, until the last time. The last time he hit her, he walloped her. He broke three of her ribs. She was supposed to stay in her room. He always sent her there before my smackdown. This time, she didn't stay, and she paid for it."

"I knew then if I didn't leave for myself, I had to leave for Josie, and the baby I carried inside of me. I couldn't stay anymore and let my girls think this was all okay. Up until then, I excused it all. I wanted Josie to grow up with two parents, something I never had. But when I saw her, against the wall in pain, I couldn't stay. We finally left. I probably should have left long before then, and I will always feel guilty I didn't, you know?"

"About guilt from the past? More than you know," he scoffed. "And Gracie never knew him?"

"No, I was pregnant with her when I left, although he left his mark on her too."

"Meaning?"

"Meaning, after Josie, Alan didn't want any more kids. He thought Josie took too much of my attention away from him. And then I became pregnant with Gracie." I picked at my nails. "He came home one night after work. Josie and I were talking about the new baby and he went nuts. He beat the crap out of me, almost beat the baby out of me. I was twenty-eight weeks pregnant, and I went into premature labor."

"Fuck me." His words howled.

"No, actually, fuck Alan." I grunted. "I don't like to talk about this."

"We don't have to. I understand."

"Do you? Because I don't." Anger boiled up inside me, and I exploded into a long over-due rant. "I don't understand at all. Why the hell should I be so fearful to say I was abused, and sometimes brutally so, by my ex-husband? Why can't I tell anyone, not even my closest friends and Randall, my ex would slap me because I looked at Josie's first-grade male teacher? Or used me as a punching bag because I talked too much to our waiter? Why can't I say—" I choked on my tears.

"Say what, sugar?"

"That he raped me, a few times? Why am I scared to admit my baby girl, Gracie, was conceived during one of those rapes, which was a good thing, a great thing because I can't imagine my life without her?" My tears came, and my voice stopped.

I wept into a throw pillow on the couch to muffle the sound of my sobs.

"Shhh." Brody cooed over and over. "I'm here."

"You know..." I hiccupped and sniffled through my words. "Alan told me he never wanted Gracie, but actually, it was because of her I finally found the courage to leave. Grace became part of all of mine and Josie's saving grace, thus her name."

"Beautiful." His voice was soft and calming. "Beautiful."

"I suppose it is." I took a Kleenex and honked out my nose.

"Geese in your house? Huh. Interesting pets, sugs."

"Jerk." I teased as any tension in me released like a slow leak in a tire. "And why the hell did I tell *you* all of this?"

"I am glad you did, sugar."

"Yeah, well, *don't*, I repeat *do not* feel sorry for me."

We fell silent. I wanted to hear a response, but I also dreaded one. What I got next solidified our friendship.

"You know, the only thing I feel is irritated and the need to go kick his ass." His words were angry and cold, neither of which matched Brody. "But I think there's already been too much violence in your life.

What I'd like to do instead is hold you, and tell you, as long as I am part of your life, he will never do this to you again."

"Thank you." My voice quivered.

"And you do know I mean friendship, right? I don't want you to get the wrong idea."

"Thanks for clarifying." I snickered. "And my brother, Hayden, already kicked his ass, which landed him jail time."

"Good. Not about the jail time but about the kicking ass part. I think I'd like your brother."

"Actually, I think you would, too."

"And sugs? I don't feel sorry for you, not in the least. Sure, you endured more than most women have or should have to and that sucks."

"But you don't feel sorry for me." My sarcasm pushed out of me.

"No, and you know why? You survived it, sugar. You lived it, you endured it, and you moved on." Brody swallowed, as if he had to get a hold of himself and his emotions. "Your girls? They're great, at least from what I've seen. Yes, Josie is acting up and, sure, part of the reason is being a teen. But she's funny, and I see how she takes care of her little sister with passion. And Gracie? Can she be any sweeter or loving? They were raised by you."

"Don't, okay? Don't patronize me. I know what I did."

"Do you? Doesn't seem like it to me. I mean, I get why you—" His voice trailed.

"Oh puh-leeze, do not stop now." I battled to hide my irritation, but I lost. "Why what?"

"I get why you don't talk about your past. It

sucked. It was painful. You don't want to be pitied. But maybe you don't fully realize what you should be proud of."

"Be proud of?" This time I did shout. "Be proud of? I went through hell and brought Josie there with me. What's there to be proud of?"

"You came out on the other side. Yeah, scarred and burned, but you got out and took Josie with you. And you know you won't go back. You are one bad-ass woman and mother."

"Don't, Brody. I'm good. We're good. I don't need placating."

"Is that what you think I'm doing?"

"Yes," I snapped with impatience. "So just don't."

"I'm not. And the bad-ass woman you're showing me right now is the woman I can't go a day without thinking about. Not one goddamn day. Hell, not one goddamn hour in a day."

"Um." I was stunned. "Okay. Wow. Thank you."

"You're welcome."

"And thanks for not asking why I stayed with Alan."

"I'm sure it is a complicated answer."

"Sure. We'll go with complicated." I sighed. "Bottom line was I held on too long because I thought our relationship was best for Josie until I knew it wasn't. Stupid, I know."

"Stupid? No. One of life's hard lessons."

"I suppose."

This conversation with Brody, a man I barely knew, got deep, too deep. And I didn't like it deep.

"You think of me all the time, huh?" I needed light. "How many rolls of toilet paper do you think your boots can hold?"

"Double or single?"

"Are you surrendering, Mr. Reed?"

"Not at all. A friend can tell another friend he thinks of her all the time, and she's bad-ass. And many friends ask questions about toilet paper."

"True." I giggled out the rest of my words, barely able to get them out. "I ask Marti all the time how many rolls of toilet paper she can fit into her winter boots."

"See, a general question." Brody chuckled with me. "I don't know, Harper. I think you want me to concede."

"You do, huh?"

"Yup. You keep taking everything I say and bringing it to the non-friend area. I also don't think your attacks on me are in the friend zone."

"Stop," I insisted. "You know I feel guilty about throwing myself at you."

"All I'm saying, Harper McReynolds, is I do believe you will regret this bet."

"I do believe you are wrong." I laughed. After all this intense shit, I needed to laugh, and I snorted as I did.

"Man, you have a great laugh."

"Snorts don't bother you?"

"No. They're fun. Laughs are supposed to be fun. Why would you—" He skipped a beat. "Ah. Alan didn't like them."

"Let's not talk about him anymore, but yes." Silence entered our conversation. I needed to shut the door on it. Alan couldn't ruin our conversation, so I asked, "How's Z's laugh?"

"Z? Well—" Brody paused. "See, here's the thing.

I broke up with Z."

"You thought it over, huh?"

"I have, for the past few days now."

"And talked it over with her?" I asked.

"For hours on end."

"And you're okay with your decision?"

"Actually, I am great with it. We've tried to make this work for far too long. I think for old time's sake. Neither of us felt anything anymore. She knew it. I knew it."

"You sure you're okay?"

"Yup, I'm good. We were headed this way for a while now, probably the last six months. We both figured out we're good friends, horrible anything else. You know, we started out as friends. Probably should have stayed friends. Oh, right. You don't believe I can have women friends." Brody reminded me.

"Well—"

"Do you believe women and men can be friends at all?"

"No. I mean if one or both are married or gay, maybe. But no, I don't."

"Wait? So, we're not friends?" He got me. He was a great friend to me.

"Maybe my mind is changing."

"Maybe," he sing-songed.

"I should go. I have to work in the morning, and I need to find a frame before I head to bed."

"A frame? As in a picture frame? I thought most people counted sheep before bed. Never heard of counting picture frames before."

"Smart ass. Gracie drew me a picture of tulips in purple and pink. She knows they are my favorite flowers and purple and pink are my favorite colors." I glanced down at the picture on my coffee table and tenderness engulfed me. I loved Gracie so much, it pained me. "I promised her I'd frame the picture and hang it in my bedroom. It'll be the first thing I see in the morning and help start my day. I also like baby's breath, but those were too hard for her to draw."

"Limited artist. I get it." Brody chuckled. "Okay. Well, have sweetness in your dreams, sugs."

"Aw." His sentiment hit me in my gut. "Thank you. You, too."

"I should be back soon." He hesitated. "I miss you."

"Thanks." He stunned me twice. "Bye, Brodes."

"Bye."

****

My alarm clock blared music at five thirty in the morning. On my third attempt, I hit the off bar before dragging myself out of bed after only four hours of sleep. Note to self, a long conversation with Brody in the late evening was not a good thing the following day. I put on my workout clothes, cranked up my songs, and danced in the front room for the next half hour.

On the way to their schools, my heart ached as I listened to Josie tell me how much she will hate the day. After I dropped the girls off, I arrived at work. Declan and Marti laughed in his office doorway when I walked by.

"Hey, Harper," Declan called out.

"Hi." I plopped down at my desk.

"You okay?" Declan stood in front of me, Marti at his side. He gave me the look he gave the troubled students he counseled.

"Yeah. No." I drew a sharp breath in.

"Wanna talk about it?" Marti asked while she flashed puppy dog eyes at me.

"Did Brody tell you?" I asked.

"You told Brody about Josie?" Marti cocked her head and, once more, reminded me of a puppy.

"So, you know," I bellowed. "Marts, who told you?"

"No one." Marti leaned on the wall of my cubicle and tried to look casual. "Okay, Hannah came over last night."

"Hanny? She came over?"

"Remember you suggested her for Career Day, a day someone wrangled me to organize?"

"You're welcome." Declan grinned.

"Anyway, I asked her to dinner to talk about it. I really like her." I knew Marti and Hannah would hit it off. Marti tended to befriend odd birds, case in point Esther. "She stayed for hours, and eventually, she told me about Josie. It came up."

"What did you hear?"

"Everything." Marti came over to me and grabbed my hand. "She was concerned for you is all. We all are. And you know we love you and Josie. Don't be mad at Hannah."

"I'm not. I would have told you eventually."

"And, no worries, I didn't say anything to Esther," Marti said. "I thought you would want to tell her."

"Thanks. For your support and keeping it from Esther. I'll tell her. Just not yet." I squeezed Marti's hands and stood up to hang up my coat.

"Anything we can do?" Declan asked. His concern warmed me. "I'm here if you wanna talk about it."

"No, just be my friends."

"You got it." Marti was a good four inches taller than me even when I wore heels, so when she pulled me into a hug, my eyes were level with her breasts. "We love you."

"I love you both." I maneuvered out of her grasp and went back to my desk.

"Hey. You're still coming to the girls' night in, right?" Marti placed her arms on the top of my cubicle wall and looked over it at me.

"I'm not sure. I don't know if I want to do anything or leave Josie alone now." I flipped through the mail.

"Who are you punishing?" Declan asked. "You or Josie?"

"Don't get all social worker on me, Mr. Reed," I warned.

"Well, I hope you join us." Marti tapped her fingernails on top of the divider. "It's not a big crowd, just me and Esther, Hannah, and maybe Bryn. I'm still working on her."

"Oh goody, Bryn. She loves me," I mumbled.

"What?" Marti asked.

"Nothing," I said. "What time?"

"About six thirty, seven o'clock. I'll be lucky to make it to nine, but I'll try."

"You are sleeping for two." Declan kissed her on her temple, and Marti fell into him.

"I know." Marti sighed. "Come on. You'll get to see the Reed boys in skirts."

"They're called kilts, and I'm not sure yet if we're wearing them," Declan said. "It was Cal's idea."

"It was a good one too. Rejoice in part of your heritage." Marti gave a nod for emphasis.

"Yay." Declan faked enthusiasm.

"Well, I can't miss seeing those legs," I said. "I will see what I can do."

"Great." Marti pumped a fist up in the air. "Oh, and did you know Brody has officially broken up with Z? From what Bryn told Declan, and I overheard—"

"Of course," Declan deadpanned.

Marti slid a look at Declan. "What I overheard is Brody tried to make it work, but neither of them had anything left for each other."

"Yeah," I said. "That's too bad."

"Too bad? Really?" Marti smirked.

"Yes, really," I said, trying to hold onto patience. "Look, we're friends. In fact, I wanted to fix him up with my sister, Hannah."

"And?"

"And he wasn't interested. But it doesn't mean I'll stop. They look good together."

"You two do too," Marti insisted.

"Marti, don't. Just, don't," I pleaded.

"Well, you do." She kissed Declan on the cheek. "I should get to my classroom. Love you."

"Love you too, babe," Declan called out after her. He fiddled with the plastic top on my divider.

"Yes, Declan?" I raised an eyebrow.

"You and Brody? Still in the heat of this bet, huh?"

"Yes, we are."

Declan smiled at me. The Reed family gift to womankind, also known as dimples, dug deep into his cheeks. "One day, Harper, you will understand, neither one of you will win this bet."

I was about to say more, when a young man, not much older than twenty, came down the hallway. A floral arrangement in brown paper blocked his face.

"I'm looking for Harper McReynolds," he bellowed.

"I'm Harper." I raised my hand as if in school.

"These are for you." He handed me the package, and I signed the clipboard.

"Later," he said as he whistled down the hallway.

"Later?" I asked Declan.

"Yeah, you know. Later." He laughed.

I took the card stapled to the paper and read it, to myself.

*Sugs—Sorry your days have been sucky. This will not be as good as your saving Grace's drawing, but I'm hoping it'll be something to look at while you work. And since you're set on a boot holding toilet paper, maybe give this a shot. See you soon. Your amigo, Brody.*

"Well, I should go." Declan glanced at the bundle still unopened on my desk.

"Okay." A smile on my face spread.

"I'm glad he makes you happy. Randall's a nice guy." Declan grinned before he walked away and headed to his office.

"Sure, but so is your brother," I muttered as I ripped down the brown paper. One dozen pink and purple tulips and baby's breath sprang from their confinement. They were nestled in a gray cowboy boot vase. I laughed and laughed until I cried.

Chapter Fifteen
Chili and Comfy Clothes

By six o'clock on Friday, after a long week at work, complete with two hours of overtime when the school's computers shut down, I was ready for my makeup to come off and put my pajamas on. A night with chili, Hannah, Hayden, Nonnie, and the girls didn't only beckon me, it screamed to me in shouts of comfort and family.

Josie's morning therapy session drained us. Sabrina slowly pulled out the memories and the nightmares she lived through. I blamed some of the nightmares on Alan and acknowledged my role as I could have woken her up from them sooner. Instead, I stayed.

I sat outside in the reception area. Josie came out of Sabrina's office with puffy eyes. She flew into my arms and asked me to hold her. She felt seven years old again, and she told me she loved me.

During our drive to Josie's school, the mood lifted. We laughed at corny jokes and sang along with every song on the radio. We bellowed at the top of our lungs, and never once did Josie critique my voice.

Over the first week of school, brief texts flew back and forth between Brody and me. We texted about the flowers—I expressed my gratitude for them, and he asked me to send him a picture. When I did, he admitted he "done good." We texted about the bet. I teased the flowers were one step closer to his loss of the bet. He joked flowers were a sign of friendship, according to the book on friendship he never read. We texted about the girls, my work load, and his production of a new album. The last text Brody sent warned me he may not text or talk because of his work schedule and nothing else. Disappointment punched me in the gut like a professional boxer, and the surprise of my reaction hit me harder.

Randall called me every day since the night Josie came home with the police. At the start of each of our conversation, Randall asked about me, then about Josie. Each time, his interest touched me. He made offers to take us all out for dinner, or a movie, or bowling, to get our minds off things. I rejected his offers and explained I needed to be with my girls. He understood my reason and supported it.

During my last conversation with Randall, he battled with impatience when I told him I wanted to stay in, with my family, on a Friday night. Randall huffed through my cell phone when I explained the exhaustion of the week caught up with me. I extended him an invitation to join us to eat a meal, play some cards, or watch a movie. Randall declined my offer and said he needed to tell me something, alone, not with an "audience." I held my ground, and he held onto his exasperation but eventually Randall relented.

When I pulled my car into my driveway the Friday night after the first full week of school, Hayden's 1980 Ford pickup was parked in the drive, and I grinned. I walked up the stairs in complete peace and thought about which one of my three sets of pajamas I wanted to collapse in. A smile spread across my face like water on a desert when I heard Gracie's giggles, Josie's laughs, and Hayden's booming voice.

"Hello, family," I bellowed as I entered. "Let's get our chili on."

"Hello, Momma." Gracie beamed up at me as she sat on Hayden's lap. She had the same blonde curls as her uncle, unruly and plentiful. Hayden's eyes were green like Hannah's, his nose was broad like a boxer's and his face had a deep scar running down his cheek. Gracie pulled on the patch of hair growing on his chin, and with each pull he kissed her neck, sending her into fits of laughter.

"Hello, Gracie Girl." I slipped off my shoes and put my purse and keys on the counter.

"Hey, Harpsichord." My brother's easy smirk lit up his face.

"Haymaker, how are you? Haven't seen you around in a while. I thought you left the country." I ruffled my brother's hair.

"Thought about Russia, but nah. Like your chili better. Russia puts too much vodka in it."

"Hey, Mother." Josie brushed my cheek with a kiss as she walked by me.

"Hello, Josephine." I took off my blazer and draped it over my arm. Hannah stood by the stove and stirred the pot of chili. She smiled a secretive smile at me. "What's going on with you?"

"Nothing." She looked at Josie and then back in the pot.

"Nonnie's not here yet?" I ran my hands down the skirt I wore—a brown tulip skirt I matched with a bright yellow, button-down blouse, and a peplum blazer.

"No, she's downstairs w—" Josie began.

"She'll be up shortly." Hannah jumped in and smiled again as if she was the cat that ate the canary.

"Oookay," I said. "I'm gonna change, and then we can talk about the secret you two are keeping."

"Why don't you keep on what you're wearing?" Hannah glanced at Josie, and a laugh escaped my daughter.

"Because I want to get comfortable." My eyes narrowed. I looked from Josie to Hannah back to Josie. "Seriously. What's going on with you two?"

"Oh, nothing." Hannah shrugged. "I like that outfit on you."

"Yeah," Josie threw in, "me, too. You should keep it on."

"Thank you?" Who were these aliens taking over their bodies?

"Momma," Gracie cooed as she played with Hayden's fingers. "I think you look bootiful in any clotheth."

"Thanks, Gracie Girl." I cupped her face with my hand and smooched her lips.

"Ya think so?" Hayden pulled back and looked down at Gracie. "Even when she wears those ugly brown sweatpants and gray Chicago Bulls T-shirt?"

"Yeth." Gracie nodded her head.

"Brrr." Hayden gave a fake shiver.

"Just for that"—I pushed Hayden's head—"this is precisely what I'm wearing tonight."

"No," Hannah called after me. "Don't."

"Mom, please don't," Josie pleaded.

"Nope. Too late." I walked into my bedroom.

"Ya happy?" Hannah asked.

"Very." Hayden let out a roar of laughter.

I stood in my kitchen doorway, makeup stripped from my face, and my hair piled on top of my head in a haphazard bun. My brown sweatpants were rolled at my waist and my gray, stained T-shirt, one of the most comfortable T-shirts I own, hung over my braless breasts. I twirled in the doorway with my hands out.

"And here she is." I spun. "The most beautiful sweatpants model in North America, perhaps the world. Going for the comfy look, this Friday evening, which is all the rave in Paris. This model oozes beauty and sophistication. Notice the stains on the gray T-shirt. It brings out the specs of blue in her eyes. The brown sweatpants scream too large, yet comfortable. Yes, this model from Noteah, Illinois, is taking the comfy look by storm."

I put my hands on my hips and exaggerated a model's walk into the kitchen. Gracie jumped off Hayden's lap, giggled, and joined in my stride.

"I would have to agree with you, sugar. You are the most beautiful friend I have."

He leaned against the kitchen counter with a glass of water in his hand. His wolf eyes blazed in heat. He took a sip of water and smiled over the rim at me.

"Me too, Momma." Gracie giggled as she continued to pivot. "I'm bootiful in my comfy look, too."

"You sure are, Gracie Girl." The words came out choked as I stared at Brody.

"Told ya to leave your work clothes on." Josie passed behind me on the way to her seat.

Any other words I wanted to say were imprisoned in my throat, slammed shut like a jail door. I wore the most ridiculous outfit ever while I gawked at Brody Reed, who looked beautiful in a blue striped shirt, cuffed at the wrists, and the most fabulous pair of tight-in-the-right-places faded jeans.

"See." Hayden snorted the same laugh as me. "This is funny."

"Shut the hell up," I said, which only made Hayden laugh harder.

"Mother," Josie admonished with fake indignation. "Swear jar."

"Brody came over about an hour ago." Nonnie walked past me and patted my upper arm. "I asked him to stay for dinner. He helped carry these extra chairs up."

"Because Uncle Hayden's too lazy." Josie slid down in the seat next to Hayden, the one I usually sit in.

"Hey." He tugged her ponytail. "I worked hard today. No offense, Brody."

"None taken." Brody looked down at the ground, then shot a look back up to me, in a plea for help. I came out of my muteness.

"I'm glad you did, Nonnie." I found my sea legs to walk by him. "Have a seat while I get the meal on the table."

"Need any help?" His breath hit my neck and my nipples puckered.

"Uh, no." I coughed, and Brody chuckled softly. "Go ahead and have a seat. I'll dish it up."

"There are two pots, Brody," Josie offered. "The red pot is the really hot chili; the way Uncle Hayden and I like it. The yellow one is mild."

"The way I like it, right, Momma?" Gracie asked.

"Right, Gracie." I looked at a still-standing Brody.

"Which way do you like it?"

"Hot." He lifted his eyebrows before he took a seat by Nonnie. "Always hot."

"Okay then." I did a small shake of my head.

"Don't fergit my muffinth." Gracie's eyes grew big in excitement. "They got chocolate in them. I apperimented."

"Yes, you did," I agreed.

"I'm not eating *your* muffins." Josie's face scrunched up. "I'm eating the corn muffins Mom made, not *your* corn muffins. Yuck."

"Oooooh—" Gracie fought back the tears.

"Josie, please." I sent her a pleading look. She looked down at her hands in embarrassment and, I hoped, in regret.

"I'll have one, Grace." Hannah reached over and smoothed out her hair.

"Me too." Hayden grinned at his niece.

"How about you, Mithter Brody?" Gracie's tongue darted out from her teeth.

"Chocolate corn muffins sound interesting, Grace." Brody smiled. "Sure, I'll try it."

"All right then." I put out the muffins, both mine and Gracie's, along with everyone's bowls of chili.

"The chili looks good." Nonnie sat down slowly.

"You fixed your stove, huh?" Hayden asked. "I'm impressed."

"No big deal. I replaced a part." I shrugged. "The element terminal block broke. It took a couple of tries, but I got it to work."

"Seems right." Hayden nodded. "What do you think, Brody?"

"Huh?" Brody looked at the muffins in front of him

as if he tried to understand them. "Um, I don't know much about stoves. Not very handy."

"Mom is. She fixes everything, and she teaches me." A pride rose in Josie's voice.

"And she hates to wait," Hayden threw in.

"If I waited for you, Josie would be off to her honeymoon before you came to fix it." I took a muffin, my muffin. Gracie's face crumbled, so I took her chocolate one. She nodded approval.

"I am a busy man." Hayden rubbed his hands together. "Now, let's eat."

The conversation rumbled through the room while we ate. Gracie talked in detail about her day as room helper. She handed out schoolwork papers, held the door, and was first place in line for the entire day. Josie spoke about the fight between Katie and Maggie, and how they tried to be her friend again, but Josie didn't want any part of it. Perhaps therapy gave her the strength. Nonnie talked about her pinochle tournament with her lady friends and a twenty-five-dollar win. Hayden spoke about an old Harley in his shop which intrigued Brody.

"I have a BMW," Brody offered. "It's a '96. Runs great."

"I didn't know you had a motorcycle," I said.

"Yup, part of my bad boy image." He winked, and my stomach almost flipped out onto the table.

"Ah," I acknowledged.

As conversation revolved around Halloween, Brody leaned into me and spoke quietly. "I hope you don't mind I came over."

"Not at all. I'm glad you did. And you get to see me at my finest." I let out a nervous laugh.

"Sugs, I wasn't kidding. You look beautiful. Always." His eyes dug into me. I flushed. "As a friend," he added.

"Of course." I snorted "How long were you here?"

"About an hour. I thought you came home at four."

"Normally, but the computers went catawampus on us," I explained.

"Catawampus. I wonder if I can fit that into a song. Great word." Brody broke a muffin in half. "I really only came to say hi, but when Nonnie asked me to stay—"

"It's fine." I slid my hand under the table and onto his knee. "I'm glad to see you, and besides, there is plenty."

"It's good, too." He squeezed my hand and kept it there. I wanted to pull away. I should have pulled away as any friend would, but instead, because it felt natural, I did nothing.

"You're left-handed?" I asked when looked at his free hand grab a spoon to scoop up some Chili.

"All my life. You know, if you had my stalker moves, you would have known."

"You'll have to teach me, oh, master."

"I will." He took a spoonful of chili and smiled. "Nonnie told me you can cook. She wasn't wrong."

"I've been cooking for a long time." I scooped in a spoonful of chili with corn chips, sour cream, and cheese into my mouth.

"Yeah?" Brody took a drink of his water.

"Uh-huh." I nodded and swallowed. "I began cooking when I was around eight or nine. My mother, well, she didn't cook. If we were going to eat, it was up to me."

"Seriously?"

"Seriously. My mom wasn't, still isn't, your usual mom as you may have guessed. Kathy wasn't home too often at night. She preferred to be out and about with friends, trying to find a man to make her feel young. So, I would cook. I was very creative." I shrugged. "Hey, I learned early and learned well."

"Always taking care of everyone, huh?"

"We all have our roles in life."

"But who takes care of you, Harper McReynolds?"

"I don't need to be taken care of, Brody Reed." I pulled my hand back.

"Aw, sugs, everyone does some time or another."

"Mom, guess what? Mom. Mom." Josie's voice screamed over all the conversations.

"What, Josie, what?" I met her loudness and gave Brody one last look.

"Coach Carlton put me at guard."

Josie continued to talk about her new role on the basketball team in the way only she told a story—with humor, sarcasm, and in great detail. She kept us all entertained. Hayden and Hannah laughed and egged her on for more. Nonnie clasped her hands together in pure delight. Gracie struggled to understand, but the hero-worship in her eyes stayed glued on her big sister.

I looked over at Brody a few times. Josie captured his attention. When he laughed, a bit of sour cream escaped, and again, like with the pizza sauce, I wanted to wipe it off with my tongue. Brody caught my stare once. His smile dropped from his face, and his eyes held me captive for a few long minutes.

"Oh," Josie said. "Coach found about the police picking me up for breaking curfew. She told me I'm going to have to sit out the first three games."

I knew it pained her to tell us as life lessons were painful sometimes.

"Well, you know—" I started.

"Don't." Hannah spoke up in defense of her niece. "Just don't, Harper. She gets it."

"And you," I pointed at Hannah, "don't tell me how to parent."

"No, it's okay, Aunt Hannah." Josie slumped a bit in her chair. "I get it. It was wrong, and the coach was right. I can't break the rules and not expect some type of consequence."

"Aw, sweetie." I smiled. "Very mature of you."

"Yeah, it is. Can I get my phone back now?"

"Not a chance." I popped a piece of my corn muffin into my mouth.

We sat around a cleared table to make room for a card game. It was a game of Hearts, one not familiar to Brody. We took turns explaining, and by the third hand, he caught on.

Gracie sat on Hayden's lap as his "partner." Hannah and Josie, while not officially partners, teamed up to stick it to me. Nonnie kicked everyone's asses with each hand, and Brody let out a few swear words for the rookie mistakes he made. Each time he did, he pulled money out of his wallet for the swear jar while we laughed in harmony. It was one of those nights where perfect would be a weak word to describe it.

"Is the doorbell out?" Randall's voice burst into the room followed by his laughter.

"Randall." I startled. "I didn't expect you."

"I know. But I had to come over." He bent down and kissed my lips, something he never did in front of an audience. He looked over at Brody and gave a short nod.

"My bad." Hayden grabbed in a pile of cards. "I guess another thing I forgot to fix."

"It's been out for a few days now," Nonnie admonished.

"Anyway, hi," Randall said. "I hope you don't mind."

"Not at all." I got up. "Have a seat. You hungry?"

"What are you wearing?" He sat down while his eyes inspected me from the tip of my head to my fuzzy flippered feet.

"It's my comfy look." I snorted and found a spot by the counter to lean on. "Don't you like it?"

"It's different," Randall said.

"Which means he's not a fan." Josie crinkled her nose.

"I don't know." Brody joined me against the counter. "I think comfy looks good on you."

"Thank you, Brody." A warmth filled me.

"Ah, Brody. Nice suck-up move, but you just don't get it." Josie shook her head. Brody threw back his head in laughter. "Randall does. But no, not you."

"Hey." I balled up a napkin and threw it at her. "Don't be taking Randall's side."

"I think you look bootiful." Gracie yawned and fell back on Hayden's chest.

"Don't be a brown-noser, kid." Hayden tickled Gracie which sent her into fits of giggles. "We all agreed, except Brody there, your mom looks funny."

"Don't listen to Uncle Hayden." I glared at Hayden. "Thank you, Gracie Girl. You're my favorite."

Both girls laughed.

"There's chili on the stove. I can heat up for you," I said to Randall. "Both hot and mild. Did you want some?"

"No, I already ate." Randall sat back and folded his arms across his chest as if something was on his mind.

"You okay?" I asked.

"You're looking kind of glum, chum," Brody said, and smiled when I slid him a look. "What?"

"Glum, chum?" I lifted an eyebrow.

"Glum's a word. An underused one."

"For a reason," I replied. "If that's how your lyrics went in Jamaica, you have some problems, Mr. Reed."

"Hmmm." Brody looked off into space in thought. " 'Turn your frown upside down, Mrs. Brown' probably won't be a hit either, huh?"

"Maybe in children's books." Everyone laughed at our exchange, except Randall.

"Hey, really. You okay?" I smoothed a hand over Randall's shoulder.

"I know we said we'd talk sometime tomorrow, but I was wondering, do you have a few minutes?" Randall asked.

"Um…" I looked around the room at my family and Brody. We were having such a great time, and the interruption of Randall took some of the fun out the room.

"Can we go and sit outside? For a few minutes?" Randall pleaded. "Please?"

"Go on, Harper." Nonnie stood up. "Randall really seems like he needs talk. I'll put Gracie to bed, and everyone else will clean up in here. Except for Brody. He's our guest."

"And a guest who will be leaving." Brody pushed

himself off the counter.

"You don't have to." And I meant it. I wanted him to stay. I wanted him to stay more than I wanted to talk with Randall, which made me an awful girlfriend, I know. But I liked Brody's ease and comfortable fit with my family. I didn't want it to end.

"No, I do." Brody's stormy gray eyes filled with disappointment. The room which was once filled with laughter and easiness grew serious. I didn't like serious. I had too much serious. A strangled smile thinned his lips. "Bye, everyone. I had a great time."

"You like to lose?" Josie teased.

"I know the game now, so expect an arse-kicking next time." Brody winked. Pink crept up on Josie's cheeks.

"What does arthe mean?" Gracie's yawns intensified with each tick of the clock.

"It's a word my father always says because he's from Ireland and it means—" Brody hedged.

"It means butt, Gracie." Randall smiled at me warmly. I rubbed his shoulder.

"A thwear." She pointed to the swear jar.

"He's good, Grace," I said. "We took enough money from him tonight to furnish your college education."

"What can I say? I swear when I'm frustrated." Brody grinned.

"I'll walk him out," I announced to the kitchen.

"Why? He knows the way out." Randall whistled a nervous laugh through his nose.

"I know, but—"

"It's okay," Brody replied. "I'll show myself out."

Then Brody did something so bold, I reeled. He

kissed me. In front of my boyfriend, on the lips, he kissed me. I suppose it was more of a peck really. It was very slight, and Randall didn't react, but it sent a wave of tingles down me and goosebumps exploded on my arm. Brody soft, yet cocky, chuckle gave me away.

"Bye, sug—Harper."

"Bye." I coughed to hide my reaction. "Bye, Brody."

**\*\*\*\***

Randall and I sat on the swing in the backyard. The night's breeze cooled off the Indian summer's heat from the day. Stars blinked in the sky's dark blue canvas. Lighting bugs put on their show for us. I cuddled into Randall and curled my feet up. He draped a hand over me. The scent his woodsy cologne lingered on him from his morning spray.

"Beautiful night, isn't it?" I asked.

"Yes," he answered sharply.

"Hey, what's going on?" I looked into his light brown eye darkening under his glasses. I followed his stare to the Rose of Sharon bush. Its buds were closed and nearly brown, readying itself for the autumn months.

"Why was Brody here?" he asked, his eyes did not move. "I mean, didn't you say it was just going to be family?"

"Hey, I invited you."

"You did. Did you invite Brody too?" Randall cracked with reserve anger.

"No. Brody just showed up." I nestled closer to him to calm him.

Randall and I never fought. He hadn't even so much as snipped at me. It's what I liked about him, about us. After Alan's temper, which flared then exploded like faulty fireworks, I wanted calm. I needed it. After three months together, arguments were going to happen. And if this was how an argument went with Randall, I was okay with it.

"Randall." I wrapped my arm around his midsection. "I couldn't have kicked Brody out. I'd be a bitch if I did."

"Rude of *him* then to just show up."

"No." I defended Brody. "Not really. He didn't know about Friday game night with my family. When he came over, Nonnie invited him to stay. You know Nonnie, she would invite a Jehovah's witness to dinner if he rang our doorbell."

I saw a small smile start to crawl on Randall's face. "I suppose you're right."

I kissed his cheek. "Did you get a little jealous again?"

"Damn it, I did. Why is that? I am not a jealous man, yet with Brody—"

"He's a friend, Randall. Nothing else."

"Are you sure? Because he is a good-looking guy, and you laugh a lot around him."

"Sure, he makes me laugh, just like Marti and Esther." I placed my hand on his cheek.

"You don't laugh that much around me."

"Yeah, I do." I didn't. I moved on. "Now tell me, what is so important, and why can't it wait until tomorrow morning?"

"This is not how I wanted to start all of this." Randall smacked a wet, hard kiss on my lips before he stood up and paced the grassy area around us. He stopped and swallowed hard. "Harpie, I am totally *in* love with you. I love you, Harper McReynolds. I love you."

His word struck me mute. I didn't know what to say, but Randall looked like he needed a response. I gave him one of the lamest ones in romance history.

"That's nice," I said, casually.

What the hell? He told me he loved me, and I came back with *that's nice?*

"Really?" Randall looked confused, hurt, even angry.

He shook his head and walked over by my tomato plants giving off one last bunch of fruit. He stuffed his hand in his pocket and looked up to the sky.

"I know. Stupid response." I went to him. "This is just all surprising, Randall. We've only been dating a little over three months. Too soon for an *I love you*, don't you think?"

"Obviously not since I said it."

"Shit, Randall, I didn't mean—"

"You know, since my wife died, I've only dated a few women, and I never felt this way about any of them." He kept his back to me. "There's something special about you, Harper. You're smart and funny. You're beautiful, and you're kind. I'm not saying this to have sex with you. You can decide when you want to have sex. I'm saying this because, well, I really do love you."

"Oh, Randall." I sighed and rubbed his back.

"I know. I'm not good with words."

"No, your words were touching." I paused. I wanted to choose my next words carefully. "And I'm honored, really. But—"

"Momma." Gracie's voice came out of the kitchen

211

window above us. "My belly hurtths. I think I eatths too many muffinths. Can you come up and rub it for me?"

"Go and lie down, Gracie. I'll be right up."

" 'Kay."

"I really should—" I pointed to the house.

"Sure." He looked at me and forced a smile. "Poor thing, huh?"

"Too many chocolate corn muffins will do that to you." I took his hands into mine. "Randall, can we talk more about this later?"

"Why don't we talk on Sunday night?" Randall asked. "It'll give you a day to think about all of this. I know you have to go to work on Monday, but we can make it an early dinner."

"Sunday night?" I chewed my lower lip.

"Something wrong?"

"On Sunday night, I'm getting my girls ready for the week."

"Right." He nodded.

"Can we make it Sunday late afternoon or early evening? Around four thirty or five o'clock? Josie has a basketball game and suspended or not, she'd probably like to go. Do you want to come with us?"

"Sure. I would love to be with you, but a game doesn't give us much privacy, now does it?"

"No, I suppose not. How about after the game I'll come over to your place after?"

"Are you sure? It's a lot for you, Harper."

"You're worth it." I nipped his lips.

He took me into his arms and kissed me, long and hard. I wanted to like it. It was an excellent response, but I was relieved when I had a reason to break away.

"Mom," Josie called out. "Gracie is crying."

"I should go."

"You should." He leaned down and gave me one last kiss. "Go. Gracie needs you."

I watched him leave. Randall Prescott was a kind and understanding man. He was a good man for me. He understood my priorities with my girls. He was patient with my time, and my need to be with them. And he loved me. He. Loved. Me. And yet, as I watched him drive away, I wasn't disappointed to see him go.

"Mommmm!" Josie yelled. "Gracie says she feels like throwing up, and I don't do throw-up."

"Coming."

Chapter Sixteen
Girls' Night In

"And then I said, 'that's nice.' " I cringed. I wanted to cover my face, but I had a facial mask on. Marti saw a recipe for a facial mask on a website. The main ingredients were mashed avocados and kosher salt. I didn't ask about the minor ones, but they must have been what made my face tingle. Marti assured me it meant the toxins were being sucked out of my face. I wasn't so sure.

"What?" Esther laughed. Marti joined her. "You said that? To a man who just professed his love for you?"

It was girls' night in. Marti, Esther, Hannah, and I were in our pajamas and Bryn came in a T-shirt and jeans. She told us she slept in the nude, and no one had reason to doubt her.

I held my first glass of wine in my hand. Hannah already downed two, and Esther had emptied three-thirds of a Chardonnay bottle. Bryn sipped from a glass of brown liquid which I assumed was whiskey. Marti drank water from a bottle.

We had a smorgasbord of food in front of us. Marti made guacamole, but I didn't try it. It looked too much like what was on my face. Esther brought onion dip, jarred salsa, and chips. Hannah arranged a variety of cheeses and crackers on a fancy plate from one of those yuppie glassware places. Bryn contributed pizza rolls out of a box from the freezer section of a grocery store, and I made chocolate chip and oatmeal raisin cookies which were nearly gone.

"Obviously you didn't want to say it back, right?" Marti dipped into the guacamole.

"No," I said, "we haven't been dating very long."

"It can happen fast." Marti crunched on her chip. "Look at Dec and me."

"True, but you two are the exception, not the rule," I argued.

"I don't know," Hannah said. "I know a lot of couples who confess love after only six weeks or less."

"The bottom line is you don't feel it." Esther pointed out the obvious. "And that's okay. It doesn't mean you're gonna break up with him."

"And if you do, that's okay too," Bryn added. "I mean, no one needs a man."

"Here we go." Marti rolled her eyes.

"Seriously. Harper, you are an independent woman. You are doing just fine," Bryn ranted. "Why does a woman need a man? Sex? You can have sex with a man without any 'I love you' attached. Companionship? I can get companionship with my friends. Kids? I guess, but as Brody and I said the other day, and no offense to anyone, but you don't need kids to complete your lives."

Her last words stung.

"Did you now?" Marti bit out.

"All I'm saying is if Harper is not on the same page, then she isn't. It is no big deal." Bryn took a sip of her whiskey. It was obvious. She enjoyed her booze and her rant.

215

"I think Harper likes Randall, just doesn't love him. It'll take time." Hannah jumped in. Her second glass of wine loosened her lips. "I think the time will eventually come. Randall is good for Harper. He is pleasant, has a great smile, and he gets along with everyone. He won't be a jerk like Alan. Randall would never hit her or her kids."

The room became still and quiet. Esther knew I left an abusive relationship. Now Marti and Bryn knew. I didn't try to hide my past; I just never talked about it.

"Your ex-husband hit you?" Marti looked at me. There it was, the sympathy in her eyes I never wanted. "Oh, Harper."

"It was a long time ago. I'm fine." I wanted to end the conversation. "We came out of it fine."

"Did he go to jail?" Bryn asked.

"Yes," I answered. "But he's out now. He hasn't bothered me."

"Only he wants to see Josie," Hannah scoffed. "It's his way of bothering you."

"Can we not talk about me?" I asked.

"Boy, have we had sucky men in our lives." Hannah obviously did not understand my request. "Kathy doesn't even know who Harper's father is."

"Who's Kathy?" Bryn asked.

"Our mom, but we can't call her Mom. It has to be Kathy, long story." Hannah puffed out a breath. "Anyway, Kathy, our mom, doesn't even know who Harper's father is. He was any of the eight guys she slept with at a Grateful Dead concert."

"Seriously?" Esther asked.

"Seriously." Hannah slurred. "Oh, it gets better. My brother's father killed *my* father in a bar fight before I was even born. Oh, Kathy sure knew how to pick 'em. We didn't have great father figures in our lives, so how the hell do we know anything about men?"

"Hey." I grabbed Hannah's hand. I knew she had pain. It always upset her she didn't have a dad or even a man she could call one. "We ended up okay."

"Did we, Harper?" Hannah looked at me through glassy eyes.

"Hanny, I love you, but you're a little drunk right now. We don't need to spill all our family's secrets." I turned to Esther. My eyes pleaded with her for help.

"Have you thought about what you're gonna say to Randall?" Esther asked.

"No, but I probably should. I'm gonna see him tomorrow afternoon," I said.

"You look sad about it." Marti dug into the salsa.

"I'm not sad. At this point, I don't love him. I like him. Love's a huge jump. I don't want to hurt him, but—"

"But nothing." Bryn twirled her the ice cubes in her drink while she spoke. "You shouldn't put his feelings before your own."

"Are you going to break up with him?" Hannah asked.

"What? No," I said. "No. I like him, a lot."

"Man entering Girls' Night In." Declan entered the room and stopped dramatically. "There are women wearing green stuff on their faces in my front room. Quick, call 911."

"Stop." Marti roared. "It's for our beauty."

"Babe, you can't get any more beautiful." He cooed. "I'm leaving now. Brody is waiting in the kitchen. Not sure when I'll be home."

My stomach flipped with excitement when I heard Brody's name—until I remembered the green gook on my face. Then, I sent out a wish to the Universe that Brody would not step into the room

"Where's your kilt?" Bryn asked.

"Brody and I decided we're not gonna wear them, but we didn't tell Cal. Shhh." Declan chuckled.

"You're so mean." Bryn laughed with him.

"Yes, you are." Marti got off the couch and went to him. Declan rested his hands on her hips and looked at her. "Have fun tonight, Dec."

"I will."

"But not too much fun." Marti played with the buttons on his shirt.

"Not too much fun, got it."

"I mean it, Dec. There will be strippers, I'm sure, and I know you will be drinking and—"

"And you are the only one I ever want." He kissed her despite the mask. "Okay? Trust me, babe."

"I do…" She hesitated. "But it's the other women I don't trust."

"All you need to do is trust me. You, and our baby inside of you, are my world." He kissed her longer and harder.

"If you two don't stop your making out, we're gonna miss seeing Ewan's last days of singlehood." Brody entered the room. Two dogs bounded ahead of him. The dogs were the opposites of one another. One of them looked more like a horse than a dog, and the other, more like a rat.

"You brought Moxy and Fifi." Marti bent down in delight. The dogs danced around her, eager to please and attempted to lick the mask off her face.

"Fifi?" The question came out of me before I realized I didn't want any of Brody's attention sent my way. So much for my hope to the Universe. Although in fairness, it wasn't the Universe's fault. I am the one who spoke up.

"Yup, Fifi," Brody said. "What? Don't like the name?"

"Doesn't fit you."

"Not supposed to fit me. It's her name." Brody scooped up the tiny dog up and nuzzled her to his broad chest. "And Fifi is a lady, aren't you?"

"You called her a bitch when you asked Declan to take care of her, and now she's a lady?" I admonished him. "Brody Reed, you are confusing the pooch."

"Ah, she has a doggie shrink. She'll be okay."

I snorted out a laugh. "Fifi's adorable."

"No," Brody whispered loudly, "she's actually ugly."

He had a point. Fifi was ugly, especially compared to Moxy. Moxy was tall, majestic, with her head hitting at Marti's rib cage. She was white with black saddles on her sides, long black ears, and beautiful sky-blue eyes. Moxy looked half Great Dane, half Weimaraner and possessed the beauty of both breeds.

Fifi, on the other hand, was tiny and unattractive. Her small body fit in most of Brody's hand. She was tan, and bald, except for a tuft of dark-brown on her head. Her bulging black eyes looked as if they would fall out of her skull in one move. She had an underbite with a pushed-in snout, which caused her to pant from her mouth.

"What breed is Fifi?" I asked.

"Not sure. I think she may be an alien."

"Well, alien or not, I'm glad she's here." Marti grabbed Fifi from Brody. "Ever since Rodger and Honey died, I miss having a pet."

Rodger was Declan's dog. Three weeks after they were married, he died when a car hit him outside their then apartment. Honey, Marti's twelve-year old cat, died a few months later. The losses broke Declan and Marti's hearts.

"Ready?" Declan ruffled Moxy's fur.

"Yup." Brody stuffed his hands in his pockets. "Have a fun night."

"You, too," I called back, unable to contain my words. "And enjoy the strippers."

"There's going to be strippers?" Brody contemplated. "Huh."

"I'm sure there will be, and I bet one of them will be named Fifi."

"Sugar, you are obsessed with my dog's name, who, incidentally, was not named after a stripper," he teased.

"Enough about your dogs." Declan shoved Brody toward the kitchen. "Cal's waiting in the car with a kilt on, and I'd rather get his ass-kicking out of the way."

"Why did we think this was funny, again?"

"Don't know."

"Probably because we're idiots." Brody groaned. "Maybe we can pick up this conversation about my dog's name another time?"

"Absolutely, my friend." I smirked.

"Good." Brody smiled, and deep dimples burrowed into his cheeks. "Oh, dig the green crap on your face, by the way."

"You do?" I touched my neck. "We were going for an amphibian look tonight. Did we achieve it?"

"Absolutely." Brody looked at his brother. "Ready?"

"Been." Declan gave Marti one last kiss. When he kissed her pregnant belly, he chuckled. "She moved."

"Of course, she did. She loves her daddy already." Marti wiped away the green on his cheeks. "I love him too."

"Bye, ladies," Brody said. "Oh, and you too, Bryn."

"Go to hell, bro," Bryn called after them, in a droll, bored voice. "And tell Ewan I said hey."

All of us, except Bryn, watched her brothers leave. Even Esther stole a glance. Nice asses are hard to look away from.

I pointed to Marti. "You have to quit being so insecure. Declan is crazy about you."

"I keep telling her," Bryn said.

"Yeah, yeah, yeah." Marti picked up a chip and threw it at me.

"You do know you two ruin it for all the rest of us, right?" I asked. "Seriously, what you and Declan have is what everyone wants, but no one really gets."

"I am lucky," Marti agreed.

"As is Declan." Esther rubbed her arm.

"Exactly," I said. "You and Declan have this crazy, I-can't-be-without-you kind of love. When one of you is in a room and the other walks in, the whole room sees how glued you are to each other. And then, just now, when he kissed you. It wasn't a lazy kiss. It was an I-miss-you-already kiss."

"They haven't been married very long, Harp,"

Hannah said. "I'd hope they still have passion."

"No, no." I turned to Bryn. "Your parents have this too, right? Marti told me the other day how they can't keep their hands off each other. She's not wrong, is she?"

"No." Bryn shrugged. "I always thought it was normal until I saw other kids' parents. The Reeds are pretty passionate."

"Precisely." I jumped up to grab a fresh napkin. It was time to take the green crap off my face. "Reed men are special."

"Yeah?" Marti laughed. "So, does that mean you want Cal? Or Brody?"

"What? Noooo." A rush of warmth blushed my cheeks.

"Well, they're both Reeds and—"

"Shut up." I begin to smear the mask into a napkin. "I used Declan and Mr. Reed as examples. I didn't say I wanted a Reed."

"Maybe you'll get the same passion from Randall, you know?" Hannah looked at me, hopefully. "Declan is crazy about Marti, but it took time, right?"

"No." Esther shook her head. "It was pretty instantaneous."

"Okay, but they are the exception," Hannah said. "Give it some time."

"You like him, Hannah. Why?" Bryn looked into the last of her liquid, swirled it, and then drank it in one gulp.

"I don't know." Hannah shrugged. "I've gotten attached to him. And he's good for Harper."

"But—" Esther pointed her glass at Hannah. "It's not about you. It's about Harper."

"I know," Hannah snapped and then took a calming breath. Wine sometimes caused nastiness to seep out of her. "I think Harper and Randall are a good, strong couple. I am excited he told her he loved her. Harp needs time. She is not used to a man loving her."

"Hanny." I hugged her. "I love you, and you're right. I need just to give it more time. Now no more talk about me. Let's get the music cranked."

\*\*\*\*

"I thought you might need this."

Brody came up from behind and wrapped a blanket around my shoulders. He sat down next to me. The roughness of his jeans through the thinness of my pajamas caused me to clench and shiver.

I sat on the back steps of Marti's house and stared into the darkness. It was two o'clock in the morning. My mind would not let me capture any z's.

"Thanks." I pulled the blanket closed. Fifi danced up to me, jumped in my lap, and curled up, while Moxy lumbered out into the yard. "Fifi, you're a beautiful dog."

"I hear the sarcasm in your voice. If I hear it, poor Fifi hears it. You'll make her insecure you know."

"Sorry, Fifi. You are beautiful, on the inside."

"Better. I think." Brody frowned. "But now Moxy is jealous."

"She doesn't look jealous." We watched Moxy prance around.

"She hides it well," Brody said. "Why aren't you asleep, sugs?"

"Too much on my mind." I looked over at him and smiled. "You just get in?"

"Yup." He reached over to stroke Fifi with his long

fingers. I held back a groan.

"No bruises. I guess Cal didn't kick your ass."

He laughed. "Nah, actually, Declan and I were the only ones who didn't have on kilts."

"That'll learn ya," I said. "Declan and Cal home, too?"

"I put Declan to bed, and Cal curled up on the floor next to Bryn in the nursery. Where are the rest of the ladies?"

"Esther's on the couch and Hannah's in the guest bed, probably took up all of it by now. How was the party?"

"Hmmm, let's see. We played poker, ate, drank, and farted. Good times."

"Sounds like." I grinned. "You put Declan to bed. Was he drunk?"

"Declan doesn't drink too often. It takes only two to three beers before he's drunk. He had four tonight, which made him pretty shit-faced."

"How is Cal?"

"He's okay. Not sober enough to drive, but okay. I drove."

"Was it hard for you?"

"Nah, I've been driving for over ten years now."

"No." I playfully slapped his arm. "To have everyone drinking around you."

"Oh." He chuckled. "Sometimes. My da was there, and it helps when he's around."

"Your dad's not a drinker?"

"Not since I've known him." Brody hesitated, then exhaled. "See, my da promised my ma, right before she became pregnant with Bryn and me, if she stopped, he wouldn't drink again. She stopped, with slip-ups here and there, and my da never took another sip."

"Really?"

"Really." His laugh was bitter. "The story goes when Declan and Cal were young, she was not in control of her alcoholism. My da thought about leaving her. Bryn and I were make-up babies."

"Sounds rough."

"Cal had it the roughest. He saw a lot more than any of us. Cal took care of her if my da got pissed and left. Hell, Cal took care of all of us when my da worked, and my ma, well, she was not able to take care of us. You know how it goes. Different illness, but same results—the oldest takes on the caregiver role."

"I suppose we do," I agreed.

"Cal's one of the best." His voice hitched. "He's seen a lot, been through a lot, and yet, his heart remains huge. I love him, ya know?"

"I can see why." I wanted to hug him. "Is your mother sober now?"

"No, not really. She has slip-ups—Christmases, birthdays, weddings, and sometimes for no reason. It pisses Bryn off, but they never had a great relationship. Declan and I avoid her when she's on one of her binges. But Da and Cal? Well, they always take care of her." I rubbed Brody's back, moved he shared an intimate part of himself. Brody looked at me and grinned. "Oh, speaking of Cal, I'm going to sing at his bar for the last time, two weeks from tonight."

"You are?"

"Yup." He leaned back and placed his elbows on the step behind him. "I thought about what you said, about performing at a bar, and I made the decision. In two weeks, it'll be the last time. You will come and see me, right?"

"Sure. Absolutely."

"Good." Brody looked off into the yard, and I knew another subject was done.

"Were there any strippers tonight?"

Brody slanted a look at me and picked up an eyebrow. "Can I fantasize about why you want to know? I mean, wow. What a vision of you and a stripper and—"

"Okay, don't tell me." I held up a hand and laughed.

"I can't." He nudged me with his shoulder. "It's in the bachelor party's code."

"There's a code?"

"You haven't heard about it? Well, there is, and if I break it, I will explode into tiny, traitor bits all over this yard."

"You will, huh?"

"Absolutely." Brody smiled. "Every guy knows this."

"Did you have fun?"

"I liked the poker and the farting parts." When I snorted, Brody chuckled. "How about you? Did you have fun tonight?"

"Sure. It was good to let loose. We danced, sang, gossiped, and watched a movie. Well, Bryn and I watched it. I think the wine made Hannah and Ester tired. They fell asleep in the middle of the movie. Marti fell asleep during the opening credits."

"You and Bryn, huh? Left all alone?"

"It was nice actually. Once we started talking, we missed most of the movie ourselves. We had a great conversation."

"About?"

"About everything and nothing." I squeezed his knee. "Mostly, about you."

"Me?"

"Sure, you're a common ground." I hesitated. "So, Mr. Bugsly, huh?"

He whipped his head to me. "Nooo. She told you?"

"Yes." I snorted. "You slept with a stuffed spider? A bug? She said it was hideous."

"He was not," Brody protested. "Mr. Bugsly had beauty on the inside."

"Like Fifi?" I asked.

"Hey!" Brody poked my ribs, and I giggled.

"No, I thought it was cute. Bryn did too." I wrapped my arm into his and rested my head on his shoulder. "I couldn't get much out of Bryn about herself. She's a bit guarded, huh?"

"Guarded is a good word to describe her."

"Not a bad thing, and I actually like her."

"I'm glad." Brody rested his head on mine. "She means a lot to me."

"You two are a lot alike."

"We are?" He pulled back in surprise.

"Sure. You're not as guarded as Bryn. You're more open than her. But she has a similar sense of humor, and you do have the same, I don't know, not shyness, but quietness to you. She's probably more outgoing, but still similar. She only talks when she's comfortable. I'm sure many people mistake it as rude. I thought it when I first met her, and I thought you were arrogant, but actually, you're both quiet."

"Maybe." Brody shrugged. "What's going on with you? Why is your mind full tonight?"

"I don't know. Lots of stuff."

"How's Josie?"

"She's okay. The grounding is going better than I thought."

"She's a good kid. She probably gets it."

"I hope so."

Some silence grew between us. It was comfortable for a while, until I spoke again. I hated to break it. Yet, I wanted to tell him since he sat down. "Randall told me he loved me yesterday. All I said back was *that's nice*."

He brought his arm back to throw the stick and stopped mid throw. "Do you love him?"

"No. I like him, but not love. At least not yet." I watched Moxy's eager face for Brody to throw the stick. "It'll be awkward between us now."

"Okay, confession time." He released the stick. "I heard your conversation in the front room tonight. I didn't mean to, but while I sat in the kitchen and waited for Dec. well, I did."

I looked at him. "How much did you hear?"

"All of it."

"Including Hannah's history lesson of our lack of male figures?"

"Yup."

"Don't feel sorry for me, okay?"

"Only because you had to go through it." I opened my mouth to say something, but Brody jumped in. "What'cha gonna do? About Randall?"

"I don't know. I feel bad for him, ya know?"

"Yup." Brody picked up the stick Moxy deposited at his feet. "He's probably embarrassed."

It was the word I grasped for all night. He would be embarrassed, and I was going to be embarrassed for him. Brody finally gave up on the stick. Moxy, knowing the game was over, lay down and panted by my feet.

"It'll be okay." Brody draped an arm around me and pulled me in.

"I hope so," I said. "Brody?"

"Hmm?"

"I could really use a friend right now, nothing else. You know?" I leaned into his chest.

"Harper?"

"Yeah."

"I'm not going anywhere." Brody drew me in and kissed the top of my head.

"Brody?"

"Hmmm?"

"This is the first time we're alone anywhere, and I didn't attack you." I snorted. "I think our tradition is ending."

"Damn."

## Chapter Seventeen
## And Here We Are Again

Randall met us at Josie's game the following Sunday. Josie sat on the end of the bench and cheered on her teammates. Gracie talked Randall's ear off and ate all his popcorn. Randall smiled every time she took a handful. It was awkward at first, but then we all settled into a nice rhythm, like we were meant to be together, maybe even as a family.

Randall walked us to the car afterward. Josie, still excited, talked about the game and threw in a lot of "did you see" or "wasn't it great when." Gracie skipped alongside her sister and nodded with each question. Randall held my hand while we walked. It was nice, familiar and comfortable.

"So," Randall began as we stopped by the car. The girls already climbed in as I leaned against the door of it. "I think we need to talk. Alone. Can you come over tonight? Just for dinner?"

"To your house?"

"Yes," Randall replied. If it were Brody, I am sure there would have been a smarter quip. I pinched the top of my hand. I had to stop the comparison.

"That'd be nice. Let me ask Hannah if she could watch the girls. If not her, I'll ask Nonnie." I smiled. "I'll figure it out. Yes."

\*\*\*\*

I pulled into the driveway of Randall's two-story, colonial house with cedar siding and dark red window shutters. It was my first time at his house. I never questioned why, but when I pulled into his cookie-cutter house, like all the other large colonials in Noteah, I thought it odd. What puzzled me as much, if not more, was why a single man would need such a large home with a three-car garage. Prestige? A homage to his late wife? Maybe both?

Once inside, I was amazed at its pristine interior. There was not a dust bunny or smudge in sight. Not a single sock, hooded sweatshirt, or pair of kicked-off shoes laid in the foyer. There wasn't even a dirty dish near the kitchen sink. It was immaculate. I'm sure Randall paid a cleaning service top dollar.

A massive brown leather couch with a matching loveseat took up half his living room. A tan and brown checked ottoman hugged the center of the sofa. A sixty-four-inch television hung from brackets on the wall adjacent to the sofa. A stark, white brick fireplace, without any knickknacks on its mantel, took up another wall. The kitchen melded into living room. A large cherrywood table with six chairs sat in the dining area. An ornate chandelier hung above it.

I picked up a framed photo off a small side table behind the sofa. It was a picture of a younger Randall in a black tuxedo, standing behind a woman in a white lace wedding dress. His arms wrapped around her from behind. Pure joy reflected in both of their eyes, the kind only newlyweds held, newlyweds deeply in love. The woman in the picture was not beautiful, rather handsome. Her blonde hair was pulled back in a bun and showed off a strong jaw, a tall forehead, and long nose. Her smiled warmed her features, and the way she looked at Randall, colored her face in attractiveness.

"That's Jean and me on our wedding day," Randall said.

"She's pretty."

"She was beautiful. I always told her, I was lucky she chose me."

A shiver crawled up my spine. It was the exact same thing he told me a few weeks earlier. I put the picture down.

"How come you never talk about her?" I walked over to the island separating the two rooms and leaned on it. I watched Randall move around the kitchen, taking down plates and glasses.

"I told you some things."

"Not very much."

"Well, I suppose it wouldn't be appropriate for me to say much more, would it?" Randall divided our Chinese takeout onto the plates made of fine porcelain. "You don't say much about your ex either."

"Ah, but my ex is a jerk. From the look on both of your faces in the picture, you loved each other very much. She was an important part of your life."

"I ordered dinner, Chinese food." He hopped over the subject of his ex. After he placed two glasses of iced water onto coasters next to linen placemats, Randall stood back to take in the table. He moved my water a little over to the right and then back again.

"Randall, seriously, we can talk about Jean."

"What do you want to know?" Randall asked. His impatience showed in his tone.

I carried our plates to the table and sat down on the chair Randall pulled out for me. Forks were already on my placemat because Randall knew I never mastered chopsticks. He sat down next to me.

"You told me you two knew each other a long time, I mean, before she died." I wanted to slap my forehead. He knew I didn't mean including while she lay dead. I smiled inwardly and thought how Brody would have laughed.

"Yes." He played with his food.

"Did you buy this house together?"

"We did. I don't know why we bought such a big house. We never had kids. She was allergic to dogs and cats too. But she wanted it, and I never could say no to her."

"Did you want kids?" I asked.

"No," Randall admitted. "Neither of us did. Jean came from a big family and loved her nieces and nephews. I loved Jean. Kids weren't in our plans. We never talked about them. They would have gotten in the way, I suppose."

"Oh." I picked up my glass and took a long gulp. Did Randall think my kids got in the way? But he was good with Josie and Gracie. He was never ill-tempered with either of them. I always assumed it was because he understood kids; he liked kids; he wanted kids.

"It was probably a good thing. I can't imagine the pain children would have while their mother deteriorated from brain cancer." Randall shoveled some food into his mouth, and then pushed the plate away. "This isn't very good? Is it me?"

"I don't like Chinese food." I cringed.

"You don't? You should have said something."

"I thought I told you before."

"I'm sorry. I must have forgotten." His eyebrows

touched. "Can I heat you up a pizza? Make you a sandwich?"

"No, I'm good." I poked at the food on my plate.

"You okay, Harpie?" Randall sat back in his chair and examined me. "Is it the talk about Jean? I knew it would upset you."

"No, it doesn't." I needed to find my voice. It's something I struggled with since Alan smacked it out of me. But Randall wasn't Alan. I needed to speak up. "But what you just said about kids. Do you think children are, I don't know, bothersome?"

"What? No. Sweetheart, I didn't mean your kids. I meant Jean and I were busy in our careers. Children weren't a part of our picture. Probably selfish of us, but we only wanted to concentrate on our careers. Those were our loves. Jean loved teaching Latin at the college, and my business was taking off. To have children wouldn't be fair to them or us. But you have to know I like Josie and Gracie."

"I do." My mind eased.

"Good." He leaned in and kissed me. It was a wet kiss, a Randall kiss.

"You know,…" I got up and sat down on his lap. "I bought some condoms before coming over here." I snickered at the play on words. Randall looked at me for a few beats and then grinned. I knew Brody would have laughed. I had to stop.

"You did?"

"Uh-huh," I answered as I began to unbutton his shirt. "And we seem hungry, but not for food. Why don't we go into your bedroom and feed our other needs?"

"Sure." He kissed me again, his tongue darted in

my mouth like a starved snake ready to gorge. "Let me clean up here first."

I held back a giggle. Typical Randall, needing to clean up before he got all dirty.

"You sure you want to clean up?" I cupped his manhood and saw his eyes droop from pleasure. "Can't it wait?"

"I'd feel better if I cleaned up this mess first."

"Well, I guess I'll just meet you in your bedroom then." I ran my thumb on the tip of a growing erection strained beneath his pants. "Don't be too late."

I shot him a seductive look over my shoulder as I headed down the hallway. I lay in Randall's king-size bed for ten minutes listening to dishes clang against each other, and the refrigerator door opening and closing at least a dozen times. I watched the darkness crawl into the room and grew bored with its starkness. A dresser sat across from the bed. A side table with phone and an alarm clock perched next to it. I smiled at the thought only Randall would have an alarm clock and a phone in the age of cell phones. The beige walls were blank canvases that begged for framed photos, or paintings from home décor stores, something to liven them up. My clothes puddled on the oak floor. I hoped this wouldn't be a distraction for Randall.

He came into the room, the buttons on his shirt still unbuttoned. His grin touched each of his ears.

"Everything's done. Now my attention is all on you." He climbed into his bed and pulled me on top of him.

He gave me a sweet, wet kiss. I deepened it, and he came to a full salute underneath me in response. I straddled him and ran my hands down his bare chest, circling his nipples with my fingernail. Randall groaned as he grew harder. I rested back on my haunches, unbuckled his belt, and released from the confines of his pants. He moaned in appreciation.

Randall's hands, soft and clear of any calluses, kneaded my breast with a gentleness of a doctor's examination—curious and tentatively. My head fell back in pretend ecstasy while I silently willed him to roughen his grip.

I reached for his manhood. The tip of it dripped with precum, a sign he was fully prepared. I wiggled down, dragged his pants and boxer shorts off him and threw them on the ground. I looked at Randall. His hooded eyes looked down at his erection which stood straight up in a welcome salute, and my heart squeezed.

"Mmm," I moaned. My hands roamed up and smoothed over the hair on Randall's legs. I followed and sat below his hard-on. "Looks like you're ready."

"I am." He took off his glasses and placed them on the side table. "Now to get you ready."

He remembered to take care of my needs. I grew excited and waited for his hands to explore me. Instead, he trailed kisses along my jawline. It did nothing for me. He suckled on the spot just below my ear. I pushed him away.

"Don't give me a hickey, mister." I giggled.

"Come on." Randall went back at it.

"Seriously, stop." I shoved at him with more force. "I'm not going home with a hickey."

"Sorry, I got carried away." He plopped beside me. "You know what, Harper? None of this feels right." We remained quiet for a time before he broke our silence and asked, "Why did you decide today was the day for us to have sex? Is it because I told you I loved you?"

"Part of it. And part of it the timing. I don't know. I thought here, at your place, we wouldn't be interrupted."

"We never talked about my confession of love for you." Randall reached over me and put his glasses back on. "Did you think sex would avoid an answer?"

"Look, Randall, if you're waiting on me to say it back, I can't. Not now at least."

"I guess if you can't, you can't." I saw hurt cloud his eyes.

"But I do like you." I propped myself on my elbow and twirled his chest hairs around my finger. "I wouldn't want to sleep with you if I didn't have feelings for you."

*That* wasn't entirely true. I slept with three men after Alan. I didn't have any feelings toward them, well, other than lust. But wasn't lust a feeling? Or was it an instinct? I guess it didn't matter.

Things grew quiet in the room for a while. I fell back onto the pillows and watched the numbers change on his alarm clock. I wonder if we would ever get back to what we started.

"Is it because of your girls?" Randall asked.

"Is what because of my girls?"

"The reason you can't say you love me."

I turned to face him. "No, it's not because of them. I don't love you right now. I like and respect you, but I can't call it love."

"You sure?"

"Yes. I'm not holding back on you, Randall."

"Okay, because sometimes, I worry about you, Harper. You always put your girls' needs first. It's not fair to you."

"Sure. They're my priorities."

"I know. I know. And most times I'm fine with it." He picked up my hand. "But sometimes, I think maybe they're the problem between us."

"Really?" I shot up from the bed and yanked my hand from his. "They're a problem?"

"Just hear me out." Randall touched my elbow. "I like Josie and Gracie. I can't say it enough. And I like to spend time with them. You know I do. But we don't have too much of what we're having now—you know, alone time, just the two of us. When we try, Gracie is throwing up, or Josie is being picked up by the police."

"Josie is not always picked up by the police. It happened once," I snapped. "That's not fair."

"I gave that as an example." He paused. "I'll be honest. At times, I wish they had an involved father, so, you know, we could have more alone time."

"Well, they don't." I looked up at the ceiling. "And believe me, it's a good thing."

"Why?"

"Randall, I don't want to talk about him." I huffed.

"Hey." Randall reached for my hand. I whipped it away. "Don't be mad. I'm sharing with you what I think."

"And what you think is starting to upset me."

"Listen, all I am trying to say is if we had more time together—" Randall stopped and inhaled. He let it out slowly. "Gracie and Josie always need something, and I don't know, it's like intrusions on our relationship."

"Holy shit. Did you just say my girls were intrusions?" I swung my feet over the side of the bed and glanced back at him. "I don't even know how to respond."

"What I mean is I wish you and I could go away together, just us, or spend the night together, but they're always around and, so, we can't."

"Always around?" I jumped got up out of bed. "Or course they are. They're my children."

"Come on. You know what I mean." Randall reached for me, only to grab air.

"Not really." I pushed my legs into my pants. "You say you like being around my girls, even said you like them, yet you wish they weren't around? I'm confused here, and I don't like where any of this is headed."

"Slow down, Harper. Slow down. You're twisting my words into one big knot. I only meant I wish we had more time for just the two of us."

"Randall." I bit back my anger. "We're a package deal here. You have me; you have them."

"I know."

"No, I don't think you do."

"No, I do." He patted the spot on the bed I just left. "Come on, don't leave. Come back to bed."

"I can't." I headed toward the door of his bedroom and turned around. "Let me ask you something, and promise me you'll be honest?"

"Of course."

"What was Jean's favorite food?"

"What?" Randall looked confused.

"What was Jean's favorite food?"

"Chinese."

"And did she like opera?" I asked.

"Yes. Harper, why are you asking me about Jean again?" Randall stood and tried to reach for me, but I held up a hand.

"Don't you see? I don't like Chinese food or opera." I fought to stay calm. "What I do like, love, are my girls. They are important to me. They will only be young once. And they don't get in the way of my life. I want them there. They *are* my life. I'm not like Jean. I want my kids. I don't put work before them."

"Well, you're not being fair. Jean had a career. You have a job. There's a difference." Right after he bit out his words, Randall cringed.

"You heard it too," I scoffed.

"I know. I'm sorry. You have a good job. I didn't mean it."

"Ya did, but it doesn't matter. And I'm not judging Jean. All I am saying is Jean and I are different."

"I know."

"Then why do you keep trying to make me her?" I jumped in before he answered. "Look, I like you, Randall. I do."

"But you don't love me, and you continue to twist my words to justify not giving us a chance." Randall's mouth thinned. "Your turn to be honest, Harper. Did you want to pick this fight, so you could leave without explaining, really explaining, why you don't love me?"

"There's nothing to explain. I just don't love you, period." I inhaled and exhaled slowly. "Listen, Randall, I think I tried to see if our relationship would develop because you're a kind and decent man. Kindness and decency are what my girls and I need. Tonight, I realized I can't keep pushing something that's not there."

"Where do we go from here?"

"Nowhere. We go nowhere. Randall, I think we're

over." I touched his cheek. "Thank you, though."

"For what?" He scoffed.

"For so much," I answered. "Remember how you told me I never talk about my ex? I don't talk about him because he was abusive, not only to me but to Josie. That's the reason the girls' dad isn't in their life and, if I can help it, will never be part of their lives.

"Randall, you are the first man I have had a relationship with since my ex. I am thankful to you for showing me good again. It's because of your good, I hung on longer than I should have."

"Harper, don't do this," he pleaded in sadness. "Let's talk about this some more."

"Only thing left for me to say is I do hope you can find a woman who can say I love you back. I really do. You deserve love."

Randall looked crestfallen. "It's Brody, right? You can't feel for me the way you do for him?"

"Brody's not part of any of this."

"Are you sure? Are you?"

When I looked into Randall's eyes, past the desperation, past the sadness, past any anger, I saw it. "You know." I sighed. "How?"

"I overheard his sister say something at the party about the two of you in the backyard. And then I saw for myself in the driveway after the Cubs' game. The way you two are together—" He shook his head. "I see it, Harpie. I know there had to be other times."

I didn't want to deny anything anymore. So, I asked, "Why didn't you say something?"

"I don't know." He shrugged. "At the party, we were just dating. And as time went on, I thought eventually you would choose me. Stupid, huh?

"No, Randall. I'm stupid. I'm so sorry. I can't tell you how horrible I feel about—" Some tears fall. "I shouldn't have done—"

"Hey." He rubbed my arm. "It's okay.

"It's not okay. It was never okay." I kissed his cheek. "You are a sweet man."

"Don't go. Let's work this all out." He gave me a final hug. "It's okay. Really. I think we both made mistakes. You are right. I think part of me wanted you to be Jean because you were the first woman I loved since her. You are the first woman I brought back to our house. The first woman I shared our bed with, shared any of this with."

"Do you hear yourself, Randall? Our house. Our bed." I cocked an eyebrow. "Is the reason why I haven't been at your house before because you felt like you would betray Jean if I came here?"

"No. Yeah. I don't know." Randall exhaled.

"You are right. We have both made mistakes," I said. "And you will keep making yours because you're not done grieving Jean. Not completely. And it's okay. Grief doesn't have a time table."

Randall nodded once and gave me a weak smile. "I really loved her, Harper."

"I know you did." I squeezed his hand.

We stared at each other for a few long moments. "Thank you for what you gave me, Harpie."

"And what did I give you?"

"The hope that maybe, someday, I'll feel love again, the same love, I had for Jean."

"When you're ready."

"When I'm ready." He nodded.

I kissed his lips one last time before I left his

house, left him. As I walked to the car, I sent out of a prayer of thanksgiving to the Universe for Randall, the man I was lucky enough to have chosen me, if only for a time.

Chapter Eighteen
Is My Lipstick Okay?

After a long morning of dancing with myself and sneaking a cigarette from my secret stash, I told Josie and Gracie about my break up with Randall. Josie, who did not show emotion often, other than anger, something I hoped with more therapy sessions would lessen, shrugged, and threw out, "It's your life." Grace, on the other hand, grew emotional after I explained Randall and I would no longer see each other. She broke down in tears and asked how I could "do thuch a thing?" and sobbed out she really liked Randall. I told her I liked Randall too, but sometimes grown-ups made decisions little girls don't always understand. My heart tore as she continued to cry.

Nonnie nodded when I told her. My explanation was short and void of details. When I was done, Nonnie's eyes bore into me with overwhelming compassion, and she said, "Honestly, Harper, I liked Randall. But I never thought you did. Not like you should. Not like a boyfriend."

When I told Hannah, she questioned my motive for the breakup. She asked if Alan ruined all men for me, or if Randall's proclamation of love scared me off. I assured her I was over allowing Alan to ruin anything else for me and admitted I wasn't scared of anything. She hugged me and petted my hair like one of Brody's dogs. I would have laughed if she wasn't so serious about her affection.

Hayden didn't care one way or another when I texted him the news. And frankly, I would have been surprised if he did. Hayden cared about me, but he didn't have any vested interest in Randall. He asked if I was okay, and when I promised him I was, our conversation switched to my doorbell's need for repair.

Esther and Marti both knew before I told them. Randall called Declan and quit the basketball team. He told Declan it would be awkward for him now that the two of us broke up. Marti texted Esther the news after she found out. They never asked for a reason, and I never gave them one.

The person I struggled to tell about my breakup with Randall was Brody. I planned to omit the details, hoped he would accept it and then move on to the everyday conversation. But one question from Brody about how I was doing after my casual mention of the breakup, and the entire, unabridged version, sans the bed scene, spilled out of me. When I finished, Brody agreed Randall was a good man and questioned my reaction to Randall's knowledge of our, as Brody called it, "tradition." I admitted I still felt guilty, but quickly assured him I was fine. Before he asked me anything more, I returned our conversation to light again.

****

"Momma, you look beautiful." Gracie sat on the bathroom vanity and applied some of my lipstick. She missed most of her lips.

"Thank you, Gracie Girl." I took a tissue and wiped off her mouth, leaving enough on to satisfy her. "You do too, although you always look beautiful."

245

"I know." She giggled. I loved her confidence. "We are going to have thuper fun at Nonnie's, aren't we, Momma?"

"I hope so."

And I did. I hoped they would have a great time at Nonnie's while Hannah and I went to see Brody perform at his brother's bar for the last time. I hoped, but an uncomfortable feeling gnawed at my gut. Even though they'd stayed with Nonnie countless times before, the memories of Josie's recent escape ate at my belly like acid on chrome. Despite all the precautions I took which included removing all electronic devices Josie used to contact the outside world, I still felt uneasy.

Josie came in and sat down on the closed lid of the toilet. "Okay, everything's finally downstairs."

"You didn't forget Ju-Ju, did you?" Gracie's favorite stuffed animal was an elephant she named Ju-Ju. Why the name? I have no idea.

"Like I could forget Ju-Ju." Josie looked at my reflection in the mirror at me. "You look nice, Mom."

"Thank you, Pumpkin Toes."

"Stop with the Pumpkin Toes." Josie laughed and held up my earrings to her ears. "Is this the pair you're wearing?"

"I don't know." I dangled a different pair from my fingertips. "Which ones do you like better?"

"The hoops."

"Hoops it is."

I put the hoops on and faced her. I needed Josie's opinion because I knew Gracie would tell me beautiful no matter what. Gracie still worshipped me, something Josie lost when she entered middle school.

"So, I'm good?"

"So, you're good," Josie answered.

"Yeah?" I turned my face in different directions in the mirror. "I suppose I will do. And thank you for dressing me so well."

Josie picked out my outfit of black cigarette pants with silver buttons on both sides of the waist. The waistband hit under my rib cage and were straight legged down to an inch above my ankles. She paired it with a lilac buttoned-down man-inspired shirt to tie at my waist. The shirt was meant to be large on me, but across my chest, it barely buttoned. Josie suggested a pair of black flats to top off the outfit, but as I only owned heels. I decided on a pair of five-inch black, patent leather stilettos. Hannah called them my CFM shoes, as in Come Fuck Me.

Underneath my outfit, I wore a black lace bra with matching panties, perfect to go under my tight slacks. They weren't my usual pair of cotton panties and boring bra. For my birthday last year, Hannah gave me a sexy set I admired in a magazine. I commented to Hannah such underwear were unimaginable. When I opened the gift, Hannah said, "Now you can imagine." In my outfit, complete with the heels, the jewelry, and the underwear, I felt sexy, something I missed feeling in my life for quite some time.

"You are welcome. Can we go now?" Josie helped Gracie off the vanity.

"Why the hurry?" I asked.

"I want to get out of here. I'm so tired of being in this house."

"We're still going to be in the houth, thilly. Nonnie liveth downthtairth." Gracie smiled.

"I know, but it's not the same. At least I'll have a change of scenery."

"Jos, you haven't been grounded very long, and for most of it, you were in school," I said.

"And your point? I have no phone, no computer. I can't even see the sunshine." Josie slumped her shoulders in exaggeration and looked up. "I live like a vampire."

"Don't go drinking anyone's blood tonight, okay?" I grabbed her face and kissed her lips, leaving a red mark on them.

"Stooooop," she whined, rubbing off my lipstick kiss.

"I want one." Gracie puckered her lips, and I planted a freshly made kiss. "Thankth, Momma."

"You have two days left." I pointed at Josie. "You can make it."

"If you say so."

"I do." I stuffed my makeup into my purse. "Let's go."

****

"Are you nervous?" Hannah held onto me as we walked toward the entrance of Cal's bar, Reed's Tavern. The early October wind whipped up the fifty-degree temperature and sent chills through me.

"I'm fine," I said as butterflies pounded against my belly.

Hannah always looked beautiful. Her beat-up blue jeans over brown pointed boots, a dark brown sweater, and teardrop earrings didn't make her look any less. Hannah's blond hair was wild and lush, and her eyelashes, surrounding her green eyes, were glazed with only one coat of mascara. She didn't need much.

She looked stunning, and I knew many men looked her way. If not, they were idiots.

When we reached the door, my heart squeezed. I looked forward to a night out and was excited about seeing my friends. Ah, hell, who was I kidding? I was excited to see Brody again. I didn't like it, nor could I fight it. I calmed myself with deep breaths before I grabbed the handle of the door and pulled it open. Marti warned me word had spread fast about Brody's last performance at Cal's bar. And from the looks of the crowd already assembled, it spread like rapid fire.

The mahogany bar wrapped around to the front and to the right as we walked in. About thirty stools were tucked underneath the lip of the bar. A mirrored wall behind the bar gave the illusion of more depth. Tall tables with stools lined up against the windows. Smaller table and chairs were scattered across the wide-plank wood floor. There was an area for dancing before a slightly elevated stage where two guitars rested in their holders alongside a microphone. A hallway disappeared to the right of the stage, which I knew from past visits to Reed's, led to a room with two pool tables, three dart boards, and of course, the restroom where I started Brody's and my tradition. Everywhere my eye traveled, people crammed the bar.

"So many people," Hannah shouted.

"Ya think?" I snorted out a giddy laugh.

We pushed through a group of young, barely legal males who hung out by the doorway. From the looks of them, they were already on their way to getting drunk. As we passed, the boys started their catcalls. Hannah and I kept moving until I stopped dead in my tracks when I saw him. Hannah bumped into my back.

He sat on a stool against the wall, not far from the entryway. His jaw moved up and down as he chomped the gum in his mouth. Those beautiful, gray pointed-toe cowboy boots encased his feet. One foot hooked on a rung of the stool and the other was planted on the floor. He wore a dark-blue, V-neck cotton sweater. It clung to his body like a second skin and fell over a pair of faded jeans. A rip in the material offered a peek of his right thigh. His hair hung loose and hit the start of his broad shoulders. My insides rolled and clenched from the look of him.

Another man, handsome in his own right, with mocha skin and deep brown eyes, sat next to Brody. Like a machine on a factory floor, they grabbed patrons' IDs, looked down at them, and then handed them back. Once the IDs were returned, Brody and the man stamped the customers' hands and sent them on their way.

"He does look good," Hannah whispered in my ear.

"Who?" I looked away.

"Who? Brody." She laughed and shove me along. "Let's get moving. These frat boys are tiresome."

Brody handed an ID back to a man barely out of his teens. I tried to walk past him, toward the mocha-skinned man, when Brody's hand shot out to grab my wrist. My stomach did an Olympic-worthy flip. He pulled me into him, and I became intoxicated with his raw, masculine scent.

"Can't wait to hear you play, bro." The carded man sounded like a beach bum, a Lake Shore Drive version of a beach bum. "I've been a huge fan for a long time."

"Thanks." Brody played more with the gum inside his mouth, and his eyes stayed on me. When he didn't offer anymore, the man walked away.

"Hey." He smiled at me, and his dimples dug into his cheeks exposing the Reed family goldmine.

"Hey, yourself," I said. A woman hurried past me, knocking me in between Brody's legs. His hands caught my hips and pulled me closer. His hand stayed on me.

"You doing okay? You know, since—"

"My breakup? The end of my torrid non-love affair?" I snorted, and Brody chuckled. "Actually, I'm great. I was never sad about my decision, and I really don't miss him. I suppose I still feel bad about it."

"Randall knowing about your attacks on me?" Brody grinned.

"Again, Reed, willing participant," I said. "Anyway, not important. How are you doing? Okay?"

"Am now." He stared at me intently, while his tongue, the one that played with mine other times before, pushed the gum around in his mouth. "I didn't recognize you. The last time I saw you, green crap was covering your face."

"I thought I'd go for a different look tonight. One less amphibian."

"Either look is good on you," he said with a husky voice. "Thanks for coming tonight."

"I wouldn't miss it. You look fantastic."

"I do? Not sexy or dreamy or badass?"

"Well, I have sexy dreams about your great ass."

"Good." He chuckled. "How's Josie doing?"

"You mean the prisoner anxious to be paroled? She's fine." I ran my hand down his light beard. "How's the album coming?"

"The album's done." He chomped his gum more

rapidly.

"That's great." I looked at him more closely. "You're nervous, and not about the album. Are you nervous?"

"Should I be?"

"There is quite a crowd here, pal."

"I'm used to crowds." He bit his bottom lip as his eyes danced around the bar.

"Hey, what's going on?" I moved to catch his eyes.

Brody exhaled. "Lots of things, I suppose, but nerves are not one of them."

"Feeling a bit nostalgic?"

"Good word for it."

"You're gonna miss playing here, aren't you?"

"Yeah, I didn't think I would, but I already do."

"Brody, I hope I didn't talk you into something you didn't want to do. Not that I have that much power."

"You do have amazing power over me." He surprised me with a nip on my lips. My nipples pinched. "What you said hit home. A recovering addict playing music in a bar? You're right. It's fucked up. I've known it's fucked up for a long time if I'm completely honest with myself. I mean, you're not the first to tell me. Other people told me this, including my sponsor. I have cravings, like all the time. All addicts do. And to be in this candy shop is fucked up. My sponsor knew it. Cal knew it. You knew it."

"Okay, but it's not our life."

"No, it's mine. And I should get a hold of it."

"You are."

"Sure, now."

"Brody—"

"Remember the meeting I said I went to in LA?"

Brody asked.

"Yeah?"

"Three people called me out on tempting fate and questioned if I got off on it. So, no, it's good I'm getting out of here. Cal encouraged me to get out of here. But—"

"But?"

"But"—a smirk lit up his face—"your butt looks great tonight. I mean fucking fantastic."

"Thanks." I ran my fingers through his hair. "But?"

"It's probably nothing."

"But you will miss Cal?"

"No...yeah. I don't know."

"Hey." I put my hand on his chest, his defined, hard chest. My fingertips caressed his hard, defined chest. The softness of the material of his sweater contrasted with the outline of his muscles. When I saw his nostrils flare, I stopped. "It's okay."

"I suppose."

"And you're going to miss performing, aren't you?" He didn't respond, but I saw my answer was in his eyes. "You know, there are other places you can perform."

"Don't know where those other places are yet."

"You will find them. I'll help." I wrapped my arms around his neck and pulled him into a hug. His head dropped to my chest, and I raked my fingernails through the back of his hair. "I'm sorry, Brody. What a tough time for you."

"I'm trying to get my head on straight, ya know?"

"I do.

"Thanks, sugs." He breathed in. "Although, I do like where my head's at now."

"You should. Your head is in the right place. The direction is shifting to—" When he laughed, I pulled back and hit him. "Moron."

"What? You've got a great chest. It's comfortable." I rolled my eyes and tried to break free from him. He laughed and pulled me in. "I'm kidding. Not about all the other shit, but about your chest. I mean, it is a great one. Never mind. I'm sorry."

"Yeah, right." I smiled.

"No, really, I am." Brody stared at me. "And I mean it. Thank you."

"What friends are for?"

"You are a good compadre. I missed seeing you these past couple of weeks. I wanted to call you, or to see you, but I kept odd hours, and I was in a groove.

"It's fine," I said and brushed his hair aside of his face. "I get it, Brody. It's your job. It's important to you."

"True, and you'd be a distraction."

"I aim to distract," I teased.

"Did I even say hi to you properly?"

"You said hey."

"*Hey* is not a proper hello." As soon as his lips touched mine, there was an instant jolt shot through me like electricity I only felt from him. He lingered on my mouth without offering me anything more, and I did not try to take. A tingle leaped from my chest to my groin. I bit back a moan.

"You've got to stop kissing me like that." I glanced down and pointed at his shoes. "Or you may not be wearing those home."

Brody let out a loud laugh. "But it's the way we greet each other, remember?"

"True." I sniffed. And then something happened. I can't explain how it happened or what made it happen, it just happened. Without any sort of hesitation, words tumbled out of me. "Can we call a truce for tonight?"

"A what?"

"A cease-fire, or in our case, a cease-bet."

"Intrigued." Brody brought his foot down from the rung of the stool and widened his thighs. "Go on."

"Let's not worry about the bet tonight. Whatever happens, for tonight, let's let it happen." I was as stunned as Brody looked.

"Sugar, did you just say—"

"I can't believe what I said, but yes, maybe we can be friends, with some benefits? Just for tonight?"

"Uh-huh." When someone on the side of us showed his ID, Brody pointed to the dark-haired man on his left. His eyes remained glued on me.

"I've been having some shitty days lately, as you know, and now I am a free woman."

"Yes, and yes."

"You're having some shitty days now, and you're a free man."

"Yes, and yes."

"I don't know, Brody." I fumbled with my words. I darted glances around his face before I focused on his eyes which were like a wolf's ready to pounce. It scared and excited me. "I just thought if we let loose, for one night, had some fun and treated it as fun, it might help us both."

"Are you saying sex?"

"You went right to sex."

"All the time."

"Maybe. I don't know." I smoothed out his stubble

with my fingertips. "Let's see where it all goes and not push anything. Bad idea?"

"Not for me. I've been thinking of you and me in all sorts of, um, fun, for a long time, but are you sure?"

"Yes. Maybe it's a bad idea."

"Maybe." Brody grabbed my hand and kissed the palm of my hand. "But as you said, let's see where we head tonight. And, sugs, anytime you want to stop, I will. You're driving the bus here."

"Thank you, because I may not think this is the best idea an hour from now."

"Is this going to be a rebound thing? Or a pity thing?" Brody grinned. "I mean, I'm okay with either."

"No, it wouldn't be." I playfully slapped his chest. "And there's nothing to rebound from. Like I said, my break up with Randall was meant to be. And as far as a pity thing? No reason for me to pity you."

"You're not fucking with me?"

"No, not yet anyway." I snorted. "Look, I know this is a shock. For me, too. Maybe we should think it over."

"No. What we shouldn't do is overthink it. For tonight, let's not worry where this will go, or if we're breaking the bet, or what others will think. Hell, let's not think at all, okay?"

"Okay. I mean, if I find another man, perhaps one of those frat boys over there, you may be out of luck."

"Smart-ass." He gently patted my ass and kept his hand there.

"Just saying. If I'm going young with you, I might as well go younger with those boys."

"Is that right? Well, sugar—"

I cut him off as I crushed my mouth over his. He

smiled on my lips while both of his hands cupped my
ass to pull me into him. His tongue rolled over mine,
and I took it; I played with it; I sucked on it. When he
withdrew, his forehead landed on mine.

"Damn, woman. I like our tradition of saying
hello."

"Me too." I gulped in some air.

"Now don't take up any more of my time." He
softly smacked my ass. "You got what you wanted. Go.
People are waiting to get in."

"It's what we groupies do, Brody Reed."

His laughter followed me as I walked away.

I looked around the bar, hoping to find a familiar
face, and caught Declan's stare. He smiled and waved
me over to a table next to a window that looked onto
Chicago street. Declan stood behind Marti as she sat on
one of the four bar stools with Hannah perched next to
her. Esther, who bit her nails as if they were a succulent
meal, sat across from them. I parked myself on the open
bar stool at the end of the table.

"Esther," Marti said, "can you come over here,
grab my ass, and stick your tongue in my mouth? It
seems to be all the rage with friends."

"I hear it's the only way to show true friendship,"
Esther chirped.

"Hell, I'd be okay with it." Declan smiled over his
mug of beer.

"Fuck you all." I shot up my middle finger and
showed it around the table.

"Come on, Harper." Hannah giggled Gracie's
giggle. "It's not like we couldn't see Brody's hands on
your butt."

"Or his tongue in your mouth," Esther added.

"Again." I flipped up my middle finger.

"Oh. Touchy." Marti pulled back in mock disdain.

"Want a beer? We got you a mug." Esther poured one and sat it in front of me.

"Absolutely. I need one," I said "Where's your better half? Where's Brit tonight?"

"She's delivering someone's baby." Esther rolled her eyes.

"How dare her." I pounded my fists on the table in fake indignation.

"That's right how dare her," Esther said and then pointed to everyone around the table. "And don't lecture me about my consequences for being in love with a resident at a major Chicago hospital. I know her time is precious, and I know, she can't leave or call in sick. Okay? I get it. But I miss her."

"I know you do." I squeezed her hand.

"I love you guys," Esther replied, obviously affected by the empty mug of beer in front of her.

"Let's get back to Brody grabbing Harper's ass." Marti's husky laugh filled the area.

"Let's not." I looked over at Hannah, who struggled to keep a straight face. "I'm your sister, damn it. Stick up for me."

"How's Josie doing?" Esther rubbed my back.

"Well, being a teenager sucks, especially for the parent," I said.

"I bet," Esther said. "Speaking of bets, I see you and Brody are still going strong, huh?"

"Stop with Brody and me." I threw a napkin at Esther. "We're friends."

"Yes, stop." Declan nodded. "But since I know you won't, I think this is my cue to go and talk with said brother. See you in a bit, babe."

"I'll miss you." Marti kissed Declan like he was leaving the country. She watched him walk across the bar to the other side and whipped her eyes toward me. "Okay, now spill."

"Spill what?" I took a long sip of my beer and then remembered I didn't like the taste of beer. I pushed it away.

"Come on." Esther leaned in closer. "We saw the kiss and ass grab."

I debated whether or not to tell them when a deep, rich voice hit me from behind. Hands, the size of bear paws, reached around me and placed two pitchers on the table, one full of beer, the other with clear bubbly soda.

"Here you go, ladies. Pitcher of beer and one of lemon-lime soda for the lady carrying my niece. On me."

"Aw." Marti choked held back the tears. "Thank you, Cal."

"Thanks, Cal." I smiled up at him.

Cal Reed stood around six foot four. His massive chest filled out his Reed T-shirt nicely. His entire body packed itself with big, thick muscles. Like his two brothers, Cal had a great ass. His auburn hair was thick with waves on top, shaved close on the sides and combed over to one side with a prominent part. His beard was a shade lighter and his eyes were the rich blue color you see in postcards of the ocean. From the stories Marti told, women were interested in Cal, and with good reason. His charisma, biker good looks, easy personality, and gentleness made him swoon-worthy. Although, according to Brody, Cal's divorce made him gun-shy about commitment. Brody doubted if Cal would ever remarry.

"You're welcome. You look great tonight, Harper. All you ladies do." Lines formed by Cal's eyes when he grinned. His smile called out only one sexy Reed dimple on his left cheek.

"As do you," I replied. "Wait. Have you met my sister?"

"No," Cal answered. "I haven't had the pleasure."

"Oh, well, Hanny, this is Cal, Brody's brother. Cal, this is my baby sister, Hannah."

"Hi." Hannah looked at him with boredom. "You're a big man."

"I am." His eyes glued onto her, pretty much the reaction of most men. "Is that a bad thing?"

"No. Not if you like big men." Hannah shrugged.

"And do you?" Cal asked. "Like big men."

"No, not particularly." Again, Hannah's say-what-you-will approach to communication crept in.

"Crowded bar," I interrupted before Hannah got any more offensive.

"It is," Cal agreed. "People must have found out about Brody's last performance here. Two local radio stations announced it and a few blogs. It wasn't the best-kept secret."

"You okay with Brody not performing here anymore?" I asked, touching his thick forearm.

"I am." Cal nodded. "But *he* looks like he's struggling with it."

"Yeah." I glanced over at Brody.

"She's filling us in on her friendship with Brody." Marti butted into our conversation. "Did you know friends can put their tongues in each other's mouths *and* grab asses?"

"Oh, not grab, Marts." Esther took her finger out of her mouth. "Seized. He seized her ass."

"Oookay." Cal dragged out the word. "I think I have more work to do at the bar. Nice to meet you, Hannah. Sorry I am not less big for you."

"Not your fault." She sipped on her beer and looked around the table.

"I suppose not." Cal laughed his deep-from-the-chest laugh. "She doesn't look like you, Harper. Your beauties come out in different ways."

"Awe, Cal. That's so sweet." I clutched my chest. "And no, we don't look alike. Different fathers."

"Ah." Cal's eyes did not leave Hannah. "Beautiful name, by the way, Hannah. Fits you."

"Thanks. My mom had this thing about H's," Hanna explained. "I guess better than D's. My name could have been Doris or something."

"I guess." Cal scratched his beard in confusion. His charm, the one like his brothers, oozed out of him like a jelly-filled doughnut, did not work on Hannah. "I hope to see you again."

"Okay" was Hannah's only response.

"I should go. I have to introduce Brody in a few." Cal backed away, his eyes glued to my sister. "Ladies."

"Ooohhh, Hannah. He likes you." Esther's eyebrows went up and down. "He's single, too, you know."

"Not my type." Hannah smiled at Esther flirtatiously. It confused me. I knew Hannah to be straight, although, from the vibe she gave to Esther, maybe I was wrong.

"Ladies and gentlemen," Cal's voice deep voice

bellowed into the microphone and filled the bar. "For the last time here at Reed's, my brother, a man I love, and I am so fucking proud of, Brody Reed."

The place exploded when Brody took the stage. He grabbed Cal into an embrace and stayed in it, like he sought protection from a storm. The applause grew louder. Declan joined his brothers as if he knew more shielding was needed. Bryn pushed her way through the crowd to be with her brothers on stage. They kept their heads down in a circle, an unbreakable one.

My belly tumbled. A lump grew in my throat as I watched Brody engulfed in love. I didn't take my eyes off them, off Brody. He looked over Bryn's shoulder at me and smiled. Some in the crowd followed his stare.

"Ya right," Marti yelled above the noise to all around the table. "Friendship. My husband's great ass."

I ignored her. Instead, I held onto Brody's armor gray eyes, smiled, and blinked both of my eyes, à la Gracie. He laughed, said something to his family which made them all look at me. My heart expanded as I made room for more in my life.

## Chapter Nineteen
## One Sexy Motorcycle

Brody and I were quiet on the ride to his place. I used the silence to reflect on the night behind me and pondered what lay ahead. It was a comfortable tranquility, one in which neither of us stirred uneasily, or tried to cover it with an awkward clearing of throats and unnecessary words. Brody appeared relaxed as he drove his Jeep.

I took in the incredible Chicago skyline, one of the most beautiful sights I knew, and reflected on the evening spent in shared laughs with girlfriends. I couldn't remember when I had a better time. The new experience of girlfriends—women who accepted me, who teased me, who laughed with me—filled a part of me I left empty for too long.

I also thought about Brody on his last night at Cal's bar. I enjoyed listening to him sing. His voice sounded better, purer, sexier in person. He sang the songs that put him on the music map, and more recent ones I knew would take him to other locations. Toward the end of his performance, Brody dedicated a new song to a special friend. With a refrain of *And her time was spent taking caring of everyone. When would it be time to take care of her? The roads she traveled were hard, and now she was betting on easy*, I knew that friend was me.

When Brody finished his set, the crowd erupted in appeals for more. My eyes clouded with tears. The words, the thought, and the emotions he put into every song moved me to a place I never visited. And while it scared and unsettled me, it touched me like a soft light to my heart.

The antenna on the Sears Tower—technically the Willis Tower, although no true Chicagoan called it that—fingered the night sky when we drove past. Brody's eyebrows furrowed, and his mouth turned down as if he was deep in thought.

"I liked your new songs, especially the one you dedicated to your friend," I said and put my hand on his knee. "Thank you. It was lovely."

"You're welcome, sugs." He picked up my hand and laced my fingers into his. "I'm glad you liked it."

There was more silence between us.

"You okay?"

"Your question for the night, isn't it?" There was a long pause before he spoke again. "I don't talk right after a night of singing. I like it quiet. It's the reason there's no radio on right now."

"Oh." I hadn't even noticed.

His features brightened as he slid me a side glance. "You okay?"

"Sure." I nodded. "I like it quiet after I proposition a man."

Brody chuckled and placed soft kisses on the knuckle of my index finger. I fought to keep down the passion bubbling up inside of me, but I lost. A moan escaped, and goosebumps sandpapered my arms. Brody smirked and placed my hand on his lap. He held it there for the rest of the ride.

We pulled up to a three-story, tan brick house. Each level had a front bay window. They peered out at the street like the eyes of the house. A brown iron fence surrounded the front. There was a narrow driveway to its side. Brody squeezed something attached to his visor. The gate opened and gave access to a long path.

With one more click, the gate closed behind us while the large door to the garage opened. I spotted a red BMW motorcycle next to me as Brody pulled in. A bicycle and lawn mower took up the empty space on the other side of the garage. Surprisingly, I didn't see another car in the garage. I thought for sure Brody would surround himself in luxuries.

"No other car?" I asked.

"Why? I only need one."

"I suppose you're right." I liked Brody's simple approach on life.

"We can get out of *this* car, you know?"

"Yeah." I laughed nervously. "I know."

"Hey." Brody looked at me with gentle concern. "Remember, you can back out any time, sugs."

"Do you want me to?"

"Hell, no." He opened his door and got out. By the time I was done fumbling with my seatbelt, the door opened, and Brody helped me out.

"We're doing this," I said in one breath.

"Come here, sugar." Brody pulled me up into him and held me. His hands caressed my back.

When I looked up at him, he cupped my face in his hands and rubbed his thumb over my mouth. His eyes stayed on mine and then traveled around my face to examine every freckle, mole, and red mark.

"I've been thinking about you, us, all night."

With the pace of a man sampling a good meal, his lips touched mine, and I whimpered. He grabbed my bottom lip between his teeth and nibbled with gentle passion. When I opened for him, and begged for more in silent prayers, he slanted his mouth over mine. The puffy goodness of his lips painted strokes of pleasure on me. I took in his soft sandpaper tongue and rolled it over mine, played with it, tasted it, sucked it with the gentleness of an ice cube. His smile danced on my mouth in appreciative pleasure. He bent his knees and drew me up to him. His erection grew against my abdomen.

Brody's needs became more—more desperate, more wanton, more filled with desire—and matched all the ones in me. When I offered him my tongue, Brody grabbed onto it, and entwined himself into our kiss.

"Sugar," he said in jagged breaths, "we need to get into the house or else I'm going to bend you over my motorcycle and take you right here, right now."

I looked up at him through my lashes without any words.

"You drive me fucking nuts."

His mouth fell on top of mine, with less patience and more need, more of everything. As his tongue played delicious games of tag and catch-me-if-you-can, his hands busied themselves pulling at the opening of my pants.

I read once, some men like their ears scraped with fingernails, teeth, or both. I never dared to try it on Alan, who was a wham-bam-with-no-thank-you kind of man, or Randall, who was very much a traditional man. I thought I would try it on Brody for no other reason than I wanted him to give him what I yearned for—

desire and need.

With a light touch, I traced my fingernails in and around his ears, every time I came to the opening of them, he groaned, and he deepened his kiss. As I was about to laugh at my victory, he began to unbutton my blouse. My breath hitched. There would be no victors in our fight to control the passion in us.

He left my mouth and traced his lips over me—on my neck, on the sensitive part below my ear, on my cleavage, and on the two mounds of breast billowed over my bra. The soft kisses he placed with his pillow lips drove me to a place of pleasure I never knew before. He drew in the skin of my breast and sucked on it. I threw my head back in want, in need of more. He obliged. There was no marking. They were kisses of passion. I flooded my panties in wetness of sweet desire and pushed into him in a desperate attempt to connect with his hardness.

"We'll get there, Harper. We'll get there."

Brody pushed my blouse off my shoulders. He spent agonizing time brushing both with his lips and his tongue. He nuzzled his mouth across my chest and placed long, lingering kisses on each. His tongue swirled around my nipple through the lace of my bra and then grabbed the nipples in his mouth. He sucked on them like a lollypop. When he bit down on one, an electrical current pulled up through my groin, and I screamed.

"Brody," I wailed into the garage, my fingers entangled in his hair and willed him to bite again. "Please."

Without an answer, Brody peeled down the top of my bra and covered my naked nipples with his soft, full lips. He alternated between light kisses and even lighter bites. I shrieked in insatiate desire.

"Beautiful," he whispered before he blew onto the wet nipple. I bucked toward him in response.

"I need you, Brody. Please."

"Easy, sugar."

He continued to trace kisses on my breasts, while his hand snaked down the opening of my pants. His long fingers neared my folds at the same time his mouth closed in on my breast. I didn't know which one I wanted him to touch first. His fingers played with my folds, like an instrument needing attention. When his soft lips covered my nipple, his thumb rubbed over my nub. Both were marble-hard, waiting for him.

I cried out as his finger entered me. I began to rock on it. A wave of need pulsated in me. I fought to hold onto my release. I wanted this to last.

"Aw, Harper." He looked up at me and grinned in victory. "You're all wet for me."

I bit my bottom lip and nodded, as I fought to control the explosion that was oh so near.

"You like this, don't you?"

I nodded again, mute from his magical touch. My eyes rolled back in sweet agony as his thumb circled faster around my nub.

"Look at me, sugar. Please." He gently commanded. I was a slave to him, all of him. I looked at him and saw his grin widen. "I want to see you come."

I shook my head, not wanting the pleasure to end.

"No? You want me to stop?"

"Don't stop." I finally found my voice.

Brody pushed down the only part of my bra still

hanging on. His mouth took in my entire left nipple. His tongue flicked up and down the tip of it while his fingers still worked magic on my lower half. He increased his speed on both and smeared my wetness over my nub. I fell back, my hands held onto the Jeep as the wave crashed out of me, and I fell apart.

"Oh fuck," I yelled in a strangled voice of deep-rooted release.

Brody stood and slowed his pace, his fingers still on me, in me. His free arm, wrapped around me, held me close to his body. I shook and trembled and shook more. I laughed as I quaked until my body's convulsions began to slow.

I landed my forehead onto Brody's ridiculously broad shoulders. "Come inside me, Brody. Please."

He answered with his jeans falling around us as I clung to him. He let go of me, but still allowed me to lean on him for support. There was crumpling, then a tear and a few seconds later, a foil packet joined his jeans. He pulled down my pants and my panties like a man in need.

In one fluid motion, he turned me toward his motorcycle and bent me over it. The tip of him teased my entrance as he reached from behind and played with my erect nipples. I pushed back on him. He entered me a little more, then withdrew, his breath became heavier. When I let out a long sigh, he plunged into me from behind. His hands grabbed my hips and pulled me toward him. With every thrust, he touched the spot in me left dormant forever. A current of pleasure seeped into me, into my soul, every time he hit the same spot. It was wonderful. He was wonderful.

"Fuck." He yelled behind me. "You feel fucking

fantastic."

He leaned in closer to me. My insides crawled out of me toward another eruption.

"Yes," I repeated a few times.

"I have wanted you for a long time, Harper McReynolds," Brody murmured near my ear.

"Brody…I think…I'm about to…" I didn't get any more words out. As Brody's last thrust hit my passion zone, my ears rang, my pulse raced, and my breath caught. All I had left in me flew out through one unbelievable escape of desire.

"Fuck!" Brody howled as his release matched mine.

For few long minutes, we didn't move. My legs trembled with aftershock. I was spent and sweaty and weak and paralyzed. Brody's body collapsed over me, his shallow breaths kept time with mine. We stayed wrapped up in each other and slowed down the continual beats of our hearts. Eventually, Brody gently removed himself from inside of me. He let out long gasps of air.

"I knew…" His voice was choppy. "It was going to be…" Deep breath. "Great, sugs…" Long breath out. "But fuck me, not this great."

"I know." I turned around with the slow exhaustion of a marathoner trotting after the finish line. "I know. And you did great to me, twice."

"I know." He smiled, then laughed. I joined in.

\*\*\*\*

As we entered Brody's three-story house, he explained the first level, the small, garden apartment was only used if friends or relatives came to visit Chicago. The first and second floor were separate flats renovated to become one house.

When we climbed the five stairs into the main house, Moxy and Fifi greeted him with the happiness of a family reunion. Brody bent down, laughed, and petted them both. Fifi trotted up to me, looked up, and danced figure eights around my ankles. I scooped her up, and she licked my face in appreciation.

"She likes you, you know." Brody scratched the back of Fifi's ears. "Ever since your Girls' Night In party, I don't think she's forgotten you called her beautiful on the inside."

"Well, she is. She's darling. My girls would love these dogs." I let Fifi cover my face in kisses.

"I will bring them over some time." Brody reached over and stroked Fifi some more. "You like dogs, huh?"

"I do. We had one once."

"And?"

"And then we didn't." I continued to pet Fifi.

"Don't shut down on me now, sugar. Not after what just happened."

"Oh, you want to know more?" I teased.

"Yes," Brody answered.

"It's gonna be a buzzkill."

"Kill away."

"Well, we had the dog for exactly three hours. It wasn't anything planned. Josie and I walked past an animal shelter every day on our way to and from her school. One afternoon, we saw and fell in love with a terrier mix. I knew Alan didn't like dogs. He told me there was no reason to have animals in a house. This dog, Peaches, begged for us to take her home. I knew it. Josie knew it. I mean, the way Peaches looked out at us from the window of the shelter screamed 'take me home,' ya know?"

Brody nodded.

"We went in, played with her and then she was ours, for a while anyway." I kissed Fifi's head. "I lied when I filled out the application and checked single instead of married. Probably prophetic, huh?"

"Probably."

"Anyway, Alan was supposed to be away for a week, and I thought I had time to get him used to the idea of a dog. I planned for Josie to talk with him. She had a way with him. But when we got home, Alan was there. His trip got canceled. Josie ran up to him, explained how Peaches was the new addition to our home. I knew he was not happy. He pursed his lips throughout dinner, throughout Josie's rant on where Peaches would sleep and what she'd eat. Josie told Alan she'd be responsible and take care of Peaches. Alan remained quiet.

"After dinner, Alan told Josie to go to her room and don't come out. His words were stern, and his eyes fixated on me. Josie knew the look. She didn't argue. Once she was in her room, Alan erupted in anger. After my beating, Alan grabbed the dog and walked out of the house. By morning, Peaches was no longer part of our family. I covered my bruises to hide from Josie like I always did, and we all acted as if nothing had happened. Josie and I never mentioned the dog again."

There was silence. It was a story I had forgotten, and yet it came back to me like a horrible flashback.

I looked over at Brody. "See, buzzkill. I ruined the mood."

"You ruined nothing, Harper." He ran a hand down my back.

As if Fifi knew what to do, she moved nearer to me, licked my face, until Brody took her out of my hands and held her up to eye level. "Hey, Fifi. You're stealing my thunder here."

"She is not." I ruffled the dog's hair.

"Sure, she is." Brody leaned over to me and busied his mouth on mine. He withdrew and sucked in a deep breath. "Woman."

"Man." I smiled up at him.

"Why don't we sit down for a while?" Brody put Fifi on the floor. "You hungry? Thirsty?"

"No, I'm good."

With the dogs at his heels, Brody walked me across a threshold dividing his kitchen from a large room at the front of the house. I stopped before an overstuffed red chair with a pilled afghan in shades of brown, golds and reds thrown over it. I took in the room.

A black lacquer baby grand piano took up most of the bay window. A guitar sat on its base to the right of the piano. A dark purple cotton sofa sprawled in front of a white bookshelf, which held some books, but mostly framed photographs and sheet music. It lined the longest wall in the room. The colors in the room were mismatched and did not go with the light-yellow paint on the surrounding walls. I wondered if Brody was colorblind or cared less about matching and more about comfort because the room was cozy.

I went through a mental checklist of what I would do differently but dismissed it when I glanced at Brody and saw the pride in his eyes.

"This is a great place, Brody."

"You like it?" he asked.

"It's so, so, so warm."

"Good word for it." Brody looked around. "The front room needs some work. Cal and my dad renovated these two stories. They just finished the kitchen. The front room is next."

The kitchen was state of the art. The appliances were stainless steel and the cabinets were ebony wood, with blue undertones. White and black speckled the marble countertops. They matched the backsplash made up of ivory subway tiles. Six black stools with backs surrounded the large ebony wood island in the middle of the room. The kitchen sink with the tall, swan neck faucet stood out and could not be ignored.

"You did a fantastic job."

"Not me, Cal and my da did." Brody sat down on the overstuffed chair in front of me. "I didn't help at all. Not a lick. They didn't want me to, not even to hand out screwdrivers."

"Ouch."

"I know. Just because I never received the handyman gene Cal, and Declan somewhat, have— even Bryn knows how to work power tools—doesn't mean they can shun me."

"Bastards."

"I know, right?" Brody reached around and pulled me onto his lap.

"Well…" I tucked his hair behind his ear and left my fingernails to play with his earlobe. His eyes grew heavy with pleasure. "You do have other talents."

Moxy placed her muzzle on my lap as if she wanted to be part of the cuddle. I petted her until her nose sniffed my crotch and the remnants of our sex. I pushed her away, but she came back for more.

"Moxy, good girl, I mean, no." Brody smiled, then

snapped his fingers and pointed to two beds by the fireplace. Moxy sighed and retreated to one in long, easy steps while Fifi followed, waddling as she lagged.

"Now what were you saying about my other talents?" Brody wrapped his arms around me.

"Well, I think you are very handy. Or would that be handsy?" I shrugged. "Doesn't matter. They are very talented hands."

"Good to know."

He pulled me into him and laid his mouth on mine. His tongue entered me, and I feasted. I tangled my hands in his hair and pulled Brody in deeper. He kissed me once more before withdrawing.

"You're doing it to me again, Harper." Brody took my hand and put it on the zipper of his tented pants, on his massive, hard, erection.

"Hmmm," I moaned as I began to massage it. "Well, I liked where it led us last time. We can give this spot a go."

"Not this time."

"Spoilsport."

"Sugs, I want you in my bed. I've dreamt of you in *my* bed." His eyes held me while the tips of his fingers brushed over my exposed skin, first my face, then my neck and then my forearms. My nipples puckered in response. "I want to taste and see you, every part of you. Would you like me to see and taste every inch of you?"

I nodded my head, unable to talk while I enjoyed his touch.

"Good." He nipped my lips. "But for now, I would like to sit here, okay? We don't need to rush anything."

"Tease." I snuggled in closer to him and took in the

scent of his crisp masculinity. "Was it hard for you tonight?"

"I was hard tonight." He chuckled and kissed my shoulder.

"You know what I mean. Was it as hard as you thought, singing there for the last time?"

He didn't say anything at first. I let him gather his thoughts while I enjoyed listening to the rhythm of his breathing.

"Yup." He stroked circles around my arm.

"You're at a good spot now, Brody." Doubt spread across his face. "What? You are. Between what you went through in LA with Z, the bachelor party, and tonight, you showed me the strength you have. I admire you."

"Don't go painting me as a saint. My past was shitty, and it's hard to let go of sometimes."

"Come on." I sat up and looked at him. "What bad thing could you have possibly done?"

"You want to know? It'd be my turn to spoil the mood."

"Good. Then we'd be even." When he didn't join my laugh, I stroked his stubble. "Hey, I have told you a lot about my past, more than I ever told anyone, and, unfortunately, I have more. Yes. I want to hear about yours."

"Fuck. It's probably time." Brody inhaled deeply. "Cal threw Declan a twenty-fifth birthday party. I came to it very drunk and very high. Declan's fiancée at the time was there. They planned on getting married in a few weeks. As soon as I got there, she hit on me, like she always did. Cal and Bryn used to tease me about it. It was harmless flirting. I mean, Declan's my brother, and I didn't ask for any of her attention, you know?"

I kept quiet and nodded.

"That day though, I was pissed at Declan. A few weeks before, he told me I wasn't going to stand up in his wedding. He decided the day after a cousin's party where I passed out in the middle of their kitchen. Declan said he didn't want me to ruin his wedding. And he was right. I probably would have gotten too drunk, or too high, or both, and done something fucking stupid. I always did. I was most pissed off he was right.

"So, Bridget, Declan's fiancée, followed me into the bathroom of Declan's apartment. We did lines of coke on his vanity and fucked on the same vanity. And, well, Declan walked in on us."

Brody looked at me. Pain still hid in the deepest part of his eyes, the part where his soul peeked out.

"Messed up, huh?" Brody played with the tips of my hair.

"Yeah, messed up."

"Thanks for always being truthful." He chuckled bitterly.

I didn't respond. Instead, I picked up Brody's fingers and intertwined them with my own.

"Anyway, Declan beat the shit out of me in the alley behind his apartment. I didn't even fight back. I knew I deserved it. Everyone else did too because no one jumped in to stop Dec, not even Cal. When the beating finished, Cal took me to the hospital. Besides two black eyes, Dec broke my nose and some ribs. I mean, I was messed up. From the hospital, Cal brought me right to rehab. I didn't argue. I knew it was time. To add to the mess I made, Declan's fiancée was Bryn's best friend. *Was* her best friend. In one swift move with my dick, I ruined two important relationships in my life, not to mention I alienated my ma and da. They didn't think it was their boy's finest hour."

"Your ma, of all people, had to understand."

"Maybe, but she didn't." Brody shrugged. "She had a moral compass I broke. It was one thing to be staggering drunk in front of your kids, but to sleep with your soon to be sister in law?"

"That's not fair of her."

"Probably not." Tears clouded his eyes, and a few of them fell. "I think my ma saw herself in me, the part she hated the most, and at times, the reason she hated me. Everyone did for a while, except Cal. Cal never gave up on me. I owe him so much. I don't know how I can repay him."

"You repay him every day. I mean, look where you're at now."

"Sure. Maybe." Brody shrugged and rubbed the tears away with the palm of his hand. "I haven't mended all the relationships I broke while I drank, but at least I got my family back."

"They love you." I grabbed his face in my hands. I wiped away the remaining tears with my thumbs. "You do know that, right?"

"Thanks for not running for the door."

"To repeat what you said to me at Marti's party the other night, I'm not going anywhere."

"Good." He kissed me quickly. "Fuck. I never told anyone about this, other than people at AA meetings."

I kissed him in gentle response.

"Can I show you something?" Brody asked.

"Yes, but I thought we were going to talk for a while."

He laughed as he shoved his hand into his shirt. He pulled a chip attached to a silver chain. "This is my sobriety chip. It means I've been sober five years. I got it when I came back from Jamaica a few days ago. I showed Cal and now you."

"Brody, that's fantastic!" I picked it up to examine it. I turned it over in my hands and brushed it with my fingertip. "You have to be so proud."

"I'm pretty fucking proud," Brody gushed.

"Did you show your parents? Bryn? Declan?"

"I haven't yet. I know my ma and da would like to see it, Bryn too. I'm afraid to show Dec though."

"Why?"

"I don't know." Brody shrugged. "It may bring back bad memories."

"Stop. It won't. Don't you see how crazy your brother is about Marti? I am pretty sure he's over it."

"I betrayed him, sugs. You don't do that to anyone. I did it to my brother."

"While your disease was active." I shifted in his lap to look straight at him. "You are healthier now. You are a good person, Brody Reed."

Brody stared at me for a long time. Our eyes communicated in need and passion. He grabbed my hands and pulled me up toward him. We headed down a hallway. The dogs got up and followed. Brody walked backward, my hands still in his.

"Now I want to show you other things." His eyebrows wiggled up and down.

"Oh, I guess." I snorted as I let myself be led up a flight of stairs, feeling free and proud of the hands I held.

Chapter Twenty
Mayonnaise and Revelations

Music drifted up the stairs to meet me when I got out of the bathroom. After more times of orgasming at the hands and tongue of Brody—twice in his bed, once in the shower, and once as he dried me with a towel—I fell asleep, exhausted from pleasure. I awoke next to an empty spot in Brody's bed.

I walked down the spiral staircase, wearing a T-shirt I found on the back of the bathroom door. It smelled like Brody and, for a moment, I wrapped my arms around myself and took in the scent of him.

He sat on the sofa with a pencil behind his ear, his gaze cast on a piece of paper. He wore only a pair of pajama bottoms. Topless, he showed off his six-pack abs, a light dusting of his golden hair and all his glorious tattoos. He was magnificent. Passion still burned inside of me. I thought it may never be put out.

I walked up to him, leaned down, and kissed him.

"Sleep well?"

"Yes, but hungry."

"I'll make us something."

"Not that kind of hunger." I knelt in front of him and slowly rubbed my hands up his legs to his hips. My eyes never left him.

"What'cha doing, sugar?" he asked.

"Shhh." I put my index finger near my lips. "Put

down your guitar, Brodes."

Brody's eyes lit on fire as he put his guitar down and leaned it against a wall. When I pulled at the elastic waistband of his pajamas, Brody bucked his hips to make it easier for me to slip the pajamas down to his ankle. I looked down at his manhood, much larger and thicker than any other man I knew. I grew hot from the sight of it.

I splayed his legs open and began to lick at the tip of his erection.

"Fuck." Brody fell back on the sofa.

I passed my tongue around the tip of his throbbing hard on and drew a part of him into my mouth. Brody's fingers knotted in my hair. I took him in deeper while I kept my eyes on his. Brody flushed and his expression grew serious with desire. The sight of him getting off in my mouth was sexy and exciting.

When Brody was near the edge, I sheathed him with a condom, straddled him, and together, we rode another great ride of mutual yearning.

****

"My shirt looks better on you than me." Brody investigated his opened refrigerator.

"You like the too-tight-across-the-boobs, down-to-the-knees look?"

"Maybe not the down-to-the-knees. I like when you show off those terrific legs of yours and catch a peek at the hidden butterfly tattoo on your gorgeous ass."

"You like the tattoo, huh?" I asked.

"No, it's the worst tattoo I think I've ever seen. Who was the person who did it?"

"An old boyfriend."

"He wasn't a great tattoo artist."

"Because he wasn't one. We did it one night out of shits and giggles with tools from his tattoo artist brother."

Brody laugh. "Well, I do like the canvas it's on. I mean, I love your ass. Did I ever tell you your incredible curves were the first thing I noticed about you?"

"Shallow of you, don'tcha think?"

"Absolutely." He turned with his hands full of food and kissed the tip of my nose. "And you're short."

"I'm five four," I protested.

"You're five three if you're lucky." Brody winked. "What's with your stunning tiger tattoo?"

"That one was done by the professional." I leaned against the kitchen counter. "A few months after Gracie was born, Nonnie and I watched a documentary about tigers. The documentary had a part on how the Chinese consider tigers to be brave and a symbol of power. During it, Nonnie told me, 'You are a tiger, Harper.' And a day later, Hannah and I went to a tattoo artist friend of my brother's to give myself a divorce gift."

"A great gift."

"I thought so. Nonnie? Not so much." I wrinkled my nose. "She thought it was too big, but I think it's perfect."

"It is perfect," Brody agreed. The room grew quiet, quiet enough to hear the grumble of his belly. We both laughed. "And I ruined the moment."

"No." I laughed some more.

"I am making a sandwich. You want one?"

"Nah, I'm good."

"Something to drink?" Brody put sandwich fixings

on the table.

"What'cha got?" I leaned on the marble of the island.

"Let's see. Lemonade, water, and more water. I would offer coffee, but I don't want your cute nose to wrinkle in disgust."

"And it would."

"You don't know what you're missing."

"Yes, I do, thus my cute wrinkled nose. Lemonade's good."

"Cups are above the sink. Think you can reach them?"

"Ha-ha." When I got to the cabinets, I saw just how high they were. "Um…"

"I got 'em." Brody came from behind me and reached up over me. When he brought down the cups, his mouth came down on mine. He gave me a long, soft, knees-buckling kiss. He walked away like it was the most normal thing in the world. He left me wanting more. "You didn't sleep long."

"How long was I out?" I sat down across from him as he made his sandwich.

"About an hour and a half."

"You didn't sleep at all. You've got to be exhausted."

"You did wear me out." He grinned as he slathered on the mayonnaise and arranged the cheese over the roast beef.

"You liked it?"

"It?"

"Tag." I rolled my eyes. "Sex."

I am not an insecure person. My marriage to Alan made me a doubting mess, but I shed the uncertainty about myself a few years after I left him. And while I was not one to fish for compliments, I cast a line to Brody. I was inquisitive and embarrassed as I waited for an answer.

"You want to know if I liked sex with you?" Brody asked.

"Forget it." I shook my head. "It was a stupid question."

"It wasn't." His voice went soft.

"It was insecure and high school and—"

"Sugs, slow down. It's fine."

"Brody, I'm forcing you to say things you don't want to. I get it. It was my moment of weakness."

"We had a great time tonight, fantastic sex. I enjoyed it probably as much as you, maybe more." A storm of passion lit up his silver eyes. "I am fucking blown away by your softness and your amazing curves. I can come by looking at you, touching you, and I have never been like this before. And, oh man, then there's the killer way your tongue does tricks on me, not to mention the little whimpers and loud moans you give out when you're getting excited, and the beauty of you when you come. Sugar, I like what we had tonight. I like it a hell of a lot."

"You don't have to lay it on thick."

"I'm not."

"Brody, you've had other women before, and probably enjoyed sex with them just as much, maybe more. I'm not naïve, nor do I want you to lie to spare my feelings."

"Unbelievable. Lie to you? Spare your feelings?" He took a huge bite of his sandwich and chewed. Pushing the food to one side of his cheek, he continued.

"I would never lie to you. Yes, I enjoyed sex with other women before, sure. Well, except for the first time. That sucked. I was fifteen, at a summer theater camp. She was sixteen. Her name was Mia Guffner. We finished in like ten seconds."

"Well, you've certainly learned to last longer since then."

"Yes, I have." He offered me a bite of his sandwich, and I took it.

"Tastes soooo friggin good." I held my mouth as I spoke.

"Right? The secret is the mayo. My ma makes it." Brody looked up. "Now, where was I?"

"Mia Guffner."

"Right. Hot damn if she wasn't curvy, too. I like curvy women."

"Good to know."

"Tonight, was different though, in a good way." Brody put down his sandwich and rested on the counter. "If I told you it was probably the most mind-blowing sex in my life, would you believe me?"

"No."

"I know." He stood up and nodded. "Which is why I never said anything tonight. I knew you would think I fed you a line. Well, and—"

His voice trailed off as he took another bite of his sandwich. Brody put the sandwich back on his plate and stared at it as if he saw the face of Jesus.

"And?" I prompted.

"And…" His eyes remained on the bread. "And this is going to end soon, so I didn't want to say aloud what I am feeling. I don't know, maybe I'm a coward and need to spare my feelings."

"What's gonna end?"

"This." He pointed back and forth to him and me.

"We're not going to end. I hope not anyway."

"Our sex is going to end. Remember, you told me, one-time deal—a reprieve, I think you called it."

"Doesn't mean we're going to end our friendship."

"The sex part will, and it's gonna be harder for me to accept friendship. You may get those boots sooner than you thought, because, sugar, I'm not so sure going back to friends is going to be easy for me."

His words kicked my heart. Questions swirled in my mind like an Oklahoma tornado. Was Brody telling me I may not see him anymore? Was all this going to end? Was I the biggest fool for suggesting it? Was he the bigger fool for not accepting what most men would kill for—no-strings-attached-sex? And how would I deal with not seeing him anymore? Why did I care so much? Why did it already hurt?

I almost spit the bite onto the floor. I took a long sip of lemonade and thought of something to quickly change the subject.

"Your dad, excuse me, da, and Cal did this room, huh?" I took a bite of tomato from his plate.

"Not gonna talk more about it, huh?"

When I looked into his smoky gray eyes, in a silent plea to let it drop, he nodded his head.

"Yup. My da was a carpenter. He retired a year ago and had no idea what to do with himself. My house is a great project to get him out of my ma's hair. She's a handful even when she's not drinking."

"Can I ask you something personal?"

"Harper, I think what we did tonight and how many times we did it, and the positions we put ourselves in gives you the right to get personal."

"See, now you're distracting me." I snorted. "Did it irritate you when you saw your mom drink? It couldn't be easy to see her drunk while you struggled with your sobriety."

"First of all, my ma has constant slip ups, so she's not done yet. And secondly, I still struggle. I always will. Did you know only eight percent of addicts stay sober?"

"No, I didn't."

"Yup, it is a constant battle."

"But you're on top of it."

"Sure. It gets a little easier, but I can never put my guard down. I still have to work the program, go to meetings, maybe become a sponsor. I know I am always one drink, one hit, away from going down the wrong path again."

"You are tough, though."

"Don't." Brody shook his head.

"What?"

"Harper, you keep painting this picture of me you want to see. I'm not a great person."

"Wow." I pulled back in surprise. "You still beat yourself up about having sex with Declan's fiancée, huh?"

"And other things, but I don't know if I'll ever put the boxing gloves away on my betrayal."

"You know, I think Bridget was as much at fault as you."

"You really want to think the best of me."

"Maybe you should try to think better of yourself and cut yourself some slack, hell, even forgive yourself."

"Tough shit to forgive."

"It seems to me other people, the important people, have and now it's time to move on." I pointed out. "Whatever happened to Bridget?"

"Bridget married some dude she met on vacation about seven months later. She has three kids with him and lives in Miami. She comes into Cal's bar from time to time when she's in town visiting. She still tries to hit on Declan, pleading with him to take her back."

"No way."

"I know. Unbelievable. And yet she says she hates me." Brody smirked. "She told me I ruined her. And maybe I did."

I didn't say anything more. The room quieted except for the tapping of dogs' nails on the kitchen floor when they entered. Moxy, probably sensing Brody's mood, leaned in on his legs as if to protect him. Fifi sat down on Brody's feet. Her bulging eyes stared up at him. I played with the condensation on my glass.

"You good?" Brody folded his arms across his chest.

"I'm great and thank you for sharing this part of you with me. You good?"

"I'm good." He looked down at Fifi and then back at me. "You know, Harper, we were great together tonight."

"I think we've already proved it, over and over and over."

"I don't mean just sex. We were great in and out of bed. And we were great in bed because we're great together out of it. I don't know why you don't see it."

"Brody, stop right there, okay?" I grabbed his hand from his chest. "Let's enjoy tonight."

"Sure, but it's my turn to ask you one thing." Brody kissed my palm. "Have you ever come like you did tonight?"

"Are you asking if I had orgasms before? Of course, I have."

"Like the ones you had tonight?"

Here is where I had an opportunity to lie and say, *of course, I had*, to tell him I orgasmed like that all the time and ask him not to read too much into it. But I didn't lie. I couldn't lie. Not to him.

"No," I mumbled.

"I'm sorry, what?"

"I said no, okay?"

"Asshole for an ex and Randy not so good?"

"They weren't you, that's for sure." I tried to hide the words under my breath.

"You need to speak up there, Harper."

By his victorious smirk, I knew he heard me.

I let out a long puff of air. "Here's the deal," I began. "Alan, the asshole ex, was a wham-bam type of guy, never waited till I was ready, and never touched me anywhere. And I already told you he raped me. Randy, damn it, Randall, well, we never had sex."

"Never? Like, never ever."

"Never ever. We were on our way the night we broke up. I'm glad we didn't. Based on our foreplay, I don't think Randall would have been very good."

"Huh. And there were other guys?"

"Three." I picked at the crumbs on Brody's plate.

"And any of these other guys? Did they taste you?"

I didn't answer. I was embarrassed. I took a drink of my lemonade and looked around the kitchen to avoid eye contact.

"Seriously?"

"Brody, these are intimate questions."

"Yes, I know."

"Shit. No, they didn't." I put the glass down with more anger than I wanted to show. "Alan said it was gross and all the other guys, I don't know, just used their hands."

"Gross? How can your deliciousness be gross?"

"Because he said it was dirty, and I would be a whore, and he didn't marry a whore and—" I shook my head. "It doesn't matter."

"No, it does. Did you go down on them? These men?"

"Are you asking for another blow from me?" It was meant as a joke, but it came out bitter.

"Sugar, did you go down on them?"

"Brody, this conversation is getting too personal, don't you think?"

"This coming from a woman who wanted to know where she stacked up against the other women in my life?"

"I didn't ask you."

"Ya kind of did." Brody squinted. "And, Harper, I will remind you again, I think the things we did these past few hours were a bit personal, don't *you* think?"

I got up and walked toward the counter space. I wanted to distance myself from Brody, yet still be near him. I stood by the counter. "Yes. Sometimes. And I did to Alan, but not because I wanted to but because…because…because…" I stopped.

"Because he made you. Fuck." Brody came to me. I put my hand up to stop him.

"Yes."

"You don't have to—"

Maybe it was the mood, maybe it was all he shared with me, or perhaps it was time to tell more of my story. I kept it locked for so long, and it only ate at me. I don't know the exact reason, but the words seeped out of me like an oil leak; it spilled out slow and ugly.

"He made me give him blow jobs, forced me to, and to do other things to him that I already went to therapy for the last five years to try to reconcile because I'll never forget. He hated being laughed at or corrected." I shook. "When I conceived Grace, it was in a restaurant bathroom where he raped me, all because I corrected him at a work dinner when he said the Fourteenth Amendment abolished slavery."

I took deep breaths and willed myself not to move or look at Brody.

"Fucking asshole," Brody whispered.

"Now do you see? I haven't had the best sex life."

I finally looked over at him, internally pleaded with him not to pity me. "And the other guys didn't mean anything to me. They were men I needed to prove to myself I could have normal sex. One guy did ask, a few times, and each time, I said no. I don't know. I heard Alan's voice in my head, or I didn't trust him. One of the two, or both."

Brody remained silent. He held my stare and said nothing. After a few moments, he opened his arms out to me. "Come here."

"No."

"Please, Harper. I want to hold you for no other reason than *I* need to."

This time I moved, pulled toward him as if he were my life's magnet. I fell into him, and he closed his arms around me. I didn't cry because there were no tears to cry. They dried up a long time ago. I stayed in his arms. I felt warm, safe, and protected.

"We've both told each other a shit load of personal crap tonight."

"Yup." Brody put his chin on top of my head. "Thanks for trusting me."

"Trust?" I snorted. "I think you dug it out of me."

"One of my stalker moves, woman. I told you. I'm good." He kissed me quickly. "Seriously. Thank you. Not just for sharing parts of your life with me, but for letting me in, even during sex."

I stayed in his arms for a few more minutes, with both dogs curled up at our feet. I would have stayed there longer, but my cell phone spit out a bird chirp, a text from Josie.

## Chapter Twenty-One
## Alan, You Prick

"Ignore it." Brody stroked my hair and gave me kisses along my eyebrows. "Let me hold you longer."

"Sounds great," I purred and pushed off him.

"But?"

"But it's Josie. She's not supposed to have her phone," I explained. "That little sneak. Now I'm dying to hear her explanation on this one."

"Don't answer it then." He kissed my lips. "That'll teach her.

"Even though that sounds tempting, I can't ignore it. What if it's an emergency?"

"Ah." He kissed my lips and let me go.

I broke completely away and walked into the front room to get my purse.

"If she is texting you about something stupid, you're going to be more upset, aren't you? I mean—" Brody called after me, but I stopped listening as I read the text.

*—Plz don't be mad I have my phone. I am w/ Dad. In his bathrm. I'm scared.—*

"What did she say?" Brody chuckled as he came into the room after me. His smile dropped when he saw me. "What's wrong?"

"It's Josie." Tears clogged my throat. "She's with Alan, and she's scared."

I ran to his bedroom, with Brody at my heels. I pulled off my T-shirt.

"Do you know where she's at?"

"I have a tracker on her cell phone."

"Good." Brody pulled down his pajama bottoms and stuffed himself into his jeans. "Tell her you're on your way."

"Shit. Right."

I picked up my phone and banged my thumbs on the keys. —*Coming soon to get you.*—

—*K*— she responded.

"I swear to you, Alan..." I scurried around the room to grab my bra and blouse. I picked up my shoes and danced to put my feet in them. "If you touched her, I will kill you. I will fucking kill your sorry ass."

I put on my bra and then struggled to put on my top as I ran down the stairs.

"Harper, wait." Brody's steps echoed behind me.

"No," I shouted back. "I can't."

"At least let me grab my keys."

"You're not going with me." I snatched my purse and stuffed my cell phone into it.

"Yeah, I am."

"Brody, I am not wasting time arguing with you."

"Then don't." He pulled his shirt over his head.

"You're unbelievable. This is my shit."

"Sugar, I drove you. You don't have a car, remember?"

"Goddamn it." I tossed him his wallet from the table in the entryway. "I knew this was a bad idea. One night to get my ya-ya's out and—"

"Where are we going?" Brody opened the door for me to bolt out of.

"I'm not sure." I pulled out my cell phone and brought up the locator app. "She's at the only hotel in Noteah. It's gonna take us too long to get there."

"I'll get us there." Brody's voice was on the side of me. I hadn't even noticed he got in the car. He gunned it out of the garage toward the expressway. "Give me directions."

Josie's ringtone chimed again. I looked down.

—*How much lngr, Momma?*—

My stomach fell to my ankles. She never called me Momma unless she was hurt. The bastard hurt her.

"Can you go any faster?" I shouted into the car.

"Tell me where to go." Brody's voice was as calm as my thoughts were chaotic.

"Right. The hotel is six blocks north of my house."

"Good."

—*Be there soon*— I texted.

—*Don't call. He'll hear. He thinks I'm taking a dump.*—

I calmed myself with a giggle. I read the text back to Brody. He smiled.

—*Good girl. B there soon.*—

—*I'm so sorry.*—

—*No worries. I have to call the police.*—

—*Alrdy txtd Lana.*—"

At first, I had to scramble to figure out who she meant, but then I remembered.

"Yes!" I yelled.

"What?" Brody hauled ass onto the expressway.

"She texted the cop who picked her up last time."

"Great." Brody's thumb moved over his phone's screen. I wondered if he forgot the directions and didn't want to tell me. It didn't matter. I let it go.

I texted Josie again. —*Good girl. c if there is window 2 climb out.*—

—*No window big enough.*—

"Shit."

"What now?" Brody glanced d over at me and as he then weaved in and out of the early-morning traffic.

"Nothing." I shook my head.

—*Ok. Remember the moves I taught.*—

—*Already used one. How much longer?*—

"How much longer?" I looked over at Brody.

"Traffic is good. Probably in a few minutes." He glanced over at me.

"Not fast enough." I banged on the console of the car.

"Easy. It'll be okay. Keep texting Josie and let her know you're there for her. The police are on their way. It'll be okay."

"Don't. Okay? Just don't."

"What?"

"Patronize me. You don't know what I'm—" My phone chirped another text from Josie.

—*Mom, u there?*—

—*We r almost there.*—

—*He's banging louder. He's so mad at me.*—

"Goddamn it!" I screamed into the car.

"It'll be okay." Brody grabbed my hand.

"How do you know? I mean really, you don't know. Hell, I don't know."

I jerked my hand away and texted some more. I was scared and pissed, and Brody was on the receiving end of it all.

—*It'll be okay.*— I typed in Brody's words to Josie. —*Sing that song you like. The one you sing to*

*Gracie when she's scared.—*

"It'll be okay," Brody repeated.

"Stop saying that and just get us there," I shrieked.

*—I'll try.—*

*—Keep singing. We're almost there.—*

Josie texted me she heard the sirens. I told her to stay put until she heard the police in the room. I asked her the room number. When she gave it to me, I said she needed to give the number to Lana, too.

What seemed like hours was only twenty minutes from when we left Brody's to when we reached the motel. Brody drove slowly as I scanned the numbers on doors, trying to find the room number Josie gave me. There was a police car with flashing lights stationed outside one of the rooms. Before Brody's jeep came to a complete stop, I jumped out and ran toward it.

"Alan." I screamed as rage pushed me into a full run toward the door. "Alan, open up."

Officer Lana Tanner, with her partner Billy, talked into the crack of the door.

"Alan," I repeated and saw his eyes in the slit of the door. "Open this door now, Alan."

"Harper," Lana said, put her hands out. "You need to let us do our job."

"And you need to let me do mine. My daughter is in there scared to death. I need to be a mother." I glared over at Alan. "Open this door now."

"Nope. No warrant. They can't come here and demand—"

"Hey, asshole," Brody bellowed. "Let her in, or I will kick the motherfuckin' door in."

Alan's brown eyes sized Brody up and down. "Who the hell are you? Harper's new fuck?"

"Where's Josie?" I shouted.

"Harper." Lana put her hand on my shoulder. "We don't know yet—"

"Let Harper see her." Brody moved in front of me. He positioned himself between me and the door.

"Please, Alan." I peeked around Brody and used my pleading, don't-get-mad-at-me voice I used for too many years. "Please."

"Asshole, let her in to see her daughter," Brody spat between gritted teeth.

"Josie wanted to see me." Alan grinned in victory. Stomach bile came up into my throat.

"The hell with this." Brody's leg shot out and kicked the door open.

"Sir, you can't kick a door in and—"

"And yet I just did."

I ran past Alan as he hollered about his rights and Lana's lecture to Brody.

"Josie?" I shouted into the separate bedroom. "Where are you? It's Momma."

When there was no answer, I screamed again, "Josie. Please."

"Here." Her voice was small, weak, and full of terror—a terror I understood.

I ran toward the voice and found her in the suite's second bathroom, crouched by the toilet, her eyes filled with horror and one of them blackened. I swallowed my rage. I squatted by her.

"Hey, Pumpkin Toes."

"Hey, Momma." Her voice was still fragile.

"It's okay. Baby, it's okay. I'm here now." I wrapped my arms around her shoulders and helped her out from behind the toilet. We sat on the edge of the tub. I held her when she began to cry.

"I'm so sorry. I should have listened to you."

"Sh." I clutched her into my chest. I rocked her like she was a small child again. "I'm here now. It's all right."

"No, Momma. It's not. I thought it would be when I called *him*," she said through her sobs. I glanced up to see Lana in the doorway. She nodded but didn't come in.

"Hey, Josie," Lana said warmly. "Thanks for texting me."

"I grabbed your number off the counter." Josie glanced up. "I was gonna throw it out, so my mom couldn't call you if Nonnie found out I left. I didn't though. I slipped it into my jeans. Lucky I kept it, huh?"

"Very." I kissed the top of her head.

"Momma, I'm sorry. I took my phone from your room. I told Nonnie I forgot my pajamas, and I snuck out. I called Grandma Kathy, and she got a hold of *him*. *He* called me and told me to meet him at the park again. I did. *He* was fine. Fun almost, you know?"

"Yeah, honey, I do." I remembered Alan's deceitful charm.

"We came back here, ordered a pizza, and watched a movie. We laughed a lot and were having a good time. There was a woman in the movie who *he* said looked like you because…because…because…" She cried harder.

"It's okay, Josie. We can talk about this—"

"Because *he* said she had your fat ass." Josie looked up at me. "I told him he was wrong. You are not fat, and you have a good ass. I laughed when I thought of Gracie and how she would have said 'swear jar.'

And then everything started to feel wrong."

"Aw, sweetie." I sighed and ran a hand over her cheek.

"He said how I needed to stop laughing. It only made me laugh more. You know, like I do when I'm nervous or something. He got madder. He said I was disrespectful, and I was a…a…cunt like my mother. I told him I am proud to be like you, and we aren't the C-word, and he should shut up about us." Anger replaced her tears. "He wasn't fun anymore, Mom, ya know?"

"Unfortunately, I do." I knew the ugly part of him, the part I ran from, too.

"And then…and then…" She cried again. Words were stuck in between her sobs.

"Then he hit you?" I pulled her back into my chest and kissed the top of her head.

"Three times. It would have been more, but I dodged him, which made him madder. When he hit me in the eye, I kneed him in his groin. Right in his groin where you showed me. He doubled over. I grabbed my cell phone and ran into the bathroom. I texted Lana. She told me to text you."

"I'm glad you did. Everything you did was good. I'm really proud of you," I said and mouthed *Thank you* to Lana over Josie's head. She nodded.

"I am sorry, Momma."

"I know you are."

She looked up. When I swept her hair to the side, the sight of the bruise punched my gut.

"Momma, I thought he changed like Grathy said. I remember how he treated you. I do. But I thought he changed. I shouldn't have—"

"Josie, you're okay now. That's all that matters."

"I love you, Momma. So much." She wrapped her arms around me, placed her head on my shoulders and squeezed.

"I love you too. So much."

We sat on the hotel's bathtub for about forty-five minutes as Lana took notes on all the answers Josie gave her. There were loud voices in the other room and some bone-on-bone action, but I was too busy with Josie to care.

Eventually, we walked out of the bathroom. Alan writhed in pain on the floor. Blood spewed from his nose, his lip split open, his left eye swelled shut, and he clutched his stomach. I scanned the room. Billy sat on a chair by the desk, writing in his notebook, not a care in the world. Brody washed his hand by the sink outside the bathroom.

"What the hell happened?" Lana asked.

"He slipped," Billy answered.

"He beat me up is what happened." Alan pointed at Brody, and then grimaced in pain.

"I did?" Brody looked at Billy.

"I dunno." Billy shrugged. "I thought he slipped."

"He did," Alan insisted, "and I want him arrested. He kicked in the door, too. The manager will be pissed."

"Manager won't care when I tell him I'll pay for everything." Brody dried his hands. "Besides, I thought I heard someone say fire, and I was all set to rescue you. And, then, well, you slipped."

Josie let out a giggle. Brody winked at her. When he caught sight of her black eye, his smile dropped, and his jaw sawed back and forth. He leaned down and bit out, "Get up, motherfucker, so I can beat some more crap out of you."

"See?" Alan pointed up at Brody. There was fear in his good eye. "You heard him."

"Mr. Reed, no more." Lana jerked Brody back.

"I want him arrested." Alan tried to get up but collapsed back down.

"You do?" Billy looked over at Josie and scratched his chin. "Now, see, there are no witnesses except me. And who is a judge gonna believe? Huh? A dick who blew an order of protection and blackened his daughter's eye? Or me? A police officer with a clean record? Huh? Who?"

"I didn't do anything. She ran into my fist. A klutz just like her mom." And then Alan let out one of his maniacal laughs he used when hit me.

Like a wounded bird, I cried, "Noooo." I flew at Alan in a fury. "You son of a bitch. You will never touch her or me again. Ever. I want to kill you. You hear me? Kill you."

"Easy, sugar, easy." Brody pulled me back by the waist and sat me on the bed.

"No. I fucking hate him."

"I know, I know." Brody stepped in front of me and squatted down to look in my eyes. "I do, too. But Josie doesn't need to see any more. She needs you."

I looked over at Josie. She was bent over in a heap, and her shoulders shook with fear or from crying, I didn't know which. I took a deep breath, wrapped her in my arms, and cooed into her ear. "It's over, sweetie. It's over."

"What the hell happened here?" Bryn Reed strode into the room and looked down at the blood on the floor. She looked at Alan. "Who the hell is he?"

"And you are?" Lana approached Bryn, hand on her gun.

"Bryn Reed."

"She's my sister." Brody ran a hand through his hair.

"And why are you here?" Lana cocked her head.

"I texted her," Brody said.

"Ms. Reed, Brody shouldn't have—"

"Relax." Bryn took out a wallet and flashed a badge.

"You're FBI?" Billy grinned. smiled. "Cool."

"Hey, Bryn." Josie gave a weak smile. "Didn't know you were FBI."

"Hey, kid. Still have the ball you caught magnificently?"

"Uh-huh." Josie laughed through her tears.

"Hi, Harper." Bryn smiled at me. Her entire face lit with beauty, especially when the Reed dimples came out. "Did this asshole give her the shiner?"

"Yeah," Josie answered for me.

"Brody, did you do that to him?" Bryn asked.

"He slipped," Billy answered for Brody.

"Huh." Bryn winked at Josie. "These floors are slippery."

"Okay, Agent Reed." Lana took her hand off her gun. "You're here because of your brother, but this isn't a federal crime."

"Kidnapping is."

With the word "kidnapping," my body buckled.

Bryn crouched down by Alan. Her gravelly voice was vicious. "You get off by hitting women and kids, huh? Well, asshole, you'll be going to prison on anything I can throw at you, got it?"

"You think you scare me, bitch?"

"I should, but if I don't, jail will. Especially when word gets out you hit kids." Bryn laughed at him, Alan's sorest spot. It was the reason he went off on Josie. It all made sense then, in the most ridiculous way.

"If I could, I would…" Alan's words trailed off.

"What, tough guy? What do you want to do?" Bryn spat out her questions laughed again. "Go a few rounds with me? Looks like someone already went a few with you."

"Nuh-uh." Billy shook his head. "He slipped."

"Keep forgetting." Bryn smirked. "Well, maybe some other time, you know, when you recover from your fall."

"Agent Reed, I think we have this." Lana's patience ran thin. She was a by-the-book type of person, and Bryn Reed was a person who hadn't even cracked the book's binding. "You can go if you want."

"It's not what I want." Bryn looked over at me. "Want me to stay?"

Before I answered, Josie threw out a desperate, "Please?"

"Sure," Bryn answered. Looked over at Lana. "Looks like I'm staying."

"Looks like," she agreed.

Bryn rubbed her hand up and down Josie's arm. "You know, from what I know of you and what Brody has told me, I think I like you. You seem smart, funny as hell, and good to your little sister. One thing though, honey, listen to your mom, okay?"

"Bryn, I don't think she needs a lecture right now," I interjected.

"No, Mom. She's right. I should have listened to you."

"Good girl." Bryn tucked Josie's hair behind her ear and looked over at Lana. "Did you call for an ambulance?"

"I did." Billy raised his hand. "They should be here soon."

"Good." Bryn nodded.

"I already took Josie's statement," Lana said. "If she's cleared by the paramedics, we're gonna need to go to the station to write up a report."

"My mom's coming too, right?"

"Absolutely."

"Okay." Josie gave a weak smile.

"And you're tough, too." Bryn smiled at Josie, and for a moment, I saw Brody in her. "They're probably gonna need reports from—"

"Agent Reed, I do know how to do my job." Lana's voice was calm, but with a little edge.

"Okay, okay." Bryn held up her hands.

Lana sat with Josie as Billy jerked Alan up and took him out of the room. I went over to Bryn.

"Thank you."

"No biggie." She nodded toward Josie. "She's something, huh?"

"She really is." I stared at Josie and watched as she talked with Lana.

"You okay, Harper?" Bryn asked.

"No." I shook my head slowly.

"No, I wouldn't think so. It's over now though. The prick will probably go away for a while."

"I hope so."

"In the meantime…" She looked over at Brody,

who stood there, his hands in his back pockets, unsure of what to do. "I don't think he's leaving anytime soon."

"Harper." Lana broke in on our conversation. "You and Josie have some long hours ahead of you. You gonna be good?"

"Yeah." I sat down next to Josie and wrapped an arm around her. "I think we're both gonna be good."

I called Nonnie to tell her what happened. I mentioned Josie's black eye. The information sent Nonnie into a tailspin of emotions. She called Alan an SOB. I agreed. She blamed herself for Josie's problem. I reassured we were all safe but didn't disagree. I swallowed my anger and my lecture to Nonnie about how her babysitting days were numbered. It wasn't really her fault. Nonnie grew older, and so did Josie and Gracie.

As Lana predicted, the next five hours were very long. We went to the police station and gave a report. Bryn stayed in the room with us. She did not say much other than words of support to Josie. Brody gave a short statement. He did not admit to anything about the marks and bruises he doled out on Alan. When asked about them, Billy offered his Alan fell theory. Once Brody finished his statement, he stayed in the waiting area, despite my constant demands for him to go. From time to time, various personnel swarmed around him like bees around a hive. They bombarded him with questions or asked for autographs. Brody obliged with patience and kindness.

In the end, Alan was arrested for violation of the order of protection, assault on a minor, and attempted kidnapping. Bryn didn't think the latter would hold, but it was enough to keep him locked up without bail.

\*\*\*\*

"Want to stop to get something to eat?" Brody glanced in the back seat and then at me as we headed home. It was past lunch, and I had not eaten in a long time. I should have been hungry, but I was far from even one stomach growl.

"No." Josie yawned out. "I had a great stale sandwich at the station."

"Delicious." Brody darted a look at me. Smiled. He looked at me. "You want something, sugs?"

"No. Thank you." I gazed out the window and tried to keep everything in me together.

"You sure?"

"I said no," I snapped.

"Got it." Brody drove his Jeep nearer my home.

"I thought since you—"

"Damn it, Brody. I said no." A tear streaked down my check.

"Got it," he repeated, this time in a whisper.

When we pulled up in front of my house, Josie jumped out of the car and ran into the arms of Nonnie, who waited on the front porch. With an arm draped around Josie, they walked into the house.

I was unable to move. Nausea racked my body. I gulped in large swallows of air in an effort to calm myself.

"Hey." Brody opened my door and squatted in front of me. "You are both home. You're safe."

"I never wanted to see him again," I said. "And I'm sorry."

"For what?"

"For the way I've acted. I was—" My head fell

back, too exhausted to get out any more words.

"I get it."

I looked up at Brody, and for the first time, I noticed a split lip and a bruise forming under his left eye. "And I'm sorry you got hurt." I reached up and ran my fingertips over both.

"What? These? Ah, they were lucky shots." He smiled. I glanced down to my lap. "Sugar, it's okay."

"Don't." I held up my hand as I struggled to get out of my seat.

"It is. It'll all be okay—"

"That's not it." I propelled out of the car and ran to the front. Violent spasms racked my body. I held onto the bumper while I vomited. The two bites of Brody's sandwich, sips of lemonade hours before, and the colas I drank at the station, emptied out of me. After I had nothing left, my body convulsed in dry heaves. One of Brody's hand caressed my back while his other held back my hair. When I finished, I turned and fell back on the hood. Brody went to the car and came back with tissues and a bottle of water.

"You good?" He handed over both to me.

"No." And then the tears broke. "No. I know what he can do. She could have…and then I…" My thoughts scrambled.

"Oh, sugar." Brody grabbed me into him and stroked my hair. He spoke with the gentleness of a mother comforting her newborn baby. "He didn't. She's home. You're home. It's good. I promise. He will never hurt you or Josie or Gracie again."

"Brody, I was so scared." My body shook with sobs.

"I know, Harper. I know."

We stood like this for a long time. I didn't want to move. At that moment, I was being cared for, and I wanted to be shielded from the world. Yes, how I got here was messed up, but the ending felt so right. For a moment, that scared me more.

## Chapter Twenty-Two
## Finding My Needs

"Do you want some more coffee, Brody?" Nonnie asked.

"Sure, if it's no trouble."

"No trouble at all."

An hour had passed since I washed the anxiety and nerves that spewed out of me off the driveway and Brody's car. Brody wanted to help, but I insisted on doing it alone. He went inside and waited for me. After I took a quick shower, I checked on Grace. She made get-well cards for Josie after I explained the night to her. I included the black eye. I didn't go into great details, but I did tell her the truth. It was something Sabrina always stressed.

Gracie cried and wondered how her dad could be so mean. I told her because he was an angry man. I told her all of this was his fault, not Josie's. None of this was Josie's fault. I ended the conversation with reassurance Josie was safe; we were all safe.

I joined Nonnie and Brody at my kitchen table. Josie went to her room the minute she came home, probably from exhaustion and avoidance. I let her be, too fatigued myself to have a difficult and messed-up discussion.

Nonnie, Brody, and I sat around the kitchen table, each lost in our thoughts. I tried to push away the horrific what-ifs and wondered what punishment to dole out. Josie was already a wreck from what happened. I questioned whether she punished herself enough. Nonnie looked out the window and shook her head, probably contemplating what she could have done differently. She sighed every now and then before she took a sip of coffee. Brody stared down at his coffee and glanced at me from time to time.

I pointed to Brody's cup. "You know, that shit will eventually eat away at your stomach."

"Says the woman who drinks cola every morning."

"Well, at least my stomach will be eaten away by something that tastes good."

"Nonnie…" Brody shook his head. "When will she ever learn about the wonderful taste from this nectar of the gods?"

Nonnie smiled, but it was weak and forced.

"Hey." I reached over and picked up her hand. "Stop beating yourself up. Josie is the one who snuck out."

"If I slept on the couch or—"

"Stop it, okay? She probably would have figured something out." My anger toward Nonnie waned, especially when I saw the pain in her eyes. I began to believe Josie's determination to see Alan was what got her into the mess, and Nonnie probably couldn't have prevented her.

"He's such a monster." Nonnie sniffed.

The hands of the clock ticked away time and filled the kitchen as each of us went back to our own silent worlds.

"Brody." I cracked our silence once again. "You don't need to stick around."

"Are you telling me to leave?"

"No." I hesitated. "Not if you don't want to."

"Sugar, if you want me to leave, I will leave."

"Without being angry?"

"Jesus. If I get angry, I would never react the same way as the ass...um, jerk of an ex did." Brody spluttered. "This is your house. Tell me what you want. If I get mad, it's on me, not you. Don't try to please everyone else, especially over yourself. And don't walk around life scared because of one incredibly messed-up and cowardly man."

"Don't lecture me, Brody." I chided. I went to the sink and dumped my cola mixture into it. This morning, it tasted rancid from the bitterness stuck in my throat. "I don't need your lectures."

"I wasn't trying to—"

"I will do what I damn well please and say what I damn well want." I scowled and cut a glare at him. "You are not my rescuer. I don't need one. I don't need a shining knight on a white horse. I can take care of myself."

"I know. You can and—"

"And what happened last night, this morning—I could have done this all by myself, without your help and without you going all caveman on him."

"I know." His voice remained calm, which pissed me off even more.

"And just because you drove me to pick up Josie, and did whatever you did to Alan, does not give you the right to tell me what I can't do or say or think. I won't take it anymore. Not from you, not from anyone."

"Great," Brody exclaimed as he jumped up. "About time."

"What the hell does that mean?" I held up my hand. "Never mind. I don't care. Forget it. Can you please leave?"

"I can, and I will." Brody nodded.

"Harper," Nonnie said, in a soft, yet stern, voice. "He did some very nice things for you. You don't have to yell at him. He's probably tired. Maybe he should lie down somewhere and take a nap."

"No, Nonnie. I am fine to drive home, but thank you." Brody bent down and kissed her cheek. My belly flipped, and my resolve weakened.

"What the fuck happened?" Hayden rushed into the kitchen, his eyes wild with anger. "Did Alan hit you? Are you okay? Nonnie said Josie snuck out to see Alan, and you went there, too?"

"Yes, she did and—"

"Oh fuck. She's hurt, isn't she? I know she's hurt. If he laid a hand on her—" Hayden ran a hand through his curls.

"He did, but—"

"I'm outta here," Hayden shouted. "I'm gonna fuck him up."

"Hayden." Nonnie stood up and grabbed took my brother's hands into hers. "Hayden, stop. You don't even know where you're going. Besides, it's over. Alan's in jail."

"In jail? What the hell happened?" His eyes were crazy with anger as they shot from me to Nonnie.

I pointed to an empty chair. "Sit down. I'll explain, but first, you need to calm down."

Hayden grabbed a chair, turned it around and straddled it. He noticed Brody for the first time. He stared at the bruise below his eye and his cut lip and then his eyes fixated on Brody's knuckles. "You were there?"

"Yup."

"And did you give better than you got?"

"Yup," Brody answered and rocked back on his heels.

"*He's* all sort of beat up. Cool, huh?" Josie came into the kitchen, her hair in a haphazard ponytail. She wore pajama bottoms and a T-shirt a size too small for her. She looked like a little girl again, and I wanted to swoop her up, only she was taller than me. "And what's up with all the yelling? Can't a girl get any sleep around here?"

"Damn, Josie." Hayden jumped up to grab Josie into a hug. When she tried to break away, he pulled her in closer.

"Stop, I'm okay, Uncle Hayden. I'm okay." Josie pushed at him. "Right, Mom?"

"You are." I tugged on her ponytail. "Uncle Hayden needs to stop being over dramatic and worrying you. He needs to let you go."

"Shit. Right. Sorry." Hayden released Josie and kissed the top of her head. "I wish I was there."

"Well, Brody was there," Josie said.

"Uh-huh." Hayden eyed Brody. "Thanks."

"Yup." Brody stared at the floor.

"Josie, Brody is not proud of what he did, are you?" When Brody didn't respond, I nudged him. "Are you?"

"Well, um."

"Brody." I put my hands on my hips. "Violence against violence is not the answer. It's never the answer."

"But he deserved it." Josie looked at her uncle. "Right?"

"Damn right." Hayden grinned.

"Listen, Josie." Brody let out a deep breath and ran a hand through his hair. "Your mom's right. What your father did—"

"What *he* did. He's not my father. Not anymore."

"What *he* did was wrong."

"It was," Josie agreed.

"Right. But how it turned out—" Brody started.

"You mean how you beat the crap out of him?" Josie asked dryly.

"Josie." I did not want her to get a kick out of another human hurt, not even a monster like Alan. I had been on the receiving end and, and, and, okay. Part of me rejoiced when I saw a messed-up Alan crumpled on the floor, but I didn't want a thirteen-year-old to be happy about it. It wasn't right.

"Mom." Josie mimicked me.

"Josie, what happened is I lost my temper," Brody said. "I don't normally lose it, but I saw the way he treated your mother, and what he said about her—"

"What did he say?" Josie and I asked in unison.

"It doesn't matter. What matters is your mom is right. You—" Brody exhaled. "Ah, hell, I can't do this. He deserved it."

"Abso-friggin-lutely." Hayden laughed.

"Josie, Brody should not have punched your...*him*." I cut a look from Brody to Hayden.

"Officially, he fell," Brody corrected me.

"He should have let Officer Tanner and her partner handle the situation," I said between gritted teeth as I narrowed my eyes at Brody. "Violence is not the answer and—"

"Mom, I know." Josie laid a hand on my forearm. "I know punching someone or slapping or yelling or anything else to make a person feel less than, is not right. I know because you tell Gracie and me this all the time. And I know Brody doesn't normally get mad. I get it. I do, and I won't go around thinking hitting is cool. And I know Brody doesn't punch all the people he gets angry at. So, stop, okay?"

"Josie, I—"

"Mom, please."

"Okay." I let out a long breath between puffed cheeks.

"Now can I go over to Maggie's house?" When I squinted a look at her, Josie held up her hands. "I kid. I kid. I don't think I'll see the outside of this house for quite a while."

"I think maybe when you get into high school." I rubbed her arm.

"Funny, Mother."

"Don't think for a minute I'm kidding." I pointed at her.

"Uncle Hayden, you should have seen Brody's sister, Bryn." Josie ignored me. "I don't know why she came, but man, she was the bomb."

"Yeah." I looked at Brody with suspicion. "How did she get there?"

"I texted her while we drove there." Brody cringed. "I know. I know. It's wrong to text and drive. Josie, don't ever do that."

"No worries. I won't." Josie looked at him as if a second head sprung out of his shoulder. "That's just stupid."

I snorted out a laugh. "Yes, it is."

"Anyway, she's an FBI agent and really badass, Uncle Hayden." Josie sat down and held Nonnie's hand. My heart jumped from the gesture.

"Really?" Hayden looked at Brody.

"I'm afraid of her." Brody smirked. He put down his coffee mug and headed toward the back door. "And Harper asked me to leave a while ago. I'm heading out."

"You don't have to leave," I said.

"Do you want me stay?"

"Um, well—"

"Harper." Brody lifted my chin. "Don't make me lecture you again."

I smiled. "I suppose we've had too many boring monologues this morning."

"I suppose we have." He smiled back, bent down and planted a quick, soft kiss on my lips.

"Oooo, look at the two of yooouuu," Josie said.

"Bye, Joze." Brody grinned.

"Bye, Brodes. Thanks for the beatdown of *him*," Josie said. When I looked at Josie, her eyes grew big. "What?"

"You are not out of the woods. You and I, Miss Josephine, have lots to talk about," I said, then turned to looked at Brody. "But first, let me walk you out."

"Hayden." Nonnie stood. "Why don't you and I go see what our Gracie Girl is up to?"

"Nope. I want to be part of Josie's and Harper's conversation." Hayden didn't budge.

"Oh, no. It's between them." Nonnie tugged on my brother's shirt sleeve.

"Yes, ma'am." Hayden rose.

"And don't come here again using such foul language." Nonnie wagged a finger at him.

"Sorry, ma'am." He kissed her cheek. "Do you know you're beautiful when you admonish me?"

"Oh, you." She smiled and patted his arm. A blush colored her face.

Hayden held out his hand out to Brody. "Thanks again for taking care of them."

"All I did was—" Brody stopped and took Hayden's hand a shake. "You're welcome."

"Hey," Josie called after me, "how long do I have to sit there?"

"Really, Josephine." I stared into her eyes, kept my voice controlled and stern. "You don't want to push me right now."

"Yes, ma'am." Josie looked down at her hands.

****

Brody and I walked to his Jeep in silence. I turned to him when I reached it.

"Thank you, Brody." A quiver crept into my voice, and I swallowed hard. "I appreciate all your help. I know I was a bitch to you, and I'm sorry."

Brody peered into my eyes without a word.

"Okay, this is where you jump in and say I was not a bitch, and all is forgiven." I laughed weakly. A car passed, and I watched it drive down the street. I knew what I had to say, and I didn't want to look at Brody when I said it. "You know, we have to go back to being just friends, right?"

"I figured."

I looked down the now empty street. "To be more would be too complicated. All I can handle in my messed-up life right now, you know."

"Okay."

"I mean it. Us, what we did last night, it won't, it can't, happen again. I don't need someone to swoop in and be my savior. I got this."

"Shit. And here I thought rescuing Josie could be our thing."

"You know what I mean," I snorted. "I can stand the friendship between us, but nothing else."

"Well, as long as you can *stand* it."

"I'm serious."

"You know, you're trying awfully hard to convince yourself."

"No, I'm not." Was I? No, I wasn't. "I mean—"

"Momma," Gracie called from the bathroom window on the second floor. She peered down on us. "Oh, why hello Mithter Brody."

"Hi, Gracie." Brody waved up.

"What'cha need?" I shielded my eyes from the sun as I looked up.

"Well, you thsee, I went lotths of poo-poos. I mean, lotths. I don't think I got it all off my butt. Can you help me finish? And I think my undieths need to be changed, too."

"I will be right there," I called back and turned to Brody. "See, this is my life. Look at all my baggage. Why would you even—-" I exhaled. "Brody, I am wrangling in a pretty wild teen, wiping the butt of a five-year-old, dealing with a shitty ex, breaking up with a boyfriend, and—"

"I get it, Harper. You've got a lot on your plate." Brody opened the door of his Jeep and leaned on it. "I am good with your break up with Randy. The Josie thing looks like it is being handled and handled well.

But—"

"But?" I nodded. "See, I knew there'd be a *but*."

"But if you don't wash your hands after wiping Gracie, I think we would have a huge problem."

"Jerk." I pushed at his chest. He caught my hand in his.

"Harper, I understand why you were angry today. I do, and I am okay on how you took it out on me. Hell, I expected it. In all honesty, I liked it. It meant you were comfortable with me. And I'm also okay with all the so-called baggage you bring to this relationship."

"There is no relationship, Brody."

"Okay, this friendship. What I have a problem with is your refusal to let anyone in your life, not let me in your life. You say you want friendship, but it's on your terms." He shook his head, and his voice grew tired. "You're terrified to open yourself up and to feel, to feel good. You're used to the sucky parts of life. You actually think it's normal. And, God forbid, you let me—"

"Don't say *take care of you* because I don't need or want anyone to take care of me. I went down the road of being taken care of, and I cannot go back there. The entire reason I married Alan was because I thought he would take care of me after the shitty job Kathy did with her kids. I liked it, wanted it, maybe needed it, especially after a lifetime of—" I didn't want to finish. It would have been selfish.

"Of taking care of Hannah and Hayden."

"I didn't say that."

"You didn't have to. And now you take care of Nonnie and the girls. You *still* think you need to take care of Hannah and Hayden. How exhausted you must

320

be. Sometimes it's good to share the load, ya know? Or maybe let someone comfort *you*, take care for *you*, make *you* feel good, like a woman. Hell, make you come."

"Brody." I flushed from embarrassment.

"Am I wrong?" Brody placed a soft, gentle kiss on my cheek.

"Call me when you get back to your place."

"I will." He got in his Jeep and took off without a glance backward. As I watched Brody's Jeep disappear down the street, I thought about what he said and knew he didn't understand. He didn't have the same commitments I did so it was easy for him to judge my choices. He didn't have a clue what my life was like. Yet part of me knew he was right. Perhaps the time came to take a closer look at my own needs and desires.

I stood in the driveway, needing to dance and have a cigarette. The next wail of my name crushed my hope for either.

"Moooommmmmmmmmmaaaaaaa, I need you."

"Of course, you do," I said to myself but yelled back, "Be right there, Gracie Girl."

Chapter Twenty-Three
Don't Box Me In

"You really took a leave from work? For how long?" Hannah asked.

She came over for dinner, and I put her to work. She chopped onions, and I stirred taco seasoning into the ground beef cooking on the stove. It had been five days since what Nonnie and I labeled "the second Josie incident." In those five days, I decided to take a leave of absence from Noteah Middle School.

During Josie's therapy session with Sabrina, it became clear Josie wasn't okay with her father or his abuse. In her sardonic, I'm-tough-everything-is-okay way, she hid it well, but not well enough for Sabrina— one of the many reasons I liked her. After an hour of our family session together, three obvious conclusions came to all of us.

First, Josie required an intensive day therapy program for teens to sort out all her emotions (Sabrina's conclusion). Second, I had to be available to drive her, Monday through Friday, forty minutes one way, and to be part of the family sessions (my conclusion). And third, Josie needed to be open and use every resource available, including me, to help her over this incredibly large hump (interestingly, Josie's conclusion). A leave of absence would also allow more opportunities for me to see Sabrina to sort out my own life and repair some of the old wounds split open.

The hoops I jumped through and the paperwork I filled out for a leave of absence were enough to change my reason from "daughter's medical needs" to "Harper McReynolds' medical needs." It took three days, but I finally received the approval.

"Yes, I'm really on leave, Hanny. For how long, I don't know. I suppose for however long it takes. I have accumulated eight weeks of paid vacation and sick time. I will still have money coming in until past the end of the year."

"But what if it takes longer? Then what?"

I knew Hannah meant well. But I wanted to snap a snarky response of *Huh, I haven't thought about it taking longer. I mean, why would I? I'm just the mother and the financial provider.* Instead, I replied, "I'll worry about it then. It might not take too long."

"What if it is longer?"

I teetered on the brink of trading in my sarcasm for a good old-fashioned scream. For once, I wanted Hannah to listen, or even tell me it will be all right, and not repeat all the fears I carried. I didn't want to relieve *her* anxiety, instead of my own.

I talked to Nonnie before I made my decision. She listened, agreed it was the best decision, and told me it would all work out. Yet her heart wasn't in her words. She couldn't let go of blame in everything that happened to Josie. Guilt festered in her, like fermented cranberries two weeks after Thanksgiving, which brought me to an opening to change my subject.

"Did Nonnie tell you she's going to Florida for Thanksgiving to be with Mona?"

"She did. I am happy for her. They haven't seen

each other in forever." Hannah looked at me. "So, you're good with all of this. "

"Stop it, Hanny. Just stop it."

"You're crabby. I get it. You've gone through a lot." Hannah finally said some words I needed to hear. "Have you talked to Brody recently?"

"Why the hell would you even ask?" I banged the wooden spoon on the pan to release some of the meat, and some of my tension.

"Nonnie said—" Hannah's words dropped. She stared at the chopped onions like they were going to applaud her for a job well done.

"Nonnie said what?"

Hannah shrugged. "Well, she said you were, I don't know, rude to him. You pushed him back after he helped you and—"

"And nothing. I didn't push him back. I told him I can handle what I need to handle on my own. I don't need anyone's help."

"Sounds like a push back to me." Hannah nodded at her own words.

"Hannah, you don't understand."

"I don't, but I think part of your crabbiness is because of—" She scraped the onions off the chopping block into a bowl and started cutting tomatoes. "Never mind."

"Because of what? Because of him? Brody Reed does not break or make my moods, Hannah. Unbelievable," I scoffed. "And I'm glad since I haven't heard from him in four days. Oh sure, there were some texts here and there, but nothing substantial, only *good morning, busy day* type of texts."

"No, I thought—"

"Oh, you thought. What? Do you think he would cause me to get all crabby because he saw the shittiest part of my life and hasn't talked to me since? Or because he slept with me and—"

No, no, no, no, no, noooooooooo. I shouldn't have said it. I wasn't going to say it. It was no one's business. As far as anyone knew, Brody and I were friends. Crap. Shit. Crappy shit.

"What?" Hannah stopped chopping. She ran to me, grabbed my hand, pulled me away from the stove, and forced me to sit down.

"Hannah, I don't want to do this. We have a meal to—"

"It can wait."

"It'll burn."

"If it does, I have a coupon for a free pizza." Hannah flapped an unconcerned hand. "Now, what are you talking about? You slept with Brody?"

I never lied to my sister. Besides, how was I going to get out of the incredibly big hole I dug with my incredibly big mouth? I sighed. "I did."

"Oh." A lazy smile began to form on Hannah's face.

"It was stupid, so stupid." I rubbed my hands over my face.

"Was it good?"

"It *was* good, so good, but soooo stupid."

"But so good, right?"

"Not the point." I shook my head. "It should never have happened. I had this idea of a reprieve from our bet. We were both having shitty times for all sorts of reasons. I asked him, well, I implied I wanted to have sex, but only for the night, as a break, and then we

325

could move on. I only wanted a release, you know? And then he doesn't call. Typical."

"Well, maybe—"

"I called him and left three messages, and all he does is text back? What the hell? I mean, sure, texting is the new way of talking, but we used to talk all the time. And his texts were lame. Well, I'm done. I'm not calling or texting him. Done."

"Done. Sure."

"It was idiotic in the first place." I sneered. "Like Brody Reed could have sex with me and then resume our friendship. He got what he wanted. I'm an idiot, a fucking idiot."

"But he was good, right?"

"Stop. Yes. It was mind-blowing, the best-ever sex. I mean, I didn't see stars, I saw galaxies." I shut my eyes for a long pause, then popped them back open. "But it doesn't matter now. Brody Reed got what he wanted, and then saw my ugly. Now he's happy with what he got. He doesn't want to be part of my messed-up life. I mean, why would he call?"

"Do you really think he used you?" Hannah's squinted in confusion.

"Yes! Brody Reed absolutely used me. He's scared, which only shows how immature he is, and I don't need a boy in my life." I released the built-up rage inside me. "He seduced me, Hanny. Me. Harper McReynolds. The one woman who swore she would never have sex with him, but I caved. Oh, boy, did I cave. Doesn't matter. We're done."

When I said the words aloud, the ones I pushed back far too many times, I almost cried, almost, but I wouldn't allow myself to cry over Brody Reed.

"Okay, if you're sure." Hannah didn't sound convinced. "Do you think he liked it, you know, the sex, as much as you?"

"I poured out my heart, and that's your question?"

"Well, do you?"

"I don't know." I shrugged. "He said he did."

"He wouldn't lie." Harper finished the onions and looked over at me. "You know, Harper, Brody's not scared because if he were, he wouldn't have stayed with you as long as he did. He would have hightailed it out of here and not even texted you. His actions were pretty damn mature."

"Shut up. You don't know what Brody would have done."

"And seduction? Ask yourself, what was *your* reason for going to the bar the other night?"

"I'm not a slut," I shot back at her.

"I never said you were." Hanny laughed. "But maybe you used him."

"But maybe you used him," I mimicked.

"All I am saying is maybe he's waiting for you to talk about it. Maybe he's confused about everything, including the intimacy, but especially about how you pulled back. Maybe you need to talk to him about what happened. And while you're at it, maybe you need to thank him for being there and being a good friend to you."

"I did."

"Not according to Nonnie.

"Nonnie was not with us when I walked him out."

"So, you did?" Hannah asked. "You told him thank you at the car? Was that before or after you told him he should go home the entire time he drank his coffee?

327

What kind of mixed signals are you giving there, Harp?"

"You're supposed to be on my side."

"I am, but not when you're wrong, very wrong. You ruined a completely great friendship."

"Yeah, well." I stared at her, not knowing what to say.

"Yeah? Well?" She lifted an eyebrow.

"I hate when Nonnie talks to you." I walked over to the stove and began stirring again. "Damn it, Hannah. The meat burned."

"Pizza it is."

\*\*\*\*

It rained Halloween. The weather did not cooperate with Gracie's decision to be a grape. I banked on Princess Penelope, but as always, Gracie surprised me. I designed her costume out of white garbage bags painted purple and a green shower cap for the stem. With the rain, the paint streaked, and Gracie became a faded grape. It didn't matter. Gracie loved it. She canvassed two more blocks than the previous year, but far less than what Josie covered at Gracie's age.

Josie sat Halloween out, feeling too old to go trick-or-treating. With all she had been through, perhaps her innocence *was* lost. She stayed home and passed out candy with Nonnie.

While I walked with Hannah and my faded grape, I thought of Brody. I texted him a photo of Gracie in her costume. He texted back a very polite and short, *she looks great.* Gracie was excited Brody liked her costume, but I was miserable.

I wanted Brody back. I wanted our fun back. I wanted our talks back. I wanted to share with him everything going on with Josie, the good and the bad. I wanted a friend. I slept with my friend, and it sure ruined us. If I had been more flexible, I would have kicked myself in my own arse, as Brody's Da would have said.

In the beginning of her outpatient therapy program, Josie remained mostly silent during our drives there. Although sometimes, bursts of rage erupted from her which sent her into a fury of rants. But as therapy progressed, our trips became livelier and calmer.

Josie grew to like her counselor, Mark, a young twenty-something man, two or three years out of college. Josie said he was easy to talk with, and they enjoyed a lot of the same music, a massive plus in Josie's world.

Two weeks into therapy, when Josie kissed me goodbye, she looked me in the eyes and said, "Momma, thank you." I wanted to grab hold of her, pull her in, and rock her as if she were the eight-year-old girl I held onto when we left Alan. But I knew I needed to release her to her own journey. An emptiness tore a hole in my heart as I drove off. It may have been the reason I turned right instead of left onto the expressway. Although, I knew where I needed to go, where I was being pulled.

****

"Yup?" Brody's voice sent a warm calmness to my heart, the way gentle familiarity often does. One knot untied, and another one started.

"Hey." I spoke into the intercom attached to the gate's entrance. "I was in the neighborhood and—"

"In the neighborhood, huh?"

"Yes. I dropped off Josie and thought, why not

visit an old friend of mine. Brody, I think his name is, but not sure. It's been a while." I released the button and heard nothing in reply. I pressed it again. "If this is a bad time—"

"No, not a bad time." He let out a long breath. "Come on in."

"Maybe I should have called first."

"Sugar, come on in."

I parked on the driveway, in front of the garage. The memory of being in the garage, bent over Brody's motorcycle, sent a shiver over me and shook my body with surprise. "Damn it," I cursed and banged on the steering wheel.

Brody stood in the open doorway, his arm slung over the back of it. His bare chest showed off a sexy golden dusting on his chest. The hair disappeared into the waistband of a pair of black sweatpants. When I saw a sculpted v on his hips with two, thick veins, I stuffed my hands in my pockets to stop them from touching his rock-hard abs. His hair was pulled back and revealed fatigue in his gray wolf-like eyes. The bruise over his eye was gone, and the cracked lip vanished like a bad memory.

"Hi." I breathed out.

"Hi."

"Hi," I repeated.

"You look nervous."

"You look tired."

"I am." Without saying more, he stepped to one side as an offer for me to come in.

"Thanks."

We spoke to each other as if we just met and not like the lovers we were weeks ago. Moxy and Fifi pranced toward me. Their tails wagged in familiarity. I crouched to pet them. Their zealous affection made it difficult to stay upright.

I snorted out a laugh and looked up at Brody. A small smile showed off the start of dimples not even the growth of his beard could hide.

"Okay, girls," he said, and snapped his fingers. He pointed to the front room and the dogs retreated but not before they gave me one last lick.

"Want something to drink?" Brody pulled a T-shirt off the back of his chair and slipped it on. I swallowed disappointment.

"Water would be good." I struggled to stand upright. "You know, I don't do coffee."

"Yup." Nothing else but "yup." The joke we usually shared about coffee went left untouched. He opened his cabinets and took down two cups.

"Did I interrupt anything, Brodes?"

"No, just finished my workout."

"Kickboxing, right?"

"Yup." He shot me a side glance. "Ya gonna keep your coat on?"

"What?" I looked down. "Oh, no."

He filled both cups with water from the refrigerator's dispenser. He handed me one and downed half of his in one gulp. He looked over at me. "Still got your coat on."

"Damn it." When I took it off, Brody's eyes danced up and down my body as he took another long sip. "This is awkward, huh? We once talked nonstop, and now—"

"Why are you here, Harper?"

"To see how you're doing. It's been a month since

331

we talked. I mean, really talked. You know, since Alan."

"I know since when."

"I see the shiner's gone. You know, I still feel bad." I went to touch below his eye with my fingertips, but Brody recoiled. I dropped my hand.

He shrugged. "Had worse. No need to feel guilty. My decision."

"What did Alan say to you anyway? You never told me."

"Nothing." He played with his ear. "Besides, did he have to say *anything*?"

"You know you touch your ear when you lie."

"Nice to know next time I play poker." He put down his cup. "You gonna tell me why you're here?"

"What's going on with you? Why haven't you called me?"

"I've been texting."

"Not much. Why haven't you called?"

"Because."

"Because? Oh well, since it is *because*." I grabbed my coat and pushed my arms into the sleeves. "This was a shitty idea to come over here."

"Why are you upset?"

"I'm not upset."

"No?"

"No." I rubbed my nose with the back of my hand.

"Do you know you wipe your nose when you lie?"

"Well, now we know each other's tell. We can never play poker together, huh?"

"You came all the way out here to say something, sugs. What is it?"

"It's not all the way out here. I dropped off Josie,

and you're like ten minutes away." Sure, it was in the opposite direction, but only ten minutes. I fought for my hand to stay at my side and not go near my nose.

"How's Josie doing? Does she like the place?"

"Fine and yes." I walked toward the door when Brody stepped in front of me. "Brody—"

"Tell me, sugar. Why did you come to see me?"

"Damn it." I swallowed back the tears. "I miss you. I miss our friendship. There were so many times these past couple of weeks where I wanted to talk with you. You are my friend, dammit, and I miss you, so much."

"Fuck." He looked up at the ceiling and closed his eyes.

"I told you my past was ugly. You got a good up-close and personal look at my ugly." I shook my head. "I knew it'd scare you."

"It didn't scare me. It pissed me off, but it didn't scare me. I don't scare easily."

"Okay, so if that wasn't it, what was?" I moved in closer. "Answer me this, did you really want to be my friend or did you—" I stopped and tried to distance myself.

"Did I what?" Brody grabbed my wrist.

"Did you get what you wanted from me?" I asked softly.

"Did I what?" He let go of my hand. I saw the hurt in his eyes. "You think I used you for sex?"

"What else am I supposed to think?" I let some tears slip out. "Why else did you suddenly stop being a friend? I mean, we were getting to be such great friends. Then, after we slept together, you pulled back."

"*I* pulled back? *I* pulled back. Classic." He clasped his hands on the back of his neck. "Harper, you were the one who told me you didn't need me."

"Well, I—"

"And you were the one who wanted sex in the first place. Wow." Brody's hands dropped as his voice raised. "What the hell do you want, Harper? Huh? What do you want from me? Tell me because I am more than a little confused here."

"Don't yell at me." I tried to hold back a shiver, but it escaped anyway.

"Fuck. God damnit, Harper. I already told you I'm not an asshole like Alan, Harper. I can raise my voice without hitting you. You've got to stop being afraid of me."

"I'm not." I knew the truth in those words, so I repeated them. "I'm not."

"Good." Brody let out a calming breath through his nostrils. His voice grew soft. "Good. So, tell me then, what do you want from me?"

"I don't know," I said.

"Well, I sure as fuck don't know either. You wanted sex and—"

"You didn't?"

"Hell, yeah I did."

"Then what's the problem?"

"The problem is—" He turned around and pressed against the countertops. His back muscles clench as he grabbed hold of the counter's lip. He inhaled deep. The next words were barely audible. "The problem is everything between us has been so fucked up—the friendship, the idiotic bet, the reprieve, the sex, telling me to back off, getting mad when I did, thinking I can't handle your shit, telling me I'm too young or a *playa*, when to call you, when not to call—you are driving me fucking nuts here."

"I know." I sat on a stool. "I'm driving myself fuckin' nuts."

"Sugar," Brody said. When he turned around, his eyes watered and his voice quivered. "I can't keep doing this. I can't keep trying to figure out what you want. You have too many roadblocks and too many rules. You don't let many people in, and I can't keep hoping I will be one of your chosen few."

"I don't mean—" I couldn't finish. If I did, I would be in tears, and not the delicate cry, but a blubbering, ugly full on wail. The truth was always the most dangerous weapon. I knew he used it to cut at the deepest parts of me. I knew my own truth from my conversation with Hannah. I knew it at Girls' Night In when Marti threw my lecture of friendship back at me. I didn't let people in. I knew this, only I didn't know how to change it.

"I know your shit past jailed all your trust, in anyone. I know it's not something you mean to do or can even control." There was sadness in his eyes. "And that's the hardest part. Hell, it's been harder than I thought. I haven't slept. I haven't written any music. Eating is not happening. All I do is beat the shit out of my punching bag and, sometimes, I let it win."

I snorted a short laugh. He gave me a strangled smile.

"Harper, I'm not sure I can keep going on with you, with us, with this friendship."

"Brody, I can't be with you the way you want me to. I need and want light from you. You're pushing me too hard, and I can't do it. I can't. My life is too messed up."

"Life is never easy. Life is messy, and the one perfect, clean moment may never come."

"Maybe not." A tear slipped down my cheek.

"Listen, I am done talking about this. I can't do or say anymore. I need space. I need—" Brody looked at the floor and then back at me. "I'll be going to Nashville tomorrow. I'll be gone for about a week, maybe more. We both should probably take this time away from each other to think."

"About?"

"What I want. What you want."

"I still want you, need you, in my life, but as a friend, only as a friend. I've told you this over and over."

"I know. I have to figure out if I want the same thing. I don't think it is."

I slipped off the stool. We stared at each other for a time. When Fifi barked at the noise of a passing car, it broke our connection.

"Bye, Brodes."

"Bye, sugs."

As I headed home, I glanced at my car's clock. An hour and a half remained before I had to pick up Josie. Although I did my forty-minute dance work out earlier that morning, I wanted to sneak in a few more minutes, maybe even a cigarette. I wanted to get rid of the feeling lying like a bowling ball in my stomach the moment I left Brody's house—the feeling that I lost my best friend.

## Chapter Twenty-Four
## Missing Him

"Why does it still matter to me? Why does he still matter?"

I cried into my pillow. I didn't want my girls to hear. Nonnie told me I moped around too much, and she was right. I wasn't really "there" when Gracie told me a story about Princess Penelope, but to be fair, not much changes in those stories. My only thought while Gracie rehashed her convoluted story was of Brody when he tried to follow one of Gracie's stories.

I struggled to listen to Josie's obsessive talk about music. When I forced myself to concentrate, my thoughts drifted to Brody, his voice, his music, and his talent. When Nonnie drank coffee in the morning, it reminded me of our jokes about coffee. The sight of cards sent me back to the night when Brody played Hearts. Even the swear jar created clouds in my eyes. Everything I saw, ate, did, all went back to a Brody memory. They made me smile, and then, made me miserable. I tried to hide my emotions from my girls. I didn't want them to worry about me, or worse, think they caused my unhappiness. Gracie picked up on my gloom and suggested I see a doctor to help me feel better. Instead, I saw Sabrina.

Sabrina listened, and in the end, she told me I needed to decide if I liked my seat on the pity pot, or if it was time for me to get off it. Sabrina also told me she agreed with Brody. It was time for me to divorce the past and move on with my life. It started with trusting other people.

"Want me to kick his ass?" Hayden lay on top of the covers next to me. He came over the night before to fix a broken pipe in Nonnie's basement. He was too tired to drive home, and Nonnie insisted Hayden spend the night. In the morning, he plopped down on my bed after hearing the cries I attempted to muffle into my pillow.

"Yes." I laughed between my sobs. "No."

"Well, make up your mind, Harpsichord," Hayden said. "And, by the way, you look awful."

"Thanks. Love you, too."

"No for real. Your face looks ridiculous. Do you still have your makeup on from last night?"

"Yes, she does, and I think it's Harper's ass you should kick." Hannah sprawled out on the other side of me. She spent the night with me and the girls. I pushed myself to dance, create hairstyles, put makeup on each other, play games, and paint toenails. I selected gray, the color of Brody's eyes. My forced efforts to have a good time was hard work. "And Gracie put the makeup on her last night."

"You do know Gracie is legally blind, right?" Hayden asked. Hannah laughed, and eventually, I joined in.

It felt good to laugh, even better to lie in bed with Hannah and Hayden like we did when we were kids, lying together as we waited for Hurricane Kathy to subside. When the signs of a storm began to brew, Hayden crawled into my bed, grabbing Hannah on his way. I drew pictures with my finger on his back to calm him down and sang to Hannah to get her back to sleep. The reasons behind our time in my bed were messed up, but the moments themselves bonded us.

"Thanks, Hannah, for letting Gracie decorate my face like a Pollock painting." I picked up my head from the pillow. "And for wanting Hayden to kick my ass."

"Why do you want me to kick our sister's ass?" Hayden hiked himself up with his elbows.

"She's the one who pushed Brody away, and now that he's away, she's all mopey. She's been mopey for this past week. I'm glad she finally cried about it. I wish she would have done it sooner." Hannah hoisted herself up to get a better look at Hayden and talked over me. "I mean, she has to decide what she wants."

"She damn well does," Hayden agreed.

"Um, I'm right here." I passed my hand between their faces.

"Well, you have to decide what you want." Hannah fell back down onto her pillow.

"You have no idea what you're talking about." I rolled onto my back and looked up at the ceiling. "This isn't all about Brody. It has been a rough couple of weeks, you know? This is pent-up emotion."

"Oh, Harper." Hannah turned on her side to face me. She grabbed my hand and played with my fingers. "But that's not what's bothering you. What's bothering you is Brody."

"You think so, huh?"

"I know so. You're not a crier," Hannah pointed out. "Something big has to happen for you to shed tears. Brody is the big happening."

"Eat shit and die," I snapped back, reverting to the

teenage girl I remembered lying there. Hannah was right. She did know me, too well.

"Good one." Sarcasm dripped from Hayden's mouth.

"You, too." I punched his arm.

"Oh, Mother." The bed moved when Josie plopped down at the edge of my bed. "You need to watch your language."

"Why are you up so early?" I peered down at her.

"How can I sleep with all the profanity coming from this room? I mean." She pursed her mouth like a librarian admonishing a loud patron. "Also, I heard a car drive by like six million times."

"I didn't hear anything." I sat up. My arms supported my upper half.

"Because you were too busy telling Aunt Hannah to eat shit and die," Josie said in mock disdain. "I think it was Brody's."

"You think what's Brody's?" Hannah joined me in my sitting-up position.

"The car driving by. I think it was Brody's. I don't know for sure, but when I looked out the window, I saw a red Jeep, like his."

"Brody is stalking you." Hannah laughed before she dropped back down to the bed. "Didn't he say he had good stalking moves?"

"Shhh." I climbed over Hayden to get out of bed and put my ear to the window.

"What'cha doing there, Sherlock?" Hayden asked.

"You shush, too." I listened closer and heard a car pull into the driveway. I peeked out a small opening in my bedroom shades. "Shit. Damn. Crap. And shit again."

"Mother," Josie admonished, shaking her head, and looked at Hayden. "And I thought I raised you better."

"These young kids nowadays." Hayden joined her in the head shaking.

"It's him." I ignored my bobble-headed daughter and brother. "It's Brody."

"Well, go down and say something." Hannah screamed.

"Should I?" I asked.

"Yes." She jumped up and pushed me toward the door. "Go."

"I only have on my pajamas."

"It doesn't matter." Hannah handed me my robe and gave me one last push. "Go. Now. You'll regret it if you don't."

"I look like I...I mean, Hayden even said I look..." I grabbed my robe from Hannah.

"*Go.*" Hannah pointed to the doorway. "And fast unless you want him to leave."

I took off down the hall and raced down the stairs as if I were in an Olympic trial run. I dodged shoes, the newspapers waiting to go into the recycling bin, and a bottle of detergent waiting to be brought down with the laundry. I jumped over Hayden's tools on the landing. I weaved out of Nonnie's way as she walked up the stairs. I ran toward Brody's car, my robe flew behind me like a superhero's cape.

Brody opened his door to get back in when I bellowed, "Brody. Wait." His eyes widened at the sight of me. Maybe it was how disheveled I looked, especially with last night's makeover from Gracie still on my face.

"Harper, I don't want to talk."

"Well, too bad." I thumped my bare feet against the pavement as I neared him. "But I need to talk to you."

"Harper, go in."

"No." I shoved his hard chest. He didn't move. "And don't tell me what to do."

Brody looked down at his chest, then back at me and cocked one eyebrow. Damn. He was sexier than ever.

"Why are you here, Brody, driving up and down my street like some teenager trying to get my attention? Well, you got it, especially since you pulled into my driveway and—"

"I left my, well, technically, your, cowboy boots on your back porch." He ran his hand through this hair and kept it at the back of his neck.

"You what?"

"I know you heard me." His hands dropped to his side. "I lost the bet, Harper, okay? I can't be your friend."

My heart stopped and blood dropped to my feet. I grabbed the passenger door handle to keep me upright.

"You okay?" Brody grabbed for my elbow, and I yanked it back.

"No. I'm not okay." I moved up into him, my face a few inches away from his minty breath fanning over my cheeks. "You denied all you wanted from me was sex, but I know differently. What a piece of work you are."

"You really think it was about sex for me?" His jaw moved back and forth.

"You're proving it now." I raised my hands up in exasperation.

"Damn it. I thought we had this conversation."

"It doesn't matter anyway," I said. "I knew it wouldn't work anyway. You don't want my kids, so having a friendship with a woman with kids, well, it's too much of an inconvenience now, isn't it?"

"What the hell are you talking about?"

"I know." I narrowed my eyes. "Bryn told me. I know."

"Well, I don't. Told you what?"

"Bryn told me at Marti's that one night about what you said."

"Sugar, I say lots of things to Bryn."

"Like you don't need kids to complete your life?" I asked.

"Sure." Brody tilted his head like a puppy hearing a noise.

"Sure? You're admitting it? I have kids, Brody."

"That's what they are?" He slapped his palm on his forehead. "Thank you. I thought they were hired actresses."

"It's not funny, Brody."

"I know." Brody's voice raised. He ran a hand through the stubble of his beard to calm himself. "Listen, I said I didn't need kids to complete my life."

"I know. I heard."

"Did you also hear there was a *but*?"

"A what?"

"A *but*. I also said, '*but* your kids are great.' They're wonderful in fact, full of spirit. And I said, when I met your kids, kids who were fun and smart and kids I liked, a lot, I changed my mind."

"Oh," I said. I sent a silent prayer to the god of circles to create one large enough to swallow me up.

"Yeah, oh." Brody released the door and walked

around in a circle. Maybe the god heard me wrong. When Brody stopped, he spoke in a voice so loud, it probably woke the neighbors two blocks down. "First you think I'm Alan, and I want to hit you. Now, you think I'm Randall, and I don't want kids. Do you need to think poorly of me, or do you just want to?"

"Everything okay out here?" Hayden came outside and stood up straight, like an alpha male.

"Yes." I could have snapped a branch with my quick, loud response.

"No." Brody shot back without unlocking his eyes from me.

"Harper?" Hayden was ready to charge.

"It's fine." I held up my hands, hoping it would be enough to hold off his approach. "I'm fine."

"You sure?"

"Yes, Hayden, I am sure." I relaxed my tone.

"Okay, call if you need me," Hayden said before he went back inside.

"And now he thinks I'm an asshole, too?" Hurt darkened Brody's eyes. My stomach clenched in pain. "Harper, I can't take much more of you thinking bad about me. I've done enough shitty things in my life, real things, to feel bad about. I don't need you to add pretend ones to my list."

"I don't think you are bad."

"Yeah, ya do." Brody narrowed his eyes.

"No. I really don't. It's just—"

"But let me straighten out some things. First, your past is shitty, and I'm not afraid of it or you. Second, because it seems I need to keep repeating this, I don't hit women, besides the occasional pinches and arm punches I gave my sister when we were young. Oh, and tripping Margaret Mulligan in first grade. I only wanted to tell her I liked her."

"Maybe flowers would have been better."

"Now you tell me." I snorted out a laugh. His face softened as did his words. "Third, I like your kids. I like them a lot. I like Gracie's crazy, zany ways, and her honest look at life. It's refreshing, and I hope she never loses it. I like Josie's humor, her independence, her I'm-not-gonna-take-any-shit approach to life, and I don't think she'll ever lose her spirit. I like your kids, and I like spending time with them."

"Thank you."

"You're welcome." He stared at me for a long minute before continuing. "The reason I haven't talked with you is because...because...ah, shit. I can't do this."

"Because?" I grabbed his arm.

"It's the same reason I gave you the boots. I lost my bet with you, sugar, not because I can't be your friend, but because I don't want to be *just* your friend. I'm in love with you, Harper. I am over the moon, completely and totally fucking in love with you. Not in like, or in lust, but in love." His voice shook, and tears fell. "I can't be around you, as just a friend. I can't. And I won't."

"I don't want to lose our friendship, Brody. I can't." My own tears I willed not to shed, came slipping down. "It'll be too hard without you."

"But it'll be even fucking harder for me to be with you." He got in his Jeep. Before he shut his door, he looked at me one last time. "I'm sorry, sugs. This past week, you are all I thought about. Hell, you're all I ever think about. I've tried to convince myself I can continue as your friend, but I can't, not while I'm in love with you. And I don't think I'll ever be out of love with you."

"Brody," I whispered his name in pain.

"And I gave you the boots to settle the bet. Don't try to see me again. It was too hard to look at you now. I can't do it again."

As I watched him drive away, my body convulsed in sobs. I fell to the ground, doubled over in agony. The backdoor slammed behind me. Hannah's arms wrapped around my body and held me while I wept. I sent out a wail of built-up tortured emotion. My brother stood beside us. His hand slid down the top of my head as if giving comfort to a wounded animal.

"Oh dear." Nonnie came out and joined us. She was unable to do more than stand beside me and rub my shoulder. "Oh dear," she repeated.

I looked up at her. "Nonnie, I hurt."

"I know you do, Harper," she said, weakly. "I do, too, for you."

"What happened?" Hannah brushed away my tears with her thumbs.

"He told me he loves me." I cried harder and fell into her chest. I struggled with my words. "I lost him, Hanny."

"Momma." Gracie yawned. I pulled myself together, as she crawled up into my lap and held up a pair of gray boots in her hand. "Why were thethe outthide the door? Whothe are they?"

"They were Brody's, but I suppose they're mine now." I fought off the shakes in my voice.

"Why are you crying, Momma?"

"I'm just sad." I kissed the top of her head.

"Why?"

"She's sad because Mr. Brody left, and she loves him." Everyone looked at Josie. "What? Am I the only one who can see it? Come on, people. It's obvious. She does."

"Momma?" Gracie twirled the ends of my hair.

"What, Gracie Girl?"

"Why ith there a roll of toilet paper in thith boot?"

I laughed through my tears.

Chapter Twenty-Five
Thanksgiving Knockout Fish

I stayed mopey and snappy—a snappy mope—the week of Thanksgiving. My usual, semi-calm self was replaced by a woman I didn't even know. Josie called me crabby pants. When I snapped at Gracie because she spilled a gallon of juice all over the floor, she yelled back I was acting like Lady Edie, Princess Penelope's mean aunt. In my defense, I told her three times I would get the juice; in her defense, Gracie thought she was helping.

I grew edgier when Nonnie left for Florida to spend Thanksgiving with Mona. It would be our first Thanksgiving without Nonnie in five years. I wanted to ask her to stay. I didn't, of course. I may have acted like Lady Edie, but I wasn't going to *become* Lady Edie.

It was the Wednesday night before Thanksgiving. Hayden took the girls to an early-evening movie to give me a break, and Josie and Gracie a break, from me. I rolled out the crust for the pumpkin and apple pies, when I announced to Hannah, "I'm done."

"Give me a minute. I still have about six more to cut." Hannah sliced another apple for the pie.

"No, I mean I'm done being a bitch." I grabbed a towel from the counter and wiped my hand. "I am done letting a man, any man, shape my mood or my life ever again. I did it with Alan. I did it with Randall. I'm not going to do it because of Brody. No more."

"Good for you, but from what I saw, you never changed anything for Brody. You just were. I don't think moving on from him is going to be that easy for you."

"But it should be, Hanny. I've been pissy at my kids. My kids. Even Gracie. What does that say about me?" I flung a dish towel over my shoulder.

"It says you're human." Hannah placed cut apples into a bowl filled with sugar and cinnamon. "With all the crap you and the girls have gone through in the past months or so, of course you were on edge. You were strong when it was happening. Now it's over, and everything caught up with you. Gracie and Josie are fine. You're the only one beating yourself up here."

"It shouldn't excuse me. I've been nasty."

"True, you have been nasty."

"Gee, thanks."

"What? I'm gonna lie?" Hannah shrugged. "All I am is saying is I remember how you used to act when you were angry. Do you know how many times you stood up to some random, prick guy Kathy brought home? You'd get all in his face and tell him off. You were filled with spunk, like Josie, until Alan."

"Who beat it out me."

"Right. And with Randall, you were just okay. I liked Randall. Remember, I was on the pro-Randall team. You were unafraid of Randall. You were content. You were safe. And okay. I thought Randall would be the one for you for selfish reasons."

"Hanny, you're not a selfish person."

"Sure, I am." She hesitated. "I'm going to say this but know I'm not proud of this. I was a little jealous of you with Brody."

"What?" I laughed in shock. "Jealous?"

"Come on, Brody is gorgeous. And maybe I had a little crush on him."

"Hannah, if you like Brody—"

"Of course, I like Brody, but not romantically. Not anymore. I said I had a crush on him. That's gone. I moved on to someone else which meant I am fickle, and I never really liked him in the first place."

"Who's the someone else?"

"It doesn't matter." She smiled with a thought of this mystery man. "Brody's good for you and you, my-always-trying-to-put-others-first sister, deserve someone like Brody. You came alive with him. You showed your spunk. You broke out of whatever shell Alan put you in and showed everyone who you are. I've been so happy to see the return of Harper McReynolds."

"You mean you like my being a nasty bitch?"

"Yes. Look, you love Brody, Harper. And not just as a friend. You...love...him. I know it. Nonnie knows it. Josie knows it. Hayden knows it. And Gracie guesses something is going on. We all see it. We're not stupid. Well, maybe Hayden." I hiccupped out a laugh. "You love Brody, probably more than anyone in your life besides your girls."

"Fuck." I screamed into the room.

"Fuck you love him? Or fuck you're mad at me? Or fuck you don't know what to do?"

"Yes."

"Well, if you're asking, I think maybe you should tell him."

"Tell him what? I'm crazy in love with him? I'm

350

pissed as hell I let him go? That I'm taking it out on everyone important in my life?"

"It's a start."

"Here's the thing I can't seem to get past, Hanny. He's younger than me. I have the girls to think about. I can't just pick up anytime I want and go to movies, or dinner dates, or weekend getaways, or all the other crap being a couple means. He can, but I can't. Brody might not want to spend all our time together with the girls."

"He might. You don't know. Besides, you don't have to spend all your time together with the girls. You know you have support. You have me and Hayden and Nonnie. We'd watch them. You know we would. Hell, even Marti and Esther would love to have them over."

"But I am ultimately responsible for raising them."

"Listen to yourself, Harp." Hannah's closed her eyes in frustration. "We're talking a few hours, maybe overnight or a weekend here and there. We're not talking like you're Kathy and will take off for days with no one to look after them."

"I know." I thought for a moment. "Okay, but what about how young and gorgeous Brody is? Huh? Don't you think he'll want to date more women than me? I'm not insecure. I'm not, Hannah. I'm too old to for casual, and what if I am casual to him?"

"He told you he loves you. He said he is in love with you. Seems pretty committed to me."

"Yeah. Maybe." I played with an apple in front of me. Time ticked away as Hannah returned to chopping apples. "It was very stupid of me to even to make the bet and—" I stopped mid-thought.

"And what?"

"That's it." I sprung from my chair and grabbed

Hannah's face. I smacked a kiss on her lips. "You, Hanny, are a genius."

"I am?"

"You am. Or I am. Or we am." I tapped a finger on my chin and paced the kitchen. "First, I'm gonna have to get Marti involved. She'll like being involved because she's all about girlfriends."

"What's going—"

"Oh shit. Before tomorrow, I'm also gonna have to find something in my closet's all knock-outy-ish."

"All what ish?"

"Never mind." I grabbed the phone. "Keep cutting the apples. I have to get some things ready beside the pies."

\*\*\*\*

"Wow," Hannah exclaimed. She and Josie sat on the edge of my bed as I walked out of the bathroom. "You do look knock-outy-ish."

"Exactly what I am going for."

I had three dresses in my closet considered knockouts. One was a purple dress I wore to all the Noteah Middle School Christmas parties. One was a yellow summer linen dress I purchased online for Declan and Marti's wedding. And one, the one I wore as I stood before Hannah and Josie, was a black wiggle dress polka-dotted with red cherries. It was the dress Nonnie wore on her first wedding anniversary. When she gave it to me, she asked me only to wear it on an extraordinary occasion. I believed this day fit the bill.

The dress clung to my body like a soft, second skin and showed the start of my cleavage. The dress was tasteful, yet sexy. The matching black and red peek-a-boo shoes completed my ensemble, my knockout ensemble.

"You do look good, Mom." Josie pulled on the neck of her sweater. "And why do we have to get dressed up?"

"Because it's Thanksgiving and we're guests." I kissed her forehead. "You are okay with this, right?"

"For the millionth time, yes, I am great with it. And, no, I didn't tell Gracie because she probably wouldn't understand and would blab about it." Josie spoke mechanical. "Did I miss anything?"

"Yes. You love me, and I am the best mom in the world," I said.

"How about, and I promise not to join the Marines?"

"Close enough." I snorted out a laugh.

"We better go." Hannah got up from my bed. She wore a classy outfit of a simple pair of black slacks with a crisp black pinstripe blouse tucked in. "Hayden is out in the car waiting and is a bit pissed off about having to wear nice clothes."

Josie got up with her. "And Gracie is outside the car. She keeps showing him how her dress spins and then keeps getting dizzy. Uncle Hayden's patience can only last so long."

"She does love her dress," I admitted. "I'm glad we kept your dress for her. Your hand-me-down is a classic and Gracie loves it."

"I wore that? Without a fight?" Josie asked.

"You wore it and—well, let's just say, you wore it."

**\*\*\*\***

We pulled up to a red brick raised ranch in the middle of a city block. Brody's Jeep was parked on the other side of the street. My heart knocked on my chest before it lunged into my throat.

"You ready?" Josie asked.

"As I'll ever be," I answered.

"I'm proud of you, Mom. However, it turns out, I am proud of you. You always tell us to take risks and damn the consequences. I'm glad you're damning the consequences."

"Aw, thanks, Pumpkin Toes, for what I think was a pep talk." I pulled her hand up to my lips and kissed it. "And you're really, really, *really* okay with this?"

"Being called Pumpkin Toes? Never. But everything else? Yes." Josie smiled. "Now stop asking."

"Momma, do you think Mithter Brody will have hith dogth here?" Gracie popped between us after she released herself from her car seat in the back. She knew we were going to the Reeds' house for Thanksgiving. She didn't know why, and she never asked.

"I don't know, Gracie Girl."

"I hope tho."

I snatched a paper bag from the back seat. "Hannah, grab the pies."

The front door opened, and a tall, thin woman with graying blond hair and eyes the color of Brody's, greeted us with a thick Scottish accent. "Harper, come in. Very glad you made it. When Marti called and told me you were joining us, I was thrilled."

"Thank you, Mrs. Reed. I hope we are not imposing."

"Not at all. We have plenty of food." She opened the door wider for us to enter. "Please, come in."

"Oh, and here." I grabbed the pies one by one and

passed them off to Mrs. Reed. "These are for you."

"Thank you."

The smell of roasted turkey and the ring of laughter hit my heart. In the front room, an older man I knew was Mr. Reed, sat on the couch next to Marti. His hair salt and pepper gray, and his dark blue eyes were animated as he told Marti a story in his Irish brogue. Marti's husky laugh erupted at the end of Mr. Reed's tale. He smiled and when he did, the Reed dimples creased his face.

"Happy Thanksgiving, Harper." Mr Reed stood up. He was an inch or two shorter than his wife, and they made an attractive couple. "And this must be your family."

As Hayden stepped up and made the introductions, Marti struggled to get off the couch. Her belly had grown even larger.

"Happy Turkey Day." She wrapped her arms around me and gave me a big hug. "How are you holding up?"

"Okay. No. I lied. I'm scared shitless."

"Don't be. You'll be great." Marti embraced me again. "Brody's with the rest of them downstairs playing pool. He doesn't know you're coming."

I nodded.

"And sthee, it." Gracie twirled around a few times and then grabbed onto Mr. Reed's hand. "Whoa."

"I see." Mr. Reed laughed, the same deep, rich laugh as Cal. "Well, since Gracie started, why don't you all take off your coats and get comfortable."

"Gracie." I pointed at her coat puddled on the floor. "Please pick that up."

"Okay, Momma. I gotth 'thited to show Mithter

Reed my dreth."

"I see that." I handed my coat over to Hayden, who collected everyone's and hung them in the hall closet.

"Do you want me to put your bag somewhere?" Mrs. Reed pointed to the paper bag by my feet.

"No, thank you."

"Okay." Mrs. Reed put the pies on top of the entertainment unit and looked over at Hayden. "Hayden, have you met my daughter, Bryn?"

"Ma." Bryn came into the room, dressed in a simple, elegant, brown dress. "Don't be raffling me off to the highest bidder. Hi, Harper."

"Hi," I responded nervously.

"Josie. How's jail going for you?" Bryn grinned.

"Haven't been sprung yet." Josie snapped her fingers. "Darn it."

"Hi, Mith Bryn," my baby girl interrupted. "Look."

Again, she spun around. Again, she was dizzy. Again, she grabbed onto Mr. Reed's hand to steady herself.

"I like your dress, especially when you twirl." Bryn ruffled Gracie's curls.

"Come on," Mrs. Reed said. "Let's sit down and relax. Dinner won't be ready for a while."

Josie and Bryn sat down next to each other. Josie talked up a storm, and Bryn listened with an engaged interest.

Gracie sat on the floor and talked with Mr. Reed, who did not stop smiling. Gracie had a positive effect on most people. Mrs. Reed and Hayden talked about the smell of the turkey. And I did not move. I stood by the entrance, my hand gripping Marti's arm.

"You okay?" Marti asked.

"Define okay."

"I'm glad you're here." Marti rubbed her hands together. "This will be exciting."

"What did you tell Dec's mom?"

"I told her you had nowhere to go?"

"Marts," I whined. "Yu shouldn't have made us out to be orphans."

"Sorry," Marti whispered. "I knew you loved him. I knew it."

"You're full of it." Declan's voice traveled up the hallway. "You cheated, Cal. You didn't call last pocket."

"You're just pissed because you suck," Cal bellowed. "Back me on this, Brody."

Upon hearing his name, I clasped Marti's hand. She hugged me for reassurance.

Moxy galloped into the room, and Fifi trotted behind her. Moxy knocked over Gracie. She giggled in pure delight. Fifi came up to me and looked up with her big bulging eyes.

"Hi, pretty girl." I bent down and picked her up. She snuggled up against me in gratitude.

Gracie giggled when Moxy lay down next to her. "Mithter Brody, I love them. I really love them."

"I'm glad, Gracie." Brody's eyes bore into me. I lifted my gaze from Fifi and locked stares with him. The room became quiet, except for Gracie's as she talked to Moxy about being happy to meet her.

We looked at each other for long beats; neither of us said a word. Brody wore a light blue sweater over a pair of navy blue pants. The colors matched the shades in his thunderstorm gray eyes. Golden stubble dusted his square jaw. He slicked back his blond hair, taming the waves.

"Hi, Brodes." I finally found my voice.

"Hi, sugs."

"Fancy meeting you at your parents' place, huh?"

"What are you doing—"

I looked around and found a chair against the wall of the living room. I held up a finger to him. "Hold that thought."

"I thought I asked you not to come today."

"Obviously that didn't happen." I boosted myself onto a chair, Fifi still comfortable in my arms, and yelled into the room, "Excuse me. I have something to say."

Everyone in the room looked at me, some like I'd lost it, some with amusement, and one, Gracie, giggled.

"I just want to say, I lost a bet to Brody Reed. I am here today, to admit, to everyone, he was right. I was wrong." I looked down at Brody, and Fifi licked my face. My voice softened. "I bet he wouldn't know how to be friends with me. But he did. He became the truest friend I think I ever had. I haven't seen him in a few weeks, and I miss him. I think missing someone, longing for them, going out of your mind because you can't imagine another day without them, missing them so much your heart aches, is a true sign of a great friend, a best friend."

"Harper." Brody looked away from me.

"What? That was our bet. Admit I was wrong and to look all knock-outy-ish. Don't I look all knock-outy-ish?" I asked, climbing down from the chair.

"Momma, what's a knockout fish?" Gracie asked.

"I've got this," Declan said. "Gracie, I think there are some brownies in the kitchen. Come on, I'll sneak you some."

"Oh yeth, pleathe." Gracie raced toward the kitchen, Moxy at her feet. Fifi wiggled to get down. As soon as I released her, she darted after them.

"Um," Cal said as he scratched the back of his neck. "Maybe we should all give Brody and Harper some privacy?"

"Nah," Josie answered. "This is getting good."

"Come on, jailbird." Bryn pulled Josie up with her when she rose. "Wanna play some pool?"

"Don't know how."

"Then I'll teach you."

"Good luck," Marti said, and then kissed my cheek before she left.

When they all left with one excuse or another, Brody and I remained. The room still separated us. I took a deep breath.

"Oh, and here." I reached into the paper bag beside me and pulled out his gray boots. "I think you should have these back too."

"As you said, a bet's a bet, sugar."

"Sure, but you see, I think we both lost. I think we have what they call a draw, so having your boots isn't fair, especially since they have a good story." I tried to lighten the heaviness in the air.

"The bet was if I couldn't stay your friend for three months. I couldn't, so I lost. The boots are yours."

"But I lost, too."

"No, you lost only if I couldn't keep the friendship going, and I couldn't."

"Ah." I put his boots on the ground. "If you recall, I said if I lost the bet with you—"

"Actually, you asked me—"

359

"Brody, please." My voice quivered, and I took a deep breath for control. "You're not making this easy for me."

"Oh, like you made it easy for me?" He ran his hand through his hair. "Harper, do I need to rehash the conversation we had in your driveway?"

"No."

"I will anyway. You know, to make it easier on you." He came up to me, his face inches from mine. I saw my pain reflected in him. "I told you I am in love with you, Harper. And you said you can't handle it. You told me we can only be friends. and it had to be your way or no way, so now it's no way. And you think it's been easy for me?"

"I know. And I—"

"Fuck, Harper. Do you know what a mess I've been without you?" Hurt flashed in his eyes. "I want to hate you, to despise you, so I can move on. But here you are, and I can't. All I can feel is love for you. Looking like a knockout fish is not helping."

I snorted out a laugh, and Brody grinned.

"I know." I looked down. "I know," I repeated.

"You know? That's all you got?" Brody shook his head. "Did you hear me? I can't be friends with you. I told you why."

"I know."

"Harper, fucking say something else besides you know." He raised his voice, and for the first time, I wasn't afraid of a raised voice. "Damn it, Harper. How many times do I have to tell you? I love you and not only as a friend. How else can I get through to you—"

"Shut up," I yelled as my head snapped up. "Shut up for one damn minute and let me explain."

Brody's eyes widened as he backed away from me.

"You know, you're an idiot." I shook my head. "Why do you think I'm here? Huh? To ask you to be friends with me again? Why do you think I brought my family to crash your Thanksgiving, like some circus act traveling through town? Why do you think I stood on the chair and yelled into the room? Huh? I told you I lost my side of the bet too because—" I let out a breath.

"Because?" He cocked an eyebrow.

"Because." Then the tears came. "Because I love you. It's the reason I am here, Brody. To tell you I am completely and madly in love with you."

"Oh, sugs. You could have led with that."

"Let me finish. I rehearsed this." I wiped my drippy nose with the back of the hand as more the tears fell. "I love you, Brody Reed. I love your humor and how you listen. I love your strength and your gentleness. I love your talent and your fight against the wrongs in this world. I love and admire how you confront the battles you had in your life. I love how you open yourself up, and how you give me time to do the same. And I love the smell of you, the touch of you, the taste of you, and the look of you. You are one gorgeous man."

He didn't answer. His gaze steadied on me.

"I love you and everything about you. And I wanted you to know all of this. These are the reasons why I'm here." I cried even harder.

He pulled me to him, and I sobbed into his hard chest. His arms surrounded me. He stroked my hair and kissed the top of my head.

"Hey, hey," he cooed. "It's all right."

"I'm afraid, Brody." I wept.

"Of what?"

"Of you. Of me. Of you and me together." I looked up at him. "I'm afraid of losing you. I'm afraid I lost you. I'm afraid I lost the only man I've ever really loved."

"Fuck." He wrapped his arms around me tighter.

While he held me, every emotion and all my senses came alive. I took in the scent of him, and when I thought I might not smell it again, I cried. I felt his hard body pressed against mine, and I wondered how often I would miss his body against mine. I cried some more. I heard his soft, soothing coos, and I knew no one ever took care of me like him. I lost control of my tears. When my sobs finally quieted, I looked up at him.

"So now what?" I asked.

"Well," he said as his fingertips brushed away my remaining tears. "I'd like to talk with Gracie and Josie for a while."

"Why?"

"I'm thinking you already told them how you feel about me? I mean, they had to know the reason you came here. Or is it your thing to crash Thanksgiving dinners?"

"We all have our traditions." I snorted, and Brody threw his head back and roared. "Josie does, but Gracie? I'm not so sure she'd get it."

"Probably not." He patted my ass. It was a great, familiar feeling. "Do you mind if I talk to them? I'd like to tell them how much I love their mom, and I'm not going anywhere."

"Not going anywhere?"

"Not going anywhere." He kissed my lips.

"Oh, Brodes, if I had any more tears left, I'd cry." I

kissed him, but not as quickly as he kissed me. "Okay, I'll call them."

"No, I'd like to do it alone," Brody said. "Josie and Grace were never in the equation with Randall, but I sure as hell want them in ours."

"*Now* you get his name right?"

"Slow to catch on." He grinned. "And maybe if you aren't here when I talk to them, Gracie and Josie will be more truthful. I mean, I think they like me, but liking me and letting me into their lives might be different, especially after all the shit they've been through. Let me do this. They're your life, and I need to make sure it's good with them, okay?"

"It's probably the sweetest thing anyone's ever done for me."

"You deserve sweet and so much more."

His soft, full lips were on top of mine. I was finally his.

****

The dinner conversation was lively and the food, delicious. The laughter was plentiful, the teases gentle, and the conversations were natural. Our two families came together as if there were years of familiarity between them.

Brody remained quiet through most of the meal, as I knew him to be in a crowd. He was not shy about his affection. He kissed me openly and frequently throughout dinner with quick nips on my lips or knuckles. We held hands throughout the meal like two teenagers enjoying their first loves.

We weren't the only ones to show affection. Marti and Declan could not keep their hands off each other. Mr. and Mrs. Reed were also quite demonstrative.

Once, when I came back from taking Gracie to the bathroom, Mr. and Mrs. Reed kissed and groped by the stove. Grace skipped past without a glance. I had to sneak a peek—okay, a gawk.

When the dishes were cleared, and dessert was about to be served, Brody stood up to speak. "Um, can I have everyone's attention?"

Brody's voice wasn't sharp enough to cut through the noise of the crowd.

Cal, Declan, and Bryn laughed at something Hayden said. Marti and Hannah chatted about Marti's pregnancy. Mr. and Mrs. Reed were in their own private conversation.

The only two quiet ones were Josie and Gracie. They were silent throughout the meal, which had me worried. Maybe Brody's talk with them didn't go so well, although all three insisted it had.

"Want me to get their attention?" I asked. "I did it once."

The corners of Brody's mouth rose before he tried again with similar results.

"Hey!" Bryn shouted above all the commotion, "Brody wants to talk."

A hush deafened the room. I had a feeling Bryn often did this for Brody.

"Thanks." Brody looked over at the girls and winked. Gracie blinked both eyes, and Brody grinned. "So Josie, Gracie, and I talked. I asked them what they thought of becoming part of the Reed family, you know, if I married their mom."

"Oh my God. Oh my God. Oh my God," Marti squealed and fanned herself with her hands.

"Yes!" Bryn pumped her fist into the air.

"Oh, Brody, I'm so happy," Mrs. Reed cried out.

"And so was Nonnie," Brody said.

"Nonnie?" I asked.

"I had her on speakerphone when I talked with your girls. She's important to you."

"Oh, Brody." I clutched my chest. My heart galloped like a hundred race horses.

"Momma, I athked if you would get married in a cathle, like Princeth Penelope," Gracie said. When Josie nudged her, Gracie looked indignant. "What? I did."

"She did, which means, I have the approvals of Grace, Josie, and Nonnie." Brody put his hand out for Bryn to place a box in it. I stopped breathing, and my hand moved to my mouth. Brody pushed his chair out of the way and got down on one knee. A choir of gasps filled the room. Tears fell on Brody's cheek, and my own join his.

"Harper McReynolds, you are my friend, my very best friend. A friend I am entirely and completely and passionately in love with. I'm in love with your courage, your dedication to family, your quick wit, and your ability to hold it together even when everything around you falls apart. I am in love with your snorts." Everyone laughed, and I snorted. "I'm in love with your rocking body and your beautiful eyes and your crazy comfy clothes. But, mostly, I am in love with the way you're raising your girls and how beautiful and smart and funny they are. I know when we have kids, they're going to be as special as them because of you."

Brody took a deep breath and released it slowly. He opened the purple velvet box to reveal an amethyst tulip ring nestled inside.

I gasped.

"Oh, Brody. A purple tulip." I reached over to touch the ring. "How? When?"

"I had it made in Jamaica. After my talk with your girls, Bryn went back to my house to get it. I thought I might give it to you at the end of our bet, like a friendship ring. But I don't know. It makes a better engagement ring, don'tcha think?" He kissed my hand. "Harper McReynolds, will you please better my life by allowing me to be your best friend and husband?"

I looked around the table, a table surrounded by the people who mattered in my life, the people who would always matter, if I allowed myself to give life a chance. I looked back at Brody. His steel-gray eyes pierced my soul in eager anticipation. My heart melted with joy and, well, thanksgiving.

"I cannot imagine my life without you in it. Of course, I will spend the rest of it with you."

I kissed his lips full and hard. I opened my mouth, wanting more of him to taste, but realized we had an audience. I clamped it closed. He chuckled against my lips.

"You know," I said, "I won't let our tradition of greeting each other ever die."

"Duh." He pecked a kiss on the inside of my hand.

Gracie slipped in between us among the cheers. Brody picked Gracie up as he rose. She hugged his neck in a tight squeeze.

Josie shuffled toward us. A girl normally stingy with her tears, she released a waterfall of them.

Brody pulled her close and we were wrapped up like the family we were going to be, we should be, we were meant to be.

"You think we're going to have more kids, do ya?"

I narrowed my eyes at him. "I don't think so."
    Brody grinned. "Wanna bet?"

**A word about the author...**

Betsy Dudak lives in the tiny suburb (more of a town) of Warrenville, Illinois, located outside of Chicago. She was born and raised on the South Side of Chicago, where she began her passion for the pretend and her curiosity of words. She has written opinion-oriented columns for local newspapers for over five years. *Wanna Bet* is Elizabeth's second romance novel, following *What the Heck, Dec?!* published in 2012.

Elizabeth has two adult children, Leah and Matthew.

You can contact Elizabeth via email at:
dudakelizabeth@gmail.com.